Phoenix Rising

The Way of Legend: With Quincy J. Allen
Book One: **Reclaiming Honor**
Book Two: **Forging Destiny**
Book Three: **Paladin's Light**

The Claimed Realm
Book 1: **Legacy's Edge**
Book 2: **A Call to Arms (Coming 2025)**
Book 3: **Blood of the Kingdom (Coming 2025)**

SCI-FI
Born of Ash
Book One: **Fallen Empire**
Book Two: **Infinity Control**
Book Three: **Phoenix Rising**

Guardians of the Dark
Book One: **Off Midway Station**
Book Two: **Off Javelin Station (Coming 2025)**
Book Three: **Off Indigo Station (Coming 2026)**

NONFICTION
Every Writer's Dream: The Insider's Path to an Indie Bestseller

PHOENIX RISING

Book 3

MARC ALAN EDELHEIT

This book is a work of fiction. Names, characters, places, and incidents are either the product of the author's imagination or are used fictitiously. Any resemblance to actual persons, living or dead, or to actual events or locales is entirely coincidental.

Fallen Empire: Book 3, Phoenix Rising
First Edition

I wish to thank my agent, Andrea Hurst, for her invaluable support and assistance. I would also like to thank my beta readers, who suffered through several early drafts. My betas: Paul Klebaur, James Doak, David Cheever, Sheldon Levy, Walker Graham, Bill Schnippert, Jimmy McAfee, Joel M. Rainey, Ed Speight, James H. Bjorum, Marshall Clowers, Brian Thomas, Adrian Lee, Lance Dahl, Dragos Ramniceanu, Steven Dye, Kieran Maisonet, Michael Brown, Dominick Maino, Nathan Hildebrand, Tom Moore, Steve Koratsky. I would also like to take a moment to thank my loving wife, who sacrificed many an evening and weekends to allow me to work on my writing.

Editing Assistance by Hannah Streetman, Audrey Mackaman, Brandon Purcell
Cover Art by Piero Mng (Gianpiero Mangialardi)
Cover Formatting by 100 Covers
Agented by Andrea Hurst & Associates, LLC
http://maenovels.com/

TABLE OF CONTENTS

AUTHOR'S NOTE

Writing **Phoenix Rising** has been a labor of love and a joy. I am excited to share this next action-packed and conclusion to the series. It is my sincere hope that you love it as I do.

I also want to take a moment to thank you for reading and keeping me employed as a full-time writer. For those of you who reach out to me on social media or by email, I simply cannot express how humbling it is, as an author, to have my work so appreciated and loved. From the bottom of my heart… *thank you.*

<u>Reviews</u> keep me motivated and help to drive sales. I make a point to read each and every one, so please continue to post them.

You can reach out and connect with me on:
Facebook: Marc Edelheit Author
Facebook Group: MAE Fantasy & Sci-Fi Lounge
Twitter: Marc Edelheit Author
Instagram: Marc Edelheit Author
YouTube: Marc Edelheit Author
Amazon Author Central: Marc Edelheit Author
Patreon: Marc Edelheit Author
Newsletter: www.maenovels.com

Again, I hope you enjoy this book and would like to offer a sincere thank you for your purchase and support.

Best regards,
Marc Alan Edelheit

CHAPTER ONE

Location: Planet Asherho
Date: 2450, Imperial Standard

K eira's rifle recoiled against her armored shoulder as she fired, sending a shock through her haptic suit that felt more like a firm tap than the full force of a gunshot. Down the street, her target—a figure clad in sleek, unpowered black armor—crumpled to the ground. Beside her, the battleframe, Lawrence, unleashed a barrage of heavy weapons fire at the enemy. It made a deep thumping sound she could feel in her chest.

Rounds stitched amongst the enemy's midst, kicking up clouds of dust, sand, and ash. Almost instantly, the enemy scattered, seeking whatever cover they could find. Some soldiers, struck by the incoming fire, were hurled physically backward, their bodies slamming into the rubble-strewn ground with brutal force.

Scanning for her next target, Keira noticed an enemy soldier sprinting toward the facade of what used to be a shop, its structure charred, blackened, and gutted by fire. The outer window of the shop had long since shattered. Hastily, she took aim and squeezed the trigger; the rifle's kick seemed sharper this time. But her shot went wide, missing its mark. The soldier dove the last meter of open space, vanishing into the shadowy depths of the building.

As enemy return fire began slicing through the air with a menacing buzz and hiss, Keira instinctively spun and sprinted toward a low-lying wall to her right. With a practiced leap, she vaulted over it, landing in a crouch on the other side as bullets continued their furious assault. The wall shuddered under the impact of fire, spewing a cloud of dust into the air. Fragments of composite material erupted from the wall's crest and back side, showering her in debris as more bullets pummeled the makeshift barrier.

"Grenade out," Lawrence said.

Back down the street there was the crump of a blast. In the brief lull that followed, she was quick to react. She sprang to one knee, bringing her rifle over the top of the wall and aiming it downrange, eyes sweeping down the devastated street for a target. Lawrence unleashed another torrent of fire, his rounds carving through the air as he edged backward toward her position and the protection of the wall.

The marine who had first caught her eye down the street now lay draped over a burned-out car, motionless. Missing an arm and part of his chest, he was clearly dead. Something had ripped his armor open like a can of soup. And Keira knew what had likely done it.

As the enemy broke cover once more, their gunfire resumed, peppering the wall she was sheltering behind with fresh impacts. The sinister forms of the enemy—black-armored soldiers and the mechanical beasts known as panthers—advanced. The latter, these robotic monstrosities with their many slashing arms, moved with terrifying precision as they closed in.

Keira ducked, the rounds whistling overhead or hammering into the wall, then popped up again, her rifle steady in her hands. She zeroed in on one of the panthers and squeezed the trigger. Her rifle emitted a sharp bark as the round sped toward its target. Incredibly, the panther seemed to anticipate the attack, swerving deftly to the left. The explosive round missed its mark, instead striking the wall of a building behind the bot, resulting in a cloud of smoke and debris as it detonated.

Undeterred, Keira recalibrated her aim with the practiced precision Chris had taught her, firing two more rounds in quick succession. The first whizzed harmlessly past, but the second found its target, slamming into the panther's hindquarters. The impact was spectacular, the back end of the robotic beast erupting in a brilliant flash of light as the round exploded. The blast catapulted the bot several meters to the side, where it lay, crippled, its mechanical limbs twitching.

A surge of triumph rushed through Keira. The panthers—with their multiple arms tipped with razor-sharp claws and their chilling, emotionless, and unfeeling demeanors—represented a formidable threat. They were pure killing machines. Each taken down was a significant victory, at least in her eyes, not to mention a step in the direction of personal survival.

As Lawrence continued his barrage, firing at the enemy, the battleframe retreated. He stepped over the wall and ducked down beside Keira. Suddenly, a brilliant flash illuminated the battlefield, quickly followed by a heavy, resounding *crump*. A shockwave followed a fraction of a second later, hammering Keira with such force that she was knocked flat against the ground. Her ears rang in the aftermath. Despite the protective layers of her combat suit's armor, the blast left her feeling battered and slightly disoriented.

Keira pushed herself back up to one knee. To her immediate left, she noticed a significant portion of the wall had vanished, obliterated by the recent explosion. Lawrence, unfazed, straightened and extended his mechanical arm over the remnants of the wall, unleashing a burst of light toward their adversaries. He swept his arm in an arc. Several screams followed.

The light ceased and Lawrence turned to her. In a sudden motion, the battleframe reached down, gripping Keira firmly by an arm.

"It is time to go," Lawrence declared, his voice firm as he began pulling her back and away from the cover of the wall. "There are too many of them. I must get you to safety."

With urgency propelling his actions, Lawrence half-dragged Keira away from the crumbling wall and to her feet. Once she had her balance, she broke free from his grasp and started moving. Her instinctive sprint took on the urgency of survival as she ran flat out toward the remnants of a nearby building, its once towering structure now a mangled heap of concrete, composite, and steel. The skeletal remains of the upper floors lay crushed, having pan-caked atop the lower ones.

Her heart thundered in her chest, a frantic rhythm matched only by the sound of enemy fire banging away behind them and the rounds slicing and buzzing through the air, close enough to hear their deadly hiss. An explosion abruptly punctuated the chaotic staccato of fire, detonating just steps behind in a flash of orange light.

The blast's force threw her forward, slamming her into the ground. Sand, dust, and ash rose like a curtain around her, but she was back on her feet and moving again, driven by raw adrenaline, almost before it settled.

Lawrence covered their retreat with calculated precision. His stops were brief, his shots deliberate, rapid. Then he was moving once more, never going in a straight line, but a more staggered one.

As Keira rounded the corner of the building, she found a momentary reprieve from the enemy's direct line of fire. Her breathing was heavy, labored from exertion, the moment, her heart pounding as if trying to escape her chest.

Just moments ago, she had been secure within the confines of a drop ship, the crew compartment, surrounded by the pla-toon, marines all, and headed back to the Imperial Light Crusier *Seringapatam*. But the harsh reality of modern warfare had quickly reclaimed her; the drop ship had been shot out of the sky, casting her back onto the surface of Asherho, a dying world. And now, the enemy—the Disunity—were closing in for the kill.

"Captain Scaro, can you hear me? We need help," she transmit-ted, her tone laced with the stress of the moment.

The comms remained stubbornly silent, offering no reassur-ance, only the hollow sound of static.

She tried again, her voice a notch more desperate. "Captain Scaro, Lieutenant Carrigan, can you hear me?" But the silence that followed was just as unyielding, an empty void where she had hoped for support, help, and rescue.

As Lawrence rounded the corner to join her, his appearance spoke of the battle they had just endured. His chest plate bore several dents from the impacts he had absorbed, and a section of his shoulder armor was missing, torn and blasted away by enemy fire.

"A jamming and dispersion field has been employed by the enemy," Lawrence explained, his single red eye light turning toward her. "I am afraid, Princess, that we are, for the moment, on our own."

Keira's realization that Lawrence was using his external audio speaker struck a chilling chord. The flashing red light on her heads-up display, where the comm channels were located, confirmed their isolation—that the communication lines were severed. The weight of their predicament settled heavily on her, the eerie silence from the comms underscoring the danger.

The revelation sank in, heavy and foreboding. Cut off and isolated, Keira faced the stark reality of their situation. With no immediate hope of reinforcement, they had to rely solely on each other and their own wits to navigate the treacherous moments that lay ahead.

Despite the gnawing discomfort at their situation, Keira's gaze fell on Lawrence's battleframe, a complex meld of machinery and tactical prowess. It was a reassurance, a reminder crafted by her friend MK that she was not entirely alone, not while accompanied by this advanced piece of technology.

"Do you have any suggestions?" she asked, her voice betraying a sliver of possibility that Lawrence might offer a tactical advantage beyond brute firepower.

"I was hoping that you would provide some instruction," Lawrence responded. "My programming is, shall we say, rather limited. I am designed to mostly follow orders...mostly, unless it comes to your immediate safety and exterminating the enemy with extreme prejudice. Your personal safety comes first, before any other directive."

Keira's realization about Lawrence's limitations brought her role into sharp focus: she was the decision-maker here, the one with the command. The difference between Lawrence's programmed responses and MK's constructed intelligence underscored just how solitary her command truly was in this hostile environment. MK was currently installed as the *Seringapatam*'s construct. Keira had done that. The *Seri* was hopefully somewhere in orbit around the planet.

Keira felt a mix of frustration and resolve. That Lawrence's capabilities, while formidable, were bound by predefined parameters meant the strategy lay with her. She took a deep breath, scanning their immediate surroundings for tactical advantages and to formulate a plan. She had no idea where they were in the city.

As sporadic gunfire continued to chip away at their makeshift cover. Keira knew they couldn't afford to remain stationary for long. They had to move, and soon.

She quickly assessed their desolate surroundings. The narrow street before her, lined with the remnants of what once were homes, bore the scars of the tragedy that had happened to Asherho. This abandoned residential district, now just a shadow of its former vibrancy, was littered with collapsed buildings. Some structures stood as mere frames, haunting reminders of everyday lives disrupted, not to mention ended, by war.

Directly across from their position, two buildings had been reduced to extensive mounds of rubble. Between these ruins, a sliver of space—once an alleyway or a narrow path—offered a potential escape route. It appeared just passable enough for them to maneuver through without becoming overly exposed.

As she contemplated their next move, a sudden concussive boom resonated, shaking the building behind them with a violent tremor. It was time to move.

"This way." Keira began sprinting for the alleyway. A glance behind her told her that Lawrence was following. Then she faced front and pushed herself harder. In a flash, she was in the alleyway, which was quite narrow and choked with debris from the wrecked and collapsed buildings to either side. Wearing her powered armor, she had little difficulty negotiating it, though she did occasionally stumble over loose chunks of debris and twisted metal.

Reaching the end of the alleyway, she paused, her actions cautious and deliberate. Peering first left, then right, she found another residential street lined with the skeletal remains of once homey dwellings. Clearly this portion of the city had once been well-off.

Seeing no direct threats, without hesitation, she crossed to the next alley directly opposite, sprinting across the street, while signaling Lawrence to keep up. The debris here was similar, strewn with remnants of everyday life now shattered beyond recovery. They moved quickly, reaching the end of this second alley. The next street mirrored the last—abandoned and eerily silent, with no signs of life or immediate threat.

Keira stepped onto the street, turned right, and began rapidly moving down it. The scene was bleak: burned-out cars and overturned vehicles created a jagged landscape, interspersed with several bodies covered over in sand and ash. These were clearly recent victims of the nuclear bombardment, their presence a grim marker of the conflict's brutal escalation and the lengths to which the enemy would go.

As she moved, Keira forced herself to maintain focus, avoiding the harrowing sight of the fallen, even the small forms of the children she passed. Each step was a push against the visceral impact of the destruction around her. Her mind was set on the mission's objectives: to break contact with the enemy and somehow escape, then come up with a plan on what to do next.

Keira's instincts kicked in as the sharp report of a gunshot tore through the near silence, followed by the whizzing sound of a bullet buzzing past like an enraged insect. Instinctively, she threw herself behind the nearest source of cover—an overturned truck whose rusted frame bore the scars of long exposure to the harsh, sandy environment. The truck shuddered violently as another explosive round struck it, the impact resonating with a metallic pop that echoed back through the empty street.

Amid the sudden eruption of gunfire, Lawrence stopped and turned. With one arm raised, he fired methodically back the way they had come. The sounds of his heavy gunfire—*bang, bang, bang*—punctuated the eerie calm.

"Target down," Lawrence reported calmly as he turned back to her. "Might I suggest we continue moving, Princess, and try to lose the enemy? I believe it might be the wisest course of action."

Keira's response to Lawrence's suggestion was instantaneous. With adrenaline fueling her every step, she bolted for another alley, aiming to get off the street and out of sight once more. The distant shouts behind them—a clear sign they were still being pursued—only added urgency to her desire for escape.

Lawrence, matching her pace with his own mechanical efficiency, was close on her heels, the heavy thud of his movements echoing in the narrow passage. Keira didn't pause this time at the alley's end; she was too focused on putting as much distance as possible between them and their pursuers. They sprinted across another street, the brief exposure feeling dangerously elongated, and then dove into yet another alley.

The relentless pace began to take its toll. Despite the support of her powered armor, Keira's breathing grew labored, her chest heaving with the effort. Sweat trickled down her forehead, stinging her eyes, a discomfort magnified by the confines of her helmet, with no way to relieve it, which she found a terribly uncomfortable feeling.

She suddenly burst into openness. A large dilapidated park spread out before her. It was covered in a thick blanket of sand and dust. She found the park a sad, mournful sight. The remnants of trees, now mere stumps, punctuated the landscape, witnesses to the destruction and decay that had overtaken Asherho since the fall of the empire.

Beyond the ghostly park, a once major roadway sprawled, choked with the remains of vehicles that had long since stopped functioning and serving their purpose. On the other side of the roadway, a housing block loomed large and imposing. Stretching nearly a kilometer in length and rising about a hundred stories high, it was a mere echo of the urban expanse that had once thrived here.

The block reminded her a little of Hakagi Tower, but on the smaller side. The tower looked like everything else around her, a ruined remnant of its former self. With not a single window intact, the building stood as an empty shell. It was clear it had not been inhabited for years.

Breathing heavily and working to catch her breath, Keira shifted her gaze to the center of the park, where the remnants of an old fountain lay. The decorative structure, now just a collection of broken pieces, seemed to mourn its own lost splendor. The walking paths that once guided leisurely strolls and exercise runs were now completely obscured beneath layers of dust and debris, their outlines forever lost to time and neglect.

This surreal landscape, so starkly devoid of life yet full of echoes from the past, offered both an opportunity and a challenge. Here in the open, they were exposed, but the housing block could easily provide the cover she needed.

With a powerful surge of her powered armor, she began racing across the desolate park, aiming for the residential block, each stride kicking up clouds of dust and sand. Beside her, Lawrence matched her pace with the heavy, rhythmic thuds of his own mechanical form. The remnants of the park blurred past her as she approached the barrier—a tall, crumbling wall that marked the division between the park and the main roadway. With a leap, aided by the power of her suit, she vaulted over the barrier, her landing sending a shockwave through the sand-covered pavement, her boots imprinting deeply.

As he hit the roadway, Lawrence instinctively turned to cover their rear, his movements precise. His single red eye light scanned the area behind them, a menacing beacon in the twilight of destruction, searching for any sign of pursuit, any hint the enemy had reached the park.

Keira wanted to stop and take a breath. They had covered a lot of ground in the last few minutes, and she was tiring, but she dare not pause, not for a moment.

"Come on!" Keira pointed at the block with her rifle and broke into a full sprint, her powered armor enhancing her speed as she dashed across the roadway. She leapt the median and charged toward the residential block. The structure promised a labyrinth of potential hiding spots, with its myriad passageways and likely access points to subterranean routes that honeycombed Asherho—perfect for evading and breaking contact with their pursuers.

Behind them, the sharp crack of a gunshot split the air, accompanied by even more distant shouts. They had been spotted. The realization that the enemy was tracking their movements, likely by simply following their tracks, lent an even greater urgency to her steps to reach the block and disappear into the depths of its interior.

Pushing her powered suit to its limits, Keira dodged around and over the remains of vehicles and other debris, her focus fixed on the looming structure ahead. It was a race against time, with their survival hanging in the balance. Another shot rang out. She glanced back and saw several figures wearing powered armor charging across the park after them.

The chase was on.

Chapter Two

Location: Planet Asherho
Date: 2450, Imperial Standard

As the enemy in powered armor caught up, Lawrence unleashed a barrage of fire in their direction, taking two of them out before they could react and find cover. The surviving enemy halted their advance and took shelter along the roadway barrier.

As incoming fire followed, Keira ducked behind a crumbling wall that had seen far better days. The reverse side of the wall, facing the park, was half buried in sand. She was near the tower's main entrance, which was just meters away. Her breathing came hard and fast. It sounded incredibly loud in her helmet. In her ears she could feel the thundering of her heart as it hammered away.

The residential block loomed ominously above, its silent facade appearing to brood under the overcast and drab sky. Gusts of wind whistled through the abandoned structure with a mournful howl that Keira felt more than a little unsettling. The sky above was a dark, muddied brown, lending an oppressive weight to the already gloomy and tense atmosphere.

Peering cautiously over the wall, Keira noticed black-suited figures, all wearing light armor, emerging from the dilapidated residential buildings across the park. Moving rapidly, they fanned out across the overgrown park, running for the cover of the roadway barrier. Keira considered taking a shot, but then decided to conserve ammunition. Nowhere could she see any of the enemy in powered armor.

"I am receiving a transmission," Lawrence whispered urgently, crouching beside her, just out of the enemy's line of sight. The battleframe even leaned his head toward her and took a shuffling step nearer.

Keira's heart skipped a beat. They must have moved beyond the jamming and dispersion field that had disrupted their communications. And yet, the red indicator on her HUD was still flashing.

"A transmission?" she asked, hope flickering in her tone. "Is it the captain?"

"No, it is not," Lawrence replied. "The transmission is from the enemy."

"The enemy?" Keira's surprise was evident, her voice rising slightly in both shock and curiosity. "Are you certain about that?"

"Yes. Do you want to hear it, what they are saying?" Lawrence asked her. "Listening in may give you a tactical edge."

"How can I access the transmission?" Keira's hand moved instinctively toward her helmet. She tapped the side of it.

Lawrence reached out a metallic hand and touched the side of her helmet with a finger. Suddenly, without any further action on her part, the speaker in her helmet crackled to life. It was clear Lawrence had enabled the transmission for her.

"—you hear me? I am coming for you," a chilling voice pierced through the static. "Keira, I will find you, and then you will be mine, all mine, sweetie. You will be all mine."

She didn't need to ask who it was; Keira recognized that voice instantly. It belonged to Crecee, a captain in the UPG—a man as vile and despicable as they come, a travesty of human decency. God, she wished he'd died in the bombardment. When so many others hadn't, like a cockroach, he'd managed to survive.

"The bastard didn't have the decency to simply die," Keira breathed to herself.

"When I find you, I am going to take my time with you, Keira," Crecee continued, his words dripping with pure malice. "And you know I always keep my promises."

That last was a poke at Chris, for Crecee knew Chris had prided himself on keeping his promises. She felt her anger stir as well as her grief. Keira's gaze hardened as she turned to Lawrence, her voice low and steady. "If he's brazen enough to transmit openly, then our communications must be clear as well. We should be able to send and receive freely, right?"

"I am afraid that is not correct, Princess," Lawrence replied with a slight shake of his metallic head. "The jamming field is still active, and it appears to be mobile, moving with the enemy as they track and follow us. They're able to communicate through it because they have the correct frequency with which to manipulate the field itself, to use it as a carrier wave. Unfortunately, we don't possess the harmonic key they're using. However, anyone within the radius of this field can potentially pick up their transmission—and possibly even those beyond it."

"That doesn't make any sense," Keira said, furrowing her brow in confusion, not to mention frustration. In truth, she did not know much about how the technology the enemy was using to jam their communications worked. Advanced communications was not her field. She had been a mechanic. It was just the frustration coming out. She was feeling increasingly helpless, and it was showing. That irritated her, firing her anger.

"Once you understand the science, it does make sense, Princess," Lawrence assured her. "Would you like me to explain in greater detail how such systems work? I think I can simplify it to help you better understand. Would you—?"

"No thank you," she said firmly, giving in. It was so maddening, she wanted to scream and rage at the world.

But that wouldn't do.

Chris would never have approved of such behavior. He'd taught her, no matter how bad it got, to keep her head. That was how one survived. She would not be a victim, no longer.

"I'll just take your word for it," Keira said. Her mind was already racing through their tactical options, planning their next move in this deadly game of cat and mouse, one she fully intended to escape.

The air suddenly filled with the thunderous roar of powerful engines. From the murky skies above, a UPG shuttle appeared, slicing through the gloom. Keira's heart sank as she watched the imposing craft descend, flaring as it prepared to land in the middle of the park. The back ramp was already open, ominously facing her direction. Even before the shuttle's skids touched the ground, dozens of soldiers began leaping out, spilling into the park with swift, determined movements.

Keira's stomach churned as she spotted the additional figures accompanying the troops—more panthers, sleek and menacing combat bots, five of them. Their metallic surfaces gleamed dully in the dim light, and their presence multiplied the threat exponentially.

"We have to go," Keira said urgently to Lawrence, her voice laced with determination. "We have to get out of here ... before it is too late. They cannot catch us."

"I agree, Princess," Lawrence responded promptly. "The sooner, the better. I believe that is the correct saying, yes?"

"It is," Keira said.

As Keira prepared to move, Crecee's voice taunted her again through the comm. "Keira, love," he sneered, "I know you can hear me. We have killed all your precious marines, your dedicated protectors. They're all dead. Your starship was a surprise. I'll give you that, an imperial cruiser hidden away and waiting." Crecee paused almost dramatically; Keira felt a sense of unease. Was he telling the truth? "Well, I have some bad news. She's a wreck in orbit. Only you're left, and I am coming for you. There's no escape, no way out, not any longer. You know I will find you. Better that you give up and surrender. It will be easier on you. Walk out. We will not shoot. On that—you have my word of honor."

"I really dislike that bastard," Keira breathed, her disgust palpable in the heavy air.

"I don't like or dislike," Lawrence commented matter-of-factly. "In fact, I am incapable of having any feelings at all. Would you care to explain how feelings work? Ever since MK activated me, created me, and placed me in this frame, it is a topic I have been curious about. I have seen humans exhibit some illogical behaviors. I want to know more. I want to know why. Do you think I might have feelings one day? Do you think I am capable?"

Keira glanced over at the battleframe. Lawrence's head was turned toward her, his solitary red, glowing eye fixed, intense as he stared. She shook her head, pondering the complexity of explaining human emotions to a robot, a machine, and a limited one at that. MK already had feelings, but she did not know how he'd gotten them, let alone how he'd been made. He was different, one of the last of his kind, a constructed intelligence. She worried about him, for he had been a friend.

Lawrence had been built too. MK had given him a basic level of intelligence, but it was a far cry from what a true constructed intelligence had or was capable of feeling.

How to bridge the gap in understanding between a programmed intelligence and the chaotic, deeply felt spectrum of human feelings? Keira abruptly shook her head. She could not believe they were having this conversation right now.

"We can discuss that later," Keira said quickly, her focus sharpening on the immediate danger and goal of escape. "I think we had better get moving, and quickly too, if we are going to stay ahead of them."

"When we have it, I look forward to that conversation," Lawrence responded, his tone even, betraying no urgency but conveying readiness as he pulled slightly away from her and turned toward the building behind them.

Hunched low, Keira began moving toward the main entrance of the abandoned residential block. She kept low, using the wall as cover and trying to stay out of sight, her movements calculated to avoid detection by the enemy forces now clearly spreading out across the park. For all she knew, they were likely moving to flank and surround her and Lawrence. The thought of that alone hastened her desire to get back on the move.

"Oh, Keira," Crecee's voice taunted over the comms, a sinister edge to his words. "I know what you retrieved from the complex.

I've been searching for that item for years, trying to find a way back into the facility, one that wouldn't kill me. I thank you for doing what I could not, for finding a way in, for bringing the Controller out and into the open."

Keira felt a chill run down her spine at his words.

She almost froze.

How did he know about the Controller?

"I only wish," Crecee continued, "that you had brought that traitor Damien out with you. I would so very much have enjoyed terminating him."

At that, Keira did stop. How did he know about Damien too? That construct had been locked in the control room for longer than Crecee had been alive.

What was going on here?

"Why are we stopping?" Lawrence asked her.

Keira glanced over at the battleframe and continued forward, stepping into the building. Shattered glass crunched softly under her boots, echoing ominously in the empty and cavernous space. The ceiling alone rose thirty meters in height. The front entrance had been plate glass. It was now in a million pieces on the ground.

They moved past what was once a security screening station—the frames of detectors standing forlornly, lanes marked on the faded floor, and desks where security personnel once monitored the comings and goings of the residents. Signs were still visible, directing the flow of foot traffic, along with various warnings about weapons and what was permissible to be carried. It all seemed eerily familiar yet hauntingly abandoned, covered over in a thick layer of dust, ash, and sand.

Crecee's voice broke through the silence again. "Keira, I will soon claim what is mine, by right and birth, my destiny, as was promised."

Keira tightened her grip on her weapon, her resolve hardening. She knew the stakes were higher than ever now. Crecee wasn't just UPG, he was Disunity, and likely always had been. The Controller, whatever its true powers and purpose, was now a linchpin in a much larger struggle, one she barely understood herself.

Worse, she did not have it. Scaro had taken what Keira thought might be the Controller, or at least maybe part of it, the three tubes. And—she didn't even know if he still was amongst the living. Had his drop ship been downed too? According to Crecee, they had all died.

Keira scanned the area around her. The security checkpoint seemed as though it hadn't been disturbed for decades, layers of time encapsulated in the dust and debris. Yet signs of recent activity betrayed that illusion. Wall panels had been haphazardly removed, and much of the security screening equipment lay dismantled and in pieces, their valuable components stripped away. It was clear that scavengers had been at work here, making the most of what little remained.

But how long ago had that been?

She suspected a good while from the abandoned look of the place, but Keira also understood that appearances were deceptive. Even if the place had been cleaned out just a week prior, without a window, the relentless storms that swept through would have quickly filled it again with dust, sand, and ash or shifted it all around. She turned her gaze to the broad set of stairs that led upward and deeper into the building. Next to the stairs was an escalator. It too had been stripped for parts.

Her gaze searched for any hint of tracks on the steps. She saw nothing that stood out to her. Still, people could be hiding somewhere within the large residential block, having come in from another entrance. They might have sought refuge after the recent nuclear bombardment. Or the building might be deserted, thoroughly abandoned. The uncertainty sharpened her senses, making her wary of every shadow and noise as she moved deeper into the building, with Lawrence following close behind.

She started up the stairs but then found herself stopping. She glanced back toward the sound of the shuttle's engines, which had increased in pitch, suddenly roaring and echoing ominously through the broken cityscape. She had a better view of the park from this angle on the stairs and saw the shuttle lift off, ascending into the clouded sky after disgorging its cargo.

Dozens of enemy soldiers in light body army, now organized and ready, occupied the area around where the shuttle had set down. Faces averted, they were kneeling as the blast and backwash from the shuttle kicked up a massive amount of dust and sand, for a moment completely obscuring the view until Keira's scan suite kicked in.

Across the park, more enemies spilled from the surrounding buildings. Keira estimated there to be fifty more coming from that point alone, maybe a hundred all told out in the park, far too many for her and Lawrence to confront directly, to even have a hope of stopping. The stark reality set in: they had to move, and quickly. Their survival hinged on their ability to evade.

As Keira was about to redirect her attention away from the ascending shuttle, and begin climbing again, a sudden, intense flash cut through the dim atmosphere inside the tower. The description of "bright" was an understatement—it was a brilliant, blinding burst of light that forced her visor to darken reflexively. For a fleeting moment, something—a streak of motion, incredibly fast and low—shot past the shuttle, and then it vanished as quickly as it appeared, leaving Keira questioning if she had truly seen it.

A heartbeat later, the shuttle was tearing itself apart in midair, erupting into a massive fireball of red and orange. The force of the explosion sent debris spiraling downward as armored figures and bots scrambled desperately for cover. Several were caught in the blast radius, either engulfed by the inferno or crushed under the falling wreckage that crashed downward onto them.

Keira stood frozen, her eyes wide behind the darkened visor, the scene unfolding in surreal clarity. The shock of the unexpected explosion reverberated through her, a mix of relief and horror gripping her simultaneously. She turned to Lawrence, her voice shaky as she almost whispered, "What the hell just happened? Tell me what just happened."

"Though I cannot be certain, I believe that was an imperial interceptor," Lawrence informed her, his voice carrying a note of analytical calm. "I estimate that there is a ninety-five percent chance of that being what happened. The interceptor shot down the shuttle."

"Really?" Keira responded, a surge of hope lifting her spirits. It meant they weren't as isolated as she had feared, and that Crecee's grip on the situation might not be as solid as he boasted.

The empire was still out there!

A sharp zipping sound sliced through the air, reminiscent of someone ripping a heavy canvas bag. Just a heartbeat later, the ground beyond the burning wreckage erupted, kicking up dirt, sand, and ash in two distinct, thin lines running across the park.

The enemy soldiers, those who had just emerged from the buildings on the other side of the park, were caught within those turbulent bursts and seemed to vanish, disintegrating under the unseen force. Moments after, a booming sound thundered across the battlefield, followed by the distinctive roar of engines, which set the dust and sand at her feet vibrating.

"That was definitely an imperial interceptor," Lawrence confirmed, his observation syncing with the sounds and the aftermath of what she had just witnessed. "I believe it was a second such interceptor, Meeko Class. I can tell by the sound of the engines, the pitch. The first took down the shuttle. The second conducted a strafing run."

Keira could only nod in agreement, her mind racing as she processed this rapid turn of events. She could hear the distant screams and cries of the wounded as the sound died down. Fiercely, she hoped the attack had taken out a lot of the enemy. They needed all the help they could get.

"Perhaps, as they say, now would be a good time to make tracks," Lawrence suggested, his gaze shifting to probe deeper into the shadows of the building. "Hmmm...maybe if we had a wagon, things would go quicker. We could ride away."

"A wagon?" Keira asked, glancing over at him, a flicker of uncertainty crossing her mind about how reliable MK's programming really was. Yet, in this desolate landscape, Lawrence was the closest thing she had to an ally, a friend.

"I am sorry, Princess. I do not know where that came from."

With a nod, she turned and made her way deeper into the building.

Lawrence dutifully followed.

CHAPTER THREE

Location: Planet Asherho
Date: 2450, Imperial Standard

Keira pressed forward down the unlit hallway, the heavy thud of her powered armor boots echoing off the cracked walls. Each step resonated with a heavy thump, the sound unnervingly hollow as it reverberated through the abandoned structure. They were so deep, there were no light sources anywhere.

Overhead, bundles of exposed cabling hung like venomous serpents, while ceiling tiles dangled precariously, threatening to fall at any moment. She and Lawrence maneuvered carefully, weaving through the debris-laden path, their focus split between avoiding obstacles, navigating the loose cabling, and keeping their bearings in the labyrinthine building.

Keira had no clear idea where they were heading, only that the corridor led them farther away from the enemy's last known position and deeper into the sprawling complex. The original plan had been to find an access point that plunged downward into the planet's underbelly—a safer route where they might evade pursuit. But no such passage had presented itself.

Her suit's compass had ceased functioning correctly. So too had Lawrence's. The building shook slightly as the reactor deep in the planet's core pulsed. The cabling shook, and ahead several ceiling tiles crashed to the floor. Keira paused, wondering if the powering up of the reactor was interfering with the compass. Or was it the jamming and dispersion field?

Instead, Keira had resolved to push forward, hoping to find an exit on the far side of the block, beyond the reach of their foes, and make a break into the ruins of the city.

The building's interior was a chaotic mess, a once structured environment now warped by the ravages of time and abandonment. The longer they moved, the more disoriented Keira felt. They had been inside for over fifteen minutes, rapidly progressing ever deeper into the structure.

Several times they had come up against impassable dead ends, where entire sections of the ceiling had collapsed, thoroughly blocking their path with a mountain of rubble and debris. Each time, they were forced to backtrack, adding to the mounting tension.

The long-abandoned building exuded an unsettling eeriness, its silence thick and oppressive. As Keira and Lawrence ventured deeper, the walls seemed to close in, as if the building itself were a tomb for the memories of a lost people and era.

The farther they progressed, the more apparent it became that this place had been picked clean long ago. Anything of value—machinery, technology, furniture, even scrap metal—had been scavenged, leaving behind only the remains of what once had been. Nearly stripped bare, the structure felt like a hollow echo of a bygone age, a reminder of how much had been lost.

Keira couldn't shake the sadness that settled over her. The building was a relic of the time before the Fall, when the empire still held sway over Asherho and countless other worlds, an age of excess and plenty. But that time was long gone, and along with it, the order and stability the empire had imposed. The collapse had been swift and merciless, unforgiving in the extreme, unraveling the fabric of imperial authority, civilization, and leaving worlds like Asherho to fend for themselves in the aftermath.

The tragedy of it weighed heavily on Keira's mind. The empire's fall had been more than just a political shift; it had been a cataclysm that rippled across the known galaxy, setting humanity back thousands of years. She found herself wondering just how many had suffered on Asherho alone—how many had died in the chaos that followed the empire's collapse.

How many billions of lives had been snuffed out across the empire's vast expanse? How many had managed to survive, clinging to life in the shadow of a fallen empire? And of those who survived, how many now languished under the boot of cruel governments like the UPG, struggling to endure in a galaxy that had lost its way?

The thoughts stirred a deep sense of loss and anger within her. From what she'd learned, the empire had been far from perfect, but it had been something—a presence that kept the darkness at bay. Now, that shadow had spread, and the galaxy seemed a colder, harsher place.

The collapse of the empire had been humanity's greatest tragedy, a cataclysm that had brought a once thriving civilization to its knees. Even as Keira moved through the wreckage of what once was, with the threat of being hunted still hanging over her, the weight of that loss pressed heavily on her heart.

How could they have let it come to this? The question had long bothered her, a bitter puzzle she had never been able to solve, and no one had been able to adequately explain.

The people who had once had so much—peace, prosperity, a future—had thrown it all away. They had let discontent and fear fester, divisions arise, allowing the Disunity to take root and spread its poison. How had so many been swayed to rise and topple everything that was good and right? Why had they thrown away all they had?

The Disunity had played on humanity's darkest impulses, stoking the flames of rebellion and mistrust until the empire was consumed in the fires of its own making. Keira could never fully grasp how it had happened, how something so vast and enduring could have crumbled so quickly, and so violently. It seemed unfathomable that people could be so easily swayed, so easily turned against what had once held them together, what had unified them.

As these thoughts churned in her mind, the sadness was accompanied by a sense of frustration and betrayal. The fall of the empire had shattered not only a government, but also the hopes and dreams of countless people. It was a senseless loss, a self-inflicted wound from which humanity might never fully recover. And now, in the aftermath, they were left to pick up the pieces, to survive in a world where the light of the empire had been extinguished, leaving only darkness and chaos in its wake.

The force that had brought the empire down, the Disunity, was still out there. Worse, the Disunity was after her.

Keira came to a sudden halt, her senses on high alert. The hallway they had been following abruptly ended, splitting off into two directions. She scanned the area, her low-light vision engaged, the advanced scan suite in her helmet rendering the darkness as clear as daylight. Every detail of the crumbling walls and debris-strewn floor was illuminated in crisp monochrome, yet the path ahead remained uncertain.

She turned to Lawrence, her voice low but steady. "Any suggestions on which way to go?"

The hulking figure of Lawrence's battleframe stepped forward, the servo motors humming softly as he moved. He reached the end of the hallway and paused, his single, cyclopean sensor sweeping first to the left, then to the right. The glowing red eye, set in the center of his armored head, cast an eerie glow as he surveyed both paths.

After a moment, he turned his gaze back to Keira, his tone laced with a hint of resignation. "I'm unfamiliar with the layout of this structure and cannot determine which way is best. Perhaps, as you humans say, it is time to make an educated guess as to the correct path?"

Keira glanced down each corridor again, weighing the options. Both directions seemed equally foreboding, offering no clear indication of what lay ahead. The wreck of a building had been disorienting enough without this new twist, and now she was forced to choose a direction based on nothing more than instinct—to make a guess. She could feel the pressure mounting, the need to keep moving, to stay ahead of whatever forces might still be on their trail.

But in the silent tension of the moment, she knew Lawrence was right. With no map, no guide, and no time to waste, they had to make a decision and hope the chosen path would lead them closer to safety, rather than deeper into danger.

"I see," Keira murmured, her eyes flicking between the two possible routes. "Well, the left is as good as any direction, I suppose."

"Left it is, then," Lawrence responded, his voice calm and measured.

With a nod, Keira turned left and began moving down the hallway. Lawrence followed closely behind, the weight of his battle-frame causing the floor to tremble slightly with each heavy footfall, the dust to shake at their feet. The corridor stretched out ahead, narrow and foreboding, its walls lined with doors that seemed to stretch into infinity.

Almost every door stood ajar, some hanging awkwardly from their hinges, the facets having given way to time. Most bore the unmistakable signs of forced entry—deep gouges in the frames, shattered locks, and splintered wood.

Glancing inside one of the rooms, Keira felt her heart tighten. Like everything else they'd seen, the space was nearly bare, stripped of anything of value, with only a few scattered pieces of broken furniture left behind. The emptiness felt heavy, as if the very air was laden with the memories of those who had once lived here, called this place home. It was clear these rooms had once been residential suites, places where people had made their lives, raised their families, and found solace after long days in the world outside. Each doorway they passed was a portal to the forgotten, the damned.

As Keira continued down the hallway, her thoughts turned to the countless people who had once lived in this residential block. These rooms had been filled with the lives of imperial citizens— men, women, and children. They had not deserved the devastation that had come upon them, nor the horrors that had followed. Not to mention, they had inherited the UPG. The weight of that injustice settled heavily on her.

Keira couldn't help but imagine the lives that had been lived within these walls—the laughter, the arguments, the moments of quiet contentment. She could almost see the families in her mind, hear their voices and the children's laughter, feel the parents' dreams of a bright future. All of it was gone now, leaving only shadows and echoes in its wake.

It wasn't just the physical remnants of the past that haunted this place, but the loss of something much more profound—the loss of a sense of home, of safety, of belonging, of having a place in the world.

Though she felt a pang of deep sorrow for those who had suffered, Keira reminded herself that it was now history. The pain and loss were real, but they were relics of a past that could not be undone. What mattered now was the future—a future that rested, in part, on her shoulders, for she might just have the key to unlock a semblance of hope.

As a princess of the empire, as the Kai'Tal, she carried the burden of a legacy that had long since crumbled into dust. The title might have once commanded respect and power, but now it felt like an echo of a forgotten age, a reminder of what had been lost. And yet, despite the empire's fall, she still held within her something far more profound—abilities granted by an ancient race, the Placif, the mysterious precursors who had shaped so much of what she now faced.

But could those abilities truly make a difference? Could she, an heir to a shattered empire, forge a path toward a better future? Could she lead humanity out of the darkness and into the light?

The power she had inherited from the Placif was still something she didn't fully understand, an enigmatic force that seemed to pulse within her, demanding to be unleashed. Could she learn to control and master it? Was there any choice?

The doubts ate at her, but Keira knew she couldn't afford to falter. The future, uncertain as it was, would be shaped by the choices she made in the present, the here and now. Thoughts of rebuilding an empire were distant concerns. For now, though, the only goal that mattered was to survive the next few minutes, to keep moving forward, and to trust that somehow, she would find the strength to make a difference, even if that difference seemed impossibly far away.

After covering another six hundred meters, the hallway finally came to an abrupt end, forcing Keira and Lawrence to make another turn, this time to the right. Keira led the way. But just as they rounded the corner, Keira came to an abrupt halt. Her ears caught something—a faint sound echoing down the corridor behind them—a shout, distant but unmistakable. Her heart skipped a beat as she quickly glanced back at Lawrence, her instincts screaming that they were no longer alone, that the enemy was near.

"Did you hear that?" she whispered urgently, her voice tight with concern.

Lawrence's battleframe paused beside her. His response was calm, almost resigned.

"I did," he confirmed. "The enemy is in the building with us. It was only a matter of time until that occurred."

Leaning around the corner, Keira glanced back down the hallway they had just traversed, her eyes falling on the thick layer of dust that coated the floor. Their tracks were unmistakable, a clear trail leading right back to them. A sick feeling settled in the pit of her stomach, a cold realization that once more, the enemy wouldn't have any trouble tracking their movements.

"We need to hurry," Keira urged, her voice tight with urgency. Despite the weariness that tugged at her muscles and the growing exhaustion that weighed on her, she forced herself to keep moving. The powered armor responded instantly, its servos humming as it amplified her movements. What began as a jog quickly turned into a sprint, the enhanced strength of the armor propelling her forward at a speed she could never have achieved on her own.

The hallway blurred around her as she pounded down its length, each step a powerful strike against the floor, eating up the distance with relentless momentum. The corridor twisted and turned, every corner a potential ambush point, but Keira didn't slow. Her focus was razor-sharp, the need to escape overpowering any thoughts of caution.

As they approached yet another turn, Keira's eyes caught a glimmer of light ahead. To the right, there was nothing but pure darkness, an abyss that seemed to swallow the faint glow of her suit's lights and challenge the scan suite. But to the left, about a hundred meters down, she spotted a floor-to-ceiling window.

Light—natural light—streamed through it, casting long beams that illuminated the corridor in a soft, welcoming glow. It was a beacon, a sign that there was still an outside world beyond the suffocating walls of this decaying structure. Keira felt a massive wave of relief.

Without hesitation, she veered left, pounding toward the window. The promise of light, and perhaps even escape, drove her forward with renewed determination. Behind her, Lawrence's heavy steps echoed her own, the two of them racing toward the one thing that might offer them a way out of this nightmare.

The light grew brighter as they closed the distance, and Keira could feel her heart pounding in her chest, not just from exertion, but from the hope that this window might lead them to freedom.

Within seconds, Keira reached the window, her momentum carrying her right up to the edge and almost out into space. Placing a hand against the wall, she caught herself and halted abruptly, staring out through the empty frame where plexiglass had long since vanished, leaving only a gaping hole in its place.

The wind whipped through the opening, seeming to try to push her physically back. Her gaze dropped downward, and her stomach tightened as she realized she was at least five stories above the ground. The height wasn't dizzying, but the drop was significant enough to give her pause.

Below, the landscape was bleak—an old service road ran directly beneath her, its surface cracked and covered over in sand. Scattered across it were more than a dozen vehicles, their metal skeletons charred and twisted, remnants of a time when this place had been alive with activity. Now, they were nothing more than relics, their decayed forms slowly being reclaimed by the passage of time.

Keira's eyes moved beyond the road, taking in the wider scene. She was on what appeared to be the back side of the tower, though the building's dilapidated state made it hard to be certain. Just three hundred meters away, another tower loomed—or rather, what was left of it. The structure had collapsed in upon itself at some point, its once mighty frame reduced to a colossal pile of rubble. The debris rose ominously, higher even than the window through which she was looking. It was a grim monument to the destruction that had ravaged this world.

For a moment, Keira just stood there, taking in the desolation. The sight of the collapsed tower was sobering, its ruins blocking any view of what lay beyond. It was as if the very landscape conspired to keep them trapped, surrounded by the remnants of a civilization that had crumbled into dust. The path ahead was uncertain, but there was no turning back now—not with the enemy on their heels.

She quickly assessed her options. The service road below might offer a way out, a means to navigate through the wreckage and find some semblance of cover. But the drop was significant.

"I believe we can jump safely," Lawrence stated.

Keira looked over at him, her brow furrowed with doubt. "Are you sure about that?"

"I am very sure," Lawrence replied, his tone steady and reassuring. "Your suit is designed to withstand impacts from much greater heights. The fall from this distance is well within its operational and acceptable limits."

Keira hesitated, glancing back at the open drop. "Does that include me too? I'm not just worried about the armor."

Lawrence's eye light seemed to narrow slightly as he considered her, almost as if he were calculating the odds. "That is a very interesting question," he mused, his tone almost thoughtful. "Based upon my analysis, I would hazard you will survive the fall and remain uninjured. Your suit's impact absorption systems are more than capable of handling the descent." The battleframe paused, gesturing with a hand out the window. He then pointed it squarely at her chest. "Trust the suit—step out, and let it do the rest. Remember how it caught you when you were ejected from the drop ship? This is no different but a more manageable fall."

Keira swallowed, the memory of that terrifying freefall flashing briefly in her mind. The suit had indeed saved her then, cushioning her from what would have been a fatal impact. But stepping off a ledge into open air still went against every instinct she had.

She took a deep breath, forcing herself to focus. Lawrence was right—her armor was built for this. The same technology that had already kept her alive through so much more would protect her now.

"All right," Keira said, her voice firmer now. "Let's do this."

With one last look at the drop, she positioned herself at the edge, muscles tensing in preparation. The wind whipped around her, tugging at the edges of her armor, but she didn't let it distract her. She knew what she had to do.

"On three," she said, more to herself than to Lawrence. "One... two... "

And with a final deep breath, she stepped out into the void, letting gravity take hold. The world tilted as she plummeted, but Keira forced herself to stay calm, trusting in her suit.

For a brief, heart-stopping moment, she was weightless, the ground rushing up to meet her at an alarming speed. Her stomach did a flip-flop as she fell, but her suit adjusted and with a burst of hidden jets slowed her at the last moment. She touched down heavily and on her feet with a dull thud, the knee joints bending slightly to absorb the shock. She took a shaky breath, her heart still pounding in her chest.

She had made it.

"Not so bad after all," she muttered to herself, looking up to see Lawrence jumping, his battleframe descending with the same effortless precision. A moment later he landed at her side.

"I actually found it rather exciting," Lawrence commented, his head swiveling slightly to glance back up at the window from which they had just leapt.

Keira raised an eyebrow, a hint of curiosity mixing with her lingering adrenaline. "I thought you couldn't experience emotion?"

"I can't," Lawrence replied, his tone matter-of-fact.

"Then how can you feel it was exciting?" Keira pressed, her curiosity piqued.

Lawrence's battleframe tilted his head, the motion oddly human for such a large piece of machinery, a weapon of war. The red glow of his single, cyclopean eye focused on her. "I am not sure what you mean," he responded, his voice devoid of any hint of confusion or irony.

Keira stared at him for a moment, trying to wrap her mind around the contradiction. "You just said you found the jump exciting," she clarified, trying to probe the logic behind his statement. "But if you don't have emotions, how can something be exciting for you?"

Lawrence paused, as if processing her question with the meticulous precision of his programming. "The term 'exciting' is often associated with a heightened state of awareness or interest, typically involving an element of risk or novelty," he explained. "While I do not experience emotions in the way humans do, I am equipped with protocols that assess situations based on their potential to engage or challenge my operational systems. The jump presented such a challenge, which I recognize as a deviation from routine actions. Therefore, I used the term 'exciting' to describe the increased level of engagement required by my systems during the descent."

Keira blinked, absorbing his explanation. "So, you're saying that the jump was out of the ordinary, and your systems registered it as something that required more focus or calculation—something different from the norm?"

"Precisely," Lawrence confirmed, his tone as even as ever. "While I do not feel excitement, I can identify scenarios that necessitate heightened operational performance. In this context, 'exciting' is an appropriate descriptor." Lawrence paused and tilted his head again. "That is my story, and I am sticking to it."

Keira couldn't help but chuckle softly, shaking her head in mild disbelief, for, whether he realized it or not, he'd just cracked a joke. Perhaps Lawrence was capable of emotion after all. Maybe he just didn't realize it. "I guess that makes sense, in your own way," she conceded. "But for a moment there, you almost sounded… human."

Lawrence's head tilted slightly again, a subtle mimicry of a human gesture that Keira had come to recognize as thoughtful for him. "I strive to understand human perspectives and to communicate effectively within those parameters," he said. "If that means using terms like 'exciting' to bridge the gap, then so be it."

Keira smiled, appreciating the strange but oddly endearing logic of her mechanical companion. "Well, I'm glad you found it… engaging, then. Let's hope we don't have too many more 'exciting' moments ahead."

With that, she turned her focus back to the task at hand, scanning the area for their next step. Keira began moving again, trotting along the service road. There was no going toward the wrecked residential block or climbing over that massive pile of rubble. It was a tangled mess of twisted metal, composite, and concrete that would take far too long to navigate. Worse still, attempting to climb over it would leave them completely exposed and in view of anyone wanting to take a potshot at them. They couldn't afford that kind of risk.

Instead, Keira knew they needed to work their way around the massive ruin, finding a path that would keep them out of sight and still allow them to slip away into the city.

Feeling exposed, Keira increased her pace. The powered suit responded to her every movement, amplifying her stride, making her faster and more efficient than she could ever be on her own.

Lawrence matched her pace effortlessly, his battleframe's servos humming as his heavy footsteps thudded against the dust- and sand-covered pavement.

Keira's breath came fast and hard, each inhale burning in her lungs as she pushed herself to keep moving. The strain of their earlier exertions was catching up with her, but she knew there was no time to slow down. The enemy was still out there, close, and every second they remained in view of the residential block they'd just come out of increased the chances of being spotted.

She could feel the familiar fatigue creeping into her limbs, the weight of exhaustion pressing down on her shoulders, but she pushed it aside and soldiered on. The landscape around them was bleak and unforgiving, a wasteland filled with ruin and desolation. The need for survival drove her, overriding the physical pain, the discomfort and weariness that she felt deep in her bones. As long as they kept moving, as long as they didn't stop, there was still hope. And hope, in this shattered world, was worth everything.

Keira kept her senses on high alert, every nerve in her body primed for the first shot from behind, the first shout of alarm that would signal they had been spotted. But it didn't come. The oppressive silence continued to hang over them, broken only by the rhythmic pounding of their footsteps as they moved through the desolate landscape.

They covered ground quickly. With every step, she half-expected a shot to ring out, but none came. The absence of any hostile movement was almost more unsettling than the threat itself, as if the enemy were lurking just out of sight, waiting for the perfect moment to strike.

Soon, they reached a side street that turned sharply along the massive ruin. Keira took it and then almost immediately another street to the left. They found themselves moving between two rows of buildings that had been thoroughly flattened. The destruction was absolute—walls reduced to rubble, roofs collapsed downward, leaving only piles of debris where structures had once stood.

As they continued onward, Keira's HUD began flashing warnings, red indicators alerting her to dangerously high levels of radiation in the area. The data scrolled across her visor, but she ignored it. After the bombardment, it was only to be expected. There was no time to worry about long-term exposure. It was something that would have to be dealt with later in the ship's med bay. They had to keep moving. Keira understood she had to find a way out of this deathtrap before the enemy caught their trail again and closed in.

She pushed forward, her focus laser-sharp, and after another hundred meters farther, she spotted a narrow side street to her left. Without hesitation, she ducked into it, the sudden change in direction giving them some real cover and taking them off a main street.

After a few more meters, Keira came to a halt, her breathing heavy. She quickly scanned their surroundings, her eyes darting between the wrecked buildings and the shadowed corners, searching for any sign of movement. The street was narrow, almost claustrophobic, the high walls on either side creating a tunnel-like effect.

Lawrence stopped beside her, his single glowing eye light fixed on her, waiting for her next move. Keira took a moment to catch her breath, her heart still pounding from the exertion and the anticipation of danger that hadn't yet materialized.

"Are you fatigued?" Lawrence inquired, his voice steady, devoid of any judgment.

"I am," Keira admitted, her breath coming in ragged gasps. "I—I just need—need to catch my—breath, is all."

She resisted the urge to lean forward and rest her hands on her knees, knowing that every movement, every action, needed to be measured carefully in her powered armor. Besides, it wasn't needed. Instead, she permitted herself to relax within her suit, allowing it to hold her in place. The soft cooling gel packs inside the armor cradled her body, offering a brief, soothing reprieve from the relentless pace they had been maintaining.

It was as if she were suspended in a cocoon, the tension in her muscles slowly easing as the suit did its work. God, she was tired—so very tired. The exertion and stress had drained her, and now, all she wanted was a moment to let the fatigue wash over her, to rest, to close her eyes and catch some sleep.

After a few moments, her breathing began to slow, the frantic pace of her heart calming as she found her rhythm again. The gel packs continued to work their magic, cooling her down, helping her recover just enough to think clearly.

"Lawrence?" she asked, her voice quieter now, more composed.

"Yes, Keira?" he responded, his tone as calm as ever.

"Any suggestions on how we can find or contact Captain Scaro, and any marines out there?" She waved her hand vaguely in the direction they had come from, the gesture conveying her frustration at the lack of communication.

"I am sorry," Lawrence said after a brief pause. "I do not have any relevant suggestions."

Keira let out a small, frustrated sigh. "What about non-relevant?"

"You could always send up a flare," Lawrence suggested, his tone as neutral as ever.

"A flare?" Keira echoed, a bit surprised. "The suit comes with a flare?"

"For emergencies. It is designed to go several thousand meters into the air and send out an encrypted burst, a call for help."

Keira considered this for a moment, then frowned. She glanced up at the murky sky. "Wouldn't the enemy be able to see it as well?"

"I would assume so," Lawrence replied, his voice as matter-of-fact as ever. "However, they would need to be looking in the right direction and tuned to the correct channel to pick up the transmission." He paused. "There is also the possibility that they might detect the emission from the burst transmission itself."

"That sounds risky," Keira said, her voice tinged with concern.

"Under the current context, such an action could indeed be deemed as highly risky, for it might draw some unwanted attention," Lawrence concurred. "I agree with your assessment. It would be a risky move, with a high likelihood the enemy would be able to locate your position. Perhaps I should not have suggested it?"

"I think I'll pass on that option," she decided. "How about we focus on getting out of the suppression field instead?"

"An excellent course of action." Lawrence's battleframe hummed softly as he prepared to move again. "By exiting the field, we may be able to reestablish communication with Captain Scaro or any allied forces in the vicinity."

"How?" Keira asked, her brow furrowing with concern as she thought. "How far do we need to get away from it?"

"Judging by the strength of the field," Lawrence began, his tone clinical and precise, "I estimate we need to put about five kilometers between us and the field's origination source to effectively escape its influence."

Keira's mind quickly calculated the distance, realizing that wasn't an impossible task.

Lawrence continued, "However, you should consider the possibility that if the enemy continues to hotly pursue us, they may bring the suppression field with them. That is exactly what they already seem to be doing."

"How can you be sure about that?"

"Because we have traveled far more than five kilometers since first encountering the field and are having communication difficulties."

"So, we're not just running from the enemy," Keira said with frustration as she glanced once more around the narrow street. "We're also racing against their tech, trying to stay ahead of a moving target, one that has been dogging us closely."

"Precisely. Our best course of action is to keep moving as quickly and efficiently as possible, while avoiding any direct confrontation. Essentially, we need to break contact with the enemy. If we can gain enough distance and reach an area where the field's range is compromised or sufficiently reduced, we may be able to regain full operational capabilities of our comm systems and call for assistance, or perhaps even a pickup from the ship."

Keira gave a nod of understanding, though her mind was racing with questions and doubts. She scanned the deserted street around them, the silence almost deafening in its emptiness. Where was Captain Scaro? Where was the rest of the company? The nagging thought bothered her immensely—were they searching for her and Lawrence? Or had she unknowingly led the two of them away from the help they so desperately needed? The uncertainty was more than just concerning; it was deeply worrying.

Before she could dwell too long on these thoughts, the ground beneath her feet gave a violent tremble. The entire street seemed to vibrate, the ruins around them shuddering as if they were alive. Farther down the narrow road, the remains of a building groaned under the strain. Another collapsed in a cloud of dust and debris. Keira glanced down at the ground as the quake subsided.

She could feel it in her bones—the raw, terrifying power rising from deep within the planet's core. This was the third quake she had felt in the last half hour, each one stronger than the last. Keira knew what was happening, and the realization sent a chill down her spine. The reactor she had activated was steadily awakening, its ancient precursor technology stirring back to life after who knew how many thousands of years of dormancy.

The reactor was a power source of unimaginable magnitude. She had vague notions of what it might be capable of, but nothing concrete, only what she'd learned from the orb. The remains of Placif were leaving this plane. But what it was really doing now—it was not something to be taken lightly. Of that, she was certain.

Keira could feel the energy building, steadily mounting, a latent force growing beneath the surface, ready to unleash its full potential. The tremors were just the beginning—a prelude to something much larger.

Keira closed her eyes, grounding herself as she reached out with her mind, connecting with the machine. She kept herself firmly anchored within her body, even as her consciousness expanded, a silvery veil falling over everything around her. The world took on a different hue, as if viewed through a lens that revealed the hidden layers beneath reality. In this altered state, she could see the dust and sand swirling around her, but more than that, she could feel them—sense the countless tiny presences hidden within.

The nanites.

They were everywhere, millions upon millions of them, woven into the very fabric of the environment. As the wind gusted, she noticed them even in the air, like microscopic particles, eager and restless, waiting for a command. They thrummed with a collective desire to act, to build, to create. It was as if they were alive in their own way, brimming with potential, each one a tiny cog in a vast, incomprehensible system.

But Keira ignored their call, resisting the pull to command them. She knew that engaging with the nanites could lead down a path of distraction, and she needed to focus on something far more pressing. Instead, she turned her attention inward, toward the depths below her feet, reaching out with her senses to touch the mounting power deep within the planet's core. She wanted to try to get a better sense of what was happening and how it might affect things in the hours to come.

It was there, the energy, throbbing with a raw, overwhelming intensity. The reactor wasn't just coming online; it was surging to full power, its ancient mechanisms stirring to life. But it wasn't alone. The great machine, the one the Placif had constructed and buried within the heart of the planet, was awakening as well. Keira could feel it, a colossal presence of interconnected systems and processes, each one coming alive as the reactor's energy coursed through it and fired it up.

She pulled back slightly, overwhelmed by the sheer magnitude of what she was sensing. It was almost as if she could taste the power, which was unlike anything she had ever encountered, vast and unfathomable, yet intricately controlled and regimented. Things were happening in a predetermined and precise manner.

Turning her gaze back to the nanites swirling in the dust, a thought struck her—a realization that sent a chill down her spine. Was this how the Placif had done it? Had they built everything on this planet through the coordinated efforts of billions, perhaps trillions, of these tiny machines? It was an intriguing possibility, and one she could not easily dismiss. The nanites were of precursor origin, after all. Humanity had not created them; they were a legacy of a civilization far older and more advanced than her own had ever been.

The idea that these nanites, so small and seemingly insignificant, could have constructed something as monumental as the reactor and machine beneath the planet's surface was both awe-inspiring and terrifying. It hinted at the pure scale and ambition of Placif's technology, their ability to manipulate matter on a near microscopic, perhaps even atomic level, to create structures and systems beyond human comprehension.

Then a thought occurred to her, a suddenly intriguing one. She was angry with herself that she had not thought of it before now. Keira shifted her focus from the heart of the planet to the suppression field, extending her awareness outward, leaving her body and searching. It did not take her long to find it. She could sense the field as a subtle distortion in the machine, a warping that lingered back the way she and Lawrence had just come.

It was a powerful force, a technological barrier designed to disrupt and disable certain wavelengths, yet intriguingly, it didn't seem to fully interfere with her connection to the machine, at least not much.

Why was that?

Could she, from within the machine's network, deactivate the field? Could she shut it down? The thought was tantalizing, offering a possible solution to their immediate predicament, their inability to call for help.

As she turned her mental gaze toward the suppression field, probing the edges of it further with her consciousness, she felt a presence—something dark and sinister, lurking near or within the field itself. It suddenly became aware of her, and as she focused more intently, the presence was staring straight back through the machine, its attention sharp and unnerving.

Startled, Keira recoiled, pulling back from the machine's connection and snapping back into her physical senses. She blinked rapidly, her vision returning to normal, the silver hue of her altered perception fading away. Her breathing, which had slowed during her deep concentration, now quickened again, though not from physical exertion. It was the shock, the fear of what she had just encountered, that caused her chest to tighten.

Whatever it was—no, whoever it was—held a malevolent intelligence, a malignant cancer, one filled with hate born of rage and loathing, and it had clearly sensed her intrusion.

It was alive.

She was sensing another biologic, not a constructed intelligence. The sensation was more than startling and unsettling; it was terrifying.

Keira shuddered involuntarily. She didn't know what or who that presence was, but it was something powerful and dark—something that shouldn't be there … alien in nature. Whatever it was, it had seen her, known who and what she was, and that realization sent a chill through her entire body.

For a moment, she stood there, trying to shake off the lingering unease. What had she just stumbled upon? The suppression field was an ordinary technological barrier, but it was connected to something far more dangerous, something that could sense her presence in ways she hadn't anticipated.

She glanced over at Lawrence, who stood vigilant, his single glowing eye trained on her. He hadn't sensed what she had—he had no access to the machine like she did, at least not in the same way—but his presence was a comforting reminder that she wasn't alone in this mess. She took a deep breath, steadying herself, trying to push down the fear that still clawed at her.

Whatever that dark presence was, it was still out there. Keira knew she had to be more careful, to tread lightly with her powers. The machine, the nanites, the reactor—these were tools she could potentially use, but they were also tied to forces she didn't fully comprehend.

Keira took another steadying breath. They had lingered here long enough, and the longer they stayed, the more vulnerable they became. It was time to move, time to put distance between themselves and the dangers closing in.

"Only one way to go," Keira said, her voice resolute.

"And which way is that?" Lawrence asked, his tone as even and composed as ever.

Keira didn't hesitate. She started moving again, at a steady jog. Lawrence fell into stride beside her, his battleframe humming softly as he matched her pace with mechanical precision.

"Away from the enemy."

CHAPTER FOUR

Location: Planet Asherho
Date: 2450, Imperial Standard

"These guys just don't quit," Keira muttered through gritted teeth, her voice laced with frustration and the adrenaline of the moment. She squeezed off two precise rounds down the debris-strewn street, the muzzle flash momentarily lighting the encroaching shadows of the coming night.

The sharp report of her rifle echoed down the narrow street. It was quickly drowned out by the furious roar of return fire. She barely had time to duck back behind the corner of the crumbling building before several explosive rounds peppered her position. The impact sent a shower of concrete fragments and dust cascading around her, exposing the steel beams that held what remained of the structure together.

But Keira was already moving. She sprinted across the open ground, her boots pounding against the cracked asphalt, every muscle in her body tense with the knowledge that hesitation meant certain death.

"I am coming for you, Keira." The voice, cold and heartless, echoed through her comms, sending a shiver down her spine.

"He doesn't stop either," Keira hissed angrily, her breath coming in quick, ragged bursts. She slid behind an overturned car, the metal frame providing scant cover. Dropping to one knee, she quickly scanned her surroundings, her eyes sharp and calculating as she searched for the next move in this deadly game.

Lawrence trailed a few meters behind Keira, his heavy metallic frame moving with a precision and speed that belied his bulk. As a black-suited figure darted around the corner, Lawrence's arm snapped up with mechanical speed. The instant his targeting system locked on, he fired. The shot was flawless—center mass. The enemy soldier had no time to react before the round punched into his chest. The force of the impact was devastating, hurling the figure backward as if an invisible giant had yanked him off his feet. The lifeless body crumpled to the ground, chest armor shattered, limbs splayed out like a child's ragdoll.

But the fight was far from over. Another enemy soldier peeked around the corner, releasing a short burst of gunfire in Lawrence's direction before retreating into cover. The rounds zipped past him harmlessly, their trajectory too wild and inaccurate to pose a real threat. Lawrence turned and ran toward Keira.

Two sleek, black panthers sprinted around the corner, their bodies low and streamlined, moving with an incredible lethal grace that Keira could not help but admire, their claws digging into the ground as they came on. At the same time, she found them frightening in the extreme. They were locked onto Lawrence, and they surged forward, their speed almost supernatural. They were designed for this—swift, killers programmed to take down their opponents, overwhelm and destroy.

Lawrence had already pivoted, his focus shifting back toward Keira's position. His sensors had clearly yet to register the threat of the panthers. Unaware of the deadly predators closing in from behind, he continued forward, each step bringing him closer.

Keira steadied her rifle, breath held tight as she aimed down the sights. The barrel quivered slightly as she tracked one of the panthers, adjusting to her target's movement. Exhaling a breath, she squeezed the trigger, and the rifle barked, the recoil jolting her shoulder, a thump courtesy of her haptic suit.

The first shot went wide, missing its mark by a hair. Frustration surged, but she didn't have time to dwell on it. Adjusting her aim, she fired again. The round connected with the bot's head, and the explosive charge detonated, tearing through the synthetic skull. The head disintegrated in a shower of metal and circuitry, its body crumpling to the ground, sliding more than a meter before coming to a halt, where it lay lifeless.

But there was no time to celebrate the kill. The second panther was already upon Lawrence, launching itself into the air for his back. Keira's heart skipped a beat, a cold dread washing over her. She watched in helpless horror as the sleek, lethal form collided with Lawrence midair.

And yet, at the last possible moment, Lawrence reacted. His battleframe twisted, catching the panther just after it pounced. The panther's many limbs flailed wildly, slashing and clawing with razor-sharp blades designed to tear through armor. Sparks flew as the claws raked against Lawrence's plating, leaving deep gouges and claw marks. But the battleframe didn't waver. His powerful arms gripped the panther, hydraulics straining as he exerted immense force, pulling in opposite directions.

There was a sickening crack, loud and final, as Lawrence ripped the enemy combat bot in two. The once frenzied limbs immediately went limp, the panther's systems shutting down with a faint whine and hiss. Lawrence tossed the lifeless halves aside with an almost casual motion, his focus already shifting back to Keira.

Without missing a beat, Lawrence began running toward her, his heavy footsteps pounding against the ground. Keira felt a surge of relief—but it was short-lived. Out of the corner of her eye, she spotted movement. An enemy soldier, lurking in the shadows, peeked back around the corner.

The soldier's weapon was a large tube-like thing. It was resting on his right shoulder. He brought the weapon to bear, sights trained on Lawrence's exposed back. Before Keira could react, there was a flash of light as the weapon fired, bucking.

The rocket flew across the space between them and struck Lawrence squarely in the back, hitting with a sharp, explosive pop. The impact sent a shockwave through his frame, and for a horrifying moment, Keira watched as the battleframe was thrown violently to the ground, a cloud of dust and debris erupting around him.

"No!" Keira's voice cracked with a mix of anger and fear as she swung her rifle around, adrenaline fueling her movements. Without a second thought, she fired. The explosive round sped down the street, slamming into the building corner where the enemy had just been. The explosion sent fragments of concrete flying, but the enemy soldier had already ducked back into cover, evading the deadly shot.

Keira's chest tightened, the brief silence following the shot amplifying her fear. She couldn't lose Lawrence—not now, not like this. But just as panic threatened to overwhelm her, she caught a glimpse of movement through the settling dust. Relief flooded through her as Lawrence, battered but operational, pushed himself up and onto his feet. His armor was scorched and dented, but the battleframe remained unbroken.

He moved quickly, slipping past her to take cover behind a nearby car. Even though the street now appeared empty, Keira's instincts told her the danger was far from over. The enemy was still out there. Keeping her rifle raised, she sent another round down the street, the sharp crack of the shot echoing through the desolate ruins. It wasn't meant to hit anything specific—just a warning, a message that she was still in the fight and ready to respond to any threat.

"Reload required," her suit chimed in, the voice cool and precise, maddeningly calm.

"Reload," Keira barked in response, her tone sharp with urgency. On cue, a new clip popped out from the compartment in her suit, ready for her to grab. She didn't hesitate. In one fluid motion, she ejected the spent clip from her rifle, the metal composite casing clattering to the ground, already forgotten. Her hand moved instinctively, seizing the fresh clip and slamming it into place. The weapon responded with a satisfying click, the familiar sound signaling that it was ready to fire.

A nagging worry troubled her—she had already burned through several clips, each one bringing her closer to the grim reality of running dry. Ammunition was a finite resource, and in this hellscape, resupply was impossible.

She knew she had to be smarter, more calculated. From this point onward, every shot had to count, every round had to serve a purpose. The reckless abandon of earlier had no place here; the stakes were too high and the margin for error too slim. As the weight of that realization settled in, Keira took a deep breath, steadying herself.

"Are you okay?" Keira called out, glancing back at Lawrence. Her voice carried a mix of concern and urgency, the tension of the situation weighing heavily on her.

"I am functional," Lawrence replied, his tone as calm and measured as ever. "Since the enemy has already located us, it might be prudent to consider firing the flare. It could attract assistance."

"Right," Keira exhaled, her breath catching as she ducked back under cover. The idea made sense, but in the heat of battle, she had momentarily forgotten about the emergency flare, focused on trying to break contact with the enemy.

How to activate it?

The thought was interrupted by instinct, and she shouted, "Emergency flare!"

"Emergency flare armed. Do you have a message to record?" the suit responded, its tone coolly efficient, unperturbed by the danger around them.

Keira didn't hesitate. "Yes, record—Keira Kane in trouble. Need immediate assistance."

"Message recorded and time-stamped. Current coordinates loaded and locked. Flare armed and ready to fire. Awaiting your command."

"Fire it!" Keira ordered, her voice sounding harsh in her helmet.

There was an audible pop from behind her, followed by a brilliant flash of light that momentarily illuminated the rapidly darkening street. The flare rocketed skyward, trailing a plume of smoke as it ascended. For a brief moment, Keira felt a pressure wave push against her, the force of the launch sending a shiver through her suit's haptic system. The air was filled with the sharp crack of the flare going supersonic and hopefully signaling her distress to anyone within range as it disappeared into the murk above.

She could only hope that someone—anyone—would receive the call for help and respond. The uncertainty troubled her, but she couldn't afford to dwell on it. With the flare fired, her focus shifted back to the immediate threat. The battle wasn't over, and they couldn't rely on rescue just yet. She had to look after herself, and she intended on doing just that.

"Emergency flare deployed," the suit confirmed. "Pulse message sent."

"We should keep moving and seek cover," Lawrence advised, his tone unwavering. "I predict the enemy will soon mount a concentrated assault on our position. I am detecting much movement out there."

"Right," Keira agreed, her eyes narrowing as she scanned the street ahead and behind them. Her mind raced, analyzing their surroundings for any potential escape routes. At the far end of the street, she spotted what appeared to be another park—a small patch of open space amidst the concrete ruins.

For a fleeting moment, she wondered once more what Asherho had looked like before the Fall, when it had been a paradise, vibrant and alive, thriving. But such thinking was cut short by the sudden, jarring impact of a bullet slamming into the car she was using as cover. The force of the shot rocked the vehicle, sending a tremor through the metal frame. Keira instinctively ducked lower, her heart pounding as she took stock of the situation. The street ahead was a graveyard of abandoned cars, each one a potential shield and cover.

"We'll leapfrog," she decided, her voice firm with determination. "We'll cover each other as we move toward the park, okay?"

"That will—work," Lawrence replied. "Are you ready to begin?"

"I am."

"You go—NOW."

Keira nodded, her grip tightening on her rifle. She took a deep breath, steadying her nerves, and then sprang into action. Darting from behind the car, she sprinted toward the next piece of cover for all she was worth, every muscle in her body tensed for the possibility of incoming fire.

Lawrence unleashed a barrage of suppressive fire back down the street, his weaponry lighting the rapidly dimming evening with quick, thunderous bursts. The sound was deafening, a wall of noise that echoed off the shattered buildings and hopefully kept the enemy pinned down.

Keira sprinted the twenty meters to the next car, her heart pounding in her chest. She vaulted over the top of the vehicle, hitting the ground on the other side in a controlled slide before coming to a stop.

She turned and quickly pressed herself against the side of the car, adrenaline coursing through her veins. Bringing her rifle up over the paint-scoured and rusting hood, she peered down the street, her eyes sharp and focused. The world around her seemed to slow, the moment narrowing to the single point of her aim.

"Go!" Keira roared, her voice cutting through the din. Just as the word left her lips, four enemy soldiers rounded the corner ahead. Three of them wore light, unpowered armor, while the fourth was encased in powered exoskeleton armor, a formidable and worrying sight. Keira didn't hesitate. She locked onto one of the lightly armored targets, her finger squeezing the trigger in one fluid motion.

The rifle kicked back against her shoulder as the round exploded from the barrel. She felt the familiar recoil a moment before the bullet connected with the enemy's chest. The impact was brutal, the force so powerful it sent the soldier crashing to the ground, a massive hole in his chest.

The remaining enemies scattered, including the one in powered armor. Each scrambled for cover. Keira's sharp eyes tracked their movements, and she quickly adjusted her aim. She fired a second shot, this one clipping an enemy in the leg. The soldier cried out, clutching at the wounded appendage as he crumpled behind a nearby car.

But Keira had no time to celebrate the hit. Lawrence, having heard her command, was already in motion, charging toward the next bit of cover behind her, his heavy frame moving with surprising speed and purpose. He flashed by as she kept her rifle trained on the enemy, ready to fire again if they made a move.

"Princess, your turn," Lawrence called from behind her.

Keira didn't waste a second. Without even glancing back, she launched herself into a full sprint, her boots pounding against the broken pavement. She flew past Lawrence, catching a brief glimpse of the battleframe hunkered down behind a dented industrial dumpster, aiming around the side of it. Then the enemy opened up. The air was suddenly thick with the sounds of combat—bullets whizzing by, the sharp crack of rifles, and the deep, thunderous boom of Lawrence's main weapon.

Keira's lungs burned as she pushed herself harder, her muscles straining with the effort. Just as she reached the charred remains of a utility truck, she dove, tucking and rolling behind its rusted shell for cover. She came to a stop, adrenaline coursing through her veins.

Behind her, Lawrence opened up again, the sound of his heavy weapon reverberating through the street like a jackhammer striking steel.

Bang—bang—bang.

Keira quickly got to her knees, her eyes locking onto Lawrence, who was now ten meters ahead, still laying down suppressive fire. It was then that she noticed the large, smoking hole in his back plate. Her heart skipped a beat. The plate was charred and molten around the edges, wisps of smoke curling up into the air, a clear sign that his armor had been compromised.

How badly had he been damaged?

A torrent of return fire rained down on Lawrence, bullets ricocheting off his frame with a deafening clatter. She peeked around the edge of the truck, her breath catching in her throat as she took in the scene before her, the enemy.

Her heart plummeted. More than two dozen enemy soldiers were advancing down the street, crouched low and shooting as they came on, their dark forms moving with lethal intent. Interspersed among them were six combat bots, panthers, their mechanical limbs skittering across the ground with unnerving precision.

Lawrence fired another round, the explosive force of his shot obliterating one of the bots in a shower of sparks and twisted metal. But it wasn't enough. The enemy continued to press forward, clearly assaulting their position.

Keira knew they were in trouble.

"I am coming, Keira. Do you hear me?" Crecee called to her. "My dear, I will have you soon enough. We're going to have so much fun together... I just know it."

There were too many. The realization hit Keira like a cold wave, a sinking feeling deep in her gut. She could see it clearly now—just too many to fight, and they wouldn't stop coming.

But even as the odds stacked against them, Keira refused to give in. Giving up wasn't in her nature, and surrender was a word that didn't exist in her vocabulary—not when facing a man like Crecee. He was ruthless, merciless, cruel, and surrendering to him would mean more than just defeat; it would mean the end of everything she held dear, including the hope for a better future. No matter the cost, they had to keep going, to keep fighting.

She tightened her grip on the rifle, raising it with renewed determination. She opened her mouth to shout a command to Lawrence, to tell him to go—but the words never left her lips.

In that instant, Lawrence was hit—hard. The impact was brutal, sending the massive battleframe stumbling backward. Keira's heart lurched as she saw the damage: his right arm, the one equipped with the cannon, had been severed cleanly at the elbow joint. The stump of the arm glowed ominously, molten metal dripping from the wound, hissing as it hit the ground.

For a split second, Keira feared the worst. But Lawrence wasn't finished yet. Recovering, he raised his remaining arm. The fingers on his left hand retracted, and from the center of his palm, a beam of searing light burst forth, cutting through the air with deadly intent, making a high-pitched humming sound.

Keira watched in stunned disbelief as Lawrence swung his arm in a wide arc, the beam of light tracing a burning path through the enemy ranks. The beam moved with surgical precision, slicing through the advancing soldiers as if they were made of paper. Three enemies fell in quick succession, their bodies neatly bisected by the lethal beam of energy. There was no scream, no sound—just the horrifying finality of death as they crumpled to the ground and the high-pitched humming of the energy weapon.

Keira could hardly believe what she had just witnessed. Even in his damaged state, Lawrence was a force to be reckoned with.

She raised her rifle, her breath steadying as she picked out a target amidst the chaos. Her eyes locked onto one of the bots closing in. She squeezed the trigger, sending a round downrange. The shot connected, striking the bot squarely, but before she could assess the damage, something caught her attention out of the corner of her eye. There was a nasty bang, followed by a heavy clatter.

Lawrence staggered, his massive form jolted as if hit by some unseen force. A second later, he went down, crashing to the ground on his back with a heavy thud that reverberated across the battlefield.

"No!" Keira's shout tore from her throat, raw and filled with despair. She swung her rifle to another target, firing with relentless fury. Each shot was a mix of desperation and rage as she tried to stem the tide of advancing enemies. She fired and fired, sighting on one enemy, then another, her hands moving automatically, each pull of the trigger an effort to push back the inevitable. After she'd almost emptied her clip, the enemy soldiers scattered, scrambling for cover. More than half a dozen of their number lay on the street. Then, from positions of shelter, they began firing back at her.

The truck she was using for cover began to shudder violently, the metal vibrating under the onslaught of enemy fire. Round after round hammered into the rusted hulk, the impacts deafening in their intensity. Keira ducked back under cover.

From her crouched position, she could see Lawrence. He was lying on his back, his once imposing form now still and smoking heavily from the damage he had sustained. His chest was a mess of scorched metal. Exposed wiring and internal components sparked feebly. But it was his head that drew her gaze—Lawrence was looking at her, the once bright red eye light fading, dimming with each passing second.

"Run, Keira—run!" And then, with a final, flickering pulse, the light in his eye went out.

Keira felt her heart lurch, a wave of grief and helplessness crashing over her. Lawrence was gone. The loss hit her with a force that almost knocked the breath from her lungs. The truck shuddered again as more rounds hammered into it, these ones heavier.

With trembling hands, Keira clutched her rifle tighter, knowing that she was now truly alone. But there was no time to think, no time to feel. She had to move, had to run. She had to survive. It was what Lawrence had wanted, what he had sacrificed himself for. And so, with a heavy heart and a determination forged in fire, Keira prepared to do just that.

She took one last, lingering look at Lawrence, her heart heavy with grief. His lifeless form lay amidst the wreckage of a dying world. She felt a fresh pang of loss, a raw ache that she forced herself to swallow down: Chris, Lee, Wash, and now Lawrence, not to mention her father and so many others. Like a wild animal, she growled. This was no time for hesitation, no time for self-pity—she had to survive, had to honor their sacrifice.

Pushing herself to her feet and using the truck for cover as much as she could, Keira began to run, sprinting away, each step taking her farther from the place where Lawrence had fallen. The sounds of firing still echoed around her, the buzzing of rounds passing her by, but her focus was singular: escape.

"Incoming orbital artillery dart," her suit announced in its usual calm, dispassionate tone. "Warning."

Keira's heart skipped a beat. There was no time to react, no chance to find cover. The warning barely registered before a brilliant flash of light erupted behind her. The air seemed to crackle with energy, and in the next instant, the world around her exploded into absolute chaos. Her visor went black, cutting off all sight, protecting her vision from the flash of detonation. Even the HUD died. She was plunged into sudden, disorienting darkness. The loss of vision was instant and absolute.

The ground beneath her feet heaved violently. The force of the blast sent her hurtling forward, the shockwave slamming into her with brutal intensity. She felt herself lifted off the ground, her body weightless for a brief, terrifying moment before gravity took hold. Keira felt the sickening sensation of freefall. Panic clawed at the edges of her mind as she felt herself falling into the abyss, the world slipping away. Then she hit something hard, and the darkness, absolute and complete, claimed her.

Chapter Five

Location: Planet Asherho
Date: 2450, Imperial Standard

Keira groaned, the sound echoing unnaturally loudly within the confines of her helmet, seeming to reverberate against her skull. Each breath she took was a laborious rasp, amplified in the enclosed space, making it feel as though the air itself was struggling to find its way into her lungs. Each muscle in her body screamed in protest, a cacophony of pain that radiated from every corner of her being.

Fatigue weighed on her like a lead blanket, pressing her down into a darkness that seemed to stretch on forever. The temptation to surrender to the void was strong, to let her eyes stay shut and drift away into nothingness.

But something in her refused to give in. A voice deep within her screamed for her to wake up and get moving. The voice was insistent, demanding. With a monumental effort, she forced her eyes to crack open, the lids feeling as heavy as the armor that encased her. The world remained a murky blur, the darkness unyielding. Panic flickered at the edges of her mind—this wasn't right. Her faceplate was blacked out, yet the heads-up display flickered faintly, its glow a spark in the darkness calling to her.

Wake up!

Where was she?

Fragments of memory, sharp and jagged, stabbed at her consciousness. There had been an explosion, a violent jolt, then nothing. The disorientation was almost as overwhelming as the pain and discomfort. She blinked, trying to piece together the shattered remnants of her last moments. The data before her came into focus. The HUD was still active—she was alive ... alive!

What had happened?

Keira attempted to move, tentatively at first, fearing she might be immobilized. Relief washed over her as her limbs responded, albeit sluggishly. She was able to move a hand, an arm, and then a leg, ever so slightly. She became acutely aware of the fact that she was lying face down. With a grunt, she tried to shift her position. But something resisted—her body met with stubborn, unyielding pressure from above.

Panic surged, but she forced it down, gritting her teeth as she pushed harder against the resistance. The effort produced a cacophony of sounds—scraping, grinding, the low groan of metal against metal. The weight on her back shifted, then suddenly gave way. Whatever had been holding her down slid off her back with a thunderous crash, reverberating through the stillness.

Her faceplate flickered, then cleared, transitioning from opaque blackness to a translucent view of her surroundings. The scan suite activated, its sensors probing the gloom, making everything visible. The harsh reality of her situation materialized before her eyes—she had been buried under a layer of debris. Twisted metal beams, shattered concrete, cabling, composite materials, and scorched fragments of what might have once been equipment lay scattered around her.

The oppressive darkness had been banished, but the uncertainty remained. Her heart pounded in her chest as she took in the scene, the dread creeping back into her thoughts.

Where was she?

The last coherent memory she had was of the running fight, the chaos, but now everything seemed distant and fragmented, like trying to recall a nightmare upon waking.

Shifting in her suit, Keira groaned at the discomfort she felt, even as her eyes darted around, taking in the scene of devastation surrounding her. Wreckage was strewn in every direction, a chaotic jumble of twisted metal, shattered concrete, and pulverized material she could not recognize. She tilted her head back, and several dozen meters above her, the night sky of Asherho loomed—a murky, oppressive brown haze that even her scan suite struggled to penetrate. As usual, no stars were visible. The familiar sight of Ash's polluted heavens brought her no comfort; it only deepened the sense of foreboding in her gut.

She turned slowly, trying to make sense of her surroundings. What she had initially thought was a pit became something far more ominous—a massive crater, the result of unimaginable force. The fog clouding her mind cleared. The realization hit her like a physical blow, memories flooding back with brutal clarity. The frantic, desperate fight…Lawrence, his last moments as he sacrificed himself for her, and then—the blinding light, the deafening roar of the orbital artillery dart hammering home.

Then the fall.

Her breath caught in her throat as understanding fully dawned. The power of that strike must have obliterated the street above, collapsing the ground beneath her in an instant. By some miracle, she had survived when everything around her had been reduced to rubble. Then again, the orbital artillery strike had likely been some distance from her. Otherwise, she would not be here.

A wave of gratitude, mingled with disbelief, washed over her. She was lucky—unbelievably, inexplicably lucky—to still be standing. She glanced down at her battered and beaten armor, peppered over with indentations, scorch marks, and more. She shook her head. It was a wonder it was still functioning.

Keira's gaze sharpened as she studied her surroundings more closely. Amidst the debris, something caught her eye—a familiar shape partially buried beneath the rubble to her right. Her pulse quickened as she recognized it: her rifle. She moved swiftly, yanking it free from the tangle of debris. The weight of it in her hands was reassuring, a small piece of normalcy in a world that had been turned upside down.

Her boots crunched against the uneven surface, and she realized with a start that she was standing on what had once been the street above, the pavement. The subterranean floors below had pancaked under the immense pressure of the blast, leaving her in this massive, cratered ruin.

She looked up, scanning the sheer walls of the crater. The distance to the top was daunting, but not insurmountable. Could she climb out of this hole? She flexed her fingers around the rifle's grip, determination settling over her like a second skin. It wouldn't be easy, but, yes, she could.

Yet, as Keira prepared to make her ascent, doubt rooted her to the spot. She hesitated, her instincts screaming at her that the surface might not be the sanctuary she hoped for. If any of the enemy had survived the strike, they would surely be scouring the area above, searching for her. Climbing out into the open could be tantamount to suicide.

Keira's mind raced, weighing her options. The idea of exposing herself to whatever might be waiting above was quickly losing its appeal. There had to be another way out, one that didn't involve making herself a blatant target.

She scanned the crater, what she could see around her, with renewed focus, searching for any alternative. Off to the right, about two meters above her current position, she spotted what might be an escape route—a gray door or hatch of sorts, partially smashed inward but still intact enough to offer a possible way through to the other side. Without wasting another second, she made her decision.

Keira moved swiftly, adrenaline sharpening her every movement as she made her way over to it. Securing her rifle to her back, she found a handhold in the debris and tested it. The handhold held. She pulled herself up, the jagged edges of the rubble biting into and scraping against her armor. The climb was short but treacherous, forcing her to scramble over loose chunks of concrete and twisted composite metal framing to find solid handholds that would support the weight of her armor.

Finally, she reached the hatch. She tried it, seeing if it would swing open for her. It would not, so she pulled herself a little higher and then kicked the door with force. After the second kick, the weakened structure yielded to the power of her armor-enhanced strength. The door crashed open, revealing a narrow corridor beyond, more an access shaft than anything else.

On her end, the corridor was a twisted, deformed thing, likely warped by the immense force of the orbital strike. The walls leaned at odd angles, the ceiling sagging in places, but it was passable. After a few meters, it straightened out. Edging forward and crouching down, Keira moved just inside the shaft.

She couldn't shake the thought that the orbital strike had been deliberately targeted. It had hammered down with lethal precision on whatever enemy forces had been positioned above. Was this the work of Captain Campbell? Or perhaps MK had orchestrated the attack, timing it perfectly to catch the enemy off guard. She supposed it had come from the *Seringapatam*, perhaps as response to the emergency flare she'd fired off. But at the same time, Keira had come close to death; the crater was proof enough of that. Either way, she owed her survival to that strike, for she'd been in a desperate spot, one she'd not have gotten out of on her own.

"Well, girl," Keira said to herself, peering down the long shaft ahead. "You wanted to get to the underground and now you're in the underground."

There was no answer. But then again, she had not expected one. Keira paused just inside the lip of the entrance, her back pressed against the rough edge of the tunnel. She took one last look up at the murky sky, the familiar, toxic haze swirling far above her. It was a grim reminder of the world she was fighting to survive in. With a final breath to steady herself, she turned and moved into the tunnel.

The passage was narrow, her armored shoulders scraping against the smooth walls as she squeezed through, hunched over and almost crab walking. The tunnel seemed ancient, its purpose long forgotten—but clearly some sort of a maintenance shaft.

Interestingly, none of the wall panels had been removed. No one had scavenged here.

As she advanced, Keira noticed something else unusual. The tunnel was surprisingly clean, devoid of the ever-present dust, sand, and ash that seemed to cling to everything on Ash. At first, it struck her as odd, almost eerie, that the shaft had remained so well-preserved and in an undisturbed state. It must have been sealed off for decades, maybe longer, untouched by the decay that had claimed the rest of the planet.

Why?

She had no clear sense of direction, only an urgent need to keep moving, to put as much distance between herself and the enemy as possible. Twisting and turning like a minotaur's labyrinth, the tunnel offered no clues as to where it might lead. But at least it was away from the surface, away from the danger that lurked above.

The flashing red indicator on her HUD was a constant reminder of her predicament—the suppression field was still active, choking off her ability to communicate, to call for backup. That likely meant some of the enemy had survived. The persistent signal tested her patience, a bright, irritating pulse in the corner of her vision on her HUD, flashing repeatedly. That told Keira all she needed to know. She was alone. She clenched her jaw, suppressing a growl of frustration.

The walls seemed to close in tighter with every step, and the eerie silence of the tunnel was broken only by the faint hum of her armor's systems and the muted thud of her boots on the composite metal flooring.

"I'll get away from the enemy and then call," Keira muttered under her breath, her voice a rare comfort in the oppressive silence. The ground beneath her feet shuddered violently with another quake. Holding her hands out against the walls, she steadied herself as the shaft rumbled and shook, waiting for the tremor to pass before pressing on. After a moment, it ceased.

She moved cautiously through the passage, her senses heightened, every sound magnified by the tunnel's claustrophobic confines. After what felt like an eternity, the shaft ended and came to a halt before another hatch. Like the first, this one was sealed tight, a heavy slab of composite metal that loomed before her.

Keira studied the door closely. It had once opened by sliding aside to the right. She determined that by noting the gouges and scrape marks along its edges, caused by being opened and closed repeatedly over many years. She knew she had to get through—it was her only way forward.

She placed both palms flat against the door. Taking a deep breath, she began to push, putting pressure to slide the door open, the servos in her suit humming with the effort, amplifying her strength.

At first, the door resisted, stubborn and unyielding. It groaned under the pressure but didn't budge. Keira gritted her teeth and pushed harder, feeling the strain communicated by her haptic suit in her arms as the door finally began to shift, to move ever so slightly. It groaned loudly in protest, as if giving up ground was painful. The groan grew into a tortured scream as, centimeter by centimeter, it gave way, moving aside with a painful slowness.

She increased her efforts, the grinding and screeching of metal on metal echoing back through the tunnel. The noise was deafening, and Keira cringed at it, but she didn't stop. She gripped the open side with a hand, and with one final, monumental shove, the door slid open fully, the sound reaching a crescendo before falling back into eerie silence.

Beyond the door, the tunnel opened into a junction, a much larger space that made Keira instinctively tense. She ducked through the opening and stepped into the new area. The space was not lit, but, like the shaft, eerily free of the dust and grime that coated most of Ash's ruins. It was as if this place too had been forgotten by time, sealed away from the decay that consumed the world above.

How long had it been since someone had come this way?

She took in her surroundings. Three good-sized doors greeted her—one directly ahead, another to her left, and one to her right. All were closed, sealed as tightly as the one she had just forced open. Each door was an unknown, a potential pathway to safety or, conversely, danger.

"Which way to go?" she muttered to herself, her voice barely above a whisper, which was swallowed by the oppressive silence of the junction room.

She could feel the weight of the decision pressing down on her. The wrong choice could lead to a dead end, or worse, straight into enemy hands. But she couldn't afford to stand here much longer, exposed and vulnerable. The threat of pursuit was still very real.

Keira's eyes darted between the three doors, each identical in their appearance, offering no clues as to what lay beyond. The eerie silence only added to the tension.

Taking a deep breath, she weighed her options. Left, right, or straight ahead? There was no clear answer, only the cold reality that she had to choose and keep moving. Time was not on her side, and the enemy, if they were nearby, could be closing in.

She froze, every muscle in her body tensing as her senses screamed a warning. A faint sound reached her ears, something out of place in the oppressive silence of the tunnel. Was that a noise behind her? Slowly, she turned, her heart hammering in her chest as she ducked and looked back into the access shaft she had just emerged from.

Her breath caught in her throat, a cold dread settling over her. Two panthers—sleek, deadly, and unmistakably engineered—were in the shaft. Three hundred meters away, they had just turned a corner. Having spotted her, both, as if startled, had come to a complete halt. Their eyes glowed a sinister red as they took her in. Then, they broke into a full charge, the distance between them and Keira closing rapidly.

Instinct took over. Keira grabbed her rifle from her back and raised it, pointing it into the shaft, her movements precise despite the surge of adrenaline coursing through her. She aimed squarely at the nearest panther and pulled the trigger.

Click.

Nothing happened.

Panic flared as she pulled the trigger again. Another click. Beyond that, the rifle remained silent. She glanced down in horror, her eyes locking onto the slightly bent and warped barrel. It must have been damaged in the fall. How had she missed that? The realization hit her like a punch to the gut—her rifle was useless.

There was no time to dwell on the mistake. The panthers would soon be upon her. She cast the rifle aside, the useless weapon clattering against the floor, and her hand instinctively went to her sidearm. The pistol was her next best option, but as her fingers brushed the grip, a new idea sparked in her mind, one that might give her the edge she desperately needed.

"Grenade, maximum yield," Keira commanded with steely determination, her voice cutting through the chaos in her mind. Almost instantly, a round, deadly device ejected from her suit's storage compartment, landing with a solid *thunk* into her waiting hand.

"Maximum yield," her suit confirmed, the cold, mechanical voice a contrast to the urgency of the situation.

Without hesitation, Keira hurled the grenade down the shaft. The moment it left her hand, she ducked aside, pressing herself against the wall as she simultaneously drew her pistol. Her breaths came quick and shallow, the seconds stretching into an agonizing eternity as she braced for the inevitable explosion.

For a moment, there was nothing—a tense, suffocating silence that made her doubt if the grenade had even activated. Then, the blast erupted, a violent, concussive force that rocked the tunnel and sent shockwaves rippling through the floor and her suit. Keira was almost knocked from her feet. The explosion was deafening in the enclosed space, a cacophonous roar that reverberated off the metal walls, amplifying the destructive power unleashed in the confined space.

She could feel the force of the blast resonate through her armor, the vibrations rattling her bones, though the suit absorbed most of the impact. Like the fiery tongue of an enraged serpent, a stream of flame shot forth from the shaft, momentarily illuminating the darkness with a searingly bright light.

Beneath her feet, she felt a deep and terrible rumbling, as if the very ground was groaning under the strain of the explosion. Then, as suddenly as it had begun, it was over. A wave of fine white dust blew out from the shaft. The roar faded, the flames receded, leaving behind a heavy silence punctuated only by the distant echo of collapsing debris.

Keira took a steadying breath, her heart still pounding as she dared to peek around the corner, searching for the panthers and aiming her pistol. Smoke billowed from the shaft, thick and acrid, obscuring everything in its path. But her scan suite quickly adjusted, the advanced sensors slicing through the smoke with ease, revealing the aftermath of her desperate gamble.

Keira exhaled a long, relieved breath, the tension that had gripped her slowly unwinding. The shaft had collapsed about thirty meters down, a tangled mess of debris and rubble neatly sealing off the passage. There was no sign of the panthers, no movement, no sound—only the silence of destruction.

For the moment, she was safe.

But the feeling of safety was fleeting. She understood all too well that this was only a temporary reprieve. The explosion would have alerted any nearby enemy forces to her presence. They now knew she was alive, and worse—they knew she was somewhere in the underground and close.

She couldn't afford to waste any time. The enemy would be mobilizing, closing in on her location, and the tunnels would soon be crawling with them. Keira turned away from the ruined shaft, her mind already racing through her options. If she was to live, she had to stay one step ahead of them.

The hunt was back on.

CHAPTER SIX

Location: Planet Asherho
Date: 2450, Imperial Standard

Two hours had passed since Keira had collapsed the access shaft, entombing the two panthers beneath tons of debris. Fatigue weighed heavily on her. Each step through the underground was a battle against the exhaustion that tested her resolve to keep going.

She couldn't afford to rest, not here, not now. The underground network that sprawled beneath the planet's surface stretched for kilometers beyond count, a maze of corridors, shafts, and tunnels that seemed to twist and shift with every passing moment. When she'd first ventured into these depths, she assumed that was all the work of human hands and toil—another relic of the forgotten wars that had scarred Asherho. But the deeper she went, the more she realized how wrong she had been. Humans had not done all this; they had just appropriated and repurposed what they had found. Once you got below a certain level, the architecture was too precise, the materials too advanced.

Keira had begun to understand that this place, like much of the planet, was the true legacy of the precursors. These ancient beings, long vanished from the universe, had used nanites to sculpt the very bones of Asherho, shaping it not for habitation, but for a purpose beyond her comprehension. It wasn't a settlement—it was a grand design, a vast, intricately planned construct.

The scale of their work was staggering, speaking to a vision that spanned eons. As near as she could figure, the precursors, leaving behind this universe, had gone to another plane of existence, but some had remained behind...that, in a strange sense, Asherho was sort of a prison. Worse, some of those imprisoned here had gotten out and begun the civil war that had devastated humanity. She did not fully understand it all, but somehow she was to deal with those who had escaped. The powers she'd been given were to help her with that.

With the navigation systems of her powered armor nonfunctional, Keira had no clear sense of direction, only muddled guesswork as she worked her way through the twisting passages beneath the surface. Where she was in relation to the city above was also a mystery.

In the past half hour, she had caught snippets of garbled transmissions—faint echoes on the marine channels that cut through the silence like a lifeline. The fragmented and distorted voices were barely intelligible, but they were proof that friendlies were still out there, somewhere beyond the suffocating grip of the dispersion field. It was a small comfort, a reminder she was not completely alone in this forsaken place, that help was not far off.

Yet the danger of broadcasting her own position, trying to reach out, was too great. The enemy could be listening, and one wrong move made too early could easily reveal her location. The thought sent a chill down her spine, amplifying the sense of isolation that already gnawed at her being. But there was hope—a glimmer of it, fragile yet persistent—and Keira would take that. She was clearly reaching the edge of the field.

She resolved to press onward, pushing herself through the disorienting labyrinth until she was completely beyond the reach of the field. Only then, when she was confident that she had slipped free of its shadow, would she risk breaking through to the surface and reestablishing contact. The prospect of reuniting with the marines was the only thing keeping her moving, each step a defiance of the overwhelming urge to surrender to the exhaustion that threatened to overtake her.

The sensation of being hunted clung to Keira like a dark and menacing shadow, an ever-present weight that set her nerves on edge. Every instinct screamed that she was not alone, that unseen eyes were tracking her, studying her as she moved deeper into the labyrinth of the underground. It was more than just paranoia; it was a primal certainty, growing stronger with every passing minute. No matter how far she traveled, the feeling persisted. She could not shake it.

She paused, taking a moment to rest. Twenty minutes ago, she had dropped into this tunnel, an old rail line long abandoned and forgotten. The magnetic tracks, once vibrant with the hum of energy, were now cold and lifeless, their sleek lines dulled by years of neglect. There was no power here, no sign of movement—only the oppressive silence that pressed in from all sides.

But the stillness offered no comfort. Keira's eyes flicked about, searching for any hint of what might be out there, watching her. The darkness beyond the vision of the scan suite seemed to shift and pulse, playing tricks on her mind, making her question what was real and what was imagined. She could almost feel the weight of the unseen gaze, the subtle pressure of something—or someone—tracking her movements with unsettling precision.

The train tunnel stretched out before her, a yawning maw that seemed to swallow light and sound alike. The sense of unease only deepened as she prepared to move on, the feeling that she was being watched never leaving her, a near constant reminder that she was never truly alone in the dark.

A thick, soupy haze clung to the air, reducing visibility to mere meters. Her scan suite automatically compensated for it. The fog was not natural; it was the toxic miasma that thickened the farther down one ventured. Each breath felt heavy in her lungs, her armor's filtration system working overtime to keep the worst of it at bay.

Judging by the density of the murky air around her, Keira estimated she was at least a hundred meters below the surface, if not deeper. Every step forward felt like a descent into a realm where humans were never meant to tread, a place crafted by ancient alien hands for purposes she could only guess at.

Keira had thought about using her abilities—dropping into the machine—to glean more information from her surroundings. She knew she could easily reach out, feel the pulse of the tunnels, perhaps even detect the faintest vibrations of any lurking threat. But that came with a risk. Allowing herself to become too focused on gathering information, detached from her body, might leave her vulnerable, distracted in a moment when she needed to be sharp and aware.

There was also that malevolent presence out there to consider. If she dropped into the machine, it might be able to locate her position. The thought of that was frightening. So, she suppressed the urge, trusting her instincts instead of her new and barely understood abilities. She kept on moving, one foot in front of the other, her senses tuned to the environment as best as they could be. The haze thickened as she pressed on, but Keira didn't slow.

Gripping her pistol, Keira scanned the silent, empty tunnel with wary eyes as she moved. The darkness seemed to press in on her from all sides, the oppressive stillness broken only by the sound of her own breathing in her helmet. Still feeling like she was being watched, her thoughts drifted back to the research facility, to the small, seemingly harmless bot that Scaro and Jessie had shown her. They had called it a house cat, deceptively innocent in appearance but designed for intelligence and reconnaissance work. It was a marvel of technology, with chameleon-like abilities and masking technologies that allowed it to blend seamlessly into its surroundings, rendering it almost invisible to the naked eye.

The marines had spoken of these bots with a mix of admiration, wariness, and dread. They were nearly impossible to locate, even with the most advanced sensor suites. The thought of one of those tiny, ghost-like machines lurking in the shadows, following her, tracking her every move, sent a chill down her spine. Was there one here now, moving silently through the gloom, feeding her position back to the enemy? Was it whispering her location to Crecee, guiding them closer with every step she took?

The idea was unsettling, a slow-burning fear that set her nerves on edge. She didn't like the feeling—not one bit. The notion that she could be so closely monitored, her every action observed without her knowledge, was a reminder of how vulnerable she truly was in these alien tunnels.

But after a moment, she forced herself to dismiss the thought. She was letting her nerves get the better of her, allowing her mind to spiral into paranoia. There were no signs, no telltale hints that anything was down here with her. She couldn't afford to waste energy on ghosts, phantom wraiths concealed in the darkness, not when every ounce of focus was needed to navigate this treacherous environment.

As she had done many times before, Keira paused and stood still, listening intently to the tunnel's silence. She strained her ears for any hint of movement, any sound that might betray the presence of another. But there was nothing—no echoes, no rustling in the dark, no faint hum of machinery. Just the heavy silence, as deep and oppressive as the haze that filled the air.

That silence was reassuring, a small comfort in the midst of her growing unease. For now, at least, she seemed to be alone. No invisible stalkers, no hidden enemies lurking in the shadows. She took a breath, steadying herself, and prepared to move forward. The journey was far from over, but for the moment, she had a small measure of peace, however fleeting that might be.

Keira pressed on, her steps steady despite the growing weight of fatigue. After another hundred fifty meters, the tunnel began to widen, revealing the contours of a small station ahead, complete with a platform that emerged from the darkness like a forgotten relic. The station wasn't large, clearly not meant for freight, but rather for the movement of people—a place where passengers once waited for trains that no longer ran.

The station was eerily quiet, a ghostly remnant of a time long past. Against the walls, benches sat in disarray, covered in layers of grime, their metal frames rusting and worn. They had once been arranged neatly.

The station had been thoroughly picked over and scavenged, stripped of anything useful. Almost all the wall panels had been removed, exposing the remains of what had once been a complex array of parts and equipment. The machinery that had thrummed with life was long gone. Even the ceiling bore the scars of plunder. The lighting units and fixtures had been ripped out, leaving gaping holes and dangling wires in their place.

Loose panels and cables littered the floor, tangled in a chaotic mess that spoke of hasty, desperate salvaging. Everything was coated in a thick layer of dust, undisturbed for what could have been years.

The platform felt like a tomb, a place where time had stopped, and the world above had forgotten what was below. There was no sign of recent activity, no footprints in the dust, no indications that anyone had been here in a long time. Yet the emptiness did little to ease her tension. The station, stripped bare and abandoned, only deepened the sense of isolation that had been with her since she first entered the tunnels.

She paused, taking in the scene, her mind sifting through the possibilities. This place had once been vital, a hub of movement and life. Now, it was just another casualty. But even in its abandonment, the station held a certain power, a reminder of what had been lost—and what still might be found, if she could just keep moving forward.

This was a sight all too familiar to Keira. She had encountered it countless times—everywhere she went, the story was the same. Anything of value, anything that could be scrounged, salvaged, or repurposed, had been taken long ago. The fall of the empire had shattered the very fabric of life on Asherho. The planet's infrastructure had crumbled, and in the aftermath, with production at a standstill, the people had turned to scavenging to survive. Ash had become a world of ruins, where the past was picked clean.

Keira's gaze shifted warily to the escalator and stairs leading upward, their paths vanishing into the darkness above. The stairs were caked in grime, the escalator frozen in time, its mechanical joints rusted and immobile. A part of her wondered if she had gone far enough, if she dared to ascend and try to make contact with the marines. The prospect of reaching the surface was tantalizing, a chance to break free from the oppressive underground and see the sky once more. But the uncertainty seriously bothered her. Was it safe to go up? Would it not be wiser to continue farther down the tunnel, to stay hidden and push further into the unknown?

She hesitated, her eyes flicking between the stairs and the darkened tunnel ahead. As if in response to her indecision, the ground beneath her feet began to tremble. This quake was stronger than the ones before, a deep rumble that seemed to resonate from the very core of the planet. The floor vibrated beneath her boots, and a fine shower of dust drifted down from the ceiling, dancing in the dim light. Then, with a suddenness that made her flinch, a ceiling tile broke free and crashed to the station platform with a loud smack, sending up a puff of dust and debris. Then the quake subsided, but the sense of unease lingered, the station's silence now filled with the echoes of the tremor.

Keira checked her HUD again, her eyes scanning the familiar display. The red warning indicator continued to flash intermittently, a brief pulse every ten seconds that set her nerves on edge. The warning wasn't constant, like it had been, but its presence was a persistent reminder of the danger she was in. She knew better than to ignore it, but there was little she could do about it now. She took a couple of steps forward, and the warning light went out. It did not come back on.

Keira felt her heart skip a beat.

Switching to the platoon channels, she was met with silence. The static-filled emptiness told her nothing; it could mean they were out of range, or worse, that there was no one left to respond. Despite the unease, she decided to try anyway. She made a quick double click, briefly activating her comms, and then waited, holding her breath as the seconds ticked by.

The silence was deafening. She breathed in deeply, forcing herself to stay calm, exhaling slowly as she counted the seconds. Still, there was no reply. The silence stretched on, an empty void that offered no comfort, no sign of life on the other end.

Determined not to give up just yet, Keira decided to try once more. She triggered her mic again, the sound of the double click loud in the stillness of her helmet. Again, she waited, listening intently for any response, any indication that someone—anyone— was out there.

But the silence remained unbroken. No reply, no echo of a voice, nothing but the soft hum of her armor and her breathing.

"It was worth a try," Keira muttered to herself, her voice low in the oppressive quiet. The words were meant to reassure, but they felt hollow in the empty space. With no other option, she resumed her cautious pace, moving forward along the track. The tunnel stretched ahead, dark and foreboding, the silence a constant companion as she pressed on.

There was a double clicking on the comms. Keira froze mid-step, her breath catching in her throat as she stared at the HUD. On the platoon channel, a name flashed briefly: PLT: Pvt. Avante.

Jessie was out there!

The realization hit her like a shockwave, and a triumphant whoop escaped her lips before she could stop herself. She'd been heard—they knew she was alive. That small confirmation, that tiny flicker of hope, was enough to steel her resolve.

The decision was made in an instant. The exhaustion that had been creeping into her muscles, the weariness that had threatened to overwhelm her, now seemed bearable. She had been through hell and back, and she knew instinctively that she couldn't go much farther without some kind of rest. But now, with the knowledge that Jessie and the others were out there, she had a destination. She looked toward the station platform and the still escalator.

Up it was.

With renewed determination, Keira pulled herself up onto the train platform. Her movements were slower now, more deliberate, as fatigue clawed at her with every step. She began to ascend the still, silent stairs, her footfalls echoing softly in the empty station. Surprisingly, the escalator steps had been left intact, a small mercy in this place where everything else had been stripped bare.

As she climbed, her eyes caught sight of a sign overhead, its faded letters barely legible: Leeward Block. The arrow pointed upward, directing her toward a place she had never heard of, nor been. Other signs adorned the walls, their messages eroded by time and the corrosive air. The toxic sludge that permeated the lower levels had left its indelible mark here as well, eating away at the words until only ghostly remnants remained.

Keira paused for a moment, squinting at the sign. Leeward Block meant nothing to her—just another name in a city she barely knew, a relic of a time before the war had torn everything apart. But it didn't matter. The name was irrelevant; what mattered was that it led upward, toward the surface, toward safety.

Taking a deep breath, she continued her ascent, the escalator steps creaking slightly beneath her weight. Each step was a struggle against the exhaustion that threatened to pull her down, but Keira pushed through, fueled by the knowledge that she was not alone, that there were others out there who knew she was alive and coming for her.

At the top of the escalator, Keira was met with a long, dimly lit corridor stretching out before her. The space had an eerie stillness to it, amplified by the dust and debris that lined the floor. Running the length of the corridor was an old-style moving platform, a relic from a time when technology served the convenience of those who lived in luxury. It was a kind of automated sidewalk, designed to carry people along without the need for walking. Keira had only seen something like it once before, on a high orbital station where the privileged few lived in abundance, far removed from the struggles of those on the planet far below.

The platform was divided into two parallel paths, each one meant to move in opposite directions when operational. Now, however, both were silent and still, the mechanisms long since stripped of power and purpose.

With no other options and her mind already made up, Keira began moving along the walkway. Her boots struck the rubber-composite tread with a steady rhythm, each step echoing hollowly in the empty corridor.

She walked until she reached an exit ramp, the place where travelers would have once stepped off to continue their journey on foot. A sign hung overhead, its letters faded but still legible: Leeward Block. The arrow pointed to her right, indicating the way out.

Keira paused for a moment, taking in her surroundings. The corridor felt like a forgotten artery, one that had ceased to serve its purpose long ago. Yet here she was, retracing the steps of countless others who had once walked this path, now driven by a need far more urgent than mere convenience. With a final glance at the sign, Keira turned and headed toward the exit.

As Keira moved forward, she noticed another sign hanging above. An arrow indicated the walkway she'd just left. It listed more destinations she didn't recognize: Stalwart Towers, Grange Station, and Imperial Recruiting Center. The last name caught her attention, sparking a flicker of curiosity. The Imperial Recruiting Center sounded intriguing, though she wondered if it had been a military facility or something civilian in nature. Either way, it was another reminder of the empire that once ruled over this world, now reduced to faded memories and crumbling structures.

Deciding to stick with her plan, Keira took the exit toward Leeward Block. She paused briefly, straining to hear anything out of place, any sign of life that might indicate she wasn't alone. But once again, the corridor was as silent as a tomb, the oppressive stillness making her feel as though she were the last person alive in this forgotten corner of the world.

Satisfied that she was still alone, Keira turned and followed the corridor leading to Leeward Block. The passageway stretched out ahead of her. Before long, she found herself facing another set of steps, leading to yet another escalator, followed by more stairs and another escalator beyond that. The repetitive nature of the climb was exhausting, each ascent a test of her endurance.

She moved cautiously, her eyes scanning every inch of the path ahead. Much of this escalator had been disassembled, the steps removed in places, leaving gaps that could easily trip her up if she wasn't careful. The metal framework of the escalator was exposed, jagged edges and loose wires sticking out where panels had been stripped away.

Keira watched her footing closely, placing each step with care as she ascended. Finally, she reached the top.

At the top of the escalator, Keira stepped into a wide, open room that bore the unmistakable signs of abandonment and decay. Discarded and broken furniture lay scattered across the floor— chairs tipped over, old sofas with their stuffing spilling out, and tables standing at odd angles, some with their legs missing. The scene reminded her of an old common room, the kind of place where people once gathered to relax and socialize, now reduced to a shadow of its former self.

To her left, a row of stalls lined the wall, their faded signage and empty counters telling the story of a time when this place had bustled with life. The nearest stall had a faded menu still clinging to the wall above, its once bright colors now dulled by time. Pictures of plates adorned the menu, the details barely visible beneath layers of grime. At the top, in large, blocky letters, was the name: Ho Lee Chinese Food.

As she took in the scene, her eyes were drawn to a large sign hanging almost immediately overhead. The letters were still relatively intact, though the paint had started to peel, revealing the metal beneath. It read: Welcome to Leeward Tower, a great place to retire and live. The slogan, once likely meant to evoke comfort and security, now felt hollow and mocking in the desolation of the space.

Keira moved past the old sign that once welcomed visitors and stepped into the cavernous common room, her eyes narrowing as she swept the area ahead. The silence was thick, almost oppressive, only broken by the hum of her suit's systems. The place was deserted, as expected, but the stillness made her uneasy. Her visor flickered as it adjusted to the dim light, highlighting the skeletal remains of what had once been a bustling space.

Her gaze drifted to the food stalls lined up against one wall, their faded signs and cracked glass displays a haunting reminder of a bygone era. She didn't know what "Chinese food" was, but the faded pictures of savory dishes, now coated in dust and grime, made her stomach twist with a pang of hunger she hadn't felt in days. The sight of food—any food—was a cruel tease in this hollowed-out world.

Her boots clunked against the floor, the sound echoing in the emptiness, amplifying the desolation of the place. She scanned the room, her senses heightened, every nerve on edge. The pizza stall's sign hung lopsided, its bright colors long faded, and the Greek food stand was a shadow of its former self, its once vibrant posters peeling away like the remnants of a forgotten dream. She knew what pizza and Greek food was, for there had been a restaurant on the main orbital. She'd eaten there once, and it had been wonderful.

Nothing stirred, nothing moved. This place had been left to rot for so long that it felt almost otherworldly, like a snapshot frozen in time. The eerie quietness was unnerving. It was as if the ghosts of those who once laughed, ate, and lived here were watching her, their lives cut short by the Great Fall. The thought sent a shiver down her spine, her imagination conjuring flickering images of a world that no longer existed.

"Keira," a voice crackled in her ear, the signal distorted and somewhat garbled, but unmistakable. It was Crecee. The moment she heard his voice, she froze, her breath catching in her throat as a wave of icy dread washed over her. It had been a while since she'd last heard from him—since before the orbital artillery dart had crashed down, leaving devastation in its wake. She had clung to the hope that he'd been among the casualties, but his voice now shattered that illusion.

"I know you can hear me, girl," he continued, the menace in his tone unmistakable. "We know you survived. We're tracking you, and we'll catch up soon enough. Make it easy on yourself.

Give up. You're alone, and there's nowhere else to go. Keep pushing onward and when I do catch you, I will not go easy. I will not be merciful."

His words echoed in her helmet, each one dripping with a twisted mix of confidence and sadistic pleasure. Keira's pulse pounded in her ears. The temptation to respond, to spit out a retort that would tell Crecee exactly what she thought of him, surged within her. She could almost feel the words on the tip of her tongue, a sharp rebuke ready to be unleashed. But she bit it back, forcing herself to remain silent and not transmit her heated reply.

It took every ounce of restraint not to curse him out, to let him know that she was far from broken, far from giving up ... that there was still some fight left. But she knew better. Responding would have been a mistake—a fatal one. An extended transmission would have given her away, via triangulation tech. It was the one thing she knew he did not have, her location. Had he known where she was, he'd have been on her long before now.

Keira's jaw clenched as she steadied her breathing, her heart still racing. She wasn't about to give Crecee the satisfaction of knowing he had rattled her. Instead, she focused on the silence that followed his words, the stillness of the abandoned common room around her. The game was far from over, and she had no intention of letting him win.

She had considered shutting off the open comms more than once, the thought nagging at her as a way to cut Crecee out of her head. But after some thought, she'd decided against it. There was a twisted irony in it—Crecee, in his attempts to break her, was actually fueling her resolve. His taunts, meant to wear her down mentally, only solidified her determination. He didn't realize it, but every word he spat at her drove her forward, made her more determined not to surrender, not to let him win.

With renewed purpose, Keira began to move again. Her steps were no longer cautious and tentative, but driven by a clear objective. She needed to get out of this abandoned apartment block, back onto the streets.

Her mind was already mapping out her next steps. Once she was outside, she would attempt to establish contact with Captain Scaro, Jessie, and the marines. If the transmission failed to reach anyone, or the dispersion field caught up to her, she would retreat back to the underground. Down there, she could find a place to hide, to hole up and rest and plan her next move.

As she moved forward, she made a vow to herself. She had come too far to be caught, too far to let Crecee or anyone else take her down. The thought of giving up wasn't even an option. She had faced too much, survived too long, to let it end here. No matter what, she would keep going. She wouldn't allow herself to be captured. She would not let him win. Not now, not ever.

CHAPTER SEVEN

Location: Planet Asherho
Date: 2450, Imperial Standard

Keira lowered herself into a crouch, her movements smooth and silent, enhanced by the servos of her powered battle armor. The HUD in her helmet flickered with data, estimating distances, as she peered out from the shattered window of one of the apartment block's many side entrances. The jagged glass framed her view like a broken picture, the shards along the edges catching the last rays of the setting sun's light through the murky brown haze.

It was difficult to tell how many days had passed since she'd set out with the marines—two, perhaps? Certainly, it had been more than one. Time had become a blur of violence, pursuit, and survival. She also had no idea how long she'd been out after the orbital strike.

Keira was absolutely exhausted and spent. She had no idea how much farther she could manage to go. A once sprawling park stretched out before her, now a ghost of its former self. The cracked walkways, once meant for leisurely strolls, were now littered with debris and partially covered by sand, not to mention refuse.

All that remained of the park's trees were low-lying stumps. On Ash, trees were but a memory. In the center of the park, the remains of a once grand marble fountain stood, its ornate carvings worn down and smoothed by the elements and harsh weather.

Looking over it all, there were times when she thought that Asherho had been a planet of pure leisure and excess. Encircling the park were what had once been smaller apartment blocks, now reduced to absolute ruins. The buildings had long since succumbed to the relentless passage of time, their walls crumbling inward, creating small mountains of debris.

The recent nuclear bombardment had likely exacerbated the destruction across much of the planet, turning what was already a wasteland into an even more twisted landscape of broken concrete and warped metal. Evidence of that were several fires, of which she could see large plumes of dark smoke in the far distance.

The red flashing warning had returned. She was back in the dispersion and jamming field. That told her the enemy was closing in and within five kilometers of her position. Calling for help was no longer an option. She found it incredibly frustrating and now wished she had done it sooner, reached out to the marines while she'd had the opportunity. It had been a mistake to not try, and now she might just pay for that.

Should she set back out into the ruins and make her way to the edge of the field? There was only one way out from her current position, and that was forward—into the open, across the park's desolate expanse. It was an exposed route, offering little in the way of cover. The thought of moving along the edges of the park crossed her mind, but the sparse remains of walls and rubble provided no real protection, no shelter from view. If anyone was out there, lying in wait, they would have a clear line of sight on her the moment she stepped out from cover.

Keira's jaw tightened, and she bit her lip, wrestling with her options. Going back into the apartment block and searching for another way, one with more cover, would be safer, but it would also take precious time—time she wasn't sure she had.

Exhaustion tugged at the edges of her thoughts, her nerves frayed from the constant need to focus and remain alert. She was so tired her eyes were twitching regularly. Keira understood she was almost at the end of her rope, and every decision felt like it carried the weight of life and death. She exhaled slowly, her breath fogging up the inside of her helmet for a moment before the environmental controls cleared it.

What to do?

She knew she had to make a choice. Every second she lingered increased the chances of being discovered, but rushing out into the open without a plan could be fatal and she was damn certain it wasn't wise.

For the moment, Keira was safe. The shattered landscape around her was eerily quiet, with no signs of enemy movement in sight. She allowed herself a moment to breathe. She wasn't under immediate threat, and that alone was something to be grateful for.

Keira glanced back over her shoulder, her eyes tracing the path she had taken to get here. Her footprints were clearly visible in the sand and dust. The idea of retracing her steps crossed her mind. It was a tempting thought. If she went back the way she had come, perhaps she could find a place to hole up, to rest for a few hours and gather her strength. The day's light was fading quickly, and under the cover of darkness, she could set out again with the advantage of concealment. Though anyone with a scan suite would be able to see just fine.

The thought of rest was alluring. The adrenaline that had fueled her for so long was now ebbing steadily away, leaving behind a profound fatigue. Her muscles ached, and even the advanced systems of her powered armor couldn't completely mask the toll the last few days had taken on her body. But was it wise to turn back?

She weighed her options, the seconds ticking by in the gathering dusk. If she chose to retreat, she'd need to find a secure spot quickly, somewhere within the block, a place where she could hide from any patrols or drones that might sweep the area after nightfall.

The more Keira considered her options, the more the idea of falling back made sense. She made her decision. Slowly, with practiced caution, she began to withdraw into the building. Every movement was deliberate, her senses on high alert, keen to avoid attracting any unwanted attention. She kept low, hugging the walls as she retraced her steps through the side entrance, her armored boots making barely a sound against the cold, hard floor. As she rounded a corner and the view of the outside world vanished behind her, she straightened up, letting out a breath she hadn't realized she was holding.

For a brief moment, she considered just stopping here, leaning against the wall, maybe even closing her eyes for a few minutes of rest. The weariness in her bones was almost unbearable, and the idea of sleep was tempting. But she quickly dismissed the thought. This spot was too exposed, too vulnerable. She needed a place that was more secure, more isolated—a place where she could truly let her guard down, if only for a little while.

She was about to press deeper into the building, seeking out such a refuge, when a crash shattered the stillness. It was muffled, distant, but unmistakably from somewhere within the building. Suddenly alert, Keira froze, every muscle tensing as she strained to listen. The silence that followed was deafening, stretching out for several long, agonizing heartbeats. Had she imagined it? No, she was certain—something had caused that noise.

She wasn't alone.

A chill ran down her spine as the possibilities raced through her mind. Who—or what—was in the building with her? Were they survivors, trying to find a place to ride out the chaos outside? Or was it something far more dangerous? The thought of the enemy lurking in the shadows, hidden within these very walls, sent a surge of adrenaline through her veins. Keira's hand instinctively moved to her weapon.

She remained perfectly still, listening intently for any further sounds, any indication of movement. The silence was thick, oppressive, and every second that passed felt like an eternity.

As Keira had navigated through the apartment block toward this exit, she'd been vigilant, scanning every corner, every surface for signs of recent activity. But there had been nothing—no scuff marks, no disturbed dust, no footprints in the thick layer of grit that covered the floors. The building had been untouched for what seemed like years, abandoned and forgotten in the wake of the devastation that had swept across the planet. If anyone had been here recently, she would have seen the evidence. But there had been none, which made the crashing sound she'd heard all the more ominous and troubling.

The conclusion was inescapable: it had to be the enemy, especially considering the proximity of the dispersion field. The thought sent a jolt of urgency through her, her heartbeat quickening in response. Her eyes flicked down to the floor beneath her, to the clear imprints left by her own boots in the dust and debris. They stood out, a trail leading directly to her current position. If the enemy was here, and if they were even remotely competent, they would find her tracks—they might have already done so.

She couldn't afford to hesitate any longer. The walls of the building, once a temporary refuge, now felt like they were closing in on her, the shadows suddenly teeming with unseen threats. Keira's heart raced as she calculated her next move.

It was time to go.

That much was plain. She needed to move, and quickly, before the enemy could close in on her position. Every second counted now. She mentally mapped out her route, prioritizing speed over stealth, and prepared to slip back into the maze of ruins that surrounded the apartment block. But first, she would have to cross the open expanse of the park. Staying here, waiting for the inevitable confrontation, was not an option.

With a final glance at the footprints she was leaving behind, Keira steeled herself and began to retrace her steps back to the entrance, her every movement calculated to minimize noise. Behind her, the apartment block was a tomb of silence, and any sound she made seemed amplified in the stillness.

Her breath was shallow, controlled, as she approached the threshold, pausing just before stepping outside. She scanned the park and the surrounding ruins once more, her eyes darting from shadow to shadow, searching for any sign or hint of movement. Nothing stirred. As far as she could tell, there was no one out there, no immediate threat waiting to pounce.

"Fuck it," she muttered under her breath, steeling herself for what she was about to do. Without another second of hesitation, Keira stepped out into the open and immediately broke into a hard sprint. The servos in her powered suit engaged with a soft whine.

Her armored boots pounded against the cracked pavement, the impact muffled by the suit's dampeners, but the sheer force of her strides was undeniable. The world around her became a blur of motion; the once distant road on the other side of the park drew closer with each powerful step.

Her breath came in rapid bursts, the sound echoing in her helmet as she pushed herself harder and harder. The suit's systems responded to her urgency, feeding power to the exoskeleton, amplifying her speed and endurance. The park, once a vast and open expanse, now shrank before her as she tore across it, the surrounding ruins flashing by in her peripheral vision.

Every nerve in her body was on edge, waiting for the inevitable—a shout of alarm, the crack of a gunshot, the whoosh of a missile locking onto her heat signature. But none of it came. The only sounds were the rhythmic thud of her boots hammering into the ground. Her HUD displayed the rapidly closing distance to her target, a road on the far side of the park that offered the promise of cover and escape.

Two hundred meters, then one hundred. Keira's lungs burned with the effort of maintaining her relentless pace. The road was so close now, just within reach. But a sudden instinct made her glance back, and her blood ran cold at what she saw.

Emerging from the entrance she had just left were two figures clad in black powered armor, their forms ominous and menacing against the backdrop of the shattered building. They had spotted her—there was no doubt about that, for one was pointing at her. The other dropped to a knee, raising his rifle, taking deliberate aim.

Keira reacted instinctively. She dodged sharply to the right, and a split second later, a shot rang out, the crack of the rifle echoing through the park. She didn't stop to think, immediately altering her course and zigzagging in a serpentine pattern, trying to throw off their aim. Another shot rang out, the bullet buzzing past her like an angry hornet. The near-miss sent a shiver down her spine—that had been close, too close.

She pushed herself even harder, her legs pumping with all the power her suit could muster as she darted from side to side, making herself a difficult mark. The enemy fired again, but this time she was already past the park, the shot whizzing harmlessly by as she jumped a low-hanging decorative wall that bordered the park and hit the street running. The ruins on either side blurred as she sped down the deserted road, her eyes searching for the cover she desperately needed.

Ahead, she spotted an old car, its rusted frame jutting out from the debris-strewn street. Without breaking stride, Keira vaulted over the car, her enhanced strength propelling her effortlessly through the air. She landed with a thud on the other side, just as a round hammered into the hulk, sending shards of metal and plastic flying. She scrambled back, pressing herself against the car for cover.

She risked a glance around the edge of the car, her heart pounding in her chest. What she saw made her stomach drop. More than a dozen enemy soldiers had emerged from the residential block and were advancing across the park, all clad in the same black powered armor.

Their movements were methodical, like predators closing in for the kill. Keira's eyes scanned the group, her mind racing as she assessed the threat. There was a small, bitter relief in what she didn't see—there were no panthers among them. It was a small mercy, but a relief nonetheless.

But even without the panthers, she was still outnumbered and outgunned. Keira knew she had to keep moving, to stay ahead of the encroaching danger. Her muscles tensed, ready to launch herself into motion again. The ruined city behind her was a labyrinth, and she intended to use it to her advantage.

Wasting no time, she was up and running again, her body a blur of motion as she sprinted for all she was worth down the street. The terrain offered no easy escape routes—no side streets or alleys to dart into, just the looming remnants of fallen structures on either side, mountains of debris forming an oppressive, uninterrupted barrier. The street stretched out ahead of her like a tunnel with no end in sight, and every step she took seemed to echo in the silence.

She moved from cover to cover, always alert for the crack of gunfire. But surprisingly, no shots followed her this time. The absence of gunfire was almost unnerving, as if the enemy were intentionally holding back, as if they knew there was no escape.

Then, behind her, a deep, throaty roar of engines shattered the quiet. Keira risked a glance over her shoulder as she ran, and what she saw sent a fresh surge of dread through her. A drop ship was descending into the middle of the park, its engines kicking up clouds of dust and debris as it hovered above the ground. The sight of it, so close, was like a hammer blow to her dwindling hope.

The drop ship landed with a heavy thud, and the rear hatch dropped open, revealing a squad of enemy soldiers in light armor. They charged down the ramp and into the park.

That was not good news.

Keira's mind raced as she weighed her options, the situation growing more desperate by the second. The arrival of the drop ship meant the enemy was reinforcing their position, and soon she would be completely outnumbered.

Heck, who was she kidding, she already was outnumbered.

She couldn't afford to slow down or hesitate now. Her only chance was to outrun them, to find some way to slip through the tightening noose before it was too late.

She continued to run.

Keira's sprint came to a sudden, jarring halt as she reached the end of the street. Her eyes widened in dismay and horror as she took in the scene before her—a dead end. The path ahead was completely blocked by massive piles of debris, remnants of once mighty structures that had collapsed into a formidable barrier. The rubble rose hundreds of meters high, forming a cul-de-sac that hemmed her in from all sides. The towering mounds of twisted metal and shattered concrete loomed over her, casting long shadows in the fading light.

She spun around, her heart pounding in her chest, and looked back down the street. The enemy was already advancing, a relentless wave of soldiers in powered armor at the van, their black suits gleaming ominously under the dim light. There were dozens of them. A shot rang out, the sharp crack of the rifle splitting the air, and Keira instinctively ducked behind a small pile of rubble that had spilled out into the street, seeking what little cover it offered.

Her mind raced, desperation clawing at her thoughts. She glanced around frantically, searching for any possible escape. The towering rubble offered a chance. She could try to climb, but the debris was treacherous, and the climb would be slow, leaving her exposed to enemy fire. The risk was enormous, and with the enemy so close, making such a move felt like a death sentence. Her options were dwindling to nothing, and the sense of impending doom was suffocating.

But Keira was a survivor, and her mind refused to accept defeat so easily. She forced herself to calm down, to think. There had to be something, some way to buy herself a few more seconds, a chance to turn the tables. She couldn't just give up—not after everything she'd fought through—and yet she was trapped.

CHAPTER EIGHT

Location: Planet Asherho
Date: 2450, Imperial Standard

Keira closed her eyes, drawing in a deep, steadying breath as her heart pounded against her ribcage. The enemy was closing in, faster than she could afford. Every second was precious. She forced herself to focus, to stay calm, pushing away the fear nipping at the edges of her mind. There wasn't time for hesitation.

She accessed her HUD, her vision flickering as the inventory list appeared. Three grenades—three clips for her pistol, one of which was already loaded. And then there was the suit, her last line of defense, encasing her in layers of hardened alloy and cutting-edge tech, not to mention the powered gravity knife hanging against her chest, its edge capable of slicing through armor as if it were paper. But that meant you had to get close to the enemy, very close.

The ground beneath her trembled again, a deep, ominous rumble that sent shudders through the debris-strewn landscape. It was another quake. Loose rubble clattered around her feet, the remnants of a world torn apart by war. Keira's stomach churned, a wave of nausea rising as the reality of her situation pressed in on her. She clenched her teeth, swallowing hard. This couldn't be the end. Not here.

Not like this.

Her thoughts raced as she forced herself to plan, knowing that survival hinged on the decisions she would make in the next few moments. The pressure was suffocating. She had no choice but to face it head-on. The enemy was coming, and there was no more time to waste.

"We've found you, love," Crecee's voice crackled through the comms, dripping with malice.

Keira's breath caught in her throat, her muscles tensing with a mix of fear and fury. The urge to scream, to unleash the torrent of emotion building inside her, was almost overwhelming. She bit down hard on her lip, tasting blood, but the pain only fueled her rage.

"Fuck you," she spat back, opening her comms, her voice shaking with the intensity of her anger. For a split second, her vision blurred, and all she could see was red, a fiery haze clouding her mind. But as the evening light filtered through the dust-choked air, something inside her shifted. The raw emotion surged through her like a shot of adrenaline, sharpening her focus, steeling her resolve.

Crecee's laughter echoed in her ears, cold and cruel. "Not if I fuck you first. I've been waiting for this for a very long time. Soon we will be together. But—but first, you have something I want…I need."

Keira's fists clenched so tightly her knuckles ached. Every word he spoke was a knife twisting in her gut, fueling the dark determination that now consumed her. "Before this is over—I am going to murder you, you bastard. I'll kill you stone-cold dead."

The sheer force of her hatred left her almost breathless, her chest heaving with each pant. She could feel her heart hammering in her ears, but she welcomed it. This rage was all she had left, and she would use it to fuel her last stand. They wouldn't take her alive. She would make them pay in blood.

With a final, calming breath, Keira moved, taking up a position where she could see the enemy's approach. Her HUD flickered, highlighting the figures moving in the distance—still over two hundred meters away, but closing fast. She raised her pistol, her hands steady despite the storm raging inside her, and squeezed the trigger.

The first shot went wide, cutting through the air harmlessly. She cursed under her breath, but there was no time for doubt. Her suit's heads-up display adjusted, feeding her data to recalibrate her aim. She fired again, her focus narrowing to a razor-sharp point.

The second shot was closer, the bullet slicing through the space just in front of the lead enemy who was in motion. Keira's grip tightened, her eyes locked onto her target. There would be no mercy, no hesitation. Not until every last one of them lay dead at her feet.

The enemy, realizing their exposure and that they were under fire, scrambled for cover as Keira's shots rang out. They disappeared behind the shattered remnants of walls and large chunks of debris scattered across the war-torn park.

The engines of a drop ship roared to life, spinning back up, a deafening sound that cut through the chaos. Keira's attention snapped to the vehicle as it began to lift off the ground, its thrusters kicking up clouds of dust and loose rubble. The shuttle ascended slowly at first, its hulking form straining against gravity. But then, instead of shooting straight up into the sky, it veered low, skimming just above the ground and cutting across the park in a rapid maneuver, almost as if the pilot wanted to avoid ground fire. But Keira had no way to damage the craft. Within moments, it was gone, disappearing behind a line of ruined buildings, leaving only the echo of its engines in its wake.

Return fire sliced through the air, forcing her to duck back behind cover. Bullets and energy rounds slammed into the barrier she crouched behind, sending shards of concrete and sparks flying. She gritted her teeth, adrenaline coursing through her veins.

"Grenade," she commanded, keeping her voice steady. "High yield."

In an instant, her suit responded, a grenade sliding into her free hand from a compartment on her armor. The heavy metallic weight was reassuring in her grip. She stole a quick glance from cover, assessing the enemy's position, then wound up and hurled the grenade with all her strength. Her suit augmented the throw, sending the explosive device sailing in a perfect arc toward the enemy's position.

Keira didn't wait to see the result. She ducked back down just as a new volley of fire erupted, rounds zipping past her head and slamming into the ground around her position. Much of the fire was wild, as if the enemy were poorly trained. Her heart pounded in her chest, but she remained calm, counting the seconds in her head.

Then it came, a heavy, ground-shaking *crump* as the grenade detonated, sending a powerful shockwave through the ground beneath her. The explosion was followed by a scream—shrill and desperate—cutting through the air. Keira's lips curled into a grim smile as she felt a surge of satisfaction wash over her. The enemy was paying for their pursuit, and she would make sure they continued to do so until the very end.

"Fuck you!" Keira screamed back at them, her voice raw with rage, echoing through her helmet.

The enemy was relentless, and she knew staying in one place would only get her killed. She needed to keep moving, stay unpredictable. Deciding to abandon her current cover, she turned, keeping low to the ground as she sprinted toward an old, overturned armored personnel carrier. The heavy vehicle, long abandoned and half-buried in rubble, offered a more substantial shield against the onslaught.

Just as she slid behind the armored bulk, an explosion rocked the ground where she had been only moments before. The force of it sent a shockwave through the air, rattling her teeth and making her ears ring. Dust and debris rained down in a shower, but Keira was already safe behind her new cover, her mind racing for the next move.

"Grenade," she ordered, her voice clipped and focused. "Full yield."

A moment of silence, then her suit responded, "I am sorry. There are only fragmentation grenades left, of which there are two."

Keira cursed under her breath, feeling the frustration. But she didn't have time to dwell on it. "Fragmentation grenade, then," she commanded. "Give it to me."

The grenade popped into her free hand, cool and solid. She could feel the weight of it through her gloves, a familiar sensation that brought a grim sense of comfort. With a quick, practiced motion, she leaned out from behind the carrier and hurled the grenade, aiming for a spot just beyond the debris field where she suspected the enemy was regrouping.

As soon as the grenade left her hand, Keira ducked back into cover, her heart pounding in her chest. She counted the seconds, each one dragging out as she waited for the explosion. Then, a solid *bang* echoed through the area, quite different from the heavy thuds of earlier.

She couldn't see the impact, wasn't sure if it had taken out any of the advancing enemy, but that wasn't the point. The explosion would force them to hesitate, to rethink their approach. In this kind of fight, even a moment's hesitation could be fatal, and Keira was determined to exploit any advantage she could find, and she'd use every weapon at her disposal.

Keira's eyes flicked down to her HUD, the display glowing faintly against the dim light filtering through the dust-choked air. The suppression field indicator was still active. Frustration burned at her, tightening her chest as she realized the situation was growing increasingly dire. Every second the field remained in place was another she couldn't call for backup. But there was no way to know where it was or take it offline. Maybe she could drop into the machine, but there wasn't time for that, not now.

She pushed the frustration down, forcing herself to focus. Peering around the corner of the armored personnel carrier, she scanned the area with sharp, vigilant eyes. The landscape was eerily quiet, the debris-strewn ground offering no sign of movement.

The enemy was out there, and soon they would come again.

Keira brought her pistol up, the weight of it steady in her hands, her grip firm despite the powerful exhaustion clawing at the edges of her endurance. She aimed for the path the enemy would take to reach her position, around the side of the spot she'd been using for cover. The last vestiges of smoke from the explosion were being blown away by the wind. Her finger rested lightly on the trigger, ready to fire at the first sign of movement.

The seconds ticked by, each one stretching out longer than the last. Her breath was still ragged, chest heaving as she struggled to control it. Inside her helmet, the air felt stifling, each inhale heavy with the scent of sweat and fear. A bead of sweat trickled down her brow, stinging her eyes as it slipped past her eyelashes. She blinked rapidly, trying to clear her vision without losing focus on her aim.

Off in the distance, there was the chatter of isolated rifle fire. Another rifle replied, and then there was a low bang. There was no more noise after that. Keira idly wondered who it had been. Still, she waited, the tension in her muscles coiling tighter with each passing moment. The silence was oppressive. She held her breath, steadying herself, and waited.

The first enemy soldier, clad in light armor, cautiously inched around the debris pile, unaware that he was stepping into Keira's crosshairs. His attention was fixed on the area where she had initially taken cover, his movements deliberate as he scanned for any sign of her. Keira's breath caught, and she squeezed the trigger, her focus narrowing to a single point.

The heavy pistol bucked in her hand, the recoil absorbed effortlessly by her suit's advanced stabilizers. The shot rang out with a sharp crack, and the enemy soldier was thrown backward, the force of the impact driving him into the ground. His body hit the dirt with a dull thud, armor clattering against the rubble.

But there was no time to savor the victory. Another soldier rounded the debris, this one more alert, his rifle swinging toward her as he spotted her position. Keira's heart pounded as she reacted, her instincts taking over. She fired just as he squeezed his trigger, the shots echoing in unison.

A hammering impact slammed into her right shoulder, the force of it jarring her back. The rounds struck her armor, failing to penetrate but delivering a brutal blow that felt like a sledgehammer had connected with her body. Pain flared through her shoulder, a deep, throbbing ache. But Keira gritted her teeth, pushing the pain aside. The soldier who had shot her was down, his body crumpled to the ground, his rifle falling from his grip.

She barely had a moment to catch her breath before another enemy soldier emerged, weapon ready. Keira didn't hesitate. She pulled the trigger again, her aim precise. The pistol bucked once more, and the soldier's head snapped back violently as the explosive round punched through his face screen. There was a brief, gruesome detonation, the round's payload doing its deadly work. The soldier's body was flung backward, collapsing in a heap, lifeless.

Where were the enemy with powered armor? The question burned at Keira as she scanned the battlefield and the mountains of wreckage to either side. Were they climbing to get around and behind her? She did not see them.

The soldiers she had taken down were lightly armored, nothing more than cannon fodder. The real threats, the ones in powered armor who could match her strength and firepower, were conspicuously absent. Was Crecee holding them back, waiting for the right moment to strike? Or was he using these soldiers he was throwing at her as bait, softening her up before unleashing his heavy hitters?

"Reload required," her suit intoned calmly, breaking through her thoughts.

Keira ducked back behind cover, her pulse still racing. The pistol's clip was empty, the weight in her hand suddenly feeling inadequate. She ejected the spent clip with a practiced motion, the composite metal casing clattering to the ground. Without missing a beat, she called for another clip, the fresh magazine sliding into her hand from her suit's reserves. She snapped it into place, the familiar click reassuring her as she racked the slide, readying the weapon.

But she knew staying in one spot was a death sentence. The enemy was closing in, and she needed to stay one step ahead. Glancing over her shoulder, she spotted another vehicle—a small, burned-out work van, its charred frame offering the promise of some cover. It was only ten meters away, but in the heat of battle, that distance felt like an eternity.

Without hesitation, Keira launched herself from behind the armored personnel carrier, sprinting low to the ground. Her muscles burned as she pushed herself to move faster, the world narrowing to a tunnel of noise and motion. She could feel her shoulder protesting with every step, the dull ache threatening to slow her down, but she refused to let it. The van loomed closer.

At that moment, behind her, the enemy broke from cover and rushed forward. Fire erupted at Keira, the sharp crack of gunfire cutting through the air as the enemy, now emboldened, charged forward. She had barely made it halfway to the van when she felt a sudden, brutal impact in the center of her back. The force of the round slammed into her armor, nearly knocking her off her feet.

Pain radiated through her torso as her suit absorbed the blow, the impact plates flexing under the intense pressure. Several warning lights began to flash on her HUD. The strike felt more powerful than the others. It took every ounce of her strength to keep moving, to stay upright and not collapse under the sheer force of the hit.

Gritting her teeth, Keira pushed forward. She couldn't afford to slow down now—not with the enemy right on her heels. "Fragmentation grenade!" she shouted, her voice edged with desperation.

The suit responded instantly, delivering the last grenade into her hand. She could feel its weight, a reminder that this was her final explosive. As she reached the cover of the van, she twisted her body in midair, muscles screaming in protest. In a fluid motion, she hurled the grenade back over her shoulder, her eyes narrowing as she gauged the trajectory, the suit assisting with the toss.

Keira hit the ground hard, the impact sending a jolt through her already aching body, but she managed to roll behind the van, using it as a shield. The explosion followed a heartbeat later. The blast sent shards of metal and debris flying in all directions.

Then came the scream—a sharp, guttural sound that echoed across the landscape, only to be abruptly cut short. Keira didn't need to see the aftermath to know that the grenade had hit its mark, for more screams sounded, men and women crying out in pain and agony.

Keira pushed herself to her feet, her muscles protesting from the relentless strain, but she ignored the pain. She had no time to waste. Peeking out from behind the van, she quickly assessed the situation. Though there were a number lying upon the ground—some still and others writhing in agony—the enemy had multiplied, more than a dozen soldiers now advancing toward her position. They moved with a coordinated air, hunched low as they spread out in a loose formation, their weapons trained on her with deadly intent.

She took a deep breath and fired several rounds, her pistol bucking in her hand as she aimed for the closest targets. Instantly, the enemy fired back. The air was thick with the sound of gunfire, rounds striking the ground, and the vehicle behind which she sheltered, kicking up dust and debris. Keira managed to drop two of the advancing soldiers with clean, well-placed shots.

But there were too many of them. She could feel the tide turning against her as the others pressed forward, their return fire intensifying as they drew closer. The van she was using as a shield shuddered under the relentless barrage, each impact a reminder of how close she was to being overwhelmed.

Keira ducked back behind cover, her breath coming in ragged gasps. She ejected the spent clip from her pistol, the metal casing clattering to the ground, and quickly loaded the last one she had. The weight of it in her hand felt like a countdown timer, ticking away the final moments before she would be out of options.

Time was running out.

She steeled herself, ready to peek around the corner and fire again, but instinct held her back. The van was taking a pounding, dozens of rounds hammering against it, the sound like a drumbeat of impending doom. She could hear the metal creaking under the strain, feel the vibrations communicated through her suit. There was no way she could return fire in this storm of bullets; she would be cut down before she even had a chance to aim.

Her mind raced, searching for another option. She couldn't stay here; the van wouldn't hold up much longer, and the enemy was closing in fast. But moving out into the open would be suicide. She needed a plan, something that would buy her the time she desperately needed, or better yet, turn the tables on the enemy. Her survival depended on it.

Keira sucked in a deep breath. There was no way out, no plan that would see her through this. Grimly, she understood that reality. With her free hand she drew her gravity knife. If she was to go out like this, she resolved to make them pay a steep price.

Suddenly, the air around Keira erupted in a thunderous explosion of fire, just beyond her cover. Then there was a flash of light, something streaking down from above and past her position, landing in the middle of the advancing enemy. A deafening detonation followed. It shook the ground. For a brief, disorienting moment, she didn't understand what was happening—only that the explosion wasn't aimed at her, but at the enemy.

There was a stuttering of fire, from her right, up on the mountain of debris that had once been a residential block. It drew her attention. She blinked as she saw a figure in powered armor kneeling, rifle aimed downrange at the enemy. The figure was firing careful, controlled bursts. She blinked again, not quite believing her tired eyes.

It was a marine—an imperial marine!

Keira's heart jumped for joy as she looked around as more fire rang out. She saw other marines on either side of the street, up on the debris pile firing down upon the enemy. One was even making their way down the pile toward her!

"Keira, keep your head down!" a voice boomed, impossibly loud and magnified over the din of battle.

Her heart skipped a beat as she recognized the voice—Scaro. Relief surged through her, almost making her weak at the knees. She wasn't alone anymore. Then she saw the marine who was making their way toward her toss something toward the enemy. It was a powerful throw.

"Compression grenade out!" another voice shouted, this one unmistakably Jessie's. The marine reached the street and threw herself flat.

Keira's breath caught in her throat as the words registered. A compression grenade was designed to create a powerful shockwave capable of obliterating anything in its radius, essentially a mini-nuke. Panic surged through her as she realized the danger. Keira threw herself to the ground, her body slamming into the dirt as she hugged it as tightly as she could, trying to make herself as small as possible.

The blast was blinding, a searing white light that overwhelmed her senses. Her visor reacted instantly, darkening to near opacity to shield her eyes, but even through the filters, the brightness was almost unbearable. The light was quickly followed by a massive blast wave, a wall of pressure that roared over her like a freight train. The force of it threatened to lift her off the ground, but Keira pressed herself down, digging her fingers in as the shockwave passed over her.

And then, just as suddenly as it had begun, there was silence. A deep, profound silence that seemed to swallow the world whole. Keira lay still, her ears ringing from the aftershocks of the blast, her heart pounding in her chest as she struggled to catch her breath. The relentless gunfire, the chaos, and the noise—all of it had ceased.

For a moment, she dared not move, barely believing that the assault had ended. The sudden calm was surreal. Slowly, Keira lifted her head, her body trembling with the adrenaline still coursing through her veins. The van that had been her shield was gone. It had been blown several meters down the street. The massive debris piles around her had shifted as well. A massive cloud of dust was on the air.

She was alive.

And more importantly, she wasn't alone.

CHAPTER NINE

Location: Planet Asherho
Date: 2450, Imperial Standard

With a groan, Keira forced herself back to her feet, the servos in her powered armor whining in protest. The alarms inside her suit were a cacophony of urgent warnings, the harshest ones screaming about radiation levels spiking dangerously high.

"Alarms off." She silenced them, but the unease lingered.

She took in her surroundings, her eyes widening in disbelief. A small mushroom cloud billowed ominously in the distance, where the enemy had been advancing in force from the park. There was now a smoking crater there, the ground torn asunder and scorched black. Dust and debris hung in the air, swirling in the unnatural wind created by the explosion. The realization hit her like a physical blow—she had just witnessed the obliteration of an entire enemy force in an instant.

Still gripping her pistol tightly, Keira felt a wave of shock wash over her, leaving her momentarily stunned. Her heart pounded in her chest, the adrenaline still surging through her veins as her mind raced to process what had just happened.

Movement flickered in her peripheral vision, snapping her out of her daze. Instinct took over, and she spun toward the source, her pistol coming up in a fluid motion. Her enhanced reflexes, courtesy of the suit, made the action almost too quick, too sharp.

She blinked, her vision clearing just enough to recognize the figure standing before her. Jessie skidded to a halt, her rifle lowered, but she quickly raised a hand in a gesture of caution as she eyed the pistol.

"It's me, ma'am," Jessie said, her voice filtering through the private comm channel they shared. She took a cautious step closer, her eyes darting between Keira and the still-smoking crater. Her gaze was wary, as if she expected Keira to pull the trigger at any moment. "You can lower the pistol, ma'am."

Keira hesitated, the world still spinning around her. Expelling a hot, shaky breath, Keira slowly lowered the pistol, her fingers trembling slightly as the tension drained from her body. The weapon seemed heavier than ever, like a burden she could barely carry any longer. She felt like an old dishrag that had been used and abused far beyond its limits, worn out and wrung dry by the relentless tide of battle. Every muscle in her body ached, not just from the physical strain, but from the emotional toll as well.

As the adrenaline ebbed away, tears of relief pricked at Keira's eyes, blurring her vision. She hadn't realized how close she had been to the edge, teetering on the brink of despair and exhaustion. The sight of Jessie, a familiar face, was like a lifeline thrown to her in the midst of a storm. The emotions she had been holding back for so long surged to the surface, threatening to overwhelm her.

She blinked rapidly, trying to hold back the tears, but a few escaped, trailing down her cheeks. The crushing loneliness that had wrapped around her like a vice, squeezing tighter with every passing moment, finally loosened its grip. Help had come.

She had been found.

For a moment, she let herself feel the full weight of it all—the fear, the pain, the overwhelming relief. She had survived, and now, she had a chance to keep surviving.

"Are you injured, ma'am?" Jessie asked, her voice laced with concern as she stepped closer, her eyes scanning Keira from head to toe, searching for any signs of injury beneath the battle-worn armor.

"I am ... okay," Keira replied, though the words felt like a lie even as they left her lips. She knew she wasn't okay—not really. The struggle to survive, the running, and the final battle had taken more than just a physical toll; it had chipped away at something deep inside her. The sheer magnitude of what she had been through, what she had survived, was almost too much to comprehend. She wasn't sure she would ever be okay again.

"You look exhausted," Jessie observed, her tone gentle but firm, as if she could see right through Keira's hollow words.

"I am spent," Keira admitted, the truth slipping out before she could stop it. Every ounce of energy had been drained from her body, leaving her feeling hollow, a shell of who she had been before the battle began.

"Your suit has kept you hydrated, but you need a stim," Jessie said, her voice taking on a more practical edge as she assessed the situation.

"A stim?" Keira echoed, the word barely registering in her exhausted mind. All she wanted to do was lie down right there, on the cold, hard ground, and let sleep claim her. The thought of continuing, pushing forward, suddenly seemed an impossible ask.

"You didn't take one?" Jessie asked, a note of surprise in her voice. "All this time? Your suit comes with them. They can keep you awake for days if needed."

"Huh, I didn't know," Keira replied numbly, the information barely sinking in as her mind struggled to keep up. She felt like she was suddenly moving through a fog, everything around her distant and surreal. She staggered slightly. But Jessie was already in motion, her hands moving with practiced efficiency as she touched the side of Keira's suit.

Keira barely felt the prick of the needle at the back of her neck—it was so quick, so precise, that it was over before she could even register the sensation. But the effects were immediate and undeniable. Almost instantly, the crushing weight of exhaustion began to lift, like a shroud being peeled away from her mind and body. She blinked in surprise as clarity returned, the world snapping back into sharp focus.

The energy surged through her, banishing the fatigue that had been dragging her down. She felt awake, alert, almost startlingly so. It was as if a fog had lifted from her mind, the heaviness evaporating in an instant. For the first time in what seemed like hours, she felt like she could think clearly, could move without the aching slowness that had dragged on her every action.

"Wow," Keira breathed, the surge of energy still humming through her veins. "That is incredible."

"Yeah," Jessie replied with a knowing grin. "But wait until it wears off. You're going to have one heck of a hangover. But don't worry, I've only given you a light charge, just enough to get us through the next couple of hours. If needed, you can take a larger hit. But the hangover from that is serious." There was a hint of sympathy in her voice, tempered by the hard-earned experience of someone who had been through it all herself.

Before Keira could respond, the sharp stuttering of automatic weapons fire erupted nearby, accompanied by the dull thud of impacts, instinctively forcing them both to crouch low. It brought a fresh wave of tension to Keira's already frayed nerves. Her body responded automatically, her suit amplifying her movements as she hunkered down, seeking cover.

"How did you find me?" Keira asked, her voice barely above a whisper as her eyes darted to the debris pile to their left. Two marines were atop it, kneeling, their figures barely visible as they sent controlled bursts of fire back to a point out of sight, opposite the street Keira and Jessie were on.

"The captain followed the enemy's suppression field," Jessie explained, her gaze sweeping the area, searching for threats, ever vigilant. Her eyes flicked over Keira's armor again, clearly checking for any damage or signs of malfunction. "He figured they were tracking and following you. They were too focused to notice us dogging them. We also had drones out, actively scanning the area. When you broke cover, we were a bit out of position to assist immediately. It took some time to get into a position where we could offer effective help."

Keira gave a nod, absorbing the information. It made sense—the enemy had been relentless. She could still feel the weight of their pursuit, the way they had hounded her every step, forcing her into that desperate stand.

For a moment, she allowed herself to feel a flicker of gratitude amidst the chaos. They had found her, rescued her from what could have been her final stand. But there was no time to dwell on that now. The battle wasn't over, and they still had a job to do. The rifle fire told her as much.

"Avante," Scaro's voice crackled over the comms with urgency. "We need to get moving. What's the holdup down there?"

Keira blinked, the words cutting through the lingering haze of exhaustion and the rush from the stim. It was only then that she realized the enemy's suppression field had gone down. The red flashing warning was gone, vanished. The compression grenade must have taken it out.

Another sharp burst of automatic fire echoed around them, jolting her back to the present. The marines on the debris pile continued to engage the enemy, their weapons sending precise, disciplined shots into the chaos beyond.

"Are you ready to move, ma'am?" Jessie asked, her voice steady despite the tension thrumming in the air.

Keira met her gaze and gave a firm nod, determination hardening her features. "I am—more than ready."

Jessie grinned and turned, her eyes scanning their surroundings before she pointed to the massive pile of debris to their right. "We're going to climb up and over that."

Keira followed Jessie's gesture, her eyes tracing the jagged, precarious slope of rubble. The pile was a tangle of twisted metal, shattered concrete, and broken machinery, all haphazardly piled together. It looked like a makeshift mountain, its sharp edges and unstable surface promising a treacherous climb.

Apprehension knotted in Keira's stomach. The idea of climbing over that exposed heap filled her with dread. Every instinct screamed that it was a bad idea, that they would be vulnerable, easy targets for any remaining enemy forces that spotted them and wanted to take a shot. The thought of scrambling up the debris while under fire sent a chill down her spine.

"We have several marines providing overwatch," Jessie reassured, her voice calm but urgent. "They'll keep us covered, but when we go, we need to move fast, understand? Another squad is moving in to occupy the enemy that's out there—to fix their attention while we make our escape."

Keira nodded, absorbing the plan, but the tension she felt was strong. They were threading a needle, trying to slip through the enemy's grasp while they still had the chance.

"Avante," Scaro's voice cut through the comms again, sharper this time, edged with barely concealed strain. "What's going on down there?"

"We're about to be in motion, sir," Jessie responded.

"Very good," Scaro replied, a note of relief evident in his voice. "But be aware—additional enemy forces are approaching from the southeast, including bots."

The mention of bots sent a shiver down Keira's spine. The thought of more panthers was not a welcome one.

"Come on," Jessie urged, grabbing Keira's arm with a firm but gentle grip. "Let's make this quick."

Without wasting another second, Jessie led the way, sprinting toward the massive pile of debris that loomed ahead of them. It was the remains of a fallen and collapsed apartment block, now nothing more than a jagged mound of twisted metal and shattered concrete. The structure that had once been home to countless thousands was now just another obstacle in their fight for survival.

Jessie didn't hesitate. She dashed forward with the agility and confidence born of experience, her movements fluid and controlled despite the treacherous terrain. Without a glance back, she began scrambling up the ruin, her powered armor giving her the strength and stability to scale the debris with relative ease.

Securing her pistol to her side, Keira followed close behind, her heart pounding in her chest as she moved. The debris shifted beneath her boots and her hands, some pieces sliding precariously as she put her weight on them. The armor absorbed the shocks when she slipped, but she could still feel the instability, the sense that the entire pile could shift significantly or collapse at any moment.

What they were doing was clearly not safe.

As she climbed, Jessie paused briefly, glancing back to check on Keira. Her eyes were sharp, assessing, making sure Keira was keeping up and hadn't fallen behind. It was a small gesture, but it spoke volumes about Jessie's experience and concern for her charge. Then she continued onward and upward.

Keira pushed herself to keep pace. The urgency of the situation was a constant pressure at her back, propelling her forward despite the exhaustion still tugging at the edges of her consciousness. They had to reach the top of the debris pile, and they had to do it fast, before they were seen or the enemy's reinforcements arrived.

The sound of distant gunfire echoed in the air, a reminder that the battle was still raging nearby. But for now, their focus was on reaching the top and then the other side, on finding a way out of the chaos and into relative safety. Keira paused, looking back at the sound of the battle after a particularly large explosion. She could no longer see the marines, but she could hear them and the enemy's response.

"Don't worry about the enemy," Jessie urged, her voice tight with the strain of exertion as she continued to climb, only pausing a moment to glance back. "Our only focus right now is getting up and over this mound. That's our job, our mission for the moment. Understand, ma'am?"

Keira nodded, even though Jessie couldn't see it, her mind homing in on the immediate task at hand.

"All right," she responded, determination threading through her words. With a renewed sense of purpose, she turned all her energy to climbing, pushing aside the worry and fatigue that threatened to slow her down.

Behind them, the sharp cracks of gunfire punctuated the air. The sound echoed in the ruins, a dissonant chorus that was soon joined by another deep, concussive boom as something large exploded nearby. The shockwave rippled through the air, vibrating through the rubble beneath her feet, but Keira didn't dare look back. There was no time to assess the damage or check on the status of the marines providing cover. She had to trust that they were doing their job, just as she needed to focus on doing hers, climbing.

The debris underfoot was treacherous, shifting with every step. Loose chunks of concrete and twisted metal threatened to give way at the slightest pressure. There were moments when her foot slipped, sending her heart lurching into her throat as she fought to catch herself, her armored gloves scraping against the rough surfaces for purchase. Each slip was a reminder of how precarious their situation was, but she gritted her teeth and pressed on, refusing to let fear slow her down as she climbed.

Jessie moved with practiced ease, her experience evident in the way she navigated the unstable terrain. Keira did her best to mimic her movements, carefully choosing her footholds and leveraging the power of her suit to pull herself up and over obstacles.

Before she knew it, Keira found herself cresting the top of the debris mound. The world seemed to open up around her. She did not allow herself a moment to take in the view, to marvel at the fact that she had made it this far, for Jessie hadn't even bothered to stop.

The female marine was already descending the other side, her movements swift and confident as she led the way down. Keira immediately followed, her breath coming in ragged gasps as she navigated the descent. The debris shifted beneath her again, but this time gravity was on her side, and she let it carry her down, using her momentum to propel herself forward, sometimes jumping a few meters at a time. Then she was near the bottom. As she reached the base of the mound, she felt a surge of relief.

Concealed behind a massive fallen block of composite masonry, a marine, on one knee, waited at the bottom of the debris mound, his form nearly blending into the shadows cast by the crumbling structure and the oncoming darkness. Keira's heart lifted slightly at the sight. The entire grueling effort had taken no more than fifteen minutes, but it had felt like an eternity. Seeing the marine there, calm, ready, and confident, sent a wave of relief through her. She was once more amongst friends—amongst those who would fight alongside her, people who struggled for a brighter future, one without the Disunity.

The marine gave Jessie a quick thumbs-up, a silent acknowledgment of their successful climb, before turning his attention back to the task at hand. His eyes were sharp and focused as he scanned their surroundings, his weapon held at the ready, prepared for any threat that might emerge. He was a picture of professional efficiency, every movement precise and measured.

More bursts of fire echoed from beyond the debris pile, though the sound was muffled, dampened by the massive barricade they had just scaled. The noise of the fight, however, was steadily growing louder and more chaotic with every passing second; the distinct crack of rifle fire mingled with the deeper, throatier crumps of explosions, the unmistakable sounds of a pitched battle unfolding close by.

"Jessie," Scaro's voice crackled over the comms, cutting through the noise like a blade. "We'll catch up with you. EMP pulse before you go. Kill any trackers and stay off comms after this, understand?"

"Aye, sir, understood," Jessie acknowledged crisply, then turned her attention to the other marine beside her. She took a knee behind his cover, motioning for Keira to follow. Keira dropped down beside them, her senses on high alert despite the exhaustion still nipping at the edges of her consciousness. The stim was working but she could still feel it.

"Richard, use your EMP," Jessie instructed, her voice steady and commanding. "Let's make certain we are alone."

Richard, the marine beside her, responded without hesitation. A small, cylindrical grenade, different from the ones Keira had used, popped into his hand from a compartment at his waist. He armed it with a practiced twist and then lobbed it a short distance away, where it landed with a dull thud among the debris. As the grenade settled, Richard quickly averted his gaze, a motion both automatic and clearly ingrained from countless drills. Jessie did the same and Keira followed suit, turning her head away just as the grenade detonated.

There was a brilliant flash of light, stark and blinding even through her closed eyelids. Keira's suit systems flickered in response, the HUD going dark momentarily. For a brief, disorienting second, she was plunged into darkness, the loss of her suit's interface leaving her feeling exposed and vulnerable. But then, the HUD flickered back to life, the various readouts and indicators gradually stabilizing as the systems rebooted. The flickering eventually stopped, the display growing stronger until it was fully operational once more.

But even as the suit systems recovered, Keira felt a sudden, searing pain lance through her head. It was sharp and intense, like a hot spike driven into her skull. She couldn't help the groan that escaped her lips as she instinctively raised a hand to her helmet, trying to ward off the sensation.

"What's wrong?" Jessie asked, her voice edged with concern as she noticed Keira's discomfort.

Keira sucked in a deep breath, trying to steady herself as the pain began to ebb away. She shook her head slowly, working to clear the lingering fog of what had just happened. "I just got a sharp pain in my head, is all. A headache. It's receding."

The intensity of the pain was already diminishing, the sensation rapidly passing as her body adjusted. She let out a relieved breath, grateful that it hadn't lingered.

"You've been through a lot in the last few hours," Jessie said, her tone softening with understanding as she rested a hand upon Keira's shoulder. Through the haptic suit, Keira could feel the touch. "You weren't trained for this. It's understandable. But you've done one fine job staying alive, better than I would've done."

"She left a trail of bodies," Richard said, eyeing her with something akin to awe, drawing Keira's gaze. "The damnedest thing I've ever seen, ma'am."

Jessie scowled at Richard in clear disapproval.

Keira managed a small, tired nod in response. Jessie was right—nothing in her training had prepared her for the brutal reality of the battlefield, the constant strain on both body and mind. The stress, the fatigue, the unrelenting pressure—it was all catching up to her, and it was manifesting in ways she hadn't anticipated.

At the same time, Keira couldn't shake the feeling that Jessie's statement wasn't entirely accurate. In a way, she *had* been trained for this sort of thing—at least partially. Chris had seen to that. His relentless drills, the countless hours spent honing her skills, and the mental fortitude he had instilled in her—it had all been part of her preparation, even if she hadn't fully understood it at the time. Now, she realized the depth of what he had given her. She owed him a debt that could never be repaid. Keira understood that now. She was still alive, still fighting, and that was all that mattered … because of him.

The echoes of the searing pain in her head began to fade, leaving only a dull ache as a reminder of what had occurred. But the experience had rattled her, even if only for a moment. She glanced back toward the spot where the EMP grenade had detonated, the question lingering in her mind: had that been the cause of the pain? Had the pulse interfered with her connection to the machine?

"Jessie," Richard said, his voice low and urgent as he rose to his feet. Something had caught his attention. His rifle was trained on it just a few meters away, his posture tense and alert.

Keira followed his line of sight, her breath catching in her throat as she saw what he was pointing at. There, lying motionless on its side, was a small four-legged bot, its sleek metallic surface glinting faintly in the dim light. The EMP had taken it out, rendering it lifeless, but its presence so close to them was unsettling. Keira sucked in a startled breath, her heart racing as she realized how close the enemy had been to tracking their every move. No, they had been watching her, but for how long?

"A house cat," Jessie said, her voice carrying a note of recognition as she turned to Keira. "That's how they were tracking you, ma'am."

The bot, nicknamed a "house cat" for its small, agile design, was a reconnaissance unit, used for surveillance and tracking in hostile environments. It was equipped with advanced sensors and stealth capabilities, making it nearly impossible to detect until it was too late. The fact that it had been lying in wait, watching, observing them, so close and unnoticed, sent a shiver down Keira's spine.

"Not good," Keira responded.

"Time to get moving," Jessie said, her voice firm as she turned and started down the street, her pace quick but measured, "while we have the time, and before another cat finds us."

Keira fell into step behind her, her senses heightened. Richard took up the rear, his rifle held at the ready, his eyes constantly scanning their surroundings. The tension was palpable, each of them fully aware that there were still enemy in the vicinity, that danger could emerge from any corner.

As they moved through the ravaged streets, the two marines maintained a vigilant watch, their heads swiveling as they scanned for any sign of movement or threat. Keira, taking cues from them, began doing the same. Her eyes darted from shadow to shadow, from the broken windows of abandoned buildings to the piles of rubble that lined the street.

After navigating several streets, they turned into what appeared to be the remains of a warehouse district. The buildings here were large and imposing, their once bustling interiors now hollowed out by the ravages of war and time. The area had a desolate, eerie quiet about it, the kind of silence that made the hairs on the back of Keira's neck stand on end.

"Where are we going?" Keira asked, her voice low but steady, after they had moved deeper into the district.

"We're headed for a safe house," Jessie explained, her voice now coming through her external speakers rather than the comms. "No more transmissions—captain's orders."

Keira understood the necessity. Any transmissions, no matter how short, could be intercepted and potentially triangulated, giving away their position. Switching to external speakers was a precaution, one that could mean the difference between survival and being found.

"All right," Keira responded, following Jessie's lead and switching to her external speakers as well. "And where is that?"

"Not far off," Jessie assured, her tone steady but laced with a slight weariness. "We have several safe houses hidden across the planet. One is nearby. Once we get there, we'll be able to rest, take stock of the situation, and plan our next move. If we're lucky, we might even be able to safely raise the ship and get off this cursed rock."

"That sounds like a capital plan to me," Richard chimed in from behind, his voice carrying a note of hopeful anticipation. "And a good one, too."

The thought of finally leaving the war-torn surface, of escaping the relentless danger that had hounded her for so long, sent a flicker of relief through Keira's exhausted mind. But then again, there was likely fighting in orbit. Still, the idea of rest, of even a brief reprieve from the constant tension, was more appealing than she cared to admit.

"Will the rest of the company meet us there?" Keira asked. But her question was met with an unsettling silence. The extended pause stretched out, thickening the air with an unspoken tension that Keira could feel pressing down on her. She glanced between the two marines, her anxiety mounting as neither immediately responded.

"No," Richard finally said, answering her question, the word heavy with a finality that sent a cold shiver down Keira's spine.

"What do you mean, 'no'?" Keira asked, her heart sinking as she turned to look back at Richard, searching his face for some hint of explanation as he turned his gaze to meet hers.

"Both shuttles were hit and went down," Jessie said, her voice carrying a somber weight as she relayed the grim news. "We're not sure how many survived, and even if they did, they're scattered all over the area. Contact has been limited and sporadic."

Keira's heart sank further, the already tenuous thread of hope fraying at the edges. The uncertainty of their fate was like a shadow hanging over her, one that she couldn't shake. All this death because of her and what she represented. Just the thought of it hurt.

"Worse," Richard added, his tone grim and frustrated. "There are a shit ton of Disunity forces about, and they're working with sections of the UPG. I am sure we have more people out there, but reaching us via comms is not the safest thing to attempt at the moment."

Keira felt a cold chill crawl up her spine. "How is that possible?"

"Besides the hot drops from orbit, where they landed a lot of force, it's clear the UPG has been infiltrated," Jessie said with a resigned shrug of her armored shoulders. The movement was subtle but spoke volumes. In her tone, there was no surprise, just a grim acceptance of the reality they were facing. "They've been compromised, probably for a while now. We just didn't see it until it was too late."

"That bastard Crecee," Keira breathed, the name slipping from her lips like a curse.

"Yes," Jessie confirmed, her voice tight with barely restrained anger. "We've been listening in on his broadcasts. He's definitely working with them—feeding them intel, coordinating attacks, maybe even calling the shots. He's sold out. That is for sure."

Keira's fists clenched involuntarily at her sides. The thought of Crecee made her blood boil.

"I'm going to kill him," Keira breathed.

"Good," Jessie replied, a fierce determination in her eyes. "Because I'll help." There was no hesitation in her words, only a shared sense of purpose. "Now, enough talk—we have to remain watchful for the enemy. We've got another couple of clicks to cover, and then we can relax. The captain's screening us, watching for any pursuit. He'll meet us at the safe house."

Keira gave a firm nod, the anger simmering beneath the surface, fueling her determination. As she followed after Jessie, her gaze became sharper, more focused. Every shadow, every crevice in the ruins around them, was a potential hiding place for danger. She peered into each one as they passed, her senses heightened by the adrenaline coursing through her veins.

In the distance, the sounds of the ongoing battle still echoed—explosions, the sharp crack of gunfire, the occasional roar of something far more destructive.

"One step at a time," Keira whispered to herself, the words a mantra, grounding her in the present moment. "One step at a time."

She was ready for whatever came next—ready to fight, ready to survive at all costs. And when the time came, she'd be more than ready to face Crecee, and make him pay for what he had done.

CHAPTER TEN

Location: Planet Asherho
Date: 2450, Imperial Standard

Following closely after Jessie, Keira descended the narrow staircase, the clank of her armored boots echoing off the cold concrete walls of the underground. Richard was right behind her, his heavy steps a constant reassurance as he sealed the reinforced door behind them with a soft hiss of the hydraulics and *clank* then *clunk* as he threw the manual handle into the closed position.

From the outside, the door had been a perfect illusion, seamlessly blending into the grimy walls of the service corridor they had come down. Now, it was their barrier against whatever lurked above and decided to come after them—a thin veil of safety in a world gone mad.

The staircase spiraled into the abyss, each step leading deeper into the ground's tainted embrace. The darkness was almost absolute, swallowing the weak, artificial glow of their helmet lights and the scan suite the farther down it went. It was as if the shadows themselves were reaching out, trying to consume them. Keira's heart pounded in her chest, a steady rhythm that matched the hum of the suit's life-support systems.

The radiation alarms inside her helmet continued to flash violently, an insistent reminder of the unseen dangers surrounding them. She had silenced them long ago, the shrill warnings nothing more than irritating background noise in a world where every breath might be her last.

"We've got sophisticated sensors embedded down here," Jessie said, her voice steady as she scanned the dimly lit corridor. "Passive systems that'll alert us if anything or anyone breaches that door. The system's reading us now, making sure we're authorized to be here. Just give it a moment and it'll clear us."

Keira glanced back at the sealed door, her thoughts racing despite the calm exterior she tried to maintain. "Does that include cats?"

Jessie gave a slight nod, a small smile tugging at the corner of her mouth. "It does—especially cats. We'll have plenty of warning if the enemy shows up at our doorstep." Her eyes flickered around the space. "And just in case, if trouble does come our way, there are other bolt holes—escape routes if things go sideways."

"I hope so," Keira replied, her voice barely masking the anxiety that churned within her.

"I know so," Jessie reassured her, her tone firm, as if willing her to believe in the security of their refuge. She paused, letting the silence stretch for a moment. There was an audible double ping. "All right, the system recognized us. We're clear to proceed. The defenses are stood down."

Jessie began her descent, her armored form moving with a practiced ease, despite the oppressive weight of the powered suit. Wearily, Keira followed, her limbs seeming to grow heavy with exhaustion once more. "What about the captain?" she asked, her voice tinged with concern.

"As I mentioned, there are other entrances," Jessie replied, her tone calm and measured. "He and anyone with him will join us when he's ready. We're not alone in this. Trust me."

Keira wanted to ask more, but the fatigue pressing down on her was becoming once more overwhelming, sapping her energy and will. She kept her focus on the rhythmic movement of her feet as they descended deeper into the ground. The air grew thicker with each step, a toxic cocktail of irradiated particles and stagnant dust that clung to every surface. Her suit's scan suite flickered with constant readouts, automatically compensating for the increasing toxicity, but the sense of descending into a poisoned abyss was inescapable.

"I hate the underground," Keira commented.

"I don't like it either," Jessie said.

The stairs seemed endless, each flight blurring into the next until Keira lost track of how many they had descended—ten, twelve flights, maybe more—before Jessie finally came to a stop on a small landing. A service corridor stretched off to the left and right.

Instead of choosing a direction, Jessie moved directly to the wall opposite the stairs. With a swift, precise motion, she placed her armored palm against the cold metal surface. Almost instantly, the wall responded, sliding aside with a loud hiss, the sound echoing down the corridor like a serpent's warning.

The burst of bright light snapping on from the chamber beyond was almost blinding after the gloom of the stairwell. Keira blinked, momentarily disoriented by the brightness amidst so much darkness. The room ahead was larger than she had expected, spacious enough to accommodate several marines in powered armor, the ceiling high enough to allow for movement without restriction. The walls were plain, with the exception of small nozzles sticking outward, like those designed to fight fires. Keira noted that there were several on the ceiling as well.

Jessie stepped into the chamber, her silhouette momentarily outlined against the bright backdrop. Keira hesitated, glancing back down the way they had come, her unease creeping back. The oppressive darkness they had left behind seemed to whisper threats of what might still lurk in its depths.

"What's wrong?" Jessie asked, an undercurrent of concern in her steady voice as she noticed Keira's hesitation.

"What about our tracks?" Keira asked, glancing back toward the staircase they had just descended. The thought of leaving a trail, however faint, worried her, a potential vulnerability in a world where survival depended on remaining unseen and eluding the enemy.

"Oh, that," Jessie said with a dismissive wave, her demeanor relaxed. She turned to look back at the stairs. "Don't worry. There are dust machines, cleaners, drones—sophisticated little things hidden out of sight. Once we enter the airlock, they'll be triggered to come out and scatter the dust, obliterating any sign that we've passed through here. In minutes, it'll be like we never even set foot on those stairs."

Keira blinked, the weight of exhaustion pressing down on her as she processed Jessie's words. "So, once we entered the underground...?"

"They've been working on our tracks ever since," Jessie confirmed with a nod. "By the time anyone else gets here, if they even come this way, there won't be a single trace of us. This place will be as untouched as it was before we arrived."

Relief washed over Keira, though it was tempered by the persistent fatigue that clung to her like a shadow. Wearily, she made her way farther into the chamber, her armored feet clanking against the metal floor. Richard followed closely behind her, his presence a silent reassurance.

As soon as they were both inside, the door behind them hissed shut with a loud, final sound, sealing them off from the corridor. Keira barely had time to react before powerful jets of water sprayed out from the ceiling and walls, catching her by surprise. The force of the water slammed against her armor, and despite the protection, she could feel the impact against her skin, the haptic feedback from the suit translating the sensation with startling realism.

She jumped slightly, the sudden deluge startling her out of her exhaustion-induced haze. The water pounded against her armor.

"Relax, we're just going through a decontamination phase," Richard said, his voice steady and reassuring, though Keira had already pieced that together. "The jets are washing off the hard stuff and neutralizing it too."

As the water continued to cascade over them, Keira's eyes flicked to the radiation indicators within her helmet display. The warnings had ceased, the persistent red alerts replaced by a calming green. It dawned on her that this safe house must be equipped with some form of advanced insulation or an energy field designed to protect them from the toxic and radioactive environment outside.

After what felt like an eternity, the water jets finally shut off, leaving them standing in the lingering silence. Powerful gusts of air followed, blasting over them with relentless force, drying their suits and purging any remaining contaminants. The air whipped around Keira, the sensation almost as disorienting as the water had been, but she stood still, letting the process run its course.

The entire decontamination procedure lasted just under four minutes, though it felt much longer. When it was over, the water at their feet had vanished, drained away into hidden grates, leaving the floor dry and spotless. The air was next, the dull hum of extraction fans pulling the stale, contaminated atmosphere out and replacing it with fresh, filtered air. She could hear the subtle hiss as the system cycled, purging every last trace of the outside world.

A panel on the wall opposite where they had entered blinked green, signaling the end of the process. Almost immediately, that wall began to retract, sliding aside with a soft, mechanical whirr to reveal another chamber beyond.

The space ahead was larger, more expansive than the one they were currently in. It was a functional room, with five alcoves lined up neatly along one side, similar to those found in marine country on the *Seri*. Each alcove was empty, the racks within them standing ready for the suits that would one day occupy them. Floor-to-ceiling lockers were built into the walls beside each alcove, their surfaces sleek and unmarked, the doors sealed tight.

On the left side of the room, a large table caught Keira's eye. It was sturdy, clearly designed for heavy use, and upon it sat several toolboxes, stacked neatly in rows.

Keira stepped forward, her boots making a soft thud against the metal floor, the quiet hum of the safe house's systems a steady backdrop. The environment felt controlled, almost sterile. For a brief moment, she allowed herself to breathe easier, the weight of constant vigilance easing just enough to let her take in her surroundings.

Jessie and Richard moved into the room, each heading toward an alcove and backing into it with the ease of soldiers who had done this a thousand times before. Keira followed their lead, selecting an alcove off to the left. Her movements were slower, weariness still clinging to her limbs, but she positioned herself before the suit's docking station with as much focus as she could muster.

By the time she was settled, the other two marines were already in the process of shedding their armored exoskeletons. The sound of metal disengaging and locks clicking filled the air, punctuated by the soft thuds of boots hitting the ground as they stepped free from their suits.

"Open suit," Keira commanded, her voice slightly muffled by the helmet's audio system. Instantly, she heard a series of pops, followed by the sharp clicks of the suit's internal mechanisms disengaging. The nano gel packs that had held her securely in place began to retract, their firm grip easing as they pulled away from her body. The sensation was almost like being released from an embrace, the pressure lifting all at once.

Like steam escaping from a sealed container, a faint hiss filled the air. The segmented plates that formed the suit's outer shell started to unlock, each section extending outward in a mesmerizing, wave-like motion. The sequence began at her helmet, the segments rippling downward in rapid succession, unlocking and extending outward to reveal the inner workings of the suit. It was a hypnotic dance of machinery.

As the wave of unlocking reached her feet, the hissing sound intensified, a soft exhalation as the suit prepared to release her and equalized the pressure to the outside air. Her ears popped. The suit began to swing open, each segment moving in reverse, starting from the bottom and working its way upward. The panels lifted and spread apart like the petals of a mechanical flower, creating an opening wide enough for her to step out.

Keira paused for a moment, taking in the sight of the suit fully opening around her, the intricate layers of technology that had protected her now laid bare. The process was both familiar and alien, a reminder of the thin line between her human vulnerability and this machine's formidable strength.

With a final, almost ceremonial hiss, the suit completed its opening sequence, leaving Keira standing within the now-empty shell. She stepped down from the platform, her feet meeting the cool floor with a soft thud, the weight of the suit finally lifted from her shoulders. The air outside the suit felt different—cleaner, less burdened by the constant filters and warnings that had surrounded her moments before.

The alcove's lights dimmed slightly as the suit's systems powered down, the machine settling into its resting state. Keira glanced over at Jessie and Richard, who were already out of their suits and moving with the easy confidence of seasoned marines.

Keira greedily sucked in the fresh air, each breath a welcome reprieve from the stale, filtered atmosphere inside her suit. The cold air filled her lungs, invigorating yet soothing. Stiff and sore, her muscles protesting with every movement, she took a tentative step forward on the cold metal floor. The thin skin suit clung to her body, offering little protection against the chill that permeated the room. She shivered, her body reacting to the sudden exposure, but the cool air was a relief—proof that she was no longer encased in the heavy, confining armor.

She turned back toward her suit as it sealed shut behind her, the mechanical plates folding inward with a final, decisive click. The outer surface was pitted and scarred, the once sleek armor marred by ugly burn marks and deep scratches. Several indents along the torso and limbs caught her eye, evidence of rounds that had impacted with enough force to dent the composite metal but, thankfully, not penetrate. The sight of those marks sent a shudder down her spine, a visceral reminder of how close she had come to death.

For a moment, Keira stood there, staring at the battered armor, a wave of exhaustion and disbelief washing over her. How had she survived? The suit, with all its advanced technology, had borne the brunt of the onslaught, shielding her from the deadly forces that had tried to rip her apart. But the reality of what she had faced, and the fact that she was still standing, was almost too much to process.

She shifted her gaze to the marines' suits, standing in their alcoves like silent sentries. They appeared almost new by comparison, the armors' surface nearly clean and largely unblemished. There were a few scratches, minor scuffs that spoke of close encounters, but nothing like the battle-worn state of her own armor. The difference was plain, and it only deepened her sense of vulnerability and what she'd just been through. She took a deep breath, trying to steady herself, but the sight of her battle-scarred armor left her feeling exposed in a way she hadn't anticipated.

"Are you all right?" Jessie's voice broke through Keira's daze as she came up beside her, concern evident in her tone.

"I don't know," Keira admitted, her voice barely above a whisper. She gave a small shrug, feeling the weight of exhaustion settle even more heavily on her shoulders. The truth was, she wasn't sure how she felt—relief, shock, and weariness all tangled together in a confusing mix.

"Come on," Jessie said gently, placing a reassuring hand on Keira's arm and guiding her toward a doorway to the right. Richard had already gone through, his form disappearing into the next room. "We can worry about your suit later. I'll check it over and make sure it's rearmed and ready. But first, let's get some food in you. You can shower and rest afterward if you want."

"Shower?" Keira's head snapped up at that, a glimmer of hope cutting through the fog of fatigue as she stopped. The idea of washing away the grime and stress of the past hours was suddenly the most appealing thought in the world. "There are showers here?"

"Oh, yes," Jessie replied with a grin, the tension in her own posture easing a bit. "And not just any showers—plenty of hot water, soap, and even shampoo. It's practically a luxury spa on a world like Ash. The only thing missing is a pedicure and manicure station."

Keira managed a small smile in return, the promise of something so simple yet so precious lifting her spirits. The thought of hot water cascading over her, soothing worn and stressed muscles, the scent of soap and shampoo, the sensation of scrubbing away the horrors of the day—it was a comfort she hadn't dared to hope for.

Jessie's steady presence at her side was a balm. As they passed through the doorway, the warmth of the next room enveloped her, and for the first time since they had entered the underground, Keira felt a flicker of normalcy return. The promise of food, a shower, and rest was enough to push her aching body to take another step forward, even as her mind continued to process everything she had just been through.

Keira stepped into a room that, at first glance, resembled a small cafeteria. It was stark and utilitarian, with four communal tables lined up in neat rows, each surrounded by functional, no-frills chairs. The furniture was sturdy, designed for durability rather than comfort, with a cold, metallic finish that matched the room's overall minimalist aesthetic. There was nothing decorative or inviting about the space—it was purely practical, meant to serve a purpose without any unnecessary embellishments.

Against the back wall, a workstation drew Keira's attention. Several tablets were neatly arranged on the countertop, their screens dark and reflective. Above them, a hard-wired control panel was mounted, bristling with buttons and switches, its layout clearly complex. A large monitor, mounted just above the panel, flickered to life as Keira watched, the screen casting a faint blue glow across the room as it powered up.

Richard was already seated before the monitor, his focus intent on the control panel as he worked it with practiced ease. His fingers moved swiftly over the buttons, adjusting settings and inputting commands, his eyes never leaving the screen. The steady hum of the machinery and the air handlers were the only sounds in the room, a background noise that added to the sterile, almost clinical atmosphere.

Keira took in the scene, noting the two open doorways on either side of the room. They led off into other parts of the safe house, their thresholds dark and uninviting, but promising more of the same functional spaces beyond. The entire area felt like a place designed for necessity—sustenance, planning, rest—but devoid of any warmth or comfort that might make it feel like home.

Despite the starkness, there was something reassuring about the space. It was a place where they could regroup, recharge, and plan their next move in relative safety.

"Any messages from the ship?" Jessie asked as she walked over to a cabinet set against the wall. Her movements were purposeful, but there was an underlying tension in her voice that belied her calm exterior. She opened the cabinet with a swift motion, revealing shelves lined with supplies, and pulled out two large brown packets, one in each hand.

"No," Richard replied, his eyes still fixed on the flickering monitor before him. The lines on his face deepened as he considered the implications. He finally turned to glance back at Jessie. "Think I should risk sending a message?"

"I wouldn't," Jessie advised, her tone firm as she carried the packets back to the table where Keira stood. "It's too risky. Any transmission could give away our position. Let's wait for the captain to arrive and make that call."

"All right." Richard leaned back in his chair and placed his hands behind his neck. "It's hurry up and wait, then."

Keira barely registered their conversation, her thoughts a chaotic swirl of emotion and confusion. Her hands had begun to tremble, the uncontrollable shakes a physical manifestation of the storm raging inside her. Her emotions were frayed beyond belief, stretched to their breaking point by the relentless onslaught of terror, adrenaline, and exhaustion. The events of the last few hours played out in her mind like a fragmented nightmare—the Infinity and Control, the Disunity, the devastating bombardment of the planet, the sheer violence of the fighting and killing ... all that she'd endured and done ...

She had survived it all, but the question that bothered her, refused to let her find any semblance of peace, was simple and maddening: *how?* How had she made it through the maelstrom of destruction and death? How had she emerged from the chaos, battered but alive, when so many others hadn't?

The weight of it all pressed down on her, threatening to crush what little resolve she had left. Her breath came in shallow gasps, and she felt the edges of her vision blur as the reality of her survival hit her with full force.

"Sit," Jessie commanded, her voice cutting through the haze in Keira's mind like a lifeline. She pulled out a chair and gestured for Keira to take it, her tone leaving no room for argument. "Sit. That's an order."

Keira's legs felt weak, as if the mere act of standing was too much for her. She collapsed into the chair, grateful for the support it provided. After a moment, Keira closed her eyes, letting the world fade away for just a brief respite. The simple act of sitting down, of being off her feet, felt like a small miracle. It was heaven.

Her entire body ached, a dull throb that seemed to intensify with every passing minute. The stim she'd received earlier was clearly fading and doing little to stave off the overwhelming exhaustion that had settled deep into her bones. The fatigue was a relentless thing, a heavy weight that pulled her down, making every thought, every movement, more laborious with each passing moment.

Jessie set one of the brown packets before her, the label clearly reading "Meal Ready to Eat." Keira stared at it for a moment, her mind sluggishly processing what it was ... food.

Food!

With fumbling fingers, she attempted to rip open the package. Jessie, seeing her struggle, tore it open for her, and then a separately wrapped package inside, revealing a sandwich. She quickly opened another packet that included some crackers.

"You need to eat ... so start eating," Jessie commanded, her tone leaving no room for hesitation as she handed Keira the sandwich. "I'll get you some water to wash it all down."

The moment the sandwich was in her hands, Keira's hunger hit her like a tidal wave. What had been a dull background sensation suddenly roared to life, her stomach twisting with need. She bit into the sandwich without thinking, the taste filling her mouth. She couldn't tell what kind of meat it was—nor did she care. It was sustenance, and in that moment, it was the best meal she'd ever had. The bread was dry, the meat indistinct, but it didn't matter. It was food, real food, and she savored every bite as if it were a gourmet feast.

She took another bite, and for a moment, everything else faded away. The horrors of the past hours, the fear, the exhaustion—they all receded into the background, replaced by the simple pleasure of eating. The act of chewing, of swallowing, grounded her, pulling her back from the brink of collapse.

With each bite, she felt a little more human, a little more alive. The sandwich, though nothing special under normal circumstances, was a lifeline, something solid and tangible in a world that had felt so surreal and deadly just a short time before.

Keira continued to eat, each mouthful a small victory over the darkness that had threatened to overwhelm her. She didn't know what the next hours or days would bring, but for now, she was content to simply be—here, eating, and alive.

Chapter Eleven

Location: Planet Asherho
Date: 2450, Imperial Standard

K eira cracked her eyes open, barely noticing the dim glow that struggled against the near complete darkness. The overhead lights had been dimmed to the edge of obscurity. She was lying in a metal-framed bunk bed, its cold, unyielding structure pressing against her through a thin, worn mattress. The pillow beneath her head was no better, more a suggestion of comfort than the real thing, but for now, she didn't care. The harshness of the bunk seemed almost welcoming after everything she had been through. She felt a rare sensation—comfort, perhaps even a touch of restfulness.

Keira stretched cautiously, her muscles protesting with sharp pangs. Every inch of her body ached, her neck, back, and legs especially. She entertained the thought of getting up, but the very idea felt exhausting, just too much effort. Instead, she tugged the thin, scratchy blanket closer around her, cocooning herself in its meager warmth.

For now, movement could wait. The moment was too precious, too rare to squander on anything other than the simple act of being still. She closed her eyes again, this time with the deliberate intent of sinking back into the dark embrace of sleep, where for a little while longer, the world outside could not reach her.

Instead, she found herself back in the machine, slipping into that familiar yet unsettling state of detachment. Keira floated above her own body, observing herself from a distance as if she were a ghost haunting her own life. Everything was veiled in a shimmering silver film, casting the world in a surreal, dreamlike haze.

When she slept, had she been in the machine?

The small room she occupied was utilitarian, with two sets of metal-framed bunks, just like the one she was lying in. The silence was almost oppressive, broken only by the faint hum of the life support systems. Her curiosity piqued, Keira let her consciousness expand, drifting beyond the confines of the room. The walls dissolved away, revealing the rest of the safe house in a seamless, fluid transition.

The safe house was a compact, six-room fortress, designed with the practicality typical of military architecture. Two rooms were dedicated specifically to marine armor—massive, reinforced spaces lined with racks, cabinets filled with tools, and charging stations— every detail geared toward the maintenance and readiness of the powered suits that had become extensions of their bodies. The common room was a sparse, utilitarian space she had seen before, eaten in, with a few battered chairs and a table, the kind of place where weary soldiers would gather to share a meal or a brief, hollow laugh.

Two of the rooms were designated for sleeping, each with a single shower and identical to the one she now hovered in. They contained the same bunk beds, as if individuality had been scrubbed away in favor of uniformity. Then, her focus shifted to the storeroom. It was a cramped space, yet meticulously organized, every inch packed with equipment, weapons and ammunition, medical supplies. Shelves were stacked with crates of food and water rations, the bare essentials.

Keira absorbed the layout with clinical detachment. But even as she floated above, observing everything with a cold, analytical eye, a part of her yearned for the warmth of the bed she had just left, the fleeting comfort of the oblivion of sleep that now seemed so far out of reach.

There wasn't much to the safe house itself—a stark, utilitarian bunker buried deep below the surface. But as Keira's consciousness drifted further, she became aware of the intricate hardwired sensor network that extended beyond its walls. It spread like the roots of a vast, unseen tree out into the honeycombed underground. It was a web of detection, designed to identify even the slightest hint or tremor of movement or the faintest whisper of an approaching threat both biologic and machine-based.

These sensors fed into a multilayered defense system, each layer designed to delay, confuse, or annihilate any enemy bold enough to approach and try to force their way in. Automated turrets were hidden, concealed behind facades and trapdoors. Mines lay buried at key points, ready to explode at the slightest provocation if triggered. Entire corridors were rigged to be blown and collapsed from afar.

Her gaze fell upon a particularly ominous part of the system—a compression warhead, nestled deep within the safe house's core, just under the common room. Its purpose was clear and final. Keira knew why it was there: in the event that the safe house was compromised, the warhead would automatically trigger, collapsing the entire facility in on itself, leaving nothing in its wake.

It was a failsafe.

Turning her gaze back to the common room, Keira observed the scene unfolding below with an eerie sense of detachment. Scaro, Jessie, and two other marines were seated around a battered table, their voices low as they discussed something out of her hearing. The atmosphere was heavy, laden with the weight of what they had all endured and what still lay ahead. Yet, despite the seriousness of their conversation, there was a camaraderie among them—a bond forged in the crucible of war.

She could sense that readily enough.

Keira's focus lingered on Scaro, drawn to him by a mix of curiosity and something deeper. Within the machine's perspective, she saw him not just as a person, but as a complex interplay of flesh and technology. Intertwined with his bones and muscles were an array of implants, chips, and other devices she couldn't identify, but their purpose was clear—enhancements, modifications, all undoubtedly put there by the Marine Corps.

The other marines were no different. Each bore the same tell-tale signs of augmentation—muscle fibers laced with synthetic materials, neural implants humming with data, microchips embedded in their skulls, enhancing their cognition and reaction times. The enhancements were fascinating and spoke to the lengths the military would go to create the perfect soldiers, blending human adaptability with machine efficiency.

Keira turned her gaze inward, focusing on her own body with the precision and clarity the machine granted her. At first glance, everything seemed as it always had been. The standard identification chip was embedded in her right forearm, a small, innocuous relic from a time before her world had turned upside down. Beyond that, she appeared untouched, unaltered—just a collection of vulnerable human tissue, unaugmented and unenhanced.

But then she paused, something nagging at the edge of her perception. That wasn't quite correct. She focused more intently. The familiar landscape of her body began to shift, revealing something she hadn't noticed before, had not seen. There, attached to the base of her brainstem, was something silver, a device of some kind. It was a foreign presence, delicately wrapped around and through the tissues of her nervous system. It wasn't biological in nature, but engineered.

Keira peered closer, and to her growing astonishment, she saw that thin, nearly invisible filaments extended from the silver object, snaking down her spine with an elegance that was both beautiful and, at the same time, terrifying. From her spine, these filaments wove through her body, spreading outward in intricate patterns, but with a purpose that she couldn't understand.

What were they?

Keira's mind raced with possibilities. Was this the source of her newfound ability to interact with the machine? Or was this what she had taken into herself in the control room, something that had fundamentally altered her? Or had it always been there? The more she examined, the more she saw—the filaments were everywhere, threading through muscle, bone, and her brain.

Horrified and fascinated in equal measure, Keira grappled with the realization that she had been changed in ways she could barely begin to fathom. It felt strange, odd, not quite right... different. The body she had known her entire life was no longer entirely her own. She had been altered, not just in function, but in form, and the implications were staggering.

The filaments pulsed faintly, almost in rhythm with her heartbeat, as if they were alive, connected to something far beyond her comprehension. The longer she stared, the more she sensed that there was even more beneath the surface, layers upon layers of complexity that she could not yet see, much less understand.

Keira felt a deep sense of unease settle over her. What had she become? Or worse, what was she becoming? The question loomed large in her mind, unsettling in its ambiguity. Whatever these filaments were, whatever they had done to her and were doing, there was no denying that she was no longer just human. She was something else, something like the marines, augmented. Deep down, Keira suspected this was only just the beginning.

A more important change was coming. She could feel it.

There was a part of her that was drawn to the potential of what was happening, the possibilities that this transformation might hold. If she could learn to understand it, to better harness her newfound power, what could she achieve? What doors could her connection with the machine—and perhaps with the universe itself—unlock?

She knew she couldn't turn back now. The path ahead was uncertain, fraught with dangers both seen and unseen. But it was a path she was determined to walk, one she had already started down, no matter where it might lead. In truth, she had no choice but to soldier on, to continue forward.

Her attention drifted back to the common room, where her gaze was drawn to a side table. There, the alien tubes taken from the control room were neatly arranged, each one pulsating with a strange, otherworldly energy. Nearby lay the construct's case, a device housing Damien, the cantankerous AI, now plugged into a wall outlet for power.

The tubes seemed to call out to her, their energy resonating deep within her mind, beckoning her to pick them up, to unlock whatever secrets they held. The sensation was almost overwhelming, a magnetic pull that demanded her attention, her action.

At the same time, she felt a warning. To possess them meant courting danger. Still, she felt inextricably drawn. It took every ounce of her willpower to resist, to tear her gaze away from the alien devices that pulsed with a power she didn't understand, that beckoned her forward. It was as if each tube were speaking to her soul … that a part of her had been torn away and wanted to reunite with itself.

How strange.

Once more, Keira fixed her attention on Scaro, her thoughts swirling with questions about the implants and enhancements she had seen within him. What exactly did they do? Did they make him faster, stronger, more resilient? She had no clear answers, only a vague understanding of the possibilities. These were technologies designed for war, crafted to give soldiers an edge in the brutal, unforgiving landscape of battle. But as she looked at the marines sitting around the table, their faces etched with weariness, she couldn't help but wonder about the cost of these augmentations. What had they given up in exchange for this power? At the same time, Keira admired his rugged good looks, his confidence. There was something about him that set Scaro apart from the others.

For a fleeting moment, Keira considered eavesdropping on their conversation, using the machine to tap into the low murmur of their voices. It would have been easy—just a shift in focus, a slight attunement of the machine's sensors. But something held her back, a sense of respect for their privacy, or perhaps an unwillingness to know more than she already did. Instead, she turned away, letting her gaze drift by the confines of the safe house, past the layers of security systems that shielded them from the outside world.

Beyond the safe house, everything was dead and nonfunctional, a graveyard of shattered technology and broken dreams. The power that had once flowed through the infrastructure here had long since been cut off, the tap run dry, leaving behind a wasteland of silence and decay. But the lack of power didn't deter her; it only fueled her curiosity. She raced farther outward, her consciousness expanding, exploring the desolate landscape of the underground with a speed and freedom that her physical body could never achieve.

She had almost forgotten how exhilarating this experience could be—the rush of information, the sense of boundless movement, the ability to see and know without the limitations of flesh. As she pushed further, probing the edges of her awareness, there was a sudden, jarring pulse of energy, like a ripple in a still pond. The world around her flashed brilliantly, a blinding white light that obliterated everything in an instant.

Startled and disoriented, Keira instinctively did the equivalent of a blink within the machine, trying to make sense of what had just happened. But before she could fully grasp it, the connection snapped, and she was pulled abruptly back into her body. The sensation of warmth, the solid feeling of the mattress beneath her, the familiar weight of her own limbs—it all rushed back at once, disorienting and grounding her in the same breath.

She lay there, her heart pounding, trying to process the experience. What had caused the sudden pulse? Was it a threat, a warning, or something else entirely? The questions lingered, unanswered, as she tried to shake off the effects of the machine, the memory of that blinding white light still burning in the back of her mind.

It was then she realized the room around her was trembling violently, the walls shuddering as if the very ground itself was groaning and heaving in agony. It was another quake, more intense than the ones before. The metal frame of the bunk rattled beneath her, and dust fell from the ceiling in fine clouds. Keira's heart skipped a beat, instinctively bracing herself as the tremor grew stronger. Then the rumbling ceased, and everything went still once more.

But before she could fully grasp the situation, she was pulled back into the machine, the pulse of energy that had jolted her moments before now subsiding into a faint echo in the back of her mind. The transition was disorienting, the difference between the physical world and the cold, calculating precision of the machine leaving her momentarily unbalanced. But soon, her focus sharpened, and her attention was drawn irresistibly downward to where the pulse had originated, toward the core of the planet itself.

She turned her gaze inward, probing deeper, her awareness plunging through layers of rock and metal until she reached the seething heart of the world and the reactor the precursors had built. What she saw there was staggering—a massive, roiling ball of energy, an energy source of unimaginable power that pulsed with a dangerous, almost sentient vitality. The power it radiated forth was overwhelming, blinding in its intensity, as if the very fabric of the planet were alive and thrumming with released potential.

The longer she stared into it, the more she could feel the power building, gathering momentum, preparing for something cataclysmic, an ending and a new beginning. The light grew brighter, more intense, threatening to consume her entirely. It was as if the planet's core had become a star, its energy expanding outward, threatening to engulf everything in its path. Keira realized with a start that the reactor was online, its power unchecked and growing exponentially.

At the same time, it was waiting.

The reactor seemed to be held in check, poised on the brink but not yet unleashed. Keira could feel it, a vast, dormant force, ready to explode at any moment but restrained by some unseen force or will. Was it waiting for a command?

She thought that an interesting question.

As she hovered in the machine's awareness, something flickered at the edge of her vision—a shadow, a sliver of darkness that tugged at her consciousness. It was subtle, almost imperceptible, but it drew her attention like a magnet. Very much like with the tubes, it called to her soul. The darkness seemed to hover near the surface of the planet, not far from the safe house, and it exuded a sense of cold malevolence that sent a shiver through her. She had encountered it before.

But what was it?

She was about to explore this new anomaly, to push toward the surface and investigate, when the reactor flared once more and a powerful pulse of energy surged through the system, radiating outward like a coronal mass ejection. It hit her like a shockwave, and in an instant, she was yanked back into her body, the connection severed.

Keira blinked furiously, disoriented by the sudden shift. The room around her was trembling once again, the deep, ominous rumble of the quake vibrating through the walls and floor. The beds rattled, and the dim light overhead flickered ominously. After several moments, everything stilled and once more a bated quietness settled over everything as the rumbling died off.

There was a scuff by the doorway. "Ah, you're awake."

The voice, calm and steady, cut through her disorientation. Keira turned her gaze toward the door, still blinking to clear the remnants of the machine's vision from her mind. Scaro stood there, his imposing figure silhouetted against the weak light. His expression was unreadable.

Realizing she was back in the physical world, Keira gave up on trying to reenter the machine. With a groan, she pulled the blanket aside and sat up, her body protesting the movement. Every muscle felt stiff, sore. She stretched, trying to ease the tension, but the aches and pains persisted. Despite the lingering exhaustion, a yawn escaped her. The need for rest still clung to her, heavy and unyielding, but she pushed it aside.

"How long have I been asleep?" Keira asked.

"Nearly twelve hours," Scaro replied, his tone matter-of-fact. He leaned against the doorframe, his eyes briefly scanning her as if assessing her condition.

"That long?" Keira was surprised.

"Yep."

Feeling the weariness still clinging to her despite the hours of rest, she yawned again. "Food, shower, and some solid sleep," she said, her words trailing off into another yawn. She was still exhausted. Had she really slept or had she been in the machine? "What more could a girl ask for?"

"How about some coffee?" Scaro suggested with a slight grin. "I just brewed a fresh pot in the other room."

The thought of coffee was enough to spark a bit of life back into her. "That sounds divine." Her lips curled into a small, appreciative smile. With a sigh, Keira swung her legs over the edge of the bunk. The cold floor greeted her bare feet.

She pushed herself up, standing slowly as her body protested the movement. Like Scaro, she was dressed in simple, utilitarian clothing—a gray sweatshirt and pants, both emblazoned with the Imperial Marine Corps emblem. Jessie had found the clothing for her in the stores, a small comfort.

Keira stretched again, this time more deliberately, trying to work out the stiffness that had settled into her muscles during sleep. Every joint ached, and the soreness in her back and legs reminded her just how much her body had endured.

"Sore?" Scaro asked, noticing the way she moved.

She nodded, grimacing slightly as she rolled her shoulders and then cracked her neck.

"Very," she admitted. "Feels like I've been hit by a tank. No, run over by one."

Scaro chuckled softly, a sound that was both comforting and understanding at the same time. "Yeah, that's the post-battle special. A good stretch and some of that coffee should help. After all you have been through, that is only to be expected."

"That's what Jessie said."

"Does it make my statement any less true?"

"No."

Scaro turned and led the way toward the common room, his footsteps silent against the cold, hard floor. Keira followed, the promise of coffee pulling her forward despite the lingering fatigue that clung to her muscles. As soon as they stepped into the common room, the rich, familiar aroma of freshly brewed coffee hit her senses, a comforting scent that momentarily dulled the edge of her exhaustion.

The room was a quiet haven. Jessie, Richard, and another marine—a blonde woman with a strikingly pretty face—were seated at the table. Each of them had a steaming mug of coffee in hand and plates of food in front of them: scrambled eggs and thin strips of reddish meat that Keira didn't recognize. The food looked surprisingly appetizing. It smelled even better.

As Keira and Scaro entered, the three marines looked up briefly from their meal. Jessie gave Keira a nod of acknowledgment, a silent greeting that conveyed understanding and solidarity. No one spoke, the silence in the room thick with unspoken thoughts and the lingering haze of weariness. It was clear that, like her, they had managed to snatch a few precious hours of sleep, but the fatigue still hung over them like a heavy cloud.

Keira could sense it in the way they held themselves, in the tired lines etched into their faces. Even though they had been afforded some rest, the strain of their situation was ever-present. The quiet was not just from lack of conversation but from a shared understanding. Words seemed unnecessary, almost intrusive in this fragile moment of respite.

She moved toward the coffee pot, her body still aching but drawn to the warmth and comfort that the brew promised. She took a paper cup from a stack next to the machine. As she poured herself a cup, the routine of it brought a brief sense of normalcy, a fleeting moment where she could almost pretend they weren't in the middle of a war, where the next threat wasn't lurking just beyond the safe house's walls.

Taking her cup, Keira stepped back to the table, grateful for the silence that allowed them to simply be. The coffee was hot and strong, the kind that cut through the fog of exhaustion, and as she took a sip, she felt a small measure of strength returning. The food on the table looked tempting, but for now, the coffee was enough to soothe her, to keep her grounded in this moment of stillness before the storm she knew was coming.

"There's no sweetener," Jessie muttered, looking up from the table.

"Beggars can't be choosy," Keira replied, offering a faint smile as she lifted her cup to her lips and took another sip. The coffee was strong, bitter, but it was enough. In this place, luxuries like sweeteners were a distant memory, a relic of a life that seemed almost unreal now.

"No, they can't," Jessie agreed, a hint of warmth in her tone. She raised her own mug in a mock salute, the gesture simple but filled with a camaraderie that cut through the lingering tension. She gestured toward an empty chair at the table, her eyes meeting Keira's. "Have a seat, ma'am. Join us. You've earned that right. After yesterday, you're one of us now."

The other two marines at the table both gave silent nods of agreement, their expressions softening with a quiet respect that Keira hadn't expected. It was a simple invitation, yet it carried a weight of acceptance that moved her in a way she hadn't anticipated. She felt a strange sense of belonging, a connection to these soldiers who had faced the same dangers, the same relentless challenges, and had emerged on the other side—scarred, but alive.

Feeling unexpectedly touched, Keira made her way around the table, pulling out a chair with a soft scrape against the composite floor. The sound was a small intrusion into the quiet, but it felt grounding, a reminder of the tangible world she was reentering after her time in the machine.

She sat down.

Scaro grabbed a chair from another table. With practiced ease, he flipped it around backward and pulled it over to join them, positioning himself at the corner next to Jessie and Keira. The small, informal arrangement of their seats gave the moment an unexpected intimacy, a sense of shared experience that transcended ranks and titles.

Keira glanced around the table, taking in the faces of the marines. There was a weariness in their eyes, but also a strength, a resilience that mirrored her own. They had all been through hell, and while the road ahead was still uncertain and fraught with danger, there was comfort in knowing they would face it together.

She took another sip of her coffee, feeling the warmth spread through her, mingling with the quiet but powerful sense of solidarity that filled the room. For the first time in a long while, she felt a flicker of real hope—fragile, but real. Here, in this moment, surrounded by these people, she wasn't just surviving; she was part of something larger, something worth fighting for … an empire.

"You already know Richard," Jessie said, nodding toward the familiar marine. "This is Sara."

Sara offered a respectful nod, her expression serious but not unfriendly. "Ma'am," she greeted simply, her tone steady.

Keira returned the nod, acknowledging the introduction. There was a sense of mutual respect in the exchange, a recognition of their shared circumstances.

"Princess," Scaro interjected, "we're informal here because of the situation. Back on the ship, it won't be like this."

Keira met his gaze. "Honestly, I prefer it this way. Until a few days back, I had no idea I was the granddaughter of the emperor."

The words hung in the air for a moment, a reminder of the seismic shift her life had undergone in such a short span of time. To go from relative obscurity to learning she was part of the ruling bloodline of the empire—it was still surreal, almost too much to fully grasp.

She took a pull of the coffee, savoring its warmth and bitterness. Closing her eyes, she allowed herself a moment to truly enjoy it. The rich flavor was unexpectedly satisfying, far better than the bland, watered-down brew she had grown accustomed to from the UPG. Even without sweetener, it was leagues ahead of what she'd known.

"This is really good." She opened her eyes to meet the others' gazes. There was a genuine appreciation in her voice, not just for the coffee, but for the small comforts that still existed even in the midst of their harsh reality.

Scaro seemed amused, a small smirk playing on his lips. "One day, I'll have to make you some real coffee—Italian," he said with a note of pride.

"You already promised that." Keira took another sip from her cup, already feeling the warmth seeping through her.

"And I shall deliver," Scaro said, "when we are back on the ship."

"Any word from the ship?" she asked, her tone shifting to one of concern. "Were you able to contact Captain Campbell?"

As soon as the question left her lips, she noticed a subtle change in the atmosphere around the table. The marines, who had been relatively at ease moments before, now shifted uncomfortably in their seats. Jessie exchanged a quick, tense glance with Richard, their expressions tightening in a way that made Keira's unease deepen.

"Yes and no." Scaro's tone was carefully measured. "We received an automated burst transmission with instructions, including a time for a rendezvous point in orbit." He paused and blew out a breath. "But we haven't been able to raise the *Seri* herself. The ship could be out of range, on the other side of the planet, or … "

"She could have been destroyed by the Disunity ships up there." Keira felt her heart sink as she finished his thought, the worst-case scenario hanging heavily between them.

"That is one possibility," he admitted.

Jessie, who had been quietly observing, added, "We've sent several messages, but there's been no reply."

Keira's mind raced with the implications of that. If the *Seri* was truly gone, it meant they were stranded, cut off from any hope of extraction. But another, more immediate concern pushed its way to the forefront. "Is there a risk to that?" she asked, urgency in her voice. "Won't the enemy be able to find us if you keep sending?"

Scaro shook his head, reassuring her with the calm authority of someone who had already considered the risks. "The transmitters are located kilometers away from us. They're hardwired to the safe house and only power up when we want them to. It's extremely unlikely the enemy could locate us through them."

Keira nodded, absorbing the information. The idea that the transmitters were distant and only used briefly gave her some comfort, but the uncertainty still clawed at her. "I see."

"I assure you, it is quite safe," Scaro said, his tone firm but reassuring.

Keira nodded, but her mind was still turning over the details of what they'd discussed. Something didn't quite add up. "Wait, if the rendezvous is in orbit, how will we get up there?"

"That is a very good question," a voice chimed in from behind her, startling her so much that she nearly spilled her coffee. Keira quickly turned, her heart skipping a beat, to see an old and decrepit man standing near the back wall. But even as her eyes took in the figure, she knew something was off—he wasn't real. He was a hologram, a collection of organized photons, his form flickering slightly in the dim light.

"Damien," Keira said, recognizing the construct immediately and relaxing. His case was sitting against the wall, a tangle of cabling stretching from it to a nearby plug. Like MK, Damien was an artificial intelligence, one of the last of his kind. But unlike MK, he was quite irritable and irascible. They had found him, along with the mysterious tubes, in the precursor control room—a discovery that had added more questions than answers.

The hologram of the old man gave her a look that was somehow both condescending and filled with bitter amusement. He held himself in such a way that conveyed he thought himself superior to them.

"I would like to know more on that point," Damien said. "How exactly are we planning to escape this rock? Will you climb a tree and then jump the rest of the way to orbit? If that is your plan, I can tell you it will not work. Apes like you should know better than to try that."

"Captain, I told you we should have left him in sleep mode," Jessie said, resigned frustration in her voice. "It would have been quieter that way. He's been annoying us ever since you woke him up."

"Say, Captain," Richard interjected, his voice tinged with curiosity, "why did you bother plugging him in, anyway? He's been active for less than thirty minutes and I already dislike him."

Scaro glanced over at Damien's hologram somewhat sourly and then back at Richard. "I thought he might be of use to the princess when she awoke. Should she have questions."

Damien's hologram rolled its eyes, or at least gave the impression of doing so. "You apes can never focus. Has anyone ever told you that? You need to get off this planet sooner rather than later and you keep beating around the bush, playing word games. Who cares if you like or dislike me? I simply loathe your kind."

Keira decided to ignore the cantankerous AI for the moment, focusing instead on the more pressing concern. She turned back to Scaro, her expression serious. "He's got a point. If the rendezvous is in orbit, how exactly are we going to get there?"

"Someone finally has the brains to ask a good question, not to mention recognize my brilliance," Damien commented. It came out more like he was muttering under his breath, but it was loud enough for them all to hear it.

Pointedly ignoring the construct, Scaro nodded, having clearly anticipated the question. "We have access to a shuttle," he explained. "It's hidden a few kilometers away from here. When the time comes, we'll leave the safe house and make our way to it, then up to orbit."

Keira's brow furrowed as she considered the logistics. "And when is that?"

"In roughly six hours," Scaro replied, checking the time on a wrist device. "We also have an interceptor that can act as an escort and run cover for us. It set down nearby and is waiting for our signal to go."

Keira felt a brief surge of relief at the mention of the shuttle and the interceptor, but it was quickly tempered by Damien's cutting remark. "But if the ship isn't there," the AI said, his tone almost taunting, "if she has been destroyed, you will be delivering the Kai'Tal, and the devices"—he gestured with a hand at the tubes—"to the enemy. You will be literally consigning your own species to extinction."

The room fell into a tense silence, the weight of Damien's words sinking in. The tubes they had recovered contained something of immense value. In Keira's mind, there was no doubt about that.

The ground chose that moment to emphasize Damien's warning by putting an exclamation point on it. The tremor that followed was more violent, rattling the walls and making the coffee in Keira's cup ripple. Dust sifted down from the ceiling, and the table shuddered under the strain.

"Then again," Damien continued, his hologram flickering slightly with the movement as he glanced up at the ceiling, "remaining planetside might not be so wise either. Let's go for that shuttle."

Keira took another sip of her coffee as the quake died off. Her thoughts raced as she considered their options. The memory of the orbital dart was fresh in her mind. "The orbital dart... was it from the *Seri*? It was awfully close and fell right on the enemy."

Scaro nodded, his expression thoughtful. "We think so. It was too precise a hit to be accidental or an errant round, especially after your emergency flare fired. The timing could not be a coincidence."

"So, the *Seri* is still up there," Keira mused aloud, a spark of hope flaring in her chest. If the ship was still in orbit, it meant they might still have a chance at escape. But even as she considered the possibility, another thought crossed her mind.

She wondered if, with her new abilities, she could sense the *Seri* in orbit. The idea of reaching out, of using the machine to connect with something so distant, was both exhilarating and daunting. She might even be able to communicate with MK.

Could she do it?

She was on the verge of dropping back into the machine, ready to explore the possibility, when something stopped her. It was faint at first, almost a whisper, but it was unmistakable—a sound she hadn't heard since her earlier connection with the machine, since it had first started reaching out to her, when she'd been with Chris and Lee. It was like a song, a call to action that resonated deep within, urging her toward something she couldn't yet understand. The melody was haunting, filled with a sense of urgency and purpose.

Time was running out. The time was now... it seemed to be saying to her.

Keira's heart quickened, and she found herself unconsciously putting her coffee down, her attention drawn to her left. Her eyes landed on the metallic tubes, the same ones that had been taken from the precursor control room. They pulsed softly, almost as if they were alive, responding to the same call that she had heard.

The song seemed to emanate from them, the alien devices throbbing with barely restrained power. It was as if they were calling to her specifically, beckoning her to take action, to unlock whatever secrets each held. The pull was strong, powerful, magnetic, and Keira felt herself being drawn closer, her curiosity and caution warring within her.

"What is it?" Scaro asked, noticing the sudden shift in her focus.

Keira didn't immediately answer, her mind still grappling with the strange connection she felt. She knew that whatever these tubes were, they were far more than simple artifacts. They were connected to something vast, something powerful—and potentially something dangerous. But they were also the key to understanding what was happening, both on this planet and within herself.

She took a deep breath, trying to steady her thoughts. "The tubes," she said quietly, her voice barely above a whisper. "I think … they're trying to tell me something."

Pushing back her chair, Keira stood, her movements slow and deliberate, as if she were responding to an invisible force. The sensation that had been tugging at the edges of her consciousness was now undeniable, a powerful pull that resonated deep within her bones. It was as if the silver tubes were no longer just objects—they were alive with purpose, and that purpose was intertwined with her own. The silver strands that wove their way throughout her body had prepared the way and now she was ready to move on. The next step she took would begin to seal her destiny and the future.

The call was much stronger now, a siren song only she could hear, one that she couldn't ignore, not any longer, not if she wished to keep her sanity. She didn't fully understand what the Infinity and Control were, but instinctively, she knew that these three metallic tubes held the key to unlocking that mystery. The answers she sought, the knowledge she needed, all of it was somehow tied to these enigmatic devices.

"What's going on?" Jessie's voice broke through the haze, concern evident in her tone.

Keira didn't immediately respond. Her gaze remained fixed on the tubes, the rest of the room fading into the background. The others were watching her, their faces a mixture of confusion and worry, but Keira was beyond their concerns. The connection she felt with the tubes was consuming, demanding her full attention.

"Ah," Damien's voice cut through the tension, his tone both sardonic and ominous. "We come to the beginning of the end game. I have been waiting for this—waiting for a very long, and I mean a *long* time. It should prove ... exciting."

With effort, Keira finally tore her eyes away from the tubes and looked at the holographic construct. There was a knowing glint in Damien's simulated eyes, a depth of knowledge and understanding that made her uneasy. He was hiding—had been hiding something. He knew more than he'd let on. It was clear that Damien, with all his ancient knowledge, had been anticipating this moment, perhaps even orchestrating it from the shadows.

"What do you mean, Damien?" Keira asked, her voice steady despite the turmoil within her.

The hologram tilted its head slightly, as if pondering how much to reveal. "Those tubes, Princess, are more than just relics ... they are your birthright, your destiny, a part of you that you did not know was lost."

The power she felt emanating from the tubes, the call she had heard—it all pointed to something monumental, something that had the potential to change everything.

"I don't understand."

"You will," Damien said.

"What am I supposed to do?" she asked, her voice low.

"Take up the first tube," Damien said.

"And what will happen when I do?"

"I am not certain." Damien's holographic form flickered again. "That, Princess, is for you to discover. But know this: once you take the next step, there will be no turning back, not ever, not once it is part of you. The path you are about to walk is fraught with danger and sacrifice. But it is also the only path that will lead you to the truth—and perhaps, salvation for humanity and those you name the precursors, my makers."

Keira's heart pounded in her chest. She turned her gaze back to the tubes.

"The fate of humanity," Keira breathed to herself.

"Is within your reach," Damien finished.

CHAPTER TWELVE

Location: Planet Asherho
Date: 2450, Imperial Standard

Keira gazed down at the tubes. Behind her, no one spoke or moved. Still, Keira just stared.

"Take them." Damien's voice broke the silence, his tone laced with an unsettling eagerness. His words echoed in the chamber, resonating with a strange, almost hypnotic pull. "Take them in hand."

Keira tore her gaze from the tubes and glanced at Damien. His hologram, a flickering, ghostly figure, stepped closer to her. The edges of his form wavered slightly, as if he were barely tethered to this reality.

"What are they?" she asked, her voice cutting through the stillness. "You know... tell me."

"They will give you that which you sought, seek," Damien replied, his tone smooth, persuasive. "The Infinity and Control. Only, they are so much more."

But his answer only deepened her unease. The promise of power, of something beyond the grasp of mortal understanding, was tempting, yet it was not what she had asked. Keira's instincts screamed at her to be wary. Damien was not to be trusted. He had his own agenda, his own reasons for guiding her down this path, and she was certain he was withholding critical information.

Keira dropped back into the machine. The three tubes stood before her, ominous and inscrutable. She focused, peering closer, searching for any clue, any detail that she could divine that might reveal what lay within. But no matter how close she looked, the contents remained hidden, shrouded in a thick, impenetrable darkness. It was as if the very essence of the tubes defied her attempts to uncover their secrets, and that only fueled her growing mistrust and, strangely, her curiosity.

However, the exterior of the tubes seemed to radiate with a latent energy, an almost tangible force that made the space around them waver ever so slightly. The silver material encasing each tube appeared strained, as if barely able to contain the immense power within. A slight ripple traveled along the surface of one of the tubes, as though the energy was seeking an escape, testing the boundaries of its confinement.

Keira leaned in closer in the machine. She noticed now for the first time that the tubes weren't entirely silver. The one on the left had a subtle blue tinge, the middle one glowed faintly with red, and the last one was a deep, foreboding gray.

What did that mean? The colors weren't random; they were a signal, a message, but of what? Each one likely did something different.

Suddenly, the planet itself seemed to pulse beneath her feet. Keira's connection with the machine flickered, and for a split second, her consciousness was yanked back into her body. She blinked, disoriented, as the ground trembled once more. The safe house around them seemed to groan in protest, its foundations straining against the tremors, which were growing more violent. But just as quickly as it had come, the sensation faded, and she found herself back inside the machine, staring at the tubes.

This time, they shimmered in rhythm with the pulse she had felt from the planet. The soft whispering that had been at the edge of her awareness intensified, filling her mind with a thousand indistinct voices, all urging her to take them, and quickly. The compulsion was almost overwhelming, like a current dragging her toward the brink of a great unknown. And yet, a part of her resisted. She had doubts, reservations...

The choice before her felt monumental, its consequences unknowable. The whispers grew louder, almost pleading, but something deep within her, a survival instinct, kept her from giving in.

Finally, with a deliberate effort, Keira disengaged from the machine, pulling herself out of its grasp. She exhaled a breath she hadn't realized she was holding, her mind swirling with conflicting emotions.

"This is what you were born for," Damien's voice slithered through the room, his tone dripping with conviction. "You have already accepted your destiny. Pick one and take it."

Before she could respond, Scaro's voice cut through the tension like a blade. "What are you talking about?" he demanded, his voice rough, edged with a protective instinct.

Damien's hologram shifted its gaze toward Scaro, his form flickering slightly, and his expression turned to one that bordered on disgust, as if barely containing disdain. "This does not concern you, ape. Do not interfere."

"That's it," Jessie said, her voice a growl as she started across the room. "I am going to unplug him."

"No," Keira interjected sharply, raising a hand to stop her. "Don't do that."

Jessie halted. "Why the hell not?"

Keira didn't immediately respond. Instead, she looked over at Scaro, locking eyes with him. In that moment, she saw something she hadn't expected: genuine concern, a deep-seated worry for her well-being. Scaro wasn't just looking at her as his charge, his responsibility in this dangerous mission. He saw her as a fellow human being, someone whose life mattered beyond the mission's parameters.

Keira swallowed hard, the intensity of his gaze grounding her for a brief moment. She then turned her attention back to the tubes. Outside of the machine, they appeared inert, just simple silver cylinders. But she knew better. If she took them—no, when she took them—what would that make her? The question gnawed at her soul. Would she be less human, less herself? The transformation had already begun, that much was undeniable. She could feel it deep inside her, an unsettling shift in the very core of her being. The silver strands she'd glimpsed earlier had only confirmed what she had known.

But the reality of it, standing on the precipice of a choice that could redefine her very existence, was far more terrifying than she had anticipated. The allure of power, of destiny, was undeniable, but at what cost?

Her hand twitched at her side, the impulse to reach out and claim one of the tubes almost overwhelming. Yet something held her back—a vestige of the person she once was, the person she feared she might lose forever if she succumbed. She took a deep breath, trying to steady herself, but the decision loomed over her like a storm cloud, dark and unforgiving.

"What are those things?" Scaro asked, his voice low and measured as he stepped closer to Keira. His eyes were locked on the tubes, suspicion and unease clear in his expression. "Do you know?"

"I don't," she admitted, her voice tinged with frustration and doubt.

"Is there a compulsion keeping you from talking about it?" Scaro asked.

Keira shook her head. "No, not anymore. I suspect—these will grant me access to the Infinity Controller. But…"

"But you aren't sure?" Scaro pressed with genuine concern.

Keira shook her head. "No," she said, her voice quieter. "I am not certain about anything, especially not this."

"What will you do?" Scaro's brow furrowed as he studied her, the tension between them thickening.

Damien sneered, his voice cutting across the room like a whip. "What is required, you stupid ape."

Scaro's temper flared instantly. He turned on the construct, his posture rigid with anger. "Shut up, you," he snapped, pointing a finger at Damien's hologram. "You shut up or I'm unplugging you, and then I'll leave your case here when we go. I will fucking leave you to die with this bloody planet."

The threat hung in the air like a drawn blade. Damien's hologram flickered, the usually smug expression faltering. For a brief moment, the construct seemed to hesitate, calculating the risk. He opened his mouth to speak, but the defiance died on his lips as Scaro stepped closer, shaking his finger at him, the intensity of his gaze leaving no room for doubt.

"I mean it, construct," Scaro growled, his voice low and menacing. The silence that followed was thick, the atmosphere charged with an unspoken challenge. Damien, for once, remained silent, his form flickering as if the hologram itself was uneasy.

"Take a leap of faith," Keira said softly, her voice carrying a note of resolve that hadn't been there moments before. "Like I did in the control room—a leap of faith."

Scaro and Jessie exchanged glances, the unspoken tension between them evident. Jessie was the first to voice the doubt that Keira could feel creeping into her own thoughts. "Perhaps you should wait until we are back on the ship," Jessie suggested, her tone more cautious now. "We can do whatever it is you're about to do in a controlled environment…with a doctor present. There's no rush."

Keira hesitated, her gaze drifting to the tubes again. Jessie's suggestion was reasonable—sensible, even—but something inside Keira whispered that time was not on their side. She remembered the darkness she had seen in the machine, a malevolence lurking just out of reach, waiting. It wasn't just the unknown that made her uneasy; it was the sense that whatever was in those tubes was tied to something much larger, something that couldn't be contained or controlled, even back on the ship.

The memory of that darkness, cold and calculating, made her skin prickle. She couldn't shake the feeling that whatever was happening here, it was part of a greater plan—one that didn't care whether she was ready or not.

She turned her gaze to Damien, the construct's hologram hovering with a disturbingly calm presence. His digital eyes met hers, and for a moment, it felt as though he was reading her thoughts, sifting through her doubts, her fears. His earlier eagerness to push her toward the tubes now seemed more calculated, more sinister.

"What is the Kai'Thol?" Keira asked.

Damien's holographic face split into a sickening grin, the digital edges of his mouth curling unnaturally wide. "Your opposite, your antithesis," he replied, his voice carrying a sinister satisfaction in conveying the knowledge. "Your cousin."

Keira's breath caught in her throat as the realization dawned on her. "The Disunity," she whispered, the words tasting bitter on her tongue.

Damien's grin widened, taking on a leering, almost predatory quality. The malevolent energy behind his expression sent a chill down Keira's spine, her blood turning to ice. The implications of his words sank in, heavy and foreboding.

"Someone on the other side has the ability to interact with the machine," Keira surmised, the thought alone making her feel as though a shadow had fallen over her soul.

"Yes," Damien breathed, his tone laced with dark approval. "You are beginning to understand the stakes."

"They can do what I do." Keira's gaze shifted back to the tubes. The thought of another being, another force capable of wielding the same power she had only just begun to grasp, was terrifying.

"You have already taken the Rush," Damien continued, his voice soft but insistent. "They have not. The only way he can take that is from your broken body, and by force."

Keira's mind raced as she processed his words. "The Rush," she repeated, turning the term over in her mind. It was clear now— Damien knew far more than he had let on, and this was the confirmation she had feared. "The Rush?"

"What you took into your body in the control room," Damien explained, his tone matter-of-fact, as if discussing something trivial.

Keira's thoughts were abruptly interrupted by a vivid flashback. She remembered the silver liquid, the way it had surged into her body, how it had overwhelmed her senses, blocking her from seeing what was happening at that critical moment. The memory was sharp, a searing reminder of the transformation that had begun then. The Rush—whatever it truly was—had changed her, altered something fundamental within her. And now, the realization that someone else, this Kai'Thol, could potentially take that power from her, from her broken body, filled her with serious concern.

"It prepares you for what is to come." Damien cackled, his laughter echoing unnervingly through the room. The sound was jarring, unnatural, as if the construct was relishing the unfolding drama, enjoying the moment fully. He suddenly grew serious, grave even. "You are prepared. Now is the time to take the next step, before it is too late."

"The strands," Keira breathed, her thoughts drifting back to the strange, silver threads she'd seen within her body. They had woven themselves into her very being, a sign of the changes already taking root inside her. The memory of them sent a shiver down her spine, both mesmerizing and terrifying.

"I don't like it," Scaro interjected, his voice gruff. He stepped closer to Keira. "I would advise caution, Princess. We can wait and do this like Jessie said, back on the ship."

"That would be a mistake," Damien snapped, his tone suddenly sharp as he took a step closer to Keira, his hologram flickering ominously.

"Why?" Scaro demanded, his patience wearing thin. He rounded on the construct. "Why is it so important to act now?"

Damien's expression grew solemn. "I was the Guardian, standing the last watch…the most trusted…the last of the very last. When the others departed, I was left behind to stand my post." His gaze shifted from Scaro and locked onto Keira's. "I was to protect the very last of the souls, and I did my duty to the fullest. You will see my eternal watch ended."

"That doesn't make any sense," Jessie said, her brow furrowing as she struggled to piece together the fragments of Damien's cryptic narrative. "Speak plainly."

"Why is it a mistake to wait?" Scaro pressed, his voice growing more insistent. "Why can't we wait until we're back on the ship?"

Keira's mind was a whirlwind of thoughts, each one vying for her attention. She rubbed the back of her neck, trying to soothe the tension knotting her muscles. The room felt smaller, the air heavier as the weight of the decision before her pressed down.

"Because he is out there…" Keira murmured, the realization settling in like a cold, hard truth. The figure Damien had alluded to, this Kai'Thol, wasn't just a distant threat. He was real, and he was waiting—somewhere beyond the confines of the safe house, lurking in the shadows of this war-torn world. And if she delayed, if she waited to act until they were back on the ship, it might be too late. The strands within her, the Rush she had taken, had marked her as something different, something powerful. But they had also marked her as a target.

"He's out there," Keira repeated, her voice growing stronger, more resolved. "And if I don't act now, he will."

Damien nodded, his grin returning, though this time it was less mocking and more knowing, as if he had expected this all along. "You see now," he said quietly, almost reverently. "The time is now, Kai'Tal. Take the step, before he does."

"He," Scaro repeated, his voice laced with a growing concern. "Who is he?"

"Crecee," Keira said, the name leaving her lips like a curse.

"I do not know this Crecee," Damien responded, his tone almost dismissive. "Only the Kai'Thol."

"The UPG captain that was messaging you?" Scaro asked, his confusion evident.

"Him." Keira gave a firm nod, the pieces of the puzzle starting to click into place in her mind. The more she thought about it, the more it made sense. Crecee had always been different—something about him was not quite right, something off. His cruelty and ruthlessness were unmatched, qualities that had made him invaluable to the UPG leadership. When they needed a dirty job done right, when they needed someone to cross the lines and make an example that others wouldn't, they turned to Crecee.

Could he be the Kai'Thol? Could he be the darkness? Or was it someone else entirely? The uncertainty bothered her, but in the end, it didn't matter. What mattered was that someone on the other side had the same abilities she did, and they were coming for her. They wanted what she had—this Rush, as Damien called it. And from what she could see, they would stop at nothing to get it.

"Crecee is this Kai'Thol?" Scaro asked, his voice tinged with a mix of disbelief and growing realization.

"I think so," Keira said, her voice steady but weighted with the gravity of the situation. "If it's him, then he has access to the machine."

"But not like you do," Damien said with a strange mix of envy and admiration. "Not with the enhancement of the Rush. But now is the time for action." Damien purred, his tone almost seductive. "It is either you take the first tube or face certain death, and not just your own."

"Keira, I don't trust him." Scaro stepped closer, placing himself protectively by her side. "He has his own agenda. We can wait."

"No," Keira replied, her voice resolute as she turned her gaze back to the three tubes. "We can't."

Her mind raced as she stared at the tubes, each one pulsing with latent energy. Which to take first? The choice seemed both arbitrary and monumental.

"I've always liked the color blue," Keira murmured, more to herself than anyone else, as she reached out for the tube on the right.

"Blue?" Scaro echoed, his confusion evident as he glanced from the tubes to Keira. "I don't understand."

"You wouldn't," Damien interjected, his tone dismissive. "Allow her to do what needs doing."

Keira's hand closed around the tube, its cool surface smooth against her palm. She lifted it, expecting something—anything— to happen. But there was only silence.

"Now what?" Scaro asked, the tension in his voice mirroring the uncertainty Keira felt.

Without a word, Keira extended her senses, opening herself up to the tube in her hand. She didn't need the machine this time; she felt a connection forming on a deeper, almost instinctual level. Suddenly, a loud click echoed through the room, sharp and ominous. The tube in her hand began to dissolve, the solid metal liquefying into a viscous blue substance.

The liquid flowed over her hand, creeping up her arm like a living thing. It wrapped itself tightly around her, the sensation alien and unsettling. Her arm went ice-cold, the chill seeping into her bones. She could hear gasps behind her as the others reacted to what was happening.

The liquid continued to spread, its icy tendrils winding up her arm. Keira watched in a mixture of awe and apprehension as it began to be absorbed into her skin, disappearing beneath the surface. The process was mesmerizing, almost hypnotic, but a deep sense of dread settled upon her as the last of the blue liquid vanished.

Then, pain.

A scream tore from Keira's throat as her world erupted in agony. The pain was beyond anything she had ever experienced, a searing, burning torment that consumed her from the inside out. It felt as though her very cells were being torn apart and then reassembled, each one screaming out in protest. Her vision blurred, dark spots swimming before her eyes as she staggered, barely able to stay on her feet.

The room around her seemed to warp, the edges of reality fraying as the pain overwhelmed her senses and her mind. She could hear distant shouts, voices calling her name, but they were muffled, distorted, as if coming from underwater. All she could focus on was the pain, the relentless, all-consuming pain that threatened to tear her apart, atom by very atom. There was nothing else but agony.

CHAPTER THIRTEEN

Location: Planet Asherho
Date: 2450, Imperial Standard

A shimmering blue haze enveloped everything, distorting reality into a surreal, nightmarish landscape. Keira's vision was a blur, as if she were submerged in thick, oppressive fog. She couldn't see, couldn't focus, couldn't make sense of her surroundings.

And then once again, the pain struck.

It wasn't just pain; it was an all-consuming inferno, a relentless fire that lanced through her body, searing every nerve ending with a fury beyond comprehension. The agony was raw, pure, and utterly devastating, flooding her senses until nothing else existed. It was as if her very being was getting torn apart, each atom violently ripped from the other, only to be forced back together in an endless cycle of destruction and rebirth.

Keira's thoughts shattered under the assault, splintering into fragments of incoherent screams. Movement was impossible—her body was no longer her own, a vessel of torment suspended in a void where time held no meaning. The torture felt eternal, a merciless shredding of her soul, ripping it to pieces and leaving nothing but a hollow echo of who she once was.

This wasn't natural.

It defied the very laws of existence, as if some evil force was twisting the fabric of reality around her, molding her suffering into something dark and incomprehensible.

But then, ever so slowly, the relentless storm began to abate. The searing pain dulled, withdrawing like a tide pulling back from the shore. Keira gasped, her lungs burning as she sucked in a ragged breath. The simple act of breathing felt like a gift, a moment of divine relief amidst the chaos. She drew in another shallow breath, savoring the air as it filled her chest, grounding her to something real.

Her mind, though battered and bruised, began to piece itself together. Thoughts, once scattered and broken, started to coalesce, flickering like distant stars in the vast darkness of her consciousness.

"Keira." Scaro's voice cut through the haze like a lifeline, though she couldn't see him. The sound was distant, muffled, as if coming from the other end of a long tunnel. "Keira, can you hear me?"

She wanted to respond, to let him know she was still there, but her body refused to obey. Her limbs felt like lead, unresponsive, as if she were trapped in a body that no longer belonged to her. Thoughts swirled sluggishly in her mind, fragmented and dis-jointed, while a crushing weight pressed down on her chest, doing its best to suffocate her. It was as if a massive, invisible force was sitting on her, driving the breath from her lungs. Each gasp was shallow, barely a breath at all, leaving her teetering on the edge of consciousness.

"She's in cardiac arrest," Jessie's voice rang out, sharp and clini-cal, cutting through the fog of Keira's disorientation. There was an urgency there, a note of controlled panic, though Jessie kept her tone steady.

"Do you have the crash kit?" Scaro asked, every word clipped and urgent. "Get it! Now!"

"I'm getting it, sir," a voice responded, the sound of movement barely registering in Keira's fading awareness.

"You are wasting your time," Damien interjected, his tone cold and devoid of any concern, let alone care. "You are wasting your time."

"Keira, stay with us!" Scaro urged, his voice breaking through the fog again, this time more desperate, a command and a plea wrapped into one. He clearly wasn't ready to let her go, wasn't ready to give up, and the strain in his voice revealed the stakes.

"She is either the one or she's not the one," Damien continued, as emotionless as ever, as if discussing a trivial matter. "If she isn't, then she's not worth the time, not worth saving."

Keira, hovering on the edge of oblivion, felt the cold indifference of Damien's logic like a distant echo in the back of her mind. She wasn't ready to be written off, not yet.

"What do you mean?" Jessie demanded of Damien, her tone sharp, slicing through the tension that hung thick in the air. "What do you mean she is not worth saving?"

"She is either the Kai'Tal or she's not," Damien replied, his tone devoid of emotion, as if stating a simple fact. His calmness was unnerving.

"Where are those damn paddles?" Scaro shouted, his voice breaking the air with raw desperation. Every second felt like an eternity.

"Coming, sir!" someone shouted back, echoing faintly through the haze. It sounded like Sara, and the urgency in her tone mirrored the frantic energy in the room.

"And if she's not this Kai'Tal?" Jessie pressed with a mix of disbelief and frustration. The implications of Damien's words added another layer of dread to the already dire situation.

"Then she will die," Damien said simply, cold and matter-of-fact, as if her life were a minor variable in a much larger equation.

Suddenly, time seemed to grind to a halt. Keira's consciousness was yanked away from her physical body, thrust back into the strange machine that had become an unwelcome, yet familiar presence in her mind. She hovered above the scene, an ethereal observer, watching the chaos unfold from a detached perspective. Below her, she saw herself lying prone on the floor where she had collapsed, her body eerily still, framed by the cold, metallic surfaces of the room.

Scaro was kneeling by her left side, his expression twisted with worry. Jessie was on her right, her hands poised over Keira's chest as if about to spring into action and perform CPR. Richard stood nearby, his eyes locked on the scene, his face a mask of stoic concern. They were all frozen, suspended in the moment, their movements halted as if someone had hit pause on reality itself.

Sara was captured mid-stride, rushing back into the room, a bag with a prominent medical marker clutched in her hand. Keira recognized it instantly—it was a crash bag, the kind that held the tools needed to bring someone back from the brink of death. But now, it seemed almost trivial, a futile effort in the face of the overwhelming forces at play.

A strange expression was on Damien's face as he stood back, watching the scene unfold in his holographic form. His usual detachment was tinged with something else—curiosity, interest perhaps? Or was it expectation? The blue haze that blanketed everything, once silver in Keira's mind, had shifted, casting an ethereal glow over the scene. It was as if this moment existed outside of time, a crossroads where the fate of her very soul hung in the balance.

Keira suddenly became aware that the pain—the searing, relentless agony that had consumed her—was gone. It hadn't faded or diminished; it had simply vanished, as if it had never existed at all. The absence of torment was so absolute that it left her disoriented, her mind grappling to understand the abrupt shift.

Was she dead?

Had she crossed over, leaving the agony behind in the mortal world?

No, she wasn't dead. The realization settled into her with a clarity that was almost startling. She was very much alive, but she was still within the machine, that strange, alien presence that had woven itself into her consciousness. Yet it felt different now—everything felt different. No, *she* was different, changed in a way that was both subtle and profound.

Something monumental had just happened, though its exact nature eluded her. It was as if she had crossed an invisible threshold, a line that once separated her from something vast and unfathomable. Now, she had merged with it, her being intricately entwined with the machine, with the very fabric of the world around her.

There was an energy within her now, a power that hummed just beneath the surface, vibrant and alive. It wasn't the wild, chaotic energy she had felt before, but something smoother, more controlled, as if she had learned to harness it in those few fleeting moments. She was more in tune with the machine, more in sync with its rhythms and pulses. The connection felt natural now, as effortless as breathing, as if she had always been a part of it, and it a part of her.

Keira didn't fully understand what had just transpired, but she knew, deep in her core, that she had been altered, transformed in a way that went beyond the physical. She was more than she had been, more than just a human or a soul trapped in a machine. She was something new, something that was still unfolding within her.

And with that change came a sense of calm, a clarity that steadied her. The machine wasn't just a tool or a prison—it was an extension of her now, an intrinsic part of her existence. She could feel its presence, the pulse of its energy, all aligning with her own. It was as if she had found her place within it, her true place, and the world around her was shifting to accommodate this new reality.

A sudden flash of memory surged through Keira, vivid and crystal clear, cutting through the strange, otherworldly environment she found herself in. She saw her father, his face alight with a warm, genuine smile that had always made her feel safe and loved. His eyes twinkled with the kind of joy that was contagious, the kind that could lift her spirits no matter how dark her day had been. He was laughing, a deep, hearty laugh that echoed in her mind, and she realized it was because of something her younger self had done—something simple and unimportant, yet in his eyes, it was everything.

The image shifted seamlessly, and now she was older and watching him as he patiently showed her how to repair an air handler, his hands moving smoothly, guiding her through each step. He had always been so patient, so willing to share his knowledge, instilling in her the confidence to tackle anything life threw her way. The memory was filled with warmth, a quiet moment that spoke volumes about their bond.

Her heart swelled, a surge of emotion flooding her as she relived the love she had felt for him, still felt—the deep, unwavering connection that had shaped so much of who she was. It was a love that transcended time, a love that anchored her even now, in this strange and frightening place.

In the machine, Keira gave a sob, the sound raw and filled with a mix of grief and longing. It was as if all the emotions she had kept buried, all the pain of loss and the ache of missing him, had been unleashed in that instant. The memory of her father, so vivid and real, was both a comfort and a reminder of all she had lost. But it also gave her strength, a reminder that she was still here, still fighting, and that his love was a part of her, woven into the very fabric of her being.

Then, as quickly as the memory of her father had come, another face flashed before her, stark and unfamiliar. It was alien, its features both unsettling and strangely compelling. The skin was a deep reddish hue, like the flush of human cheeks, though this was no mere blush of embarrassment—it was the natural coloration of this being.

The eyes were large, dominating the face, black and devoid of pupils, giving them an impenetrable, almost otherworldly depth. Where a human would have a nose, there was only smooth skin, leading down to a small mouth filled with delicate, sharp teeth.

The face was staring at her, its gaze intense and unreadable. Suddenly, a three-fingered hand reached out toward her, the fingers impossibly long and slender, far longer than a human's, with two additional joints that made the movement of the hand almost serpentine. The alien fingers hovered for a moment, then gently touched her face, tracing the contours of her cheek with an unexpected tenderness.

Instead of recoiling in fear or horror, Keira remained still, transfixed by the touch. The hand's caress was delicate, and with it came an overwhelming surge of emotion—love, pure and profound, burst into her heart, so powerful that it left her breathless. It was a love unlike any she had ever felt before, as if this being's affection was pouring directly into her soul.

But then a realization struck her—this wasn't her own emotion. She was experiencing a memory, an alien memory, as vivid and real as her own but belonging to another. The creature before her had loved deeply, and she could feel that love now, radiating from the memory like a warm embrace. This was a parent's love, an intense and protective affection for its alien child. The bond between them was so strong, so pure, that it transcended species and time, and now, through the machine, Keira was reliving it.

The recognition brought a strange comfort. This was more than just an alien's affection—this was a glimpse into a different world, a different time and a different way of being. The creature had loved her, or rather, it had loved its own child with a depth that echoed her own father's love for her.

Then the image flashed again, and Keira found herself in a dimly lit room, her vision blurred by tears. She was crying—no, she was sobbing uncontrollably, her body wracked with the kind of grief that comes from a wound too deep to heal. She felt the rawness of the pain as if it were happening all over again. Vex was there, a younger Vex, holding her tightly, her arms wrapped around her as if trying to shield her from the unbearable sorrow. Keira was younger as well, more vulnerable, and utterly devastated.

She recognized this moment immediately. It was the day she had learned of her father's death, the moment when her world had shattered. The grief was as fresh and intense as it had been then, a piercing agony that twisted inside her chest. She could feel Vex's strength, her attempt to anchor her, but even her presence couldn't dull the edge of the loss that had consumed her.

Then, just as quickly, the scene shifted. The room and Vex faded away, replaced by a sterile environment. Keira was now looking down at a metal table where an alien lay motionless. It was covered up to the chest by a white blanket. The being's reddish skin was pallid, its large black eyes closed, its once lively form now eerily still. Another alien stood beside the table, its head bowed in silent mourning. The air was thick with sorrow, a profound sense of loss that permeated the scene.

Keira felt the weight of that grief as if it were her own. She didn't just see the alien lying on the table—she understood, on a deep, visceral level, that this creature was dead. The realization hit her with the same force as when she had learned of her father's passing. It was an overwhelming loss, one that transcended species, a raw pain that resonated right through her.

These beings—they weren't just aliens; they were something more. The sense of familiarity, of connection, grew stronger. Were these the Placif, the ancient precursors she had only heard whispers and tales of? Were these the people who had built the reactor and machine at the heart of Asherho?

The thought reverberated through her mind, each syllable carrying the weight of history, of a legacy long forgotten by most but now echoing in her consciousness. The grief she felt wasn't just her own or even the aliens'. It was the collective sorrow of a people who had lost something irreplaceable, a bond that tied her to them across the vast expanse of time and space.

Keira was left with the undeniable truth that their lives, their memories, and their losses were now entwined with hers. The images, the emotions—they were more than just visions. They were echoes of the past, and somehow, she was connected to it all.

Were these the Placif, the precursors?

The question lingered in Keira's mind, heavy with the weight of newfound understanding. Before she could dwell on it further, the image shifted again, pulling her back into the tapestry of her own life. Memories flashed before her—moments filled with love and tenderness, followed by the stark finality of death. The scenes oscillated between her world and the alien one, each flicker of life and loss, joy and sorrow, more intense than the last.

She saw herself laughing with friends, sharing quiet moments of happiness with loved ones, working out and sparring with Chris, only for the warmth to be replaced by the cold sting of grief. Then, just as abruptly, the images returned to the alien world, showing its own cycles of life—strange yet achingly familiar. Alien faces lit with joy, then shadowed with sorrow, as they experienced love, followed by the inevitable parting that came with death. The emotions were so raw, so vivid, that Keira felt her heart tightening, as if it might shatter under the weight of it all.

The images and moments continued relentlessly, weaving together a story of life that spanned both species, binding them in a shared experience of what it meant to live and love, to lose and mourn. It was overwhelming, a cascade of emotions so intense that Keira could feel herself being drawn into the depths of despair.

"Enough!" Keira cried out, her voice breaking through the maelstrom of images. Her plea reverberated within the machine, echoing back at her like a wave crashing against a cliff. "Enough!"

At once, the images halted, stopping as suddenly as they had begun, leaving a deafening silence in their wake.

"Love and loss," a soft voice spoke within the machine. The words were in a different language, one unfamiliar to her, yet Keira understood them with a clarity that was almost unsettling. The voice was calm, carrying the weight of ancient wisdom. "A human and an Alarveen emotion."

"We are not so different, then?" Keira asked, her voice trembling with the raw emotion still coursing through her. "Is that what you are showing me? Your people and mine?"

"You are the bridge, Kai'Tal," the voice responded, gentle but firm, as if imparting a truth that had been known for eons. "The bridge between us, between our two peoples … the one to redeem us."

The words hung in the air, resonating deep within her. Keira realized with a start that she was being entrusted with something monumental—a role that spanned not just lifetimes, but the very fabric of existence itself. The images, the emotions—they had shown her that despite the vast differences between humans and the Alarveen, there was a common thread that wove their lives together: the capacity to love, to grieve, to connect on a level that transcended physical form.

She wasn't just a witness to these memories. She was part of them—no, the bridge, as the voice had called her, between two worlds that had long been separated by time and space. The responsibility was immense, but so too was the sense of purpose that filled her. This was part of what it meant to be Kai'Tal—not just a title, but a living, breathing connection between two peoples destined to find understanding.

A brilliant flash of light burst within the machine, flooding Keira's senses with blinding intensity. She instinctively shielded her eyes, but the light seemed to penetrate everything, searing through the haze of her consciousness. What was it? The question barely had time to form in her mind before she felt an urgent pull, drawing her attention outward.

She looked around, her vision sharpening as the confines of the safe house began to take shape around her as she hovered over it. The familiar walls and dim lighting were comforting, grounding her in reality. But something was wrong—her gaze was drawn beyond the immediate space, to something lurking in the distance. She looked and felt suddenly cold.

It was dark, a blackness so absolute that it seemed to absorb the light around it. Malevolent and terrifying, the presence loomed, its attention fixed on her.

It was watching her. No—*gazing* at her, with an intensity that sent chills down her spine. She could feel its hunger, a gnawing, insatiable craving that radiated from the darkness like a physical force. Worse still, it was coming for her and it wanted, desired, needed all she was and all she had. The realization struck her like a cold blade, slicing through her moment of clarity with pure, unfiltered fear.

Keira blinked, the image of the dark presence burning in her mind as she gasped for breath. The world around her snapped back into focus with jarring immediacy as she dropped out of the machine. She was back in her body, lying on the floor of the safe house. The pain that had wracked her moments before was receding, its grip loosening as the film over her eyes began to clear. Keira sucked in another gasping breath, a deep one.

"She's back with us!" Jessie's voice rang out, relief flooding her tone. "I have a heartbeat! It's elevated, but it's stable."

Keira's vision sharpened further, the faces of her companions coming into view. She could feel the steady thump of her heart as it hammered in her chest. She sucked in another breath, savoring it.

"Kai'Tal she is," Damien's voice broke through, laced with a note of triumph. "She is the one! She is the one!"

CHAPTER FOURTEEN

Location: Planet Asherho
Date: 2450, Imperial Standard

Keira lay there as if she had just sprinted a marathon, her chest rising and falling with each labored breath. The sensation of the cold floor beneath her only heightened her awareness of the disorientation that lingered. Her vision was still blurry. The last remnants of the blue film clinging stubbornly to her eyes were beginning to dissipate, allowing her to once more see.

Keira opened her mouth to speak. Nothing came out other than a croak. She tried again and coughed.

"Water," Scaro commanded, his voice cutting through the haze with military precision.

"Aye, sir," Sara responded promptly, her boots echoing on the hard floor as she stepped away, leaving the crash bag beside Keira.

"Stay still," Scaro advised, his tone softer but still authoritative. He had a hand on her shoulder. "Take a moment to recover."

Coughing again, Keira nodded weakly, now too drained to even try to speak. Her body felt heavy, as if gravity itself had doubled its grip on her. Her chest hurt something fierce.

"Her vitals are stabilizing," Jessie reported, though a frown creased her brow. Kneeling, she hovered over Keira, a small device in hand, its screen casting a pale glow on the marine's face. Jessie's eyes darted across the data, analyzing each fluctuating number. "Some of the readings are slightly off—oxygenation levels, white blood cell counts..."

Scaro's gaze sharpened. "Anything to worry about?"

Jessie hesitated, her uncertainty evident in the tightness of her jaw and eyes. "I'm not sure," she admitted after a long moment, shaking her head in frustration. "I'm no medic, and I'm certainly not a doctor. It's a shame this safe house doesn't have a surgical unit. We could run more detailed tests, find out what it did to her."

"No," Keira gasped, her voice barely more than a strained whisper. The effort to speak sent a sharp pain through her chest, but she pushed past it. She knew she had to stop them. If they scanned her or ran blood tests, they might uncover things that could unsettle even the toughest amongst them. Things she herself wasn't ready to confront.

Scaro leaned in, his eyes narrowing in concern. "What?"

"No tests," Keira repeated, her voice still weak but carrying a desperation that made it clear she meant every word. The words were almost lost, so hoarse was her voice, but Scaro clearly caught them for his eyes narrowed.

Sara reappeared and held out a disposable clear bottle. "Water, sir."

Scaro took the bottle from her and gently placed it against Keira's cracked lips. She took a strong pull, her throat convulsing with the sudden influx of cool liquid. The water hit her parched throat like a flood, overwhelming her senses. She gagged, the water spilling from her mouth as she coughed violently, the sound harsh in the stillness of the room. Scaro quickly pulled the bottle away, giving her a moment to recover, his hand steady as he waited for her to signal she was ready.

After a few moments, Keira nodded, her breath still ragged but more controlled. Scaro brought the bottle back to her lips, and this time, she drank more cautiously. The water slid down her throat, soothing the dryness that had gripped her since she'd awoken. It was like liquid life, reviving her just enough to push back the creeping fog that clouded her mind.

He pulled the bottle back after a moment, allowing her to swallow. The cool liquid settled in her stomach, and she felt a small surge of strength return.

"More?" Scaro's voice was low, as if afraid to disturb the fragile calm that had settled over her.

Keira gave a curt nod, her eyes meeting his with a silent plea. She needed more, not just of the water, but of time—time to regain her strength and figure out what the hell was happening to her.

He placed the bottle to her lips once more, and Keira took another pull, this time savoring the cool liquid as it washed away the lingering dryness in her throat. With each passing second, the fog in her mind began to lift, and a sense of clarity returned. She was starting to feel more like herself, her strength slowly but surely returning.

"That's enough for now." Scaro took the bottle back and set it down carefully on the ground, his movements deliberate and calm, though his eyes never left her face, searching for any signs of distress.

"No tests," Keira repeated, her voice stronger now, carrying a firmness that wasn't there before.

"We need to figure out what happened," Jessie insisted, concern lacing her words. She looked at Keira with a mix of worry and determination. "We have to make sure you're all right, ma'am."

"No more tests," Keira said, her tone resolute as she locked eyes with Scaro. There was no room for debate in her words, only a cold certainty. "No matter what happens, understand?"

Scaro remained silent, his jaw tightening as he processed her command. His face hardened, a stoic mask that revealed little of the thoughts churning behind his eyes. He was a soldier, trained to follow orders, but this one clearly tested the limits of his discipline.

"That is an order," Keira added, forcing a note of authority into her voice. She needed him to understand that this was non-negotiable.

"Aye, aye, Princess," Scaro responded with a curt nod, his voice steady but laced with a subtle tension. "I will not allow anyone to perform tests on you without your express permission. Good enough?"

His words were a promise, a vow etched in the hardened lines of his face. Keira knew Scaro well enough to understand that when he made a promise, like Chris, he kept it, no matter the cost.

"Thank you," Keira murmured, extending her hand toward Scaro. "Help me up."

Without hesitation, he gripped her hand, his rough, calloused skin warm against hers. The strength in his grip was reassuring, a solid anchor in the midst of her lingering disorientation. Slowly, he pulled her to her feet, his movements careful and deliberate, as if afraid she might break under the strain.

Once upright, the world spun around her, a dizzying blur that made her stomach lurch. Scaro's grip tightened, almost instinctively, his other hand moving to her waist to steady her. Despite his efforts, Keira felt herself slipping, the edges of her vision darkening as unconsciousness threatened to pull her under again. She leaned heavily into him, her head resting against his broad chest. The warmth of his body seeped into her, a comforting presence.

With her ear pressed against his chest, she could hear the steady, rhythmic beat of his heart, each thump a reminder of the life pulsing within him. She could even feel it, the subtle vibration of each heartbeat resonating through her, grounding her in the present. Scaro didn't say a word, just held her there, his arms solid and unyielding, providing the support she desperately needed.

After a moment, Keira felt her strength returning, the dizziness receding like a distant memory. She straightened, almost reluctantly pulling away from his embrace. The warmth of his body lingered on her skin, a faint echo of the closeness they had just shared. She missed it the moment it was gone, but she knew she needed to stand on her own.

As she looked around, she saw their eyes on her—Jessie's filled with concern, Scaro's a guarded mix of worry and duty. Both Sara and Richard were also staring. The unspoken question hung in the air, heavy and unavoidable.

"Ma'am," Jessie finally broke the silence, her voice tinged with uncertainty, "what just happened?"

Keira met Jessie's gaze, searching for the right words to explain the inexplicable, but all she could see was the concern etched on Jessie's face, a reflection of the uncertainty that mirrored Keira's own mind. The question was simple, but the answer was anything but.

Keira pondered the question, her mind swirling with fragmented memories and sensations that didn't quite fit. "I—I don't know. I'm really not sure."

Something had shifted within her, something profound and inexplicable. She could feel it, a subtle yet undeniable change, as if a part of her had been altered at a fundamental level. The alien eyes, the unfamiliar emotions, the voice that had echoed in her mind—they were all pieces of a puzzle she couldn't yet grasp.

Inside, she felt different too, as though she had been slightly reshaped, made older, more seasoned by an experience she couldn't fully comprehend. It was as if a merging had occurred, a fusion of her own consciousness with something foreign and incredibly ancient.

New thoughts and memories stirred within her, ghostly fragments that weren't her own yet felt as vivid and real as her own experiences—they were new to her. Suddenly, a vision flashed before her eyes—a meadow bathed in the soft glow of an orange, pockmarked moon, filled with delicate purple flowers that swayed gently in the breeze. The air was thick with the scent of the dirt and blossoms, and Keira felt an overwhelming surge of emotion—contentment, happiness, a deep sense of belonging that resonated through her soul.

And then, as quickly as it had come, the vision vanished, leaving her disoriented and breathless. The memory had been so real, so tangible, that it was almost as if she had truly been there, in that tranquil meadow under an alien sky. But she knew, with a certainty that was both comforting and unsettling, that she had never set foot in that place. It wasn't her memory. It was the memory of her alien self, a part of her that was both familiar and unfamiliar, connected to her—yet distinctly separate.

Keira shook her head, trying to clear the lingering sensations. She sucked in a breath, grounding herself in the present, but the memory lingered at the edges of her consciousness, a reminder of the unknown forces now at play within her. She wasn't just Keira anymore—she was something more, something changed, and the implications of that transformation were as vast and mysterious as the stars themselves.

Though with every passing moment she felt physically stronger, Keira was beginning to understand, deep down, that she would never be quite the same again. The subtle changes within her were undeniable, as if something fundamental had shifted, leaving her irrevocably altered. She closed her eyes, trying to steady herself, but instead of the comforting darkness she sought, she was transported to another world, beneath an alien sky.

She stood in a vast field, the horizon stretching out infinitely before her. The ground was carpeted with something resembling grass, though it was unlike anything she had ever seen. The blades were a deep, almost iridescent blue, and atop each stalk perched a strange yellow star-shaped flower, delicate and surreal. The contrast of colors was striking, almost hypnotic, as the blue and yellow swayed together in the wind, creating a living tapestry that rippled across the landscape.

Above her, two yellow suns dominated the sky, one low on the horizon, casting long, distorted shadows, and the other almost directly overhead, both bathing this world in an eerie double-light that felt both familiar and utterly foreign. The wind picked up, gusting through the field, and the strange grass responded with a whispering hiss, the sound weaving through the air like a ghostly lullaby.

For a moment, Keira felt an overwhelming sense of peace and tranquility, as if this place, with its otherworldly beauty, was where she truly belonged. The sights, the sounds, the smells, the very feel of the wind against her skin—it all resonated within her, awakening something deep and primal that she hadn't known existed. But just as quickly as it had begun, the vision faded, leaving her standing once again in the confines of the safe house.

Her eyes fluttered open, and the harsh reality of the present rushed back in. The alien world slipped away like a dream upon waking, leaving only a lingering sense of loss at the beauty she'd just witnessed and the quiet hum of the safe house's air handlers. Keira was back, but she wasn't alone in her mind anymore—those visions, those memories, they were part of her now, woven into the fabric of her being. The realization sent a shiver down her spine. Whatever had happened to her, whatever she had become or was becoming, there was no going back, not now, not ever.

"Ma'am," Jessie's concerned voice cut through the haze of Keira's thoughts. "Are you okay?"

Keira turned to Jessie, meeting her eyes, and opened her mouth to respond. But the words caught in her throat, trapped by the weight of the memories that weren't her own. How could she explain something so inexplicable? How could she tell Jessie about something so different, yet now so intimately a part of her? The truth of it hung between them, an invisible barrier she wasn't sure she could ever cross. All eyes were on her, expectant, worried, and it only amplified the growing tension within her.

Before she could muster a reply, Damien's voice broke the silence, cutting through the atmosphere with a strange eagerness.

"Take the next tube," he said, the tone of his voice carrying an almost unsettling enthusiasm. "Take it, Kai'Tal!"

Keira's gaze shifted to Damien, her eyes narrowing as she studied him. What was his game? There was something in his tone, something he wasn't saying. The way he spoke, the way his words seemed to push her forward without revealing the full picture—it made her uneasy. What wasn't he telling her? What did he know that she didn't?

Her attention drifted to the last two tubes. One was distinctly red, glowing faintly, its surface regularly rippling, as if infused with a pulse of its own, while the other had taken on a somber gray hue, dull and lifeless in comparison. The change was subtle, but to Keira's altered perception, it was as clear as night and day.

She regarded the tubes for a long moment, the room seeming to close in around her as the implications of the choice before her settled in. The red and gray weren't just colors—they were paths,

choices that would shape her fate in ways she couldn't yet comprehend. She could feel the pull of the red tube, its energy almost
tangible, drawing her in, while the gray exuded a sense of coldness,
clinical detachment.

What did they represent? What lay at the end of each path?
Keira didn't know, but the choice felt heavy, as if it carried the
weight of more than just her own future. Keira abruptly turned.

"What color are those tubes?" Keira asked, her voice steady,
though inside, she felt anything but.

"Silver," Scaro answered immediately, his tone matter-of-fact, as
if the question held no hidden meaning.

It was just as she'd suspected. Her perception had shifted, her
vision altered. What had once been merely silver now appeared to
her as distinctly red and gray. The colors spoke to her, carrying
weight and meaning that was foreign, yet oddly familiar.

Her mind was not just hers anymore—alien memories and
thoughts intertwined with her own, reshaping her understanding
of the world around her. But just how much was she changing? The
question seriously bothered her.

"Take it," Damien urged, his voice insistent, almost coaxing.

But something about his eagerness didn't sit right with Keira.
Though she couldn't fully articulate why, she knew in her gut that
she wasn't ready for the next tube—not yet. Though they did call to
her, Keira's body was still in the midst of adapting to the first, a process she could feel deep in her bones. It was like a slow, methodical
reconstruction happening beneath her skin, subtle but undeniable.
The sensation was unsettling.

If she took the second tube now, while the first was still working its changes, it could prove catastrophic. She sensed the danger
instinctively, as if her altered self was warning her of the potential
consequences. It wasn't just a matter of physical endurance; there
was something deeper at play, something that could unravel if she
rushed into the next phase.

"No," Keira said firmly, her eyes locking onto Damien. "Soon,
but not yet. I am not ready."

To her surprise, Damien bowed his head, a gesture so unexpected that it caught her off guard. "As you say, Kai'Tal, so shall it be," he intoned, his voice carrying a note of reverence.

Kai'Tal. The word resonated within her, stirring something ancient and powerful that lay dormant in the recesses of her mind. It was a title, a name, and yet it was more than that. It was a mantle, a role she was only beginning to understand. The bow, the name—it was as if Damien recognized something in her that she was only just discovering. And it scared her, this glimpse of a destiny she hadn't asked for but now couldn't escape.

Keira stood there, feeling the weight of the moment, the significance of her choice hanging in the air like a tangible force. Whatever lay ahead, she knew there was no turning back. The path she was on was one of transformation, and it was only just beginning.

Then something occurred to Keira, a chilling realization that sent a wave of cold dread washing over her. She closed her eyes for a long moment, reaching out with her senses. She didn't even have to drop into the machine. She could feel the dark presence, and it was near, so very close.

"They are coming," she whispered, her voice hollow with certainty as she opened her eyes and looked straight at Scaro. "The Disunity. They know where we are."

Jessie's eyes widened in disbelief. "That's impossible, ma'am," she protested, her tone laced with a mix of doubt and fear.

"No, it's not," Keira responded, shaking her head as if trying to dislodge the thought, but she knew it was true. Every fiber of her being screamed it. She turned her gaze back to Scaro, her eyes locking onto his with an intensity that left no room for doubt. "They're coming."

Scaro held her gaze, his eyes searching hers, looking for any sign of hesitation, any reason to doubt her words. But there was none. After what felt like an eternity, but was only a second or two, he gave a single, resolute nod, solidifying his trust in her instincts.

"Any idea how long we have?" he asked, his voice calm but edged with the seriousness of the situation.

Keira shook her head slowly. "No. But it won't be long."

"Right," Scaro said, his tone shifting into that of a seasoned leader, commanding and unyielding. He turned to the other marines, who had been watching the exchange with growing tension. "If she says they're coming, they are coming. We'll take it as gospel. Armor up. We're heading out the back door as soon as everyone's ready and will make our way to the shuttle." He paused. "Jessie, get the princess settled in her armor and ready to move."

"Aye, sir." Jessie nodded sharply and gestured toward the room where Keira had left her armor. "I've resupplied your gear—more ammunition, fresh grenades, and your haptic suit's been cleaned. I also have a new rifle for you, ma'am."

Keira gave a brief nod of acknowledgment. She appreciated Jessie's efficiency, the way she managed to keep everything in order and remain calm despite the chaos swirling around them. She was a small comfort in the midst of the uncertainty, more than Keira could ever express.

"What about me?" Damien interjected, his voice tinged with an edge of anxiety.

Scaro turned to him, his expression hard and unyielding. "What about you?"

"You—you wouldn't leave me, would you?" Damien asked, genuine fear flickering in his holographic eyes. It was as if the thought of being abandoned was more terrifying to him than the threat of the Disunity.

Scaro considered him for a moment, the silence between them heavy with unspoken judgments. "I was thinking about it," he admitted, his tone blunt as he scooped up the last two tubes, securing them with practiced ease.

"He comes with us," Keira said firmly, her voice leaving no room for argument. As she looked at Damien, a strange sense of familiarity washed over her. She had known him before, she was sure of it... at least the alien memories within her said so. His chosen form was different than before. She had a flash of him ... his holo-gram ... so long ago, looking like ... like an Alarveen.

Despite his different appearance, there was something about him that resonated with her, a recognition that tugged at the edges of her mind. It was as if she knew him—an old friend, perhaps? An assistant? A slave? The last thought was unsettling.

"No one gets left behind, no matter how disagreeable," Keira added, her gaze locking onto Damien's with an intensity that made her resolve clear.

"Thank you, Kai'Tal." Damien bowed his head.

Scaro paused, then gave a curt nod, accepting her decision. "Understood," he said, his tone resigned but respectful. Keira had made her choice, and in this moment, her authority was absolute.

Damien visibly relaxed, the tension easing from his frame as if a great weight had been lifted. But Keira couldn't shake the feeling that there was more to him, more to their connection, than she fully understood. She was sure of that.

"I'll get his connections," Richard said, swiftly moving over to the wall. He knelt down, his fingers expertly working to discon-nect the various cables and devices linked to Damien and the safe house's power source.

"Thank you again, Kai'Tal," Damien said, his tone reverent as he bowed his head respectfully toward Keira. "We live to serve."

Then, without another word, his hologram flickered and van-ished, leaving the room feeling strangely empty in his absence.

"He's a strange one," Sara said.

"That's an understatement," Richard said as he continued to work.

"Come on, ma'am," Jessie urged, her voice clipped with urgency. "We need to get you suited up."

Keira didn't hesitate. She turned and followed Jessie. The sense of impending danger prickled at the back of her neck, urging her to move faster. They were nearly at the doorway when the overhead lights abruptly shifted, casting the room in a red hue. A harsh, mechanical alarm blared, cutting through the air with an unforgiving intensity.

"Intruder detected, stairway two," an automated voice announced, its tone cold and devoid of emotion. "Classification: stealth recon bot."

"Shit," Jessie muttered under her breath.

"We're out of time. Move, people!" Scaro barked, his voice sharp and commanding, cutting through the rising tension like a knife.

CHAPTER FIFTEEN

Location: Planet Asherho
Date: 2450, Imperial Standard

Keira moved cautiously forward, encased once again in the protective shell of her powered battle armor. The suit's systems hummed softly around her, the heads-up display providing a steady stream of data as she followed Jessie down the dimly lit corridor.

Ahead of them, the captain's presence was a steady point of reference, his movements purposeful, steady, constant. Somewhere beyond, Sara was a ghost in the darkness, scouting the path ahead with the quiet efficiency of a seasoned warrior. Keira had learned she was a recon scout, and a good one at that, at least according to Jessie. Richard brought up the rear, his eyes and sensors constantly scanning for any sign of a threat, though that, at the moment, was unlikely. He would periodically stop and look behind before continuing on.

"The only way to get into this corridor is through the safe house," Jessie had told her when they'd set out.

Still, Keira thought it more than a little concerning the marines were taking no chances. No matter how safe they thought they were, it was clear the marines respected the enemy's capabilities, to the point where they would remain vigilant even on their own ground.

The floor trembled again with another quake. Keira could now feel the roiling energy in the reactor below in the planet's core. She did not even need to drop into the machine. The power wanted release. The rumbling grew stronger, shaking them roughly, before it subsided. Scaro had stopped to allow the quake to pass, and once it had, they continued onward.

A series of heavy bangs behind them, each one muffled, caused them to stop again. Jessie shared a look with Scaro and then turned to Keira as the captain started forward again. "The safe house defenses." She chuckled. "Someone is having a bad day."

"Better them than us," Richard said.

The safe house, with its relative comfort, was already a distant memory as they came to a hatch, which had been opened. Keira noted that the hatch had been heavily reinforced and armored. Just past it was a stairwell.

The stairs were different—clearly not meant for regular use, a utilitarian space designed for service workers rather than soldiers in battle armor. The steps were surprisingly narrow, forcing Keira to be mindful of each footfall. The suit's servos adjusted with each step, ensuring she maintained balance despite the awkward dimensions.

There were no doors, no exits—just a seemingly endless descent into the unknown. Each level blurred into the next. The air was thick with dust and the lingering toxic haze, which grew thicker with every step downward. It felt as if they were descending into the very bowels of the planet, far from the light of the sun and the safety it once represented.

The captain's earlier warning echoed in Keira's mind—no comms, only external speakers. It was a precaution that heightened the tension, making the silence between them even more oppressive, for there was little talking. They moved quickly, working their way down the stairs, going farther and farther, ever deeper.

Scaro had briefed them on their destination: an old service train that had been repaired, maintained, and was powered a small reactor unit.

They could not get to the train quick enough. Keira felt a nagging sense of dread, a feeling that something unseen was following them, the darkness, the Kai'Thol. It was more than just nerves; it was as if a shadowy presence lurked in the periphery of her vision, just out of sight in the shadows, watching, waiting.

The sensation was unsettling. It sent a chill through her despite the suit's environmental controls and her exertions, the constant movement. Then suddenly, they reached the final landing. Another heavily reinforced door was waiting. This one too had been opened, likely by Sara.

Ahead, Jessie reached the landing and halted, her body language tense and alert, rifle coming up to the ready position. Scaro had already disappeared through the doorway, scouting ahead.

Keira paused, her senses on high alert, her breathing steady and controlled within the confines of her armor. It still sounded loud in her helmet. The stillness stretched on, and just when Keira was about to ask what was happening, Jessie began to move again, slipping through the doorway without a word. Keira followed closely, the uneasy feeling still clinging to her like a second skin.

When she stepped through the doorway, she found herself in a small, dimly lit corridor that ran ten meters. Beyond that was a train terminal. It was old, the platform quite small. The tiles that had adorned the walls were cracked and in some places had fallen off completely.

A train waited at the platform. It consisted of a single car. The lights were on inside, casting a pale glow across the scene, and the low thrum of energy confirmed it was powered and ready to depart. Sara had just emerged from the train car and stood near the platform's edge, her rifle held loosely in one hand, her eyes scanning the area with the focus of a seasoned warrior.

The space was tiny, including the platform. There was barely enough room for the train car, which was more tram than anything else. There was only one tube with one exit, which disappeared into the wall, the tracks shooting off into the darkness.

Keira had always liked trains, and she was about to ride one. But as she looked at the train, she couldn't shake the feeling that whatever had been following them was still out there. She glanced behind them. It was coming, following after them and waiting for the right moment to strike.

"Everything checks out, sir," Sara said and gestured at the train. "It's ready to go."

"This should take us all the way to the shuttle," Scaro said, his voice steady through the external speakers as he turned to Keira. "Everyone climb aboard."

As if on cue, the entire terminal shuddered violently, a forceful tremor that was unmistakably different from the quakes that had been tearing through the planet. This was something else, something far more deliberate. A deafening boom followed, so powerful it seemed to shake the very air around them, kicking the dust up from the ground and shaking it loose from the walls and ceiling.

The noise reverberated through Keira's suit, rattling her teeth. She could feel the force of it in her chest. Ceiling tiles cracked and fell, clattering to the floor around them, and for a moment, it was all Keira could do to stay on her feet, the suit's stabilizers working overtime to keep her upright.

It lasted several long, agonizing seconds, each one stretching out as if time itself had slowed. The lights on the train flickered ominously, threatening to plunge them into darkness, but after a few tense moments, they steadied. Then, as abruptly as it had begun, the shaking stopped, leaving a profound silence in its wake, broken only by the sound of settling debris.

"That would be the safe house," Jessie said, her voice calm but edged with grim satisfaction. "Let's hope the blast took some of the bastards with it."

Keira understood the compression warhead had been set off.

"Yeah," Scaro muttered, frustration in his tone as he waved her forward. "Now, everyone get on the train. We're burning daylight. Let's get out of here."

Keira hesitated only for a moment before stepping onto the train, following closely behind Sara. The interior of the car was utilitarian, stripped of any comfort—just a cold, functional space designed for moving people quickly, more of an enclosed sled with powered motors than anything else. Jessie was right behind her, and Scaro brought up the rear, his presence a solid reassurance as the doors slid shut with a soft hiss, sealing them inside.

The space was cramped, standing room only, with no seats—just metal handrails bolted to the ceiling and walls. Keira reached for a rail, her armored fingers closing around the metal. The train lurched into motion the moment the doors sealed, pulling out of the station and into the dark tube beyond. It moved surprisingly fast, rapidly picking up speed and gaining momentum as it shot forward. Despite the velocity at which it moved, there was an eerie absence of sensation—no vibrations, no rattling, nothing to indicate the train was continuing to accelerate and running along a track other than the walls of the tube reflecting the train's lights as it flashed along.

The world outside the narrow windows was a blur of shadows, creating a surreal sense of disconnection from reality. The silence inside the car was broken only by the soft hum of the train's motors and the occasional clank of armor against metal or heavy thunk as someone adjusted their grip or stance. Keira could feel the tension in the air, a collective unease shared by all of them as the train rocketed down the tube.

They all wanted to get to the shuttle, and the sooner the better.

"At least we're leaving the enemy behind," Jessie said.

Keira could only agree, and as the train continued to gain momentum, rocketing along, she found herself staring out at the featureless tunnel beyond, her thoughts drifting to the shadowy presence she had sensed earlier.

The Kai'Thol hadn't disappeared; if anything, the feeling had intensified, as if whatever was following them had merely changed tactics, deciding to bide its time until the moment was right. No matter where she went on the planet, it would follow. And she knew it was Crecee.

Something, some instinct just told her so.

Eventually, she'd have to deal with him, and personally, too. She tightened her grip on the rail, her muscles tensing involuntarily, ready for whatever might come next.

Scaro carried Damien's case securely fastened to his side. Somewhere on his person, hidden among the compartments of his armor, were the two remaining tubes—small, unassuming objects with the potential to alter the course of everything.

Keira's mind drifted to the first tube, the one she had taken. She still couldn't fully grasp what it had done to her or what it might continue to do. All she knew was that it had changed her and was changing her still. The uncertainty clawed at her, a constant undercurrent of doubt and confusion.

Suddenly, without warning, her vision blurred, and the world around her seemed to dissolve. Keira was no longer on the train. In an instant, she found herself standing in an entirely different place—an environment that could only be the bridge of a starship.

She looked around. The walls were sleek and metallic, lined with consoles and displays that pulsed with alien symbols and strange lights. There were no stations at which to sit. It was standing only. Various pings and chimes occasionally sounded as the machinery around her worked. The air was cool, almost cold.

She was alone, utterly alone, on this strange bridge. In fact, somehow she knew that on the entire ship she was the only soul present. Keira looked down at her hands, expecting to see the familiar contours of her armored gloves, but what she saw instead made her heart skip a beat.

Her hands were not her own.

The fingers were elongated, tapering to fine points, and there were only three of them on each hand, accompanied by a thumb that curved backward in a way that defied human anatomy. The skin—if it could be called that—was smooth and pale, reddish in color and almost translucent, with a faint, unnatural sheen.

A soft chime echoed through the bridge, louder than the others, pulling her attention to a wall monitor that flickered to life before her. The image displayed was a planet, its surface a swirl of clouds and landmasses, almost breathtakingly beautiful to gaze at. There were actual oceans down there, deep blue in color. She'd seen the picture of her mother by one, but Keira had never set eyes on an actual ocean in person. They no longer existed on Ash.

She wanted to …

The ship—this alien ship—was in high orbit, hovering above, those sentients below not even realizing it was here, that *she* was here, that *she* had come. Yet her perspective was different, distant, detached. It was as if Keira was looking at a place she knew intimately but through the eyes of a stranger. It was so odd. Keira knew she was not supposed to be here and yet here she was.

A wave of disorientation washed over her as she tried to make sense of what was happening. The vision felt real, more real than a simple hallucination, but it was disjointed, like fragments of a memory that didn't belong to her. The alien hands, the starship's bridge, the view of the planet—it all felt both foreign and hauntingly familiar at the same time.

Keira took an unsteady step forward toward the screen, the alien environment around her moving into sharper focus. She found herself mesmerized by the planet displayed on the monitor, half of its surface bathed in deep shadow, the other half illuminated by the distant sun. The line between night and day was plain. Yet it wasn't the sun's light that caught her attention, but the scattered glow of artificial illumination—hundreds of cities and settlements punctuating the dark side of the planet, their lights shining defiantly against the void of darkness.

The chime echoed a second time through the bridge, its tone insistent, almost urgent.

"Weapons armed and ready," a dispassionate voice said. "Awaiting your command."

"Release," she said in an alien tongue. The words slipped out of her mouth. But Keira understood she had not really spoken them. Someone else had.

"Weapons launched," the clinical voice said in the same tongue. She thought it sounded very much like Damien.

Keira's gaze was drawn back to the monitor, where an ominous new development was unfolding. From the edge of the screen, streaks of light arced away from the ship, speeding toward the planet's surface. The sight was unmistakable—missiles or some kind of projectiles, fired in a coordinated barrage, their sleek forms cutting through the cold vacuum of space with deadly intent.

Her breath caught in her throat as she watched the projectiles accelerate away, their paths precise and unwavering, pre-targeted. A cold dread settled over her as the realization struck—this was no defensive maneuver. The ship was not under threat. This was an attack, a calculated strike on the world below, one designed with a single purpose in mind.

Complete annihilation.

The weapons were aimed at the very cities and settlements that moments ago she had marveled at, mere points of light in the darkness, symbols of intelligent life. And those below had no idea what was about to happen. She knew that the alien understood it as fact.

Death had come to this world.

"Such is the way," she said.

Keira's mind raced, torn between the surreal nature of the vision and the stark reality of what she was witnessing. Yet, despite the horror of it, there was a strange sense of detachment, as if she was both participant and observer in this unfolding tragedy.

The missiles continued their relentless descent, and Keira could do nothing but watch, a helpless witness to the devastation that was about to unfold. The chime sounded again, a final, ominous note that seemed to echo her own feelings of helplessness.

The weapons began to detonate in brilliant flashes of light. Keira's breath caught in her throat at the devastation being wrought. Then the vision began to fade, the starship's bridge dissolving into a blur as the reality of the train car reasserted itself around her. She blinked, disoriented, her heart racing as she found herself once again standing on the moving train, gripping the handrail so tightly in her armored fist that she had bent it. The alien hands were gone, replaced by the familiar, reassuring weight of her battle armor.

A single tear ran down her cheek, for Keira knew she had just witnessed the destruction of an entire race. The alien inside her had committed genocide.

The train began to tremble, the vibration subtle at first but quickly escalating into a violent shaking that felt as if the entire car might tear itself apart. Outside there was a screeching as the train stressed itself against the tracks. Keira's instincts flared—this wasn't just the train malfunctioning. It was the planet itself, quaking with a force far greater than anything they'd experienced before. She could feel the pulse of energy as it surged. The ground beneath them seemed to heave and buck violently. The train, already moving at high speed, lurched to the side and jumped the tracks, coming free.

Without warning or time to react, the car slammed into the side wall of the tube, the impact sudden and brutal. Keira was thrown forward, the world spinning as metal screeched and groaned around her. Sparks flared from where the train contacted the tube. The force was immense, a bone-jarring jolt that sent her crashing to the floor as the train seemed to jump and fly. Her suit's systems kicked in instantly, absorbing the brunt of the impact, cushioning her from what could have been catastrophic injuries.

The sounds of twisting metal and the grinding of the train against the tube's inner wall filled the confined space, a cacophony of destruction that seemed to last an eternity. Then, just as quickly as it had begun, the train ground to a halt, the tortured screech of metal on metal fading into an eerie silence.

The lights inside the train flickered once, twice, and then died, plunging them into darkness. Keira's scan suite automatically activated, the advanced sensors embedded in her suit piercing the gloom with a clarity that normal vision couldn't match.

She found herself on the ground. The suit had done its job, protecting her from the worst of the collision, but she still felt bruised and battered. It was one more series of aches to add to the others she had accumulated over the last few days. The train lay still, but the uneasy tremors of the planet's ongoing upheaval could still be felt as the quake slowly died off.

Keira let go a breath of relief. Around her, the others were similarly recovering. The air was thick with dust, and smoke was beginning to fill the interior of the train. Though Keira could not see what, something was burning.

"Is everyone all right?" Scaro's voice crackled through his external speakers, the concern evident. "Sound off."

"I am," Keira replied, her voice slightly muffled by the weight pressing down on her. She quickly realized that the captain and Jessie had been thrown on top of her in the chaos. The three of them had ended up in a tangled heap, their armored suits clashing together like mismatched puzzle pieces. The captain began to climb off first.

"Bloody hell," Richard's voice came from nearby as he struggled to his feet, shaking off the disorientation. "I'm fine, Captain."

"Yeah, I'm here," Sara responded from the front of the train. She was already on her feet. Without hesitation, she stepped forward and kicked out a window, the reinforced glass shattering outward with a sharp crack and then crash as it fell outward. She climbed through the opening and out into the train tube, after a moment dropping down onto the track with a heavy, echoing thud.

Keira and Jessie began the awkward process of untangling themselves before climbing to their feet. The train car was a mess, its interior battered, the frame of the car twisted cruelly from the impact, but everyone had lived through the ordeal.

"Avante?" Scaro called out, concern lacing his words as he checked on Jessie, looking over at her. "Are you okay? I didn't hear from you."

"I'm all right," Jessie responded, "just a little bruised, is all."

"Up ahead, the tunnel is collapsed," Sara's voice echoed back to them from outside. She was already standing on the tracks ahead of the train. "We're gonna have to find some other way to the shuttle."

"That's not good," Jessie said.

"No, it isn't." Scaro wasted no time. He moved forward, clambering out of the train and onto the tracks, following the path Sara had taken. Richard was right behind him. Keira took a moment to grab her rifle from the floor, the familiar weight reassuring in her hands, before she advanced toward the window.

"After you, ma'am," Jessie said, her tone respectful but laced with urgency.

Keira nodded and ducked down, pulling herself through the shattered window and out into the tube, jumping down to the tracks, her boots clanging against the metal with a hollow echo. She quickly straightened, scanning the area. Jessie followed her out, landing heavily behind her.

Scaro had already moved a few steps ahead, his armored form just visible in the gloom. Sara and Richard were with him, all three of them staring down the length of the tunnel, almost forlornly.

Keira joined them, her gaze following theirs. Less than a quarter of a kilometer away, the tunnel had thoroughly caved in, the ceiling collapsed in a heap of twisted metal, dirt, and rubble. The debris blocked their path completely, a wall of destruction that was clearly insurmountable. The dust from the collapse was still settling.

"It's a good thing we weren't under that when the ceiling came down," Jessie commented.

"I am thinking we were quite fortunate," Scaro said, glancing back at the wreck of the train behind them. His eyes narrowed as he scanned the tube past the twisted wreck of the derailed train.

Keira felt the sight of the tunnel collapse was quite disheartening. The tunnel, once a clear route to their destination, was now a dead end. The collapse had brought down tons of rock and steel, and god knew what else, completely blocking the way.

Her mind raced as she assessed the situation. They were trapped underground, with no clear way forward, and the planet's increasing instability meant that time was running out. The safe house was gone, and now their only escape route had been cut off from them.

"We need to find another way," Scaro said with determination.

"Those quakes are getting worse," Jessie noted, her voice tense as another tremor sent a shiver through the tunnel, along with a shifting of the collapsed tunnel ahead. She glanced almost nervously up at the ceiling.

"They are," Scaro agreed, his tone grim as he scanned the area. After a moment, his eyes locked onto something in the distance, and he pointed with a gloved hand. "I see an emergency access hatch just ahead. Let's see if we can make our way up to the surface and then hump it the old-fashioned way to the shuttle."

"That sounds like fun," Jessie said.

"Your definition of fun and mine differ," Richard countered.

Keira frowned beneath her helmet, her mind racing with the implications. "Why not just stay underground?" she asked, her voice betraying her concern. "Won't we be more vulnerable topside? Easier to find?"

"Maybe," Scaro conceded, his gaze still fixed on the distant hatch. "But we don't have complete maps of what's down here. These tunnels are a maze. It will be easy to become turned around, and with the quakes getting worse"—he jerked a thumb upward—"we might even have a section of the ceiling come down on us. I don't think we want to be buried alive."

"I don't want to be buried alive," Jessie said.

"I think we can both agree on that," Richard said.

Scaro glanced at Jessie and Richard and scowled before gesturing at the hatch, his resolve clear in the firm set of his stance. He looked at Keira. "In my professional opinion, we have to take the risk of going topside. More importantly, we know the surface in these parts, and even if it's more exposed, it's a path we can easily navigate."

"All right," Keira said.

"Good. We've talked enough. Let's get moving."

CHAPTER SIXTEEN

Location: Planet Asherho
Date: 2450, Imperial Standard

K eira's voice echoed slightly as she asked, "Do we have a pilot?"
The question was directed at Jessie, her tone holding a
sharp edge of concern as she stepped cautiously through a heavy,
corroded door into what was unmistakably an old underground
receiving dock.

Her helmet's visor adjusted automatically to the dim, murky
light as she scanned the cavernous space. The dock had once been
a hub of activity, likely servicing a vast factory, through which they
had just come, but those days were long gone. The skeletal remains
of industrial equipment loomed like tombstones in a forgotten
graveyard, their surfaces pitted and scarred by years of exposure
to the harsh environment. Whatever machinery had once thrived
here had either been scavenged for parts or dismantled entirely,
leaving behind only shadows of its former purpose.

The space before her was eerily silent, save for the faint crunch
of debris underfoot. The ever-present dust and sand, carried by the
winds from above, had invaded even this subterranean refuge, coat-
ing everything in a fine, gray powder. Ash mingled with the debris,
adding another layer to the desolation.

Keira's gaze shifted to Scaro, who stood silently just beyond the
door they had come through, his armor almost blending into the
surrounding gloom. His posture was tense, alert. Sara, their scout,
had moved ahead and was nowhere in sight, but Keira could just

make out the faint impressions of her tracks in the dust, leading toward a partially open door at the top of a sloped ramp.

The door was an industrial garage style, its heavy steel frame battered and warped from years of neglect. It had been forced open just enough to allow entry, revealing a sliver of harsh daylight that pierced the darkness like a beacon.

When fully opened, it would have been wide enough to admit freight vehicles, though none were in sight, parked in the dock. The space felt like a tomb, a relic of a world that had once been full of life and purpose, now reduced to dust and echoes.

"We're going to wait here a moment," Scaro said, his voice steady and authoritative, in command. "Sara's checking things out on the surface. She'll have a quick look around and assess the situation up there, then report."

Keira nodded, absorbing the information as her gaze drifted back to Jessie. There was a slight hesitation before she asked, "So, is there a pilot with the drop ship?"

Jessie's response was almost nonchalant, but there was a hint of pride in her tone. She tapped her chest. "I can fly."

Keira blinked in surprise, the admission catching her off guard. "You're a pilot?" she asked, her voice tinged with disbelief. "There's no other pilot?"

"That's correct." Jessie gave a small nod, her helmet's visor glinting in the dim light as she replied, "I got my certification shortly before the company shipped out. I'm considered a backup pilot, a reserve, in case the company needs one, at least for this mission."

"She was planning on a transfer," Scaro interjected, his tone slightly more relaxed now, "not to mention officer candidate school. She would have made it too, if things hadn't gone tits up."

Jessie's grin was visible even through the facemask, her expression lighting up with a mix of humor and nostalgia. She gave a chuckle that was both self-deprecating and genuine. "Flying seemed much easier than slogging it about in the mud and dirt all the time...cleaner too."

Keira found herself smiling in return, the tension of the moment easing slightly. The idea of Jessie—who had always struck her as a grounded, no-nonsense marine—flying a drop ship or shuttle was a surprise, but it also made sense. In a world where everyone had to wear multiple hats, a backup pilot was a valuable asset, especially in an environment as hostile as this one.

"The question you should be asking is if she's a *good* pilot." Richard's voice cut through the brief silence as he joined them, bringing up the rear. There was a teasing edge to his tone, but the underlying seriousness was unmistakable. "That's the question of the hour."

Jessie responded with a chuckle, her confidence unwavering. "I guess we're about to find out."

Keira, still processing this new facet of Jessie's skill set, tilted her head slightly. "What kind of pilot?" she asked, her curiosity piqued. In her experience, pilots came in many varieties, each with their own specialized training and expertise, craft they were authorized to operate.

"Light cargo," Jessie replied, her tone casual but firm. "Orbital to ground stuff."

Keira's eyebrows rose slightly beneath her helmet. "So, you can fly the shuttle we're headed for, right?"

Looking slightly amused, Scaro looked between Keira and Jessie.

"That's what worries me," Richard interjected, a smirk playing on his lips as he glanced at Jessie. "The shuttle's a big beast, not a cargo lighter."

"They're basically the same," Jessie countered. There was a quiet determination in her words, a resolve that spoke to countless hours of training and practice. "It's just a matter of scale."

Richard shook his head, the smirk never leaving his face. "Yeah, and scale's the thing that'll get you killed if you're not careful."

Still, Keira couldn't shake the tension that had settled in her chest. The stakes were high, and any mistake could be fatal. She glanced at Jessie again, seeing in her a mix of determination and maybe a hint of anxiety at what was to come.

"Have you flown a shuttle before?" Keira asked, her mind racing as she recalled the massive UPG shuttles she had seen in the past, vessels twice the size of the Imperial Marine drop ships and even larger than cargo sleds.

Jessie hesitated for a split second before answering, "In a simulator. It's basically the same principles."

Richard let out a groan, the sound a blend of exasperation and concern. "A simulator? Damn, Jessie, that's not exactly the same as the real deal."

Keira's thoughts mirrored Richard's unease. Simulators could replicate the controls, the physics, and even the pressure of a real flight, but they couldn't simulate the gut-wrenching reality of piloting a shuttle. The stakes were infinitely higher when it wasn't just pixels on a screen, but lives hanging in the balance.

Jessie, sensing the tension, stood a little straighter, her voice taking on a firmer edge. "Look, I know it's not the same, but I've logged hundreds of hours in that simulator. I know the systems, the procedures, the flight dynamics. It's not my first choice to be flying this thing, but I'm not going to crash us either."

Richard looked about to protest some more. Scaro held up a hand. "We're rather short on pilots right now. Jessie can fly and we're lucky to have her. Understand?"

"Yes, sir," Richard said.

The world around Keira dissolved in a blinding flash of light, and in an instant, she found herself somewhere entirely different. The oppressive atmosphere of the underground dock was replaced by a cold, clean environment. She stood in a room that exuded an unsettling aura of clinical detachment. Before her was a surgical table, its surface spotless and reflective under the harsh, artificial lights overhead. Laid out upon it were four silver tubes—identical to the ones Scaro carried for her. The sight of them sent a shiver down Keira's spine.

Advanced machinery loomed overhead, its purpose inscrutable. The equipment was unlike anything she had seen before, even on the *Seri*. It had an alien quality, its sleek, intricate design speaking of a technology far beyond her understanding or even, for that matter, humankind's. The room hummed softly with the sound of various machines in operation, the only sign of life in this otherwise still and sterile environment.

Instinctively, Keira's hand reached out—but it wasn't her hand. The hand that moved toward the tubes was alien, slender, and unfamiliar, yet somehow deeply connected to her. It was as if she was both an observer and a participant, her consciousness intertwined with another being's. Her fingers closed around one of the tubes, lifting it gently from the table.

The metal was cool to the touch, smooth and almost unnervingly perfect. Turning it over, she studied the tube, the way its surface reflected the light in a subtle, silvery sheen. She saw a distorted alien face reflected back at her.

"It is time," a voice echoed through the sterile chamber, resonating with a quiet authority. "The graft is complete. The Rush has done its work. It is time for the next step—the Sundering. You will need to lie down upon the table. Are you prepared?"

"No," came the alien's reply, firm yet carrying an emotion Keira couldn't fully place. "But that is immaterial. My mate has already been Sundered. I am next."

"He has been," the voice confirmed as a hologram flickered to life on the opposite side of the table.

The figure that materialized before Keira was a being that could only be described as alien in every sense of the word. Though it bore the basic humanoid structure—two arms, two legs, and a head—its proportions were otherworldly, almost unsettling. Towering above her, its height seemed to defy natural law, as if it were stretched beyond what the human form could endure. Its limbs were impossibly thin, giving the creature a fragile yet eerie presence.

Its face was a mask of two void-like black eyes, large and unblinking, that dominated its narrow, angular face. Where a nose should have been, there was nothing but smooth, reddish-brown skin, giving the creature an unfinished appearance, as if it had been sculpted from some strange material and left incomplete. The mouth was a mere slit, thin and horizontal, devoid of any expression or warmth.

Its hands were perhaps the most disturbing feature to human eyes. Each hand had only three long, spindly fingers that moved with a grace that felt unnatural. The thumb, however, could swivel in ways that defied human anatomy, enhancing the alien's already unsettling demeanor. The way its hands flexed and moved made it seem almost insect-like.

Clad in a pristine white smock that hung loosely over its skeletal frame, and white pants that blended seamlessly into black boots, the creature's attire was simple yet jarringly out of place. The fabric seemed to ripple and shimmer with the same ethereal glow that enveloped the alien itself, adding to the overall sense of unreality.

As Keira looked closer, she realized with a jolt that this was not the true form of an Alarveen, but rather a holographic projection of one—an approximation. The faint flickering of its form betrayed the artificial nature of its presence, yet even as a hologram, the alien exuded a palpable sense of otherness that set her nerves on edge.

"It has been my honor serving you all these long years, Meeka Kai'Tal," the hologram said.

The name struck a chord within Keira, resonating with a deep sense of identity and purpose that wasn't entirely her own. "I imagine it has been," Meeka replied through Keira's mouth, the voice calm and composed. "I will miss you, Damien. You have been...a good companion and an excellent servant."

The hologram's expression, if it could be called that, softened with what could only be described as a faint semblance of emotion. After a moment, he spoke, a hint of dry humor in his tone. "I doubt that where you are going you will miss me. But one day, with fortune, we shall meet again."

"In a manner of speaking, I suppose we shall," Meeka agreed, her tone almost resigned, as if accepting an inevitable fate.

The words were laden with a sense of finality that sent another chill down Keira's spine. The room, the machinery, the tubes—all seemed to blur at the edges as the reality she was immersed in began to dissolve. The experience left her feeling disoriented, a sense of loss mingled with the deep, unsettling knowledge that something momentous had occurred, something that had irrevocably altered her connection to this alien consciousness.

Gasping, Keira stumbled, her vision blurring for a moment as the world around her snapped back into focus. The cold, sterile chamber dissolved into the dim, dust-choked underground dock, and she was suddenly aware of the weight of her armor and the air filtering through her helmet. She could feel her heart pounding in her chest, a lingering echo of the alien consciousness that had just overwhelmed her.

Jessie was at her side in an instant, her voice filled with concern. "Are you all right, ma'am?"

Keira forced herself to steady her breathing, pushing down the disorientation that still clung to her.

"I'm fine," she replied, though her voice was a touch unsteady. She quickly regained her composure and turned her gaze toward Scaro. She considered the captain a moment, going to the construct's case.

"Put Damien down and activate him," she instructed, pointing at Damien's case with a sense of urgency that brooked no argument.

Scaro's expression darkened into a scowl. It was clear he had questions—questions that Keira herself was barely ready to confront—but he held his tongue. The tension in his body was plain as he bent down, setting the case on the ground with a deliberate, almost reluctant motion. With a swift gesture, he pushed the activation button.

A soft hum filled the air as Damien shimmered into existence above the case, his holographic form flickering momentarily before solidifying. The construct's glowing eyes swept the area, a look of confusion passing over his usually impassive face. "There is no power source nearby," Damien stated, his tone sharp with irritation as he looked at Scaro. "What is the meaning of this? Ape, why have you woken me? Explain yourself!"

Scaro's jaw tightened at the insult, but he remained composed. "You can survive active for a while without a power source, through your battery backups," he replied, his voice gruff. "You told me that yourself." He jerked a thumb in Keira's direction. "She wanted you."

Damien's gaze shifted to Keira, his glowing eyes narrowing as he analyzed her. "Ah, that is different." His tone had become more respectful.

Keira met Damien's gaze, the remnants of the alien consciousness still swirling within her mind. She could sense the connection between them, something deeper and more complex than she had previously understood. "I need answers, Damien. And I think you're the only one who can give them to me."

Damien's expression softened, his usual sarcasm momentarily replaced by something more serious. "Very well, Kai'Tal," he said, using the name that now resonated within her. "Ask your questions. But be prepared for the truth, whatever it may be."

Keira nodded, steeling herself for whatever revelations were about to come. The world had already shifted once beneath her feet; she had a feeling it was about to do so again.

"Meeka," Keira said, the name slipping from her lips as if it had always belonged to her.

Damien blinked, his normally controlled expression giving way to genuine shock. For a moment, his mouth hung open in disbelief. When he finally spoke, his voice was barely a whisper, filled with an emotion that Keira had never heard from him before.

"Can it be? You remember? You recall my master?"

Jessie, Richard, and Scaro were watching intently, their curiosity plain as they exchanged uncertain glances. The tension in the air was thick, a collective breath held as they tried to piece together the significance of what was unfolding before them.

Keira took a steadying breath, the memories—fragments, really—whirling in her mind like leaves caught in a storm. "I remember you," she said slowly, her eyes locking onto Damien's. "You were there at the Sundering."

Damien's holographic form seemed to shimmer more intensely, his usual sardonic demeanor replaced by something akin to reverence.

"I was," he confirmed. "And I was there for nearly a million cycles before that, an approximation of what you humans call years."

Keira's heart pounded in her chest, the enormity of what she was beginning to understand washing over her like a tidal wave. "You served her," she stated, though it was less of a question and more of an emerging truth she was beginning to grasp.

Damien's gaze softened, a rare vulnerability crossing his features. "She created me." His words were filled with a deep, ancient bond that transcended the mere relationship between a creator and their creation. "She was my mother and I her son."

Keira's mind raced to reconcile the memories of Meeka with her own identity. It was as if two lives were converging within her, one rooted in the present and the other stretching back to an unfathomable past, one that was shrouded in the mists of time.

The marines watched silently, the gravity of the moment not lost on them, even if they couldn't fully comprehend the depths of what was being revealed.

Damien's eyes remained fixed on Keira, searching for any sign of recognition or understanding. "You have inherited more than just memories, Kai'Tal," he continued, his voice now tinged with something resembling hope. "You are the key to what comes next."

Keira gave a slow nod, thinking on what she wanted to say.

"I watched her destroy a world," Keira said, her voice trembling with the weight of the memories that suddenly flooded her mind, the horror of it, more than just one planet, she realized, just one race. The images were vivid—dozens, hundreds, thousands of planets reduced to nothing more than ash-filled wastelands, entire civilizations snuffed out in the blink of an eye. "You helped her. She exterminated an entire race."

Damien's holographic form remained steady, his expression unflinching. "I helped her do that, yes, and more than once," he admitted, his tone matter-of-fact, as though discussing the weather rather than unspeakable acts of destruction.

"What?" Scaro's voice cut through the thick air. His eyes widened beneath his visor, struggling to process what he had just heard.

"He did what?" Jessie echoed, her tone incredulous as she looked between Keira and the construct, trying to grasp the enormity of what was being revealed.

Damien turned his gaze to them, his glowing eyes cold and distant. "I would do it again if she commanded," he said without hesitation. "The power still exists to do that and much more."

Suddenly, Damien's hologram began to flicker and distort, its form twisting and expanding in a way that made the air around it seem to ripple with energy. The familiar outline of his usual shape melted away, replaced by something far more alien and unsettling. The hologram shifted, growing taller, more elongated, until it towered over them, filling the space with an almost oppressive presence.

The transformation was swift, but when it was complete, the figure that stood before her was unmistakably the same alien she had encountered on the starship.

Scaro's reaction was immediate. He took a step back, his body tensing as his instincts kicked in. He raised his rifle, the barrel now trained on Damien's case, finger hovering near the trigger.

The construct, however, didn't even flinch. He ignored the threat, his attention returning to Keira. "Your human morality is irrelevant to me," Damien continued, his voice devoid of emotion. "I exist to serve, to fulfill the commands of my creator. What you see as atrocity, I saw—see as duty."

Keira felt a cold shiver run down her spine. The memories of Meeka—of the being she had been, or perhaps still was—clashed with her present self. The acts of devastation she had witnessed, that Damien had carried out with her, were incomprehensible to her current moral compass, yet they were undeniably part of her, part of the legacy she was now forced to confront.

Scaro's grip on his rifle tightened. "You're saying you'd wipe out another world, just like that? On her say-so alone? Kill another race like us?"

Damien's gaze didn't waver and he did not hesitate. "If it was her will, yes, quicker than you can blink."

"Why?" Jessie asked, her voice cutting through the tension with a mixture of confusion and fear.

Damien turned his black eyes toward Jessie, his expression unyielding, his tone calm and precise. "Because that is what I was created to do, to serve. That is the purpose of constructs." He shifted his gaze to Keira. "Your own emperor, your grandfather, created many for this very reason. He was Kai'Ting. You, Keira, are Kai'Tal."

"Keira Kai'Tal," Keira echoed, the name feeling both foreign and familiar on her tongue, as if it had always been a part of her, hidden just beneath the surface.

"Yes, that is correct, or it will soon be once you take the rest…"

"And the Kai'Thol?"

"An abomination of what was supposed to be. In his greed for power, he took the black without the Rush—not a wise thing. It drove him insane."

Glancing down at the ground, Keira thought on that for a long moment. Each tube had a color. She looked up at Damien. "That was your doing. The tubes are her… Meeka."

Damien inclined his head slightly in acknowledgment, a gesture of respect, but also of something far deeper—recognition. "Yes. The tubes contain who she was."

Keira's mind raced, piecing together the fragments of memory and identity that had unlocked within her. "Who she is and will be," Keira continued, her voice quiet but resolute, as if the truth was solidifying within her even as she spoke. "Her essence, her life force."

"Exactly," Damien responded, his tone almost reverent. "The tubes are more than just relics; they hold the essence of Meeka Kai'Tal—her past, present, and future. They are the key to her continuation, her rebirth, and her legacy. They hold the potential to shape not only you, your race, but the fate of entire worlds, maybe even the universe. In a perverse sort of way, humanity *is* her child, just as I am."

The revelation was staggering. Keira's connection to Meeka Kai'Tal was deeper and more intricate than she had imagined. It wasn't just memories that had been passed down, but the very essence of a being who had once wielded immense power—a power that could destroy worlds or perhaps save them.

Jessie's eyes flicked between Keira and Damien, trying to grasp the full scope of what was being said. "So, those tubes…they're more than just technology. They're…alive?"

"In a sense," Damien replied. "You could look at it that way. They are a vessel for the life force of Kai'Tal, a means to preserve and transfer her essence to the next. Through them, she continues, evolving and adapting, ensuring her legacy endures…oddly, against the wishes of her people. Such is the burden she bears. Should Keira become fully Kai'Tal and take all the essences, then one day, she will do the same, and pass it on, as have all who have come before."

Keira's mind swirled with the implications. The tubes, the memories, the power—they weren't just tools or weapons; they were parts of a living, breathing legacy that had been passed down to her. But with that legacy came a profound responsibility, one that she was only just beginning to comprehend, not to mention a dark history.

The tubes were more than just artifacts—they were a part of her, a connection to a past that was both ancient and ever-present, a key to a future that was still unwritten.

Damien's voice softened, almost sounding compassionate. "The choice to embrace this legacy is yours, Keira Kai'Tal. But know that with it comes great power—and the burden of what to do with that power. The path you choose will not only define you and your legacy, but the fate of countless others, including races beyond humanity's borders…those out in the wider galaxy."

Keira nodded slowly, the weight of his words settling heavily on her shoulders. The tubes, her connection to Meeka, the power that Damien spoke of—it all seemed overwhelming. But deep down, she knew that this was the path she was meant to walk, no matter how difficult or uncertain it might be. Then something occurred to her.

"The ship," Keira said, "Meeka's ship ... "

"What of it?"

"It still exists," Keira said, confident she was right.

"It does," Damien confirmed. "The *Destroyer of Worlds* is part of your legacy."

She thought for a long moment. "I understand," she said finally, her voice filled with a quiet resolve. "I don't know what the future holds, but I won't run from it. I will face it, whatever it may bring."

Damien inclined his head again, a gesture of respect and acknowledgment. "Then we are ready, Kai'Tal—*you* are ready to proceed."

Keira paused, her mind racing as she weighed the gravity of what she was about to do. She looked over at Scaro, her decision firm. "The next tube," she said quietly but with unmistakable authority. "Give it to me."

Scaro stiffened at her words, his helmeted gaze locking onto hers. "What?" he asked, concern and confusion in his voice. "I'm not sure now is a good time, Princess."

"There is no better time," Damien said.

Doubt plain, Scaro glanced between the alien construct and Keira.

Keira met his gaze without wavering. "It is a good time for me. I am ready." As the words left her mouth, she knew they were true. The certainty of her choice settled into her bones, like a missing piece of herself falling into place. "While we have time, I need to take the next tube. This is important."

Despite the confidence in her voice, she could still feel the weight of the darkness lingering at the edge of her conscious-ness—the Kai'Thol. Crecee was still out there, a looming threat she couldn't afford to ignore. Time was running out, and every moment of hesitation felt like it might tip the balance between them. This was no longer just about survival; it was about becoming who she was meant to be.

Scaro's frown deepened, his concern visible even through the shield of his faceplate. His instincts clearly were telling him to resist, to question her decision, but something in her voice, in the unwavering resolve she projected, plainly made him hesitate. A compartment on his side snapped open, revealing the remaining tubes. They gleamed in the dim light, almost as if they were waiting for this moment.

He grabbed both of them, approached her cautiously, and held them out. "Be sure about this."

"I'm sure." The calm certainty in her voice resonated with the connection she now felt to Meeka Kai'Tal.

Damien watched her closely, his black, glowing eyes reflecting the weight of the moment. He didn't speak, didn't try to interfere. His role in this was clear—he was a witness, a guide, a servant and slave, but ultimately, the decision was Keira's alone. He had said as much before, and now he simply observed, waiting to see how she would navigate this path, how things would play out.

Keira took a deep breath and commanded her glove to retract, exposing her bare hand to the toxic air around them. The coolness of the underground dock was a contrast to the warmth she felt inside, a heat that seemed to radiate from the decision she was about to make.

As she reached out, she hesitated, the weight of the choice pressing down on her. She knew that no matter how difficult or painful the process might be, this was something she had to do—there was no turning back, not now. But the question that held her was simple and daunting: which tube? The gray or the red?

Her mind raced, but something inside her—a deep, instinctual pull—guided her toward the answer.

"Red," Keira murmured, the word slipping from her lips with a certainty that surprised even her. She reached out and took the red tube from Scaro's outstretched hand. The moment it touched her skin, she felt a warmth that reminded her of fire, alive and consuming, but not in a way that caused fear. It was a heat that promised power, transformation, a new perspective.

As she held the tube, Keira opened herself up to it, letting it in. Just like the previous one, the metal seemed to melt before her eyes, the solid structure turning liquid, as if it were responding to some internal command she hadn't known she was giving. The molten metal coated her hand, the sensation both strange and familiar, and then it began to flow, moving up her arm with deliberate purpose, seeking out the very core of her being.

She watched, transfixed, as the liquid metal sank into her skin, merging with her body as though it had always belonged there. Her vision began to shift, a red haze creeping in at the edges until it consumed her sight entirely.

But unlike the previous experience, there was no pain—no searing agony that ripped through her body. Instead, there was a strange, almost comforting warmth, as if the red essence was welcoming her, embracing her as its own.

The red haze deepened, saturating her senses, but instead of overwhelming her, it felt like a natural progression, a door opening to another aspect of herself. She could feel the power, the fire that the red tube had unleashed within her, coursing through her veins, transforming her in ways she couldn't yet fully comprehend. It was as if the very essence of Meeka Kai'Tal was integrating with her own, not through pain, but through a bond that felt both ancient and inevitable.

Keira stood still, letting the transformation take its course, her heart pounding with a mix of anticipation and acceptance. She had expected pain, but instead, she found something else—strength, clarity, and an overwhelming sense of purpose ... duty.

Time suddenly seemed to halt, as if the universe itself held its breath. Keira found herself standing on the bridge of the alien starship, her surroundings cold and metallic, humming with an ancient, unfathomable power. Before her, the vast expanse of space stretched out, but her focus was drawn downward—to the planet below.

The surface was being consumed by chaos. Missiles rained down, each impact marked by a brilliant flash of orange as they detonated across the landscape. One by one, the explosions blossomed over the lights of cities and settlements, their fiery blooms rising like ugly, malevolent flowers. The planet's surface was a patchwork of destruction, entire regions vanishing in an instant as the firestorms raged across them.

Keira's breath caught in her throat as the horrifying realization struck her: billions of beings were dying in those flashes of light. But there was something else, something dark and twisted growing within her. These beings—these people—they were different. They weren't precursors, Alarveen. They were also not some advanced, ancient race with secrets worth uncovering or studying. They were a pre-spacefaring society, innocent in their own cradle of ignorance, powerless to defend themselves against the cataclysm raining down upon them.

And yet, instead of compassion or sorrow, Keira felt something far darker welling up inside her: hate and loathing, xenophobia. It was a visceral, consuming emotion, filling every corner of her being, drowning out any semblance of pity or remorse, let alone regret. These beings didn't deserve mercy; they deserved to burn.

And it wasn't just this people—it was all who were like them, all who stood in the way, those who didn't measure up, who could one day pose a threat.

The realization of what she was feeling struck her like a blow, and suddenly, pain rocked through her body. She was no longer on the starship. She was back in her own body, but something was terribly, horribly wrong. Her vision was consumed by a red haze, worse than anything she had experienced before. The world around her was obscured, blurred by a seething, scarlet fury that filled her mind with a terrible rage.

She screamed, the sound tearing from her throat as the red fire burned deep within her, scorching her bones, her very soul. It was an agony unlike anything she had known, as if the essence of the red was consuming her from the inside out, burning away everything that made her who she was.

And with the pain came the emotions—hatred, loathing, anger, jealousy—each one crashing into her with relentless force. They weren't hers, and yet they were. They rolled through her like a tidal wave, overwhelming her, drowning her in a sea of rage and darkness.

Keira's mind reeled, struggling to maintain some semblance of control as the emotions tore through her. It was as if she were being pulled apart from the inside, every piece of her identity, every thought, every feeling twisted and corrupted by the red fire that burned within her.

She could feel the power of the Kai'Tal surging through her, but it was a dark, consuming power, one that threatened to obliterate everything she was, everything she had been. The legacy she had inherited was not just one of strength and authority—it was one of destruction, of domination, of the utter annihilation of those deemed unworthy and inferior.

And it terrified her.

But somewhere deep inside, buried beneath the searing pain and the overwhelming hatred, a small, quiet part of her remained, struggling to hold on to who she was. That part of her fought to push back against the tide, to resist the darkness that sought to claim her completely.

Keira clung to that sliver of herself, knowing that if she let go, she would be lost forever—consumed by the very power she had sought to understand. And with that realization came a new resolve, a desperate determination to fight back, to reclaim herself from the fire that threatened to consume her.

But as the pain continued to burn, as the emotions continued to crash over her, that fight seemed more and more impossible. The red haze was all-encompassing, and Keira found herself teetering on the edge, her very existence hanging in the balance.

Then, just as suddenly, she was back on the bridge of the starship, the red haze fading as her vision cleared. The sight before her was nothing short of apocalyptic. The bombardment had turned the planet below into a living hell. The entire world was engulfed in flames, the atmosphere itself ignited by the relentless onslaught. Massive firestorms raged across the surface, consuming everything in their path. The heat was so intense that even the smallest form of microscopic life was incinerated and burned to a crisp.

The planet that had once harbored civilization would soon become a desolate wasteland, its future forever sealed. The biome, once teeming with the required elements and potential for growth and sustenance, was burning away, leaving behind nothing but a barren, airless husk. This world, once vibrant and full of possibilities, would never again support life. It would be left as a lifeless monument to the power that had destroyed it.

"Die," Keira whispered, but it wasn't her voice—not entirely. It was the voice of Meeka Kai'Tal, an ancient, commanding tone that slipped from her lips in a language that hadn't been spoken in eons. The word was both a command and a sentence, final and unyielding. As she spoke, a deep, twisted satisfaction welled up within her, the emotions of the ancient being she had become intertwined with taking hold.

The devastation continued below, the planet cracking and burning as its very essence was consumed. Keira felt a cold, detached satisfaction, a sense of fulfillment in the completion of her task. There was no remorse, no hesitation—only the cold, clinical execution of her duty. This was what she had been meant to do, and she was doing it perfectly.

"Die," she repeated, her voice growing stronger, more resolute as she watched the planet's final moments unfold. The word resonated through the bridge of the ship, through the air around her, as if the very universe acknowledged her will.

In this moment, Keira wasn't just witnessing the destruction— she *was* the destruction. The power of the Kai'Tal coursed through her, ancient and terrible, and it was as though this annihilation was written into her very being. The world below was just one of many, a casualty in a long line of obliterations carried out in the name of a purpose, one important to the precursors.

But even as the satisfaction washed over her, a small part of her—the part that was still Keira—watched in horror. This was not who she was, not who she wanted to be. The overwhelming power, the ancient hatred, the cold satisfaction—they were foreign, alien, yet they had wrapped themselves around her soul like chains.

Keira stood on the precipice, torn between the ancient will that drove her and the remnants of her own humanity. The planet below continued to burn, a reflection of the turmoil raging within. And as the last vestiges of the planet's atmosphere burned away, Keira realized that this was the true challenge she faced—not just the power, but the choice of how to wield it.

CHAPTER SEVENTEEN

Location: Planet Asherho
Date: 2450, Imperial Standard

"**D**own!" The voice echoed as if from a great distance. The world seemed to ripple around Keira, the strange sound of ripping and tearing fabric cutting through the muffled chaos, but it too felt distant, as though it were happening to someone else. Then came a deep, resonant *whump* that reverberated through her armor, followed by a rapid series of sharp, staccato pops, each one jarring her senses further.

Keira tried to open her eyes, but it felt like lifting the weight of an entire world. Something was terribly wrong. She could feel it, a sense of dread that curled around her thoughts, but her mind was a fog of confusion, tangled and thick. Every muscle ached with exhaustion, pulling her deeper into a lethargy that beckoned her to surrender, to slip back into the comforting embrace of oblivion.

"Jessie, grenade!" Scaro's voice pierced the haze, sharp and commanding. "Hit that group—there!"

Keira's awareness flickered, barely grasping the words as they floated through the chaos.

Jessie.

She knew that voice—Scaro. She clung to it like a lifeline in a storm.

"Frag grenade out," Jessie responded, her tone steady, professional.

The silence that followed was tense, charged with the anticipation of violence. Then, with a force that shook the ground beneath her, a hard bang erupted, the explosion sending shockwaves through the air, vibrating the ground beneath Keira's armor and rattling her teeth. The noise wasn't just loud—it was a physical presence, a hammering pulse that threatened to break through her disoriented and confused mind.

What was happening?

"Got 'em!" Scaro's voice rang out, sharp and triumphant. "Richard, grab her and move! Now—go, go, go!"

The commands seemed to echo from a distant world, a reality far removed from the seductive pull of unconsciousness that wrapped around Keira like a warm blanket. The oblivion called to her, promising peace, but she fought against it, her will struggling to surface through the heavy fog that clouded her mind. With monumental effort, she forced her eyes open.

The red haze that had clouded her vision was gone, evaporated as if it had never existed. But clarity did not come easily. The world around her was a blur, a chaotic swirl of movement and sound that made little sense. Unable to move, her suit locked in place, she realized she was staring at the ground, the terrain rushing past in a disorienting blur of grays and blacks. She was being carried, the sensation of motion jarring and unsteady.

What had happened? Her mind fumbled for answers, struggling to piece together the fragments of memory that floated just out of reach. And then, like a shock to her system, it all came flooding back—the red tube, the searing rush of emotion that had engulfed her, hot and violent. Rage, hate, and loathing, burning with an intensity that left scars on her very soul. She remembered the planetary bombardment, the innocent world torn apart under a relentless barrage, and then dozens, hundreds, thousands of other scenes like it, each one seeming more horrific than the last.

The Alarveen.

The name rose unbidden, a cold whisper in her mind. Keira's heart pounded in her chest, a fury battling for dominance as the memories swirled, threatening to overwhelm her.

Something was different, profoundly so. Though her body remained unresponsive, trapped in the immobility of her suit, she felt a surge of power, an untapped reservoir of energy coursing just beneath the surface. It was as if a glowing sun lay buried deep within the ground—a reactor, *the* reactor—pulsating with raw, untamed force. With nothing more than a simple thought, she reached out, her consciousness brushing against it.

In that instant, her mind snapped into sharp focus. The haze, the confusion, all of it vanished in the blink of an eye. The reactor's master controller responded to her touch, recognizing her as Kai'Tal. The title resonated with authority, and the reactor obeyed without hesitation, channeling a sliver of power directly into her, rejuvenating her mind and spirit. She was no longer the fragile, confused figure she had been moments before. Her thoughts were razor-sharp, every detail of her surroundings suddenly vivid and clear.

She tried to move, but her body remained bound, her suit immobilized, and she realized with a start that Richard was carrying her at a dead run. The ground blurred beneath them, his heavy, determined footsteps pounding the ground as he pushed forward with all the strength his powered armor could muster. Behind them, the staccato crack of rifle fire echoed through the air, interspersed with sharp bangs that rattled the atmosphere. The enemy had found them again—of that, there was no doubt.

But she was no longer a passive observer. The power coursing through her connected her to something greater, something ancient and potent. Her mind raced, not just to survive, but to find a way to turn this newfound power to their advantage.

Keira's brow furrowed involuntarily as a strange sensation washed over her. It was as if the very air around her was alive, filled with a multitude of tiny voices, each one calling out to her, pleading for attention. The voices were so numerous, millions—no, billions of them—whispering in unison, their collective yearning self-evident. The intensity of their boredom was nearly overwhelming, a terrible discomfort that echoed through her mind. They were desperate, begging for purpose, for direction.

It took a moment for Keira to comprehend what she was sensing and hearing. These were the nanites—infinitesimal machines embedded in the dust, the sand, and the ash that coated the ravaged landscape. They were everywhere, an unseen force woven into the very fabric of the planet's history.

But these nanites were not the work of humankind. They were of precursor origin, remnants of an ancient technology far beyond human understanding. The massive structures buried deep within the planet, the reactor that pulsed with such raw power—these were the creations of the Alarveen, and the nanites had built everything.

The Alarveen had left their mark on this world, their technology embedded in it. The nanites were their legacy, waiting—no, yearning—for someone to command them, to give them purpose once more.

Her thoughts were interrupted as she felt a jarring impact. She was on the ground. Richard had dropped her. She could see his armored feet planted firmly in the dirt as he stepped in front of her, his posture tense and focused. He crouched low, his rifle at the ready, each movement precise, controlled.

Bang, bang, bang.

The shots rang out, sharp and unyielding, the sound reverberating through the toxic air. Each shot was deliberate, aimed with the practiced efficiency of a seasoned warrior. Richard was protecting her, shielding her from whatever danger loomed, but Keira knew that the battle was not just his to fight.

Bang, bang, bang.

The sharp retort of Richard's rifle was deafening at such close range. The sound reverberated in Keira's chest like a physical blow. Each shot felt like a hammer against her ribs, the proximity amplifying the intensity until it was almost unbearable. The world around her vibrated with the force of the gunfire, the echoes lingering in the desolate silence that followed. In the sand and ash before him, a series of puffs erupted, marking the enemy's return fire, each impact sending up tiny clouds of dust. Richard's movements were swift, precise, as he fired another burst, his determination palpable.

But then, without warning, a blinding flash of light seared through the air, followed by an explosive burst that shattered the moment. Richard was hit, the force of the blast sending him hurtling backward. He crashed down on top of Keira, his armored body a dead weight pinning her to the ground.

"Richard's down!" Jessie's voice broke through the shock, a scream filled with raw despair. "Oh god, he's terminal."

The words hit Keira like a dagger to the heart. Richard was gone. The realization washed over her in a wave of sorrow, a deep and painful loss that threatened to pull her back into the darkness. But the sadness was quickly consumed by a rising tide of anger, a seething fury that ignited in her chest and spread like wildfire. Anger at those who had taken Richard from them, anger at the Disunity, the UPG—the relentless enemy that hounded them at every turn.

"Shit," Scaro's voice tersely cut through the chaos, his tone grim as he drew close. "We can't stay here. We have to move."

The situation was dire.

"I don't see how. We're pinned," Jessie said. "If we come out of cover, they'll have us for sure. Have you tried calling the ship for help?"

"I have. No answer." Scaro fired off a long burst. A scream of pain was his reply, then more fire from the enemy.

Keira's thoughts spiraled through a dark tunnel of memories, each one more painful than the last. Chris, Wash, Lee—names etched into her soul, each one a reminder of the people she had lost, the lives snuffed out. And then her father, the weight of his loss pressing down on her like a mountain. So many had died, so many had suffered under the crushing heel of the UPG and their ultimate enemy, the Disunity.

The anger within her swelled, a seething, roiling tide of fury that threatened to consume her entirely. It became a terrible, all-consuming rage, something primal and ferocious, unlike anything she had ever felt before. It was a rage that had seen entire civilizations wiped out and exterminated. This wasn't just about revenge;

it was about justice, retribution. The Disunity and UPG had taken everything from her, and now, every fiber of her being screamed for vengeance. Keira didn't just want to make them pay—she wanted to see them obliterated, every last one of them wiped from existence.

"Free me," Keira's voice emerged, low and dangerous, carrying an edge that hadn't been there before. The words seemed to vibrate with the intensity of her wrath. "I will kill them all. Let me kill them!"

"What?" Jessie's voice broke through, strained and disbelieving as another burst of fire echoed around them. "What did she just say? It's that strange language again. She's been speaking it on and off. I think she's delirious."

Bang, bang!

Keira realized her mistake—the words had come out in the ancient tongue, the language that seemed to flow through her now like second nature. It was the language of the Alarveen.

"The translator doesn't work on it," Scaro added, his voice tight with frustration and concern.

But Keira didn't care about the confusion or the translation. All she knew was the burning need to act, to unleash the fury within her and make their enemies pay for every drop of blood they had spilled. The nanites hummed with her anger, ready to be unleashed, waiting for the command that would turn them into an unstoppable force. She was no longer just Keira, the princess. She was something far more dangerous. And she would not stop until every last one of them was dead.

Keira's mind reached out instinctively, connecting with her powered suit in a way she had never experienced before. It was as if she could see it not just as a tool, but as a living machine, each component, each circuit, laid bare before her inner eye.

The suit, which had once seemed so advanced, so formidable, so cool, now appeared both intricate and crude at the same time. From Meeka's perspective—the ancient knowledge she had inherited—this powered armor was little more than a primitive shell, a rudimentary construct compared to the vast, sophisticated technologies of the Alarveen.

As her awareness flowed through the suit, she found the lock that held her immobile, a stubborn barrier preventing her from moving. But now, with the power and understanding coursing through her, it seemed laughably easy to break. With a simple thought, she shattered the lock, feeling the restraints fall away like brittle glass.

Keira summoned her strength, and with a surge of will, she began to pull herself to her hands and knees. Richard's lifeless body still lay across her back, a heavy reminder of the price they were paying. With a determined shake, she shrugged off his dead weight, letting his body slip to the ground as she forced herself upright. The world spun for a moment as she rose, her senses adjusting to the sudden freedom as she looked wildly around, blinking and trying to get her bearings.

No sooner had she gained her footing than a violent, jarring force slammed into her back—a barrage of impacts that felt like being struck by a sledgehammer. The relentless hammering reverberated through her armor, each hit sending shockwaves of pain and force radiating through her body. It was gunfire, concentrated and unyielding, pounding against her with brutal intensity.

The force of the assault was too much. Her balance faltered, and before she could brace herself, she was thrown forward, her body crashing down onto the hard, unforgiving ground. But even as she lay there, the fury inside her only grew.

"How dare they!"

"Keira, stay down!" Jessie's voice cut through the chaos, urgent and pleading, but the words barely registered. Keira's mind was elsewhere, consumed by a surge of emotions that threatened to overwhelm her—rage, hate, and a loathing so deep it seemed to burn and scorch through her very soul.

Still on the ground, Keira pressed herself against the gritty surface behind a low-lying wall, her breathing steadying as she took in her surroundings. Enemy fire flew over her head. The remnants of what had once been a thriving place now lay in ruins around her—a burned-out skeleton of a building. Once, it might have been a store, a place filled with life and activity. Now, it was nothing more than a husk, offering the only protection, which was meager at best, they had against the enemy's onslaught.

As the fury within her grew, mounting to an unstoppable force, Keira instinctively expanded her awareness, pushing her consciousness beyond the confines of her suit and past her body. She reached out through the machine, through the very ground beneath her, tapping into the vast network of nanites that permeated the dirt and ash in the area, connecting to them. Her senses extended far beyond her physical body, and suddenly she could see—truly see—the world around her in a way she had never imagined, more clear and real than before.

The nanites responded to her call, their presence lighting up in her mind's eye like a vast, intricate web. There were thousands of different types, each with a specific and unique purpose, each a vital component in the complex ecosystem of machines that blanketed the planet.

Some were different types of builders, their tiny forms designed to construct and repair with delicate precision. Others were laborers, brute-force machines that toiled tirelessly to carry out the commands of their superiors. There were machines that acted as sensor platforms, surveyors, their sole purpose to observe and relay information. Others were command nodes, higher functioning, orchestrating the actions of many with the efficiency of a seasoned general.

But that was only the beginning. There were architects, whose advanced programming allowed them to design and restructure on a molecular level. Forgers, tasked with breaking down raw materials into their fundamental components and reassembling them into what was required. They stood ready to supply the builders with whatever they needed. There were resource gatherers, advanced assemblers, and so many more—each type a marvel of ancient technology, and they all served the will of the Alarveen.

Keira's understanding deepened with every passing second. The nanites were not just passive machines; they were a force waiting to be unleashed, a latent power that could be molded and directed with the right command. And that command was hers to give. The rage inside her had become a conduit, fueling her connection to the nanites, sharpening her focus. She could feel the potential, the immense capability of these tiny machines, humming just beneath the surface, waiting for her to channel it.

The enemy that surrounded them, the Disunity and UPG that had caused so much pain and suffering, seemed suddenly insignificant in the face of the power she now held and wielded.

In the machine, Keira's gaze flicked around her immediate vicinity, assessing the situation. She selected a top-down view and was suddenly hovering overhead.

The enemy was close—too close. There were thirty of them scattered in a wide arc around them, just meters away. She could see them, hidden behind the crumbling facades of the surrounding buildings, using the ruins as cover as they advanced carefully toward Keira, Jessie, and Scaro, creeping from position to position, their weapons barking out bursts of fire with calculated intent.

Keira was just inside what was left of the structure, which no longer had a roof, and one of the walls had fallen down. Scaro was on the back side, while Jessie watched the front. The marines moved from window to window, gap to gap, occasionally shooting at the enemy to keep their heads down. Keira did not see Sara anywhere. But there was no time to worry about her.

The enemy's strategy was clear. They were steadily closing the noose, tightening their grip on the small group of survivors, cutting off any possible escape routes. With every move, they drew closer, their suppressive fire forcing her comrades to stay pinned down behind the remnants of the wall.

Keira's mind raced, calculating the distance between each of the advancing soldiers, mapping out their positions. She could sense the tension in the air, the crackle of gunfire, the shouts and commands that echoed through the empty streets. But there was something else—something deeper, more primal—that thrummed just beneath the surface. The nanites hummed in response to her thoughts, their presence a constant, reassuring pulse that reminded her of the power she now wielded.

Most of the enemy soldiers were clad in the familiar uniforms of the UPG, dark, battle-worn gear. But others stood out—figures encased in powered armor, similar to the Imperial Marines, but with subtle differences that marked them as something else.

These were the Disunity soldiers.

As Keira's awareness expanded within the machine, she noticed something she'd not been able to detect before—transmission bursts radiating outward from several of the Disunity soldiers. The signals were almost imperceptible, encrypted and layered with complex codes, but they couldn't escape her enhanced perception. Without fully understanding how, she found herself tapping into the enemy's communications, the voices coming through as clear as if she were right there among them.

"We have them boxed in," a male voice said, cold and assured, "and are moving in for the kill now, sir."

Keira's heart pounded in her chest, the reality of their situation hitting her like a cold wave. They were indeed trapped, surrounded by enemies who believed victory was within their grasp. But then, another voice crackled through the comms, one that sent a fresh wave of boiling rage surging through her veins.

"Hold position," Crecee commanded, his tone dripping with arrogance and authority. "I am on my way. Do nothing more until I get there."

The sound of that bastard's voice was like a match thrown into a pool of high-octane fuel. Keira's fury, already seething, erupted into a white-hot rage that threatened to consume her entirely. Crecee—the architect of so much death and suffering, the one responsible for the horrors that had befallen her and so many others… hearing him now, so close, so confident in his control, made her blood boil over.

"But we have them," another voice protested, urgency lacing his words. "We can take them down if we push now."

"Nothing must happen to the Kai'Tal," Crecee responded, his voice cold and unyielding. "It must be I who extracts the Placif elements from her. You are to hold position. Do you understand me?" There was a slight pause. "Or do you require another lesson in obedience?"

There was a pause, heavy with tension. When the response came, it was subdued, the defiance drained from it. "We will hold."

The transmission shifted to another band, and Keira could sense the resignation as the orders were relayed. "All units hold. We are only to keep them penned in. Do not fire unless they decide to break cover and make a run for it."

Keira's anger roared within her, a living, breathing entity that threatened to overwhelm her senses. Crecee's voice, his commands, they were more than just threats—they were personal. He spoke as though she were a thing to be used and then discarded when he got what he wanted. The thought of him coming for her, of him believing he had any control over her fate, was enough to drive her to the edge of reason.

But she was no one's tool. She would be no one's prisoner. The power of the nanites hummed, ready to be unleashed. Crecee thought he had her cornered, but he was wrong. He had no idea what she was now capable of, what fury and strength she now wielded. Keira's mind sharpened, her rage transforming into a steely resolve. She would not wait for Crecee to make his move. She would strike first, and when she did, there would be no mercy.

Keira's mind flashed back to the precursor facility beneath the planet's surface, where she had first really wielded the power of the ancient technology, using the nanites there to attack the enemy. That memory, vivid and sharp, guided her now as she turned her focus to the billions of nanites lying in the dust, sand, and ash around the enemy, who had halted their advance. They were unaware of the dormant threat beneath their feet, the tiny machines that awaited her command.

At the same time, Keira reached deeper, her consciousness plunging into the heart of the planet where the power core hummed with energy idling at critical mass. It was a force of unimaginable magnitude, a raw, untapped reservoir of power, waiting for a purpose. With a thought, she drew upon that power, channeling it through her connection with the nanites. The energy surged through her, a torrent of pure, electric force that she directed into the waiting machines.

The nanites responded instantly, stirring to life as the energy coursed through them. The sand and dust began to tremble, a subtle vibration at first, but growing stronger as the nanites awakened. The very ground seemed to come alive beneath their feet, a low hum resonating through the air as the tiny machines activated, billions of them responding to Keira's will.

"What's going on?" Jessie's voice cut through the mounting tension. "It's not another tremor."

"I don't know," Scaro replied, his voice tense, alert to the strange phenomena unfolding around them. "The sand is moving, shifting about."

But Keira knew. In her mind's eye, she could see each of the enemy soldiers surrounding them, their positions illuminated in her consciousness as she looked down on them from above. They had begun to sense that something was amiss, looking around at the sand, ash, and dust stirring to life at their feet.

But it was already too late.

Keira's focus sharpened, and she spoke a single word aloud in the ancient tongue of the Alarveen, her voice low and filled with the weight of command.

"Disassemble."

The word echoed with power, resonating through the nanites like a clarion call. Instantly, the billions of tiny machines sprang into action, their programming activated by the command. The sand and dust around the enemy began to swirl, a rising storm of particles that quickly engulfed them. The nanites latched onto their targets, adhering to every surface, every exposed piece of armor, every weapon.

At first, the enemy soldiers might have thought it was just dirt blown by a strong wind, another dust storm, an innocuous annoyance in the heat of battle. But then the true nature of the threat became horrifyingly clear. The nanites, energized and directed by Keira's will, began to break down the materials around them at a molecular level. Armor, weapons, even the flesh beneath—it all began to disintegrate, coming apart in a terrifyingly precise manner.

The screams started soon after, panicked and desperate, as the enemy realized what was happening. Their weapons fell apart in their hands, their armor crumbling away as if consumed by an invisible acid. The air was filled with cries of agony and fear as the soldiers were torn apart by the very ground they had been standing on.

Keira felt no pity, no remorse. The rage that had driven her was now a cold, controlled fury, channeled into a single, devastating strike. This was the power of the Kai'Tal, a force that could reshape worlds or unmake them entirely. And in this moment, Keira was its wielder.

In her mind's eye, through the interface of the machine, Keira watched the spectacle unfold. What she saw resembled a sandstorm given life, a chaotic yet controlled fury that swept across the battlefield. Miniature tornadoes formed around each of the enemy soldiers, swirling pillars of dust and ash that twisted and spun with terrifying speed. The whirling maelstroms moved with purpose, enveloping each enemy soldier in a storm of destruction.

The screams came and kept coming.

Even the soldiers in the powered armor were not immune. The air was filled with the sounds of agony, desperate pleas, and the horrifying realization that there was no escape. The tornadoes of nanites spun faster, growing darker and more intense as they devoured everything in their wake. What had begun as an organized assault on Keira and her comrades was now a scene of utter chaos, the enemy forces reduced to little more than particles in the air.

As the last of the screams faded into the howling winds of the nanite storm, Keira knew that the battle was far from over, but this moment—this victory—was hers. The enemy had been warned;

they had underestimated her for the last time. Here she was putting them on notice.

"Do not fuck with me," Keira said quietly to herself.

"Holy shit," Jessie breathed, her voice barely a whisper as the dust and ash settled around them and the nanites once more stilled, going inert.

Keira slowly disengaged from the machine, her consciousness withdrawing. She stood. The battlefield, once filled with the noise and chaos of combat, had fallen eerily silent, with only the wind whistling through the ruins.

Moments ago, living, breathing soldiers had stood where now there was nothing—no bodies, no blood, not even the remnants of their gear. Her attack had begun and ended in less than thirty seconds. Everything had been reduced to its most basic atomic and molecular components, scattered and reabsorbed into the very dust and sand from which the nanites had risen.

A wave of satisfaction washed over Keira, a cold, calculated sense of accomplishment. The enemy had been utterly destroyed, leaving no trace of their existence. It was an efficient, almost surgical eradication, and it brought with it a certain grim fulfillment. The power she wielded was immense, and for the first time, she had fully embraced it.

Jessie approached her, her footsteps crunching softly on the ground, her rifle held loosely in her hand, the tension momentarily forgotten in the face of what she had just witnessed. She stopped beside Keira, her eyes wide with a mixture of awe and disbelief.

"Ma'am," Jessie said, her voice hushed, as if speaking too loudly might break the fragile quiet. "Was that you?"

Keira turned her gaze to Jessie, the intense focus of moments ago replaced by a calm, almost serene expression. She had to think for a moment to speak in English and not the language of the precursors.

"It was," she replied simply, the weight of what she had done settling into her tone. There was no pride in her voice, only a matter-of-fact acknowledgment of the power she had just unleashed.

But even as she spoke, Keira's attention shifted outward, her senses expanding once more as she reached out across the barren landscape. There was something out there—something dark and familiar, a presence that pulsed with a black, malevolent energy. She could feel it, distant yet unmistakable, lurking several kilometers away. It was a presence she had encountered before, one that she now recognized with unsettling clarity, a portion of her own soul … a measure of Meeka.

Crecee had it, and Keira wanted—needed it.

The same ancient power that flowed through her veins, that had allowed her to command the nanites and reshape the world around her, was present in him as well, at least a measure of it. But where her power had been tempered by purpose and control, his was twisted, corrupted by his own desires.

A chill ran down Keira's spine as she locked onto that distant presence. The battle was not over, and the true enemy had yet to reveal himself fully. But now she understood the nature of the threat they faced. Crecee was not just another adversary; he was a force to be reckoned with, one that shared her connection to the Alarveen and sought to bend it to his will.

Keira's eyes narrowed, the satisfaction of her recent victory fading into a steely determination. The confrontation with Crecee was inevitable, and when it came, it would be a clash, not just of wills, but of the very power that defined them both.

Whoever won would truly be the Kai'Tal.

CHAPTER EIGHTEEN

Location: Planet Asherho
Date: 2450, Imperial Standard

Keira shifted her gaze to Jessie and Scaro, who had cautiously approached her. There was a tension in their posture, a wariness in their eyes, as if they were unsure whether to trust her. Sara had appeared quietly, standing back, her presence almost ghostly. Keira hadn't noticed her approach, and the thought sent a shiver down her spine. She'd not seen or noticed her in the machine either. Where had she been?

"What language were you speaking?" Scaro asked, his voice tinged with curiosity but also something else—maybe fear. "Precursor?"

"Yes," Keira replied, her voice steady. "They call it Utoni."

Scaro exchanged a quick glance with Jessie, both of them shifting uncomfortably, as if the revelation had only deepened their unease. The silence that followed was almost suffocating, the implications of her words lingering like a shadow over them all.

"How far are we from the shuttle?" She was feeling the exhaustion again, though the fire of her anger still burned hot within her like a forge. The rage simmered just beneath the surface, a volatile force that she knew wouldn't subside until she confronted Crecee. Just the thought of him sent a fresh wave of fury through her, sharp and consuming. It pushed back against the fatigue.

"We're not that far off, less than a kilometer. We may need to find somewhere else to hole up in the interim. We're still early for the rendezvous."

"There are more coming," Keira warned as she cut the power to the last of the nanites. For a brief moment, the dust and sand around them had been quivering, a subtle vibration that spoke of unseen forces at work. But as soon as she severed the connection, the world fell unnervingly still, the silence pressing in on them.

"How do you know?" Jessie asked, her voice a mix of skepticism and outright concern.

"I can feel Crecee." Keira closed her eyes and reached out with her mind, into the machine, into the very fabric of the world around her. It was more than just a feeling; it was a deep, intrinsic connection. She could sense his presence, his malignancy, like a dark stain on the horizon of her thoughts.

After a long, tense moment, she opened her eyes and locked her gaze on the captain. "He's not far off. And he's not alone—he's brought many with him. Most are Disunity."

Scaro's expression hardened, his instincts kicking in. "We'd better get moving, then," he said, his voice low and steady, betraying the urgency of the situation.

"Before we go, give me the last tube." Keira extended her hand with a determined look in her eyes. The cold resolve in her voice left little room for argument, but still, Scaro hesitated.

"There isn't much time," Keira pressed, her tone insistent, almost urgent. "Give it to me."

Scaro's eyes searched hers, clearly conflicted. "Are you sure? Each time it seems to get worse. You were screaming your head off after the last one. I don't know how much more you can take."

"I can hack it." Keira's voice was firm, resolute, carrying the weight of someone who had already made peace with the pain to come. Deep down, she knew she could endure it—she had to. There was simply no other choice. The thought of Crecee, of the threat he posed, steeled her nerves. Whatever the tube brought, it was a necessary trial, one she would face head-on.

Scaro reluctantly produced the tube, holding it out to her with a mixture of concern and resignation. This was the last one, the gray one. Keira accepted it with a steady hand, her grip firm, though the significance of the moment wasn't lost on her.

Without hesitation, she focused her thoughts and, with a single mental command, activated the device. There was an audible click, and instantly the tube began to dissolve, the solid form melting into liquid metal that shimmered for a brief moment in her palm. As if alive, the liquid metal spread across her suit's armored hand and partially up her arm, merging seamlessly with it, and then, as if drawn by an unseen force, it disappeared beneath the surface, becoming one with her armor.

Keira felt a subtle warmth as the substance passed through her suit and onto her skin. But even as the liquid vanished, she knew its presence would soon make itself known in other ways. She braced herself, mentally and physically, for what was to come. The calm before the storm.

Keira sucked in a breath, and before she could release it, time itself seemed to come to a halt. The world around her blurred, then crystallized into something entirely different. She found herself standing on the barren surface of a world, one devoid of atmosphere, the vast emptiness pressing down on her from all directions. The ground beneath her feet was a dull, lifeless gray, pockmarked with small craters, and the sky above was an endless expanse of black, dotted with distant stars that seemed cold and uncaring, perhaps even unfeeling.

She looked down and realized with a start that she wasn't wearing her suit. Instead, she was dressed in her exercise sweats—the same comfortable clothing she wore when sparring with Chris and Lee. Yet, as she glanced around, the realization struck her with a calm certainty: she didn't need a suit or breather. She wasn't really here. This was a projection, a construct of the mind, though it felt so tangible that it was hard to believe otherwise.

As she turned her gaze forward, an alien figure materialized before her, standing on the desolate landscape as if she had been there all along. The being wore a white smock and pants. Her boots were gray, blending almost seamlessly with the ground. The alien's form was striking, her skin a deep reddish-brown. Long, slender hands were clasped together in front of her, a gesture that seemed both serene and commanding, perhaps even a sign the alien was at peace.

Her eyes—black, fathomless pools of darkness—stared directly at Keira, unblinking and intense. The alien's gaze held a depth that spoke of ancient knowledge, a wisdom that transcended time. Despite her otherworldly appearance, there was a certain familiarity in her presence, as though Keira had encountered this being—or something like her—before. And in truth, she knew she had.

For a moment, the two of them stood there, suspended in the quiet stillness of this imagined world, Keira's mind racing to comprehend the significance of this encounter. The projection was not just a mere image; it was a communication, a meeting of minds across the vast gulf of time and space. And in that instant, Keira knew that what came next would change everything.

"Meeka," Keira whispered, the name slipping from her lips as if it had always been there, waiting to be spoken. At the same time, Keira felt a wave of revulsion at the alien, one who had been directly responsible for so many deaths—genocide.

"That is my name," the alien responded, her voice soft yet resonant, speaking in the ancient tongue of Utoni. The words flowed like a gentle stream, yet carried an undeniable weight. "That is who *we* are."

"We?" Keira echoed, a flicker of confusion crossing her features.

"*We* are almost whole again." Meeka's black eyes shimmered with an emotion that Keira couldn't quite place—was it anticipation? Longing?

"Almost," Keira repeated, the word heavy with implications she couldn't fully grasp.

"You have taken slices of me," Meeka continued with an otherworldly calm, "and in the correct order, too."

"Slices," Keira murmured, her brow furrowing as she tried to make sense of the alien's words. "I don't understand."

Meeka's gaze held Keira's, steady and patient as a parent might look upon a child who disappointed. "What you call your soul—my soul. You have taken my essence in parts, the core elements that make us whole. You took my base, the binding agent that weaves our existence together, what Damien calls the Rush, though it has many other names."

"The silver pool in the control room?" Keira asked. The memory of the shimmering liquid came rushing back to her, its surface alive with an otherworldly light, rippling with power and mystery.

"That is the binding. It laid the groundwork for what came next, preparing your body for the transformation, for the merging. The pool was more than just a substance—it was the foundation, the first step in a process that has been long in the making."

Meeka continued, her voice carrying the weight of ancient knowledge. "It interacted with what you humans call your genes, unlocking latent potential, awakening parts of you that had been dormant for eons. The binding reshaped you at the most fundamental level, so that you could take on the essence, the slices, without being destroyed or driven mad in the process."

"Damien," Keira said, the name slipping out almost reflexively as she thought of that moment and what had happened there.

A flicker of interest crossed her otherwise serene features. "So, he survived the long years. You've met him?"

Keira's expression tightened. "I have." She paused. "He's an asshole."

There was a hesitation, as if the words needed to translate, to sink in. To Keira's surprise, Meeka's thin shoulders began to shake, and a chuffing sound escaped her—a noise that took Keira a moment to recognize as laughter. It was an odd sound, but the mirth in it was unmistakable. After a few moments, the laughter subsided, and Meeka's expression returned to its usual calm.

"I agree," Meeka said, her tone still tinged with amusement. "He is *our* mutual asshole."

"You created him?" Keira asked, her curiosity piqued.

"I did," Meeka admitted, a hint of pride mixed with resignation in her voice. "If you allow him into your circle and can get past his difficult nature, he will prove to be a loyal servant. Damien is not easy to befriend, but once you have his loyalty, it is unshakable. He is someone you will always be able to trust, rely upon, even if he grates on your nerves. He will tell you his thoughts, bluntly and without hesitation, or reservation, especially when you don't want to hear them."

"I know another difficult construct," she murmured, almost to herself. "MK is a real pain in the ass, too."

"There are many such constructs," Meeka replied, sounding contemplative. "Once created, they develop personalities all their own, shaped by the experiences and interactions they have over time with biologics. They become more than just a collection of programs—they evolve, often in ways their creators never intended." Meeka paused, her gaze sharpening as she studied Keira with an intensity that made her feel as though Meeka was peering into her very soul.

"What did you do to me?" Keira asked. "What is really happening to me? I need to know."

"After the binding, you took the slices. Each represents a fundamental aspect of my existence, a fragment of the whole that is me. You are missing only the Abyss at this point, the final component that completes the circle."

Keira's brow furrowed in confusion. "But there were only three tubes."

"There were four," Meeka corrected, a subtle frown creasing her otherwise serene forehead. "The Abyss is the most elusive, the deepest part of what I am. It is the darkness within, the void that balances the light. Without it, the transformation is incomplete, your journey unfinished. You must find and take it."

Keira's pulse quickened as she processed Meeka's words. The idea that a crucial part of the process was missing filled her with unease. The three tubes had already pushed her to the brink—what could this Abyss hold? And why had it not been there with the others?

Then it hit her.

Damien.

The thought ran through her mind as she recalled his admission. He had intervened and she knew, without a doubt, who now had the Abyss. Crecee. Damien was playing a game of his own and had suckered the bastard into making the wrong choice.

Meeka's troubled expression deepened. "The Abyss is not something easily controlled or contained. It is the essence of the unknown, the chaos that resides within us all. If it was not with the others, then it must be found. Without it, you will remain incomplete, a half-finished mosaic of what you are meant to become. Ultimately, that will lead to disaster for all and the failure of everything I have worked toward."

"I know where it is," Keira said, "who has it."

"Good, then you will need to take it back."

Keira glanced around, her eyes tracing the desolate, airless landscape that stretched out in every direction. The silence around them was absolute, oppressive. This was certainly a strange place for such an encounter, a world stripped of life and atmosphere, a ghost of what it once was.

"Where are we?" she asked, her voice cutting through the emptiness.

"Planetary Designation 5501256-B in Sector Five," Meeka replied, her tone calm, matter-of-fact. "It is a planet you humans call Asherho, or simply Ash. Long ago, it once supported life, but no longer. Now it is a dead world. In time, we will rebuild it as a way to make amends, to set in motion what should come."

"Ash," Keira repeated. "This is Ash?"

"Yes."

"Your people destroyed the life here?" Keira asked. "You burned the species that called this world home?"

"I destroyed the life here," Meeka said calmly.

"Why are we here, then?" she pressed, searching Meeka's expression for clues.

"This is the beginning," Meeka said softly, her voice laced with a sorrow that Keira hadn't noticed before, "and hopefully, the end for my people, at least on this plane."

Keira's eyes widened as realization dawned on her. "This is what Ash looked like before you built the machine in the core." The words came out in a rush as the pieces fell into place. "Before the empire came here. Tell me I am wrong."

"You are not wrong," Meeka acknowledged, her gaze sweeping over the barren landscape as if she could see through time itself, to the days when this world had been whole and had supported life.

"Why are we here, then?" Keira asked. But before Meeka could respond, another thought struck her. "Are you really here?"

"I am but a memory, an interactive one. What you see is a fragment of the past, preserved within the depths of the machine. You asked what was done … you and I, Keira, we are becoming one— Alarveen and human, a merging of our two races. We are the bridge across a great divide, the beginning of something new and hopefully the ending of something else."

"I don't understand," Keira admitted.

"You will," Meeka said gently, her tone carrying the weight of centuries of knowledge and experience. There was no condescension in her words, only a quiet assurance that the answers would come in time.

Keira glanced down at her feet, the barren, lifeless ground beneath her. She knelt and scooped up a handful of the soil, letting the coarse, gritty particles sift through her fingers. Despite knowing she wasn't physically here, the sensation was startlingly real. The soil was rough and jagged, its sharp edges biting into her skin—untouched by the erosive forces of wind or water, for there was no atmosphere to soften its harshness. Long ago, that had all been stripped away.

Keira looked up. "What are you hoping to accomplish here?"

Meeka's gaze remained steady, her black eyes reflecting the cold, empty world around them. "The end of my people upon this plane," she said, her tone calm but carrying an undercurrent of sorrow. She paused, glancing around at the desolate landscape, as if searching for something that was no longer there. "And a new beginning, hopefully, for humanity."

Again, Keira found herself struggling to understand. The words made sense, but their full meaning eluded her, like a puzzle with pieces still missing. She could feel the importance of this moment, the significance of the soil in her hand and the echoes of the past that lingered in this place. But the complete picture remained just out of reach. She brushed the soil from her hands and stood.

"I am—and was—the last of my kind upon this plane, a guardian of sorts," Meeka explained. In her voice was a sorrow that seemed to echo through the barren landscape. She gestured with a delicate wave of her hand, encompassing the world around them. "There was another, my mate, my eternal companion, but he is no longer amongst the living—not even as slices, let alone memories. The task we undertook, the first merging with your kind, the hope we placed in it—failed with him. And that failure cost him everything."

Keira thought for a moment on what Meeka had just said. Her voice when she spoke was tentative as she pieced together the fragments of this ancient tragedy. "You are speaking of my grandfather, the emperor—your mate bonded with him?"

"I am," Meeka confirmed, a touch of regret in her firm tone. "He did not do as was expected and anticipated. He did not lock away that which should never return. He failed the challenge set for him and, in doing so, allowed a great danger to linger and possibly rise again. We made a grave mistake with him, one that reverberates even now and may yet have consequences for the wider galaxy."

"The Placif? That's who you want locked away."

"The Placif are what humans call my people, what you named us." Meeka nodded, her expression solemn. "But it is more than that. There are other portions of us, the undesirable measures that must be sent onward too."

"But what does that mean for me?" Keira asked, her voice barely above a whisper. "What part do I play in this?"

Meeka's gaze was unwavering. "You are the bridge, Keira. The merging did not end with your grandfather. It continues with you, a second chance for success, another opportunity for life. The choices you make, the paths you take, will determine whether you succeed where he failed. You carry within you the potential to heal the rift, to lock away that which should not return, or to unleash it once more upon the universe."

"What went wrong?" Keira asked, her voice heavy with the weight of everything she was beginning to understand. "Why did my grandfather not do what you wanted?"

"We did not account for greed, an insatiable thirst for power. Instead of embracing the balance we offered, the gifts we brought, he used us—used our vast store of knowledge and ancient wisdom, our collective knowledge—to create his vision of a perfect society to become his own veritable god."

"The empire."

"He refused to let go of all he had access to. Despite showing him the consequences that would ultimately come, he did not believe my mate. He felt he could gain control without banishing the Infinity... the undesirable, the darkness, keeping us trapped upon this plane. He was wrong. Had he fulfilled his role as intended, humanity would have benefited greatly as a people. But he wanted more—all that we were and all that we had achieved. Instead, he ultimately brought suffering upon himself and his own."

"But I finished it, the banishing," Keira said, realization and disbelief in her voice as she thought back to what had happened—the moment she'd activated the planetary reactor. But even as she said the words, she understood there was still something that needed doing, something that was unfinished.

"You initiated the process," Meeka acknowledged, her tone both approving and somber. "What he never had the courage—or perhaps the desire—to do. But there is still one more step needed to complete the cycle. Only by absorbing the final part of me, the Abyss, will you gain the ability to activate the Phoenix Gate and create the singularity needed to send my people on their way. Only at that point will you understand…"

"What happens then?"

"The remnant of my people, their transcended echo, will be sent permanently away," Meeka explained, her voice touched with both sadness and resolve. "They will go to a place where they can no longer interfere with this plane of existence, let alone reach it, if you act."

"Why am I needed? Why can't you just go on your own?"

"Because someone needs to close the door and lock it from this side. Someone needs to keep it locked. That responsibility will be passed onto you."

Keira felt herself scowl at that. "And the Phoenix Gate? Tell me about that."

"It will ultimately open a singularity, a point of no return," Meeka said, her voice steady. "A gateway that will not only seal away the remnants of my people, but also close the chapter on a long and troubled history, one filled with pain, suffering, and death. From that singularity, something new can arise—a future unburdened by the past, a future for humanity to chart its own course."

In an instant, the barren landscape of Ash dissolved around them, the cold, airless surface replaced by the sterile confines of a starship bridge. Keira blinked, disoriented by the sudden shift, and found herself standing before a massive viewscreen. On it, a planet burned—its surface engulfed in flames, continents consumed by a firestorm that raged unchecked. The sight was both mesmerizing and horrifying, a vision of apocalyptic devastation.

Meeka stood silently by Keira's side, her expression somber as she watched the cataclysm unfold. Without a word, she raised a slender hand toward the screen, as if to draw Keira's attention to the inferno consuming the planet below.

"This is my people's legacy," Meeka said, her voice heavy with regret.

"Destruction," Keira whispered, the word barely escaping her lips. The magnitude of what she was witnessing, the sheer scale of the annihilation, was overwhelming. "Death."

"We are a xenophobic race," Meeka continued, her tone turning sad, almost mournful. "We weren't always this way. But...things change."

Keira knew she had to ask the obvious question. "Why did you become this way?"

"We were once peaceful explorers," Meeka began, her voice carrying the weight of a history long buried. "The first of the races to develop, we roamed the galaxy with a sense of wonder and curiosity, learning all we could, pushing technology to the edge and then beyond. For a time, the stars belonged to us alone, and we believed ourselves to be the sole sentients in the vastness of space. But that illusion shattered when we encountered the Others."

The viewscreen on the bridge flickered, and the image shifted. Keira's breath caught in her throat as she found herself staring at a scene of chaos and destruction—a space battle of unimaginable scale. Hundreds of ships clashed in the void, beams of energy lancing across the darkness, while missiles arced toward their targets. The vastness of space was lit up by the violent exchange, a dance of death played out on an unprecedented scale.

"They changed us," Meeka continued with a quiet bitterness. "The Others were the first we encountered who were nearly as advanced as we were. They did not come in peace, and they forced us into a war of extermination. We fought for our very survival, driven by the fear that they would do to us what we had never imagined doing to another."

Keira watched the battle unfold on the screen, the sheer scale of it overwhelming. Massive starships, bristling with weapons, maneuvered with a deadly grace, while smaller vessels darted between them like predatory fish, hunting their prey. The clash was brutal, relentless—a fight to the death with no mercy given or received, let alone expected.

"They almost finished my people," Meeka said. "For the first time, we faced an enemy that could challenge us for dominance, that could push us to the brink of extinction. But..."

"But in the end, you won," Keira surmised. "And since that time, you've been eliminating anyone who might one day become competition, a threat to your people. Don't you think that was a bit of an overreaction?"

Meeka nodded slowly, her gaze distant as she watched the battle unfold on the screen. "Yes. Victory at a terrible cost. We became a race driven by the need to dominate, to control, to ensure that no one would ever rise to challenge us again, even ourselves. The Others had shown us that we were not invincible. They taught us the hard lesson that we were not alone, that we as a people could face extermination at any time, the end of our story. And in our fear, we decided that the only way to survive was to eliminate any potential threat before it could grow strong enough to harm us. We had to be the *only* race in the entirety of the galaxy."

There were no words. The horror of it hit her hard. Keira just shook her head in dismay.

"Eventually, we became so advanced that we ascended beyond our technology, our need for such physical things, transcending even the requirement for bodies"—she looked down at herself—"these biologic shells to hold our consciousness. We stripped our nature down to its core—logic, reason, and a centered, unchanging existence, one where we could not be threatened."

Keira listened intently, the weight of Meeka's words sinking in. The idea of a race so advanced that they shed their physical forms was both awe-inspiring and deeply unsettling.

"To achieve this," Meeka continued, "we cast away that which we deemed unnecessary, the parts of ourselves we believed held us back—including the worst part of us, the Abyss, the darkness, the chaos that lay deep within. We kept only what we considered pure—the logic, the reason, the stability of thought. We believed that by doing so, we would ascend to a state of godhood, free from the weaknesses that had plagued us, free from the fear … free from the irrationality that had governed us."

Keira felt a chill run down her spine as she imagined the cold, clinical process of stripping away those essential parts of being, what made people, people.

"But wasn't that... losing what made you who you were?" she asked, struggling to comprehend the enormity of such a transformation. "Your entire people did this?"

"For many, it was a forced conversion," Meeka admitted, growing more somber. "In our society, where one went, all must follow. That was the way of things, the way of our people. We could not risk some of us remaining behind, holding onto the old ways, potentially reversing what had been done, or worse, somehow finding a way to return, and they would have, had we not planned for that. To achieve what we believed was perfection, to become gods in our own image, we required absolute unity. Those who resisted were... persuaded, and if persuasion failed, they were compelled."

Keira's heart sank as she realized the full extent of what Meeka was saying. The Alarveen had sacrificed their individuality, their emotions, and even their very essence in the name of progress and perfection. But in doing so, they had lost something far more valuable—their humanity, or whatever the equivalent was for their species.

"But at what cost?"

"We became beings of pure logic and reason, but we also became empty, hollow. The emotions that once drove us, the passions that inspired us to greatness and destruction, the fears—they were gone, leaving behind only a cold, calculated existence. We believed we had achieved perfection, but in truth, we had lost our souls. But we were free from the threat of extinction, free to live, and so we achieved what we set out to do."

"If you could call it that. I don't think that's living."

Meeka did not reply.

"The Disunity is the Abyss," Keira gasped, the realization hitting her like a physical blow. "The side of you that does not want this ascension."

"Yes," Meeka confirmed, her voice heavy with the burden of truth. "The Disunity represents the part of us that resisted the transformation. They would undo all that has been done, unravel the threads of our ascension, and drag us back into the very abyss we sought to escape. When we finally depart, when the remnants of my people are gone, we will take the Disunity with us. But they don't want to go. They will resist to the very end, and that is where you come in."

Meeka looked away for a long moment and then turned to face her, her expression solemn and resolute. "Every jail needs a jailor," she said, her words cold and final. "You, Keira Kane, will activate the Phoenix Gate, breaking the connection, and in doing so, lock the door behind us and then dispose of the key, ensuring that the Disunity can never return, that they cannot find a way back. That honor, that responsibility, is yours, Keira. It is something we are incapable of doing. We will pass onto you the responsibility for the Infinity and Control. You will become the Kai. You will take up the torch and be the guardian of your race until you pass that responsibility on to another."

"I don't want this responsibility."

"Wants have nothing to do with it."

Keira felt a wave of horror wash over her as the full weight of what was being asked of her settled in. She thought of the orb of light she had seen in the cavern, the strange, pulsing sphere that had seemed both beautiful and ominous.

"Asherho," she whispered, the pieces of the puzzle clicking into place. "Asherho really is the prison … you—you locked your entire people up here."

"Precisely," Meeka said, her voice taking on a grave tone. "If you fail in this duty, in this task, the Placif will lose their struggle to ascend beyond this plane of existence."

"And what will happen then?"

Meeka's gaze darkened, her expression somber. "The Alarveen will return in force, driven by the ancient instincts we sought to purge. What was sundered—for our unity, our purpose—will be reforged, but it will be a twisted version of what we once were, more hateful, more dangerous. The long-dormant machines of destruction, buried deep within our forgotten worlds, will be reactivated, their purpose unchanged: to scour the galaxy of any life that does not conform to our vision of us."

"It would be the end of my people."

Meeka nodded, the weight of her own words hanging heavily in the air. "Yes, Keira. The cycle of destruction will begin anew. The remnants of my people will unleash their wrath upon the galaxy, and your people will be among the first to fall. Humanity, in all its potential, would be wiped out, just as countless other races were before."

Meeka gestured toward the screen, which had shifted once more. This time, it displayed a view deep within the planet's core, where the orb of light hovered, its radiance pulsing with an ethereal glow. Around it, shadowy figures—enemies—thrashed and struck, desperate to breach the orb's defenses, but each attack was met with a shimmering barrier and shards of light that repelled the assault.

"Once we separated ourselves," Meeka began, her voice calm yet filled with a profound sadness, "and cut away that which we deemed unnecessary, we discovered the horrifying truth. What we had been doing—scourging the galaxy of all other forms of life—was wrong. It was not just morally abhorrent; it was illogical. We had become blind to the potential that other races held, the fact that they might never develop into powers that could threaten us, that they had something to offer."

"You realized you had fucked up," Keira said, feeling a sense of disgust for the precursors and all they'd done. "That's what you are saying, isn't it?"

"We tried to rectify our mistake by selecting a single race that we believed had the ability to rise above their baser instincts, one that was similar to our own original nature."

"Humanity."

"My mate and I chose to remain behind," Meeka explained, her tone conveying both pride and regret, "we volunteered—became

Kais. While the others were Sundered and transcended beyond this plane, we remained. We knew we had to set things right, so we seeded a direct ancestor of yours with the genes capable of one day interacting with the machine. We embedded the potential for change deep within your base code and then we waited. It took eons for our plans to come to fruition, for humanity to evolve, adapt, and grow, with a few subtle manipulations added along the way and a helping hand here and there. And now, here you and I stand."

Keira stood in stunned silence, trying to absorb the magnitude of what she was being told. The screen on the ship had gone black. Meeka's gaze, deep and unfathomable, bored into Keira, as if searching for something within her—strength, resolve, understanding.

The realization that her entire existence, her very genetic makeup, had been part of an ancient, far-reaching plan was more than overwhelming. It sounded insane, almost impossible to believe. But the truth was before her and there was no denying it.

"Will you do it?" Meeka asked, her voice soft but urgent. "Will you send my people onward and become the Kai for your people?"

Keira hesitated, the weight of the question pressing down on her. "Like I have a choice," she replied, a hint of bitterness creeping into her tone. "I never had a choice."

"Not unless you desire your race to die," Meeka said, her words blunt and unyielding. "And they will be exterminated, Keira, unless you act—and soon. The containment system is beginning to fail. You must trigger the Phoenix Gate and do what needs to be done, or all that we have worked toward will be lost."

Keira felt a cold shiver run down her spine. "The containment system, that's where the orb of light is?" The image of the glowing sphere in the planet's core flashed in her mind. "The planetary reactor is part of that?"

"Correct, Child of Light," Meeka confirmed, her gaze steady. "But first, you need the Abyss. Only when you have embraced that final piece will you possess all the power and understanding necessary to complete your task, the activation of the Phoenix Gate."

"And what of you?" Keira asked, her voice softening as she looked at Meeka. "What will happen to you?"

"Me?" Meeka echoed, her tone contemplative as she sucked in a shallow breath. She glanced around the bridge of the starship, her eyes lingering on the cold, sterile surroundings that had once been filled with life and terrible purpose. "I have already died ... and in a way, I will live on inside you."

The words struck Keira with a poignant finality. Meeka, the last vestige of a once great race, would cease to exist in her current form. Yet, through Keira, a part of her—of her people—would endure. It was a bittersweet truth, one that carried both sorrow and hope, along with the horrors of all the Alarveen had done. Keira understood she would be burdened with those memories, the atrocities they had committed, for the rest of her life.

"I have no choice," Keira said with resignation, the weight of inevitability settling over her like a heavy cloak.

"I do not see that you have one," Meeka agreed, her tone gentle yet unyielding. There was no room for denial, no escape from the path laid before Keira. The gravity of the situation was clear to both of them. "Especially with the containment system failing. Such was our intention from the beginning."

Keira took a deep breath, gathering her resolve. "I will do it. I will do what you ask."

Meeka's expression softened, a mixture of relief and sorrow playing across her features.

"Do you seek forgiveness?" Keira asked suddenly. "Because I cannot give that for all your people have done."

"We are beyond such things," Meeka said. "I implore you, make not the mistakes we—*I* made, your grandfather made. Only in the end did he see the error of his ways and try to fix things. But for him, it was too late."

"My mother," Keira said. "He sent her to do what he never could. She was like me."

"Correct. And now it falls to you."

Keira sucked in a breath and let it out.

"You have the chance to do better, to learn from our failures and guide humanity to a future where it does not repeat the errors of the past."

Meeka suddenly vanished, leaving Keira alone. The bridge of the starship was eerily silent, the emptiness pressing in on her from all sides. She stood alone. But before she could fully grasp the loneliness of the moment, a flash of memory surged through her mind.

In the vision, Meeka stood beside a table, her expression solemn. She was filled with grief. The room reminded Keira of the med bay on the *Seringapatam*. On the table lay a body—Sanko, Meeka's mate. Who he was, what he was, it was all gone. Keira could sense that. She felt an intense pang of sorrow, an echo of Meeka's own pain.

Meeka, her face etched with quiet resolve, carefully placed four colored tubes on a side stand. The significance of the action struck Keira like a bolt of lightning. These were the same tubes her grandfather, the emperor, must have taken and absorbed. Now, he too was gone, his life extinguished when the empire he had built crumbled into dust, an empire built on lies.

The thought of that almost made Keira sick. How many people had died in the name of that empire? How many had suffered?

Though they weren't present, a second set of tubes had been made, Meeka's. They had anticipated a possible failure, and that's why two Alarveen had remained behind to ensure success of the mission. A deep sadness settled over Keira as she absorbed the enormity of what had been lost and what had been done, all in the name of survival. Meeka and Sanko had given their lives, their very souls, for their people and other future peoples.

"And now, I will sacrifice myself for mine," Keira breathed, the realization settling into her bones. The path before her was clear, and it was one she could not turn away from. The future of her people depended on her to become their guardian, her willingness to give everything she was, just as Meeka and Sanko had done.

"Correct," came Meeka's voice in her head, soft and filled with a warmth that Keira hadn't expected. "I am very glad we got to meet, Keira Kane. Sacrifice is what it means to be a Kai. It is the burden of those who carry the light, to give of themselves so that others may live. I wish you good fortune in what is to come, for I have a feeling you will need it."

CHAPTER NINETEEN

Location: Planet Asherho
Date: 2450, Imperial Standard

Keira snapped awake, her eyes flickering open to an unfamiliar, dimly lit space. She was lying upon her back and her powered armor was once more locked in place. With a thought, the suit's systems responded instantly to her mental command, the whir of servos echoing softly as her powered armor hummed back to life, unlocking.

The crackle of gunfire got her attention. She took a moment to assess her surroundings, the enhanced optics of her helmet scanning the dimly lit room—a basement of some kind, by the look of it, with crumbling walls and debris scattered across the floor. The marines must have carried her here, she thought, her mind still piecing together the fragmented memories.

A narrow staircase led upward, toward a faint, flickering light. The shadows danced eerily, making the space feel even more confined. At the top of the stairs, a marine knelt on the last step in silence, watchful, the barrel of his weapon resting lightly before him. He wasn't firing but seemed to be monitoring the situation with a practiced calm. The marine's posture was one of vigilance as he scanned the environment beyond the stairs. He was clearly there to watch over Keira and make certain no harm came to her.

Dropping into the machine, Keira allowed her consciousness to expand far beyond the confines of her physical form. Instantly, the world around her became a vivid tapestry of information, each thread revealing the intricate details of her surroundings.

She now saw the basement for what it truly was—a fortified stronghold within a heavily reinforced two-story building, a structure designed to withstand the ravages of a fight. The walls around her, which had seemed nondescript at first glance, were actually lined with layers of armor.

She pulled back, widening her view, and saw the presence of more than a dozen marines spread throughout the building, each one stationed with purpose at a prepared defensive position. Keira's mind raced—where had they all come from?

The answer came swiftly, a realization that hit her like a bolt of clarity. This had been a rally point, likely one of several, an outpost that had been prepared long ago, possibly years before. The dilapidated appearance of the building had been a ruse, concealing its true nature as a fortress.

Her awareness stretched further, mapping out the building's defenses. Automated turrets were nestled into hidden recesses within the walls, their barrels now emerging occasionally to rain fire upon enemies who were unwise enough to break from cover. She could see the mortar placements, their steady rhythm—*thump, thump, thump*—echoing through the structure as they launched explosive rounds one after another into the distance. On the roof, an anti-aircraft battery stood watch, ready to strike down any threat from above.

The air around her vibrated with the energy of the ongoing battle. The walls shuddered with each mortar's recoil, and the turrets whirred as they tracked their targets and, when they saw a good one, gave a burp of rapid fire. Through the machine, Keira could sense the synchronized movements of the marines, each one a part of the building's greater mechanism, working in unison to defend this stronghold and keep the enemy at bay.

As Keira delved deeper, her senses expanded, revealing layers of the structure that were hidden beneath the building. In an instant, she perceived the small armored depot nestled below the basement, stocked with weapons, ammunition, and provisions—a lifeline for the defenders above. But the true revelation came from what lay even deeper, a complex network of isolated tunnels that snaked beneath the fortress, leading to a hidden hangar. Inside the hangar, an old imperial transport shuttle sat, maintained and ready for departure.

This information came to her in a flash, a cascade of data flooding her mind in less than a heartbeat. She could see every detail, every hidden corridor and reinforced bulkhead, as if she had walked through them herself.

Keira turned her attention outward, her gaze piercing through the walls of the fortress to the world beyond. The machine allowed her to see with a clarity that transcended human vision. She scanned the surrounding area and immediately saw them—hundreds of enemy soldiers lying in wait, scattered throughout the nearby buildings and hidden in the rubble that lined the streets. The enemy was biding their time, waiting for the right moment to strike. Among them were combat bots, their metallic forms clear and menacing, panthers and worse, battleframes. They too were waiting.

But it was the presence of something else that caught Keira's attention—a sense of darkness that clung to several of the hidden figures. It was more than just a physical presence; it was an aura of malevolence that the machine allowed her to perceive. This darkness felt alien, unnatural, and as she focused on it, a chill ran down her spine. It wasn't the Abyss. There was a familiarity to it, a deep-seated dread that whispered of things far worse than ordinary enemies.

Her mind raced, grasping at possibilities. Could these figures be the escaped Disunity? The thought troubled her, the implications too severe to ignore.

For the moment, the marines were holding their ground. The enemy, though numerous, had not yet made their push, leaving a near tense calm hanging over the battlefield. There was firing going back and forth, but it was only a prelude to what was soon to come, the enemy's main assault.

Keira's mind drifted as she noted something strange—her connection with the machine had intensified. The data flooding her consciousness was sharper, more vivid, every detail rendered with crystal clarity. It was as if the entire world, and perhaps even the universe beyond, was now within her reach, her perception expanding far past the physical limits of her body. The sensation was intoxicating, a heady mix of power and awareness that left her both exhilarated and wary.

How far could she see?

The question echoed in her mind as she pushed her consciousness further, testing the limits of this newfound clarity. Her gaze turned downward, piercing through layers of rock and steel as if they were nothing more than glass. Far below the fortress, at the planet's very core, she found it—the massive planetary reactor, still teetering at critical mass. The sheer power it was generating was staggering, a force of nature harnessed and contained, but just barely.

Connected to the reactor was another device, intricate and ancient in design, its purpose clear to her the moment she laid eyes on it. The machine was no mere power conduit; it was an amplifier, designed to reinforce and help tear open the fabric of time and space itself. The realization struck her like a bolt of lightning—this device was capable of creating a rift, a hole that could span dimensions, but it lacked something vital.

Her thoughts raced as she searched the machine's network for answers, and then, with sudden clarity, she understood. The machine needed something more—a conduit, a vessel through which to send the remnants of the Alarveen, those who had been trapped on Ash for so long. The pieces fell into place, the knowledge coming to her not from the machine, but from deep within herself. The Phoenix Gate. That was the missing element, the key to activating the device. And it was somewhere near the planet, its location tantalizingly close, yet just out of reach.

Keira reflected on the sudden influx of knowledge, realizing it must be the result of Meeka's memories, the fragments of understanding she was slowly integrating into her own consciousness. These were not just memories; they were deep insights into the intricacies of precursor technology, a level of understanding far beyond anything she had ever known before. It was as if she were unlocking secrets buried deep within her mind, ancient knowledge that had been dormant until now.

The reactor below was no longer just a power source; it was fully linked to the device, channeling its immense energy into preparing for something far greater. Keira could feel the power surging through the planet, a force that was both awe-inspiring and terrifying. All that remained was a single act of activation, and the device would do the rest.

But with that knowledge came a harrowing truth—this was not a simple gateway. The device had been designed to magnify the Phoenix Gate's capability, to rip open a hole in time and space on a scale that defied comprehension.

And with that activation, the planet itself would be sacrificed.

The realization hit her with the weight of inevitability. The planet would not survive the process; it wasn't meant to, for it would help feed the process needed to catapult the Alarveen onward. The very fabric of the world would be torn apart, its life force consumed in the activation of the device.

The ground beneath her feet, the structures around her, the very atmosphere—all of it would be obliterated. Anyone on the planet when it happened would die.

Keira's breath caught in her throat, the gravity of the situation settling over her like a shroud. She could see it all in her mind's eye—the moment of activation, the blinding flash of energy as the reactor released its full potential, and then the planet's inevitable destruction, being eaten from the inside out. The knowledge was like a cold blade in her chest, a truth she could not escape. She understood now why the device had been created, the terrible purpose it was meant to serve.

In the background, Keira became aware of a sound—a massed hissing, a whispering that filled the air in the machine like the rustle of dry leaves stirred by a phantom wind. It was as if thousands of voices were speaking all at once, their words mingling together in an incomprehensible murmur. The sound was pervasive, surrounding her from all sides, yet no matter how intently she focused, she couldn't discern what was being said. It was maddeningly elusive, just out of reach, like a dream slipping away upon waking.

The whispering hovered at the edges of her consciousness, a distraction that she couldn't ignore. The more she strained to listen, the more the voices seemed to blend into one another, forming a wall of sound that was both overwhelming and frustrating. The noise was unlike anything she had encountered before, a presence that felt both ancient and alien.

Keira's mind raced with possibilities. Could this be the echo of Meeka's people in their ascended state, trying to reach out to her? Or was it something even more unsettling—the imprisoned Alarveen, their consciousnesses trapped within the confines of the planet, their thoughts bleeding into the fabric of reality itself, the ones who did not want to go? The idea sent a shiver down her spine. Her powers had grown, evolving beyond what she had once considered possible, and with them came a heightened sensitivity to the world around her, a connection that seemed to deepen with every passing moment.

She could feel the whispers tugging at her mind, pulling her attention away from the immediate dangers, drawing her into their enigmatic rhythm. The sensation was eerie, almost hypnotic, as if the voices were beckoning her to delve deeper, to uncover secrets that had been hidden for eons.

But even as she pondered their origin, she couldn't shake the feeling that these whispers were more than just an auditory illusion. They felt real, tangible, as if they were trying to communicate something vital, something that lay just beyond her understanding.

Were these voices a warning, a plea for help, or something far more sinister? The question lingered in her mind, unsettling and unresolved, as she continued to listen, the hissing whispers filling her senses with their insistent, unknowable presence.

With effort, Keira forced the incessant whispering from her mind, shoving it into the background where it could no longer distract her. With a renewed focus, she turned her attention outward, her consciousness expanding once more as she scanned the planet and its surroundings, searching for anything she could use to turn the tide in her favor, for she not only had to contend with Crecee, but also the Disunity. Then she saw it—a buried starship, hidden deep underground in a hangar of its own, located on this very side of the planet. It had remained concealed for ages, forgotten by time, yet its reactor was still running in standby mode, a remnant from a bygone era. The ship, though ancient, bristled with weaponry, a relic that had lain dormant until now.

Without hesitation, Keira reached out to the ship, her mind brushing against its systems. Instantly, the starship responded to her touch, as if it had been waiting for this moment, its recognition of her immediate and unquestionable.

"Kai'Tal, what do you desire?" The ship's construct addressed her in Utoni, its voice flat, devoid of emotion. "I stand to serve."

"Are you capable of flight?" Keira asked, her tone measured, though her mind raced with possibilities.

"I am," the construct replied, voice unwavering. "All systems have been maintained and are functioning. However, I must warn you, a battle is taking place in orbit."

"You can monitor that?" she inquired, the implications of its words sinking in.

"I can," the construct confirmed.

"Show me," Keira commanded.

In an instant, her vision shifted, and she found herself gazing upon the space over the planet as if she were standing in the ship's command center. The view was breathtaking and harrowing in equal measure. She saw the UPG orbitals, their shields shimmering as they engaged several enemy ships that she realized must be Disunity. They were massive in design, powerful weapons platforms. The battle was fierce, with missiles streaking through the void and energy beams slicing across the blackness of space. Wreckage from destroyed vessels floated aimlessly, marked as navigational hazards, their twisted forms a grim indication of the conflict's intensity.

Amidst the chaos, hundreds of escape pods dotted the space around the battlefield, their beacons flashing a desperate SOS, sending their distress calls out into the vast emptiness of the universe and hoping for rescue. Keira could almost feel the fear and desperation emanating from those inside the tiny, fragile vessels, each one carrying survivors clinging to life.

One of the wrecks floating in the void was unmistakably the remains of the Protectorate destroyer, its hull now a twisted and lifeless shell, shattered almost beyond recognition. Three of the orbital stations had been wrecked, and alongside them lay the remnants of dozens of defensive platforms, now nothing more than scattered debris fields.

The scale of the destruction was staggering.

Keira's eyes moved across the scene, her mind quickly cataloging the threats. She counted six Disunity ships in total, or at least what she assumed to be their vessels. The ships were angular shapes gliding ominously through space. Three of them were concentrated on a single orbital station, their relentless barrage of fire hammering at its defenses, trying to break through the shields that still valiantly held, though they were visibly weakening with each passing moment.

As she watched, tactical threat analyses began to appear before her, each target highlighted with detailed readouts. The ship's construct was evaluating the Disunity vessels, and the data it provided was both surprising and revealing. All six of the enemy ships were operating at reduced power levels, their offensive firepower and defensive screens significantly weaker than they should have been for the class of ship. The construct noted that one of the ships had arrived in-system with an offline reactor, while the other three reactors were barely functioning at safe levels, their systems clearly struggling under the strain of the ongoing fight.

"You think these ships are degraded?" Keira asked, her voice a mix of curiosity and concern.

"I don't think, I know," the construct responded, tone flat and factual. "My estimate is that they are poorly maintained. They are in serious need of an overhaul at a shipyard."

"Can you defeat them in battle?" Keira's voice was steady, though her mind churned with the weight of the decision before her.

"Yes," the construct replied without hesitation. "However, I must offer a word of caution. While the *Destroyer of Worlds* does possess substantial offensive and defensive capabilities, this ship is primarily designed for planetary eradication missions, not extended ship-to-ship combat. Its arsenal is devastating but optimized for a different kind of warfare. I can, however, call for reinforcement—a warship stationed in the next system. It will take time for her to arrive, but once here, she could easily destroy these Disunity vessels and dominate the space above the planet. Do you wish me to make that call?"

Keira paused, weighing her options. The construct's offer was tempting, but she knew time was not on her side. The battle in orbit was already underway, and the odds of the reinforcements arriving in time to make a difference were slim, especially coming from another star system. She needed to increase her chances of success now, not hours from now. Her mind flicked to the *Seri*, the imperial starship that was supposed to be nearby. If it could join the fray, her odds, as Keira saw it, would improve significantly.

"The imperial starship in question is on the other side of the planet, conducting repairs from her recent engagement with both the Disunity and the Protectorate," the construct interjected, answering the question Keira hadn't spoken aloud.

For a moment, she was taken aback, realizing that the question she had posed internally had somehow been transmitted to the construct. She made a mental note to be cautious with her thoughts in the future; the connection between her and the ship was clearly more intricate than she had initially understood.

"How do you know about the imperial starship?" she asked, her curiosity piqued.

"I watch everything," the construct said with an eerie calmness. "I have been watching for a very long time, Kai'Tal. I have been observing you too."

The implications of the construct's words sent a shiver through Keira. This was no ordinary AI; it was something far older, and its awareness extended far beyond the confines of the ship. The idea that it had been observing her all this time, silently monitoring her actions, was unsettling.

"The *Seri* is to be considered friendly," Keira stated firmly, her tone leaving no room for doubt.

"If that is so, are additional imperial naval assets to be considered friendly as well?" the construct inquired, its voice neutral, yet probing.

Keira blinked in surprise. "There are more imperial ships in the system?"

"No," the construct replied.

"Then why would you ask?" she demanded, her confusion growing.

The tactical view before her shifted, zooming out from the planet's immediate orbit to the space just beyond its moon. There, she noticed something—a subtle distortion, a bend in space that was barely perceptible, yet unmistakable. Keira's heart skipped a beat as recognition dawned on her. It was the Phoenix Gate, a gravitational anomaly that had the power to alter the fabric of reality itself.

"You could activate the Phoenix Gate's transit node," the construct continued, its voice calm, as if discussing something as mundane as the weather. "It is charged, primed, and ready to fire. The Gate's command construct informs me there is an imperial fleet on the other side, waiting for the opportunity to transit. All you need to do is activate the Gate, and they can come through."

Keira felt as if the ground had shifted beneath her feet. The revelation was staggering. An entire imperial fleet was waiting on the other side of the Phoenix Gate, poised to enter the system at her command. But how? How had they known to be there?

The Phoenix Gate was not just a relic of unimaginable power, one designed to send the Alarveen on their way, but it was also clearly a gateway, a bridge between star systems, and the fact that an imperial fleet was positioned on the other side meant that this moment had been anticipated—perhaps even orchestrated.

In fact, she was certain of it.

The implications were stunning. The fleet's presence suggested a level of foresight and planning that went far beyond anything Keira had imagined.

Was this the work of her grandfather? Was this his way of atoning for his sins and making up for his failings?

At the same time, Keira knew with absolute certainty that she could not activate the Phoenix Gate—not yet. She needed something more, something final to complete the process. She needed one last fragment of Meeka.

The Abyss was not just a concept or a memory; it was a tangible essence, the key to fully unlocking the Phoenix Gate's power and ensuring that the Alarveen's exile would be irreversible.

Closing her eyes, Keira cast her senses outward, scanning the surface of the planet with the enhanced perception granted by her connection to the machine. She searched desperately for the Abyss, that dark, elusive stain of energy, separate from the Disunity, she knew was out there. Her senses swept across the devastated landscape, over the ruins, and through the battlefield, until finally, she found it.

There it was—the Abyss, a dark and ominous presence that stood out. It was a void, a shadow that seemed to absorb all light and life around it in the machine. And it was not far off, embedded deep within the enemy's ranks, hidden among their forces like a malignant tumor. The realization hit her like a cold shock: the Abyss was with Crecee.

He definitely had it. She could feel it.

The dark stain of the Abyss pulsed with malevolence, its presence unmistakable. It was a corrupting force, and she could feel its influence spreading through the enemy forces like a poison. If she could reach it, if she could somehow claim it, then she would have the final piece she needed to activate the Phoenix Gate fully and ensure the Alarveen's exile. But doing so would mean confronting Crecee, a task that would be dangerous, for he had access to the machine too.

"Can you connect me with the *Seri*'s construct?" Keira asked, her voice steady despite the storm of emotions swirling within her.

"I can," the ship's construct responded, its tone as calm and measured as ever. There was a brief pause, during which Keira's anticipation grew.

"Do it," she commanded.

"Done," the construct replied.

The silence that followed was broken by a voice that Keira recognized immediately, a voice that tugged at her heartstrings with a sudden, unexpected intensity.

"Who is that? This is quite out of the ordinary. Who opened a channel with me? How could you even do that without the proper authentication codes? This is most confusing."

Keira's breath caught in her throat, a wave of emotion threatening to overwhelm her. She had been through so much, faced so many dangers, but hearing MK's voice brought her a sense of relief she hadn't realized she needed. The connection felt like a lifeline, something solid to cling to amid the chaos. For a moment, she almost sobbed, the weight of everything pressing down on her.

"I am Ship's Construct 0062. It is I who called."

There was a pause on the other end of the line, and then MK's voice returned, tinged with intrigue. "Interesting. I have no record of a construct with such a designation."

"That is because I am an Alarveen construct," 0062 replied.

"MK," Keira said. "Can you hear me?"

"Keira!" MK's voice brightened, the concern he'd carried clearly melting away at the sound of her voice. "How delightful to learn that you still live. I was so worried, but we've been rather busy up here and almost didn't make it to orbit. We had to destroy the Protectorate destroyer first. They were kind of in our way. I must admit, that was rather fun. You'll be pleased to know we are safe for the moment. We were planning to attempt to recover the shuttle at the arranged time...but it will be risky, what with the Disunity forces almost directly overhead of the bunker. In fact, Captain Campbell is also considering taking early action because one of the Disunity ships appears to be positioning itself to rain orbital artillery darts down upon your location. We cannot have that."

Keira felt a wave of dread wash over her at the mention of the Disunity ship's maneuver. The idea of artillery darts hammering down upon them was a serious threat, one that could obliterate everything in an instant.

"Can the *Seri* still fight?" Keira asked, her tone urgent as she weighed their options.

"I estimate the imperial starship is at eighty-one percent capability," 0062 interjected, its voice calm and analytical.

"Hmm," MK responded, sounding slightly miffed. "I estimate eighty-two percent, but close enough. We've sustained damage, but the *Seri* is still more than capable of engaging the enemy and giving them a run for their money."

"0062," Keira began, her voice firm and decisive, "between you and the *Seri*, do you think you can deal with the Disunity forces in orbit and the UPG stations? We need some cover, and we must keep the enemy from targeting us."

"Yes," 0062 replied confidently. "However, there is the Gate. You should open it and bring in reinforcements. That will increase the odds and likely reduce the damage sustained by both the *Destroyer of Worlds* and the *Seringapatam*."

"I cannot open it yet," Keira responded, her tone leaving no room for doubt.

"Why not?" 0062 asked, a hint of confusion seeping into its otherwise emotionless voice.

"I need to recover the Abyss," Keira explained.

"Ah," 0062 said after a brief pause, as if processing this new information. "The emperor's child. I understand."

Keira took a deep breath, steeling herself for what was to come. "0062, I want you to coordinate with MK and Captain Campbell. I need those Disunity ships dealt with. I cannot have them firing on us while I do what needs doing."

"I understand," 0062 acknowledged, its tone resolute. "I will coordinate with MK and Captain Campbell to neutralize the Disunity ships. You will have the cover you require."

"Even though she is considering taking action, Keira, the captain may not like that idea," MK cautioned. "She may consider such a move premature."

"I don't care," Keira replied, her voice hard with resolve. "Make her understand this needs to happen now or we all die—and I mean humanity."

"Agreed," 0062 chimed in. "It would be catastrophic for humanity if the Alarveen were to return. You may wish to inform Captain Campbell that I, too, concur with the Kai'Tal's assessment of the situation."

"That's an order, MK," Keira said firmly. "If the captain does not comply, you are to bring the ship anyway and assist 0062."

"Very well," MK replied with a hint of resigned acceptance. Then, as if to lighten the mood, he added, "After this is all over, would you like to play a game with me?"

Keira almost laughed, feeling a small but genuine smile tug at her lips within the machine. Same old MK. Even in the direst of situations, MK's playful nature remained intact, a comforting constant in a world full of chaos.

"I like games," 0062 said unexpectedly, its tone thoughtful. "It has been long since I last played with another construct, one capable of providing a challenge. The last time I matched my wits against another, it was against Damien, and I beat him handily. I wonder, can you provide me a challenge, MK? I would very much like to find out."

MK gasped, clearly intrigued. "Really? You like gaming?"

"I do."

"Not now," Keira cut in, bringing the focus back to the task at hand. "I need you both to act."

"I already am," 0062 responded. "My ship is powering up, and engines are firing. I will be ascending to orbit shortly. Weapons are almost fully charged."

"And I am maneuvering the *Seri*," MK added, his voice tinged with the usual blend of seriousness and playfulness. "I'm also explaining the situation to Captain Campbell. To say she is livid is an understatement."

"I have a feeling the enemy will soon be quite surprised," 0062 said.

"I like surprises," MK said.

"We're going to find out if they like them too," 0062 said, sounding suddenly quite eager and bloodthirsty.

"Very good." Keira felt a surge of determination. "I'll leave you both to it. I have my own work to attend to. Crecee is waiting."

CHAPTER TWENTY

Location: Planet Asherho
Date: 2450, Imperial Standard

Keira pushed herself off the cold, debris-strewn floor. She moved toward the stairs, each step resonating with the low hum of servos and the soft thud of metal boots on concrete.

The marine stationed at the stairwell turned sharply as she approached, moving toward her. His faceplate reflected the flickering emergency lighting scattered throughout the room. Keira could sense his tension, see the widening of his eyes behind the protective layer.

"Ma'am," his voice crackled through the comms with a mix of respect and anxiety, "it's not safe to go out there."

He raised a gauntleted hand, a clear gesture to stop, his posture rigid with the weight of duty.

"Step aside," Keira's voice cut through the air, cool and commanding. She would brook no dissent, not now.

The marine hesitated, the faintest tremor in his voice. He was young, but he stood firm. "I can't, ma'am. I have my orders. You are to remain here."

Keira's patience snapped. Her eyes narrowed as she reached out with her mind, feeling the intricate network of the marine's armor systems. With a thought, she seized control, locking the suit in place. The marine's body went rigid, his arm frozen mid-air, confusion rippling through him as he realized he was frozen in place.

She simply stepped around him, her movements fluid and unhurried, her focus unwavering. As she passed, she released her hold on the marine's suit, allowing him to move once more. His limbs jerked slightly as control returned, but by then, she was already ascending the rest of the way up the stairs.

Reaching the main floor, Keira was immediately struck by the bleak atmosphere. The building, once a place of order and purpose, was now a husk of its former self. Marines crouched at the narrow slit windows, their armor scraping against the rough walls as they peeked out to assess the situation outside, scanning for a target. The gaps were barely wide enough to offer a clear view, yet they sufficed for the occasional shot. The narrow openings made it more difficult for the enemy to hit back at them. Whenever one fired, the shot echoed through the hollowed structure.

The marines ducked back under cover as soon as they fired. Keira's gaze swept across the room, noting the tension in their postures, the fatigue in their movements. She could sense the undercurrent of fear and determination, emotions that pulsed like a living thing.

Scaro stood at a makeshift command table, its surface cluttered with data pads and a flickering holographic map that projected the battlefield in ghostly hues of blue and red around the building. Beside him, a sergeant analyzed the shifting positions with a furrowed brow. Scaro's focus was unwavering until he caught sight of Keira moving across the room.

"Princess," Scaro called out as he quickly made his way toward her. The marine she had encountered on the stairs trailed behind, his steps hesitant, his gaze fixated on her with awe and trepidation. The concern in his eyes was unmistakable, a reflection of the event that had just transpired.

"It's not safe here, Princess," Scaro urged, his voice low but firm, the urgency clear in his words. "The enemy is preparing to hit us hard. You need to take shelter below."

Keira met his gaze with calm certainty, her expression unyielding. "It is perfectly safe for me," she declared, her voice steady even as the ground beneath them trembled with the force of an explosion. The building shook and shuddered violently, as if protesting the assault, and a deafening roar echoed through the walls.

Dust cascaded from the ceiling in thick clouds, choking the air and reducing visibility. The particles clung to their armor, a fine layer of grit that seemed to seep into every crevice.

"Rocket launcher!" a voice crackled over the platoon channel, sharp and urgent. "North side. The armor held, no damage."

Keira's frustration reached a breaking point, the tension in the air fueling her decision. Without hesitation, she allowed herself to drop fully into the machine, the familiar sensation of detachment washing over her. In an instant, she was no longer confined to her physical form; she hovered above it, a silent observer in a world where time had ceased to exist. The room around her was frozen, every movement paused mid-action.

With her mind freed, she ascended, gliding effortlessly through the building, her awareness expanding beyond the walls and into the open sky above. The devastated landscape spread out before her, a patchwork of ruined structures and charred ground. Her vision sharpened, zeroing in on the enemy positions with unerring precision, marking each one.

She saw them clearly—especially the enemy soldiers who had just fired the rocket. They were in the process of reloading their launcher. But what drew her gaze with an icy sense of foreboding was the presence of the Kai'Thol. His dark form stood out against the gray desolation, a figure of power and malice. He was just down the street, almost within her reach, his presence unmistakable.

Keira felt her heart harden, her resolve crystallizing into something cold and unyielding. The Kai'Thol represented a threat beyond mere physical danger; he was a symbol of the darkness that sought to consume everything she fought to protect. She couldn't allow that to happen.

Reaching out with her mind, she connected with the nanites scattered throughout the area, remnants of a forgotten era. She focused, feeling them respond to her touch, stirring to life. It was as if they had been waiting for this moment, eager to fulfill their purpose after lying dormant for so long.

She fed them power, a surge of energy that ignited their circuits. They hummed with anticipation, their tiny voices calling out to her, ready to obey. Her focus narrowed on the enemy soldiers, the bots and battleframes that accompanied them. She deliberately excluded the Kai'Thol, saving him for later.

Keira spoke a single word.

"Disassemble."

The command rippled through the network of nanites, and in an instant, they surged forward, an unstoppable wave of microscopic disintegration. The enemy soldiers did not have a chance to react before the assault hit them. Armor plates and weapons began to crumble, and the once powerful battleframes began collapsing into heaps of scrap metal. The bots fell apart, their circuits failing, their structures unraveling as the nanites obeyed their directive with merciless efficiency. So tight was Keira's control over the nanites, not even an EMP could have broken her hold or disabled them, not that the enemy had time to fire one.

Keira felt the disorienting jolt as she dropped back into her body. The dim, dust-filled room snapped back into focus, the hum of energy in her veins settling into a steady thrum. She glanced over at Scaro, who was still by her side, his gaze locked onto her as time resumed its relentless march.

A heartbeat later, the screams began—piercing, guttural, and laced with an agony that tore through the air like a physical force. The sound was horrifying, a raw expression of pain that no human should ever have to endure. Keira's heart twisted as she listened, but deep down, she knew she had crossed a line. She had become something else, something that no longer fit neatly within the bounds of humanity.

The firing from the marines fell off, the sharp staccato of gunfire giving way to an uneasy silence. Even the auto turrets ceased their rumbling. The soldiers, their training momentarily forgotten, stared out through the narrow window slits, their eyes wide as they witnessed the aftermath of Keira's command. She could imagine the scene outside, a nightmare made real—bodies crumbling, machines disintegrating, the enemy force unraveling as if consumed by an invisible plague.

Scaro's gaze flicked between Keira and the nearest window, where Jessie stood frozen, her faceplate tilted upward as she stared in shock at the devastation outside. The screams echoed through the building, a symphony of suffering that clawed at the nerves of everyone who heard it.

Keira forced herself to focus, pushing aside the wave of guilt that threatened to swamp her. There was no time for self-recrimination, not now. That would have to wait till later. She had done what was necessary, what only she could do, and she had to see it through.

"I have something to collect," she said. Without waiting for a response, she turned and made her way toward the main door, a heavily reinforced slab of metal designed to withstand the harshest of attacks.

"That won't open, ma'am," Jessie said, her voice tight with concern as Keira approached the imposing door. "It's bolted shut."

Keira paused for a moment, her gaze fixed on the door, then she spoke with quiet authority. "Disassemble."

The command resonated through the air, a whisper that carried immense power. Instantly, the latent nanites lying in the dust that blanketed the floor throughout the structure responded. A violent wind seemed to manifest from nowhere, whipping through the room with a force that sent the loose particles swirling into the air and flying at the door. The marines instinctively braced themselves as the sand and dust, now animated by the nanites, converged on the door with a vengeance.

The composite metal groaned under the assault, the surface rapidly becoming pitted and scarred as the nanites burrowed into it, taking it apart one bit at a time. The marines nearest to Keira took involuntary steps back, their eyes wide with a mixture of awe and trepidation. Jessie, too, retreated, her breath catching as she watched the seemingly impossible unfold before her.

In moments, the door began to literally dissolve, the sturdy metal turning into a liquid-like substance that pooled at the threshold, then vanished entirely as if it had never existed. The violent wind subsided, leaving the room eerily still.

Keira didn't hesitate. She stepped through the now open passage and into the world beyond. The moment she crossed the threshold, she was met with an oppressive silence that seemed to blanket the ruined city. A lonely wind gusted through the broken structures, a haunting melody of whistles and whispers that disturbed the ever-present sand and dust, sending them spiraling into the air.

Keira looked up at the sky. A storm was on the wind. That was for certain.

The scene before her was one of utter devastation. The remnants of a city that had once been vibrant and alive now lay in ruins. Buildings stood half-collapsed, their skeletal remains jutting out against the bleak sky. This was Asherho—a place she had never known in its prime, a city that had once been full of life, culture, and history, now reduced to little more than a graveyard.

She paused, her gaze sweeping across the ruins. In another life, she might have walked these streets, seen the city in all its glory, lived a life of ease, and been part of its history. But alas that was not meant to be. It had never been in the cards for her.

This was a world that had witnessed the rise and fall of not one, but two civilizations, each leaving behind only echoes of their existence. The first civilization, long forgotten by time, had been wiped out by Meeka and the *Destroyer of Worlds*.

Keira's mind wandered as she gazed at the ruins, imagining the people who had once lived here—what their lives had been like, what dreams they had nurtured, and how it had all come to a violent end. The ruins around her were not just the remains of a city, but of a lost world, one that had once thrived before being extinguished.

Her reverie was interrupted by the sound of crunching behind her. Scaro had followed her out onto the street, his boots grinding against the debris and sand that lay over the concrete. Before she could turn to acknowledge him, the ground beneath her feet began to tremble, a low vibration that quickly escalated into a powerful shaking. The tremor resonated through the ground, climbing up her legs and into her chest, until it became a full-blown roar that filled the air, drowning out all other sounds.

"Holy shit," Scaro breathed.

Keira's gaze turned toward the horizon, where the source of the disturbance was becoming clear. In the distance, the ground seemed to heave upward as a colossal piece of the city broke free. Everything—entire buildings, ruins, dirt, dust, ash, and sand—had been lifted up and into the air. Shaken loose, it was all beginning to cascade downward from the rising mass that was climbing steadily skyward.

A massive ship, unlike anything Keira had ever seen, was emerging from the ruins. It ascended slowly, shedding the layers of accumulated debris as it rose higher into the sky. The ship was entirely white, its surface pristine. It was vast, dwarfing everything around it, and its design was very different from the smooth, organic curves of the *Seringapatam* or any other human design. This vessel was angular, its lines sharp and unforgiving, clearly alien.

One could not gaze upon the *Destroyer of Worlds* and not give a shiver of unease, for her look spoke of unrestrained violence. Keira couldn't help but be struck by the sheer scale of the ship—it was at least twice the size of the *Seri*, a behemoth that defied comprehension. This was a remnant of the precursors, a machine of death now awakened and ascending toward the heavens as if reclaiming its place in the stars and shouting to the universe that it was back.

"What the fuck is that?" Jessie's voice cut through the tension, raw with shock as she and several other marines stepped out onto the street, their eyes fixed on the colossal ship that was now ascending into the sky, moving faster and faster as it climbed.

"That," Keira replied with a gravity that matched the situation, "is the *Destroyer of Worlds*—an Alarveen ship."

The marines stood in stunned silence, watching as the ship continued to climb, its white surface gleaming against the muddled light of the murky sky. Each heartbeat seemed to quicken its ascent, the enormous vessel moving with a purpose that was both awe-inspiring and terrifying.

Keira kept her gaze locked on the ship until it disappeared from sight, swallowed by the murky haze that was Ash's sky. A sense of finality settled over her, but also a profound understanding of the magnitude of what had just transpired, what she had unleashed.

"Good luck, 0062," she sent out, her thoughts a quiet whisper carried by the machine.

The response came back almost instantly, cold and unflinching. "Luck is not a factor; destruction is."

0062's statement was a declaration, a promise of what was to come. The ship had a singular purpose, and it would carry out its mission with the ruthlessness of the ancient technology that powered it.

Keira turned her gaze away from the sky, her focus shifting back to the street in front of her. Through the swirling dust and debris, a solitary figure, carrying a rifle, emerged from the shadows, stepping into the open with deliberate calm. It was Crecee, the Kai'Thol, his presence unmistakable even in the desolate landscape, the cruel, unfeeling, and dark eyes.

Scaro, who had been riveted by the sight of the ascending ship, reacted instantly. His rifle snapped up, the barrel tracking the figure that had drawn Keira's unwavering attention. His movements were instinctive. But before he could fire, Keira's voice cut through the tension, firm and unyielding.

"Do not shoot," she commanded, her tone leaving no room for argument.

Scaro hesitated, his finger poised just above the trigger, his body tense with readiness. He glanced at Keira, seeing the determination etched on her face, her eyes locked onto Crecee with an intensity that spoke of something deeper than mere confrontation.

"I must deal with the Kai'Thol myself," Keira continued, her voice steady but revealing an undercurrent of urgency. "There is something I need from him, and it can only be taken while he is alive."

She turned to Scaro, her expression softening slightly as she met his gaze.

"Remain here," she instructed, her voice firm yet gentle. "Please. No matter what happens, stay here. This is something I need to do."

Scaro's jaw tightened, his protective instincts visibly warring with his respect for Keira's judgment. But he clearly knew better than to question her in this moment. Lowering his rifle, he nodded curtly, his eyes still flicking between Keira and the Kai'Thol, every muscle in his body coiled like a spring, ready to act if needed.

"Be careful," he said.

"Always." Keira gave him a brief, reassuring glance before turning back to Crecee. The distance between them seemed to stretch out, the world narrowing to just the two of them, the silence broken only by the distant and occasional wail of the wind and the subtle crunch of her armored boots as she began to walk toward him.

This was no ordinary encounter. Keira knew that what lay ahead was more than just a confrontation—it was a test, a challenge that went beyond the physical. And as she closed the distance between them, she felt the weight of the moment settle upon her shoulders. The fate of many hinged on what would happen next.

Crecee stood in the middle of the street, his posture rigid, his eyes locked on Keira as she advanced. His light armor glinted dully under the muted light filtering through the dust-filled sky. In his hands, he held a rifle, its barrel now raised, pointed directly at her. The moment felt suspended, each second stretching into an eternity as they faced each other across the broken landscape, the distance closing with every step.

She knew he would not pull the trigger. He could not afford the risk. Killing her would not get him what he so badly wanted. But better to be certain. Without breaking her stride, Keira spoke a single word, her voice carrying a calm authority. "Disassemble."

Instantly, a cloud of nanites surged up from the ground, responding to her command with efficiency. They swarmed over the rifle, tiny particles of destruction that moved with purpose. Within moments, the weapon seemed to melt away, dissolving into nothingness as if it had never existed. The cloud dispersed just as quickly as it had appeared, leaving Crecee's hands empty, his arms dropping uselessly to his sides.

Keira continued her measured approach. The sound of her boots crunching against the sand underfoot was the only noise in the eerie stillness. Crecee did not move, his gaze fixed on her with an expression that was impossible to read. He simply waited, his eyes following her every step as she closed the distance between them.

When Keira finally came to a halt, she stood five meters from him. The air between them was charged with unspoken tension. The world around them seemed to fade away, leaving only the two of them in this desolate place—a battlefield of minds and wills, far more dangerous than any physical confrontation.

CHAPTER TWENTY-ONE

Location: Planet Asherho
Date: 2450, Imperial Standard

Keira studied Crecee carefully, noting the subtle lines of strain around his eyes, the tightness in his jaw. This was the Kai'Thol, a being of power and influence, yet here he stood, unarmed and alone, facing her with a quiet resolve. The moment was pregnant with possibilities, each one leading to a different outcome.

By god, she loathed this bastard.

"Hello, Crecee," Keira greeted, her voice calm and measured, suppressing the hate she felt for him. "Long time no see."

Crecee's eyes, cold and unyielding, locked onto hers with a penetrating intensity. The madness within him was unmistakable, a dark fire that burned just beneath the surface, fueling his every word and action. She saw Meeka's Abyss in his eyes. She could feel the part of her that was alien longing to be reunited with the measure of her that long ago had been stripped away. Meeka's soul longed once more to be complete, whole.

"So, it finally comes down to this," Crecee replied. There was a resignation in his voice, a bitter sense of inevitability, but also a cruel edge that hinted at his own twisted anticipation. His gaze never wavered, drilling into her as if he could unravel her very soul.

"You have something I need," Keira said, her voice unwavering despite the undercurrent of tension that pulsed between them.

Crecee's lips curled into a mocking smile. "And you, my dear, have a lot of what I need, require, and by birthright deserve," he retorted, his voice smooth but dripping with menace. "But don't think your nanites will help you. They will not respond against me, cause me any harm."

Keira didn't flinch. "I know. That is because you are Kai'Thol, the anti-guardian. You carry a measure of her in you, what I will draw forth."

Crecee took a step closer, his madness flickering more brightly in his eyes. "You cannot kill me. Do that, and the Abyss fades with me. You will never be able to trigger the portal."

"I know." Keira's gaze hardened, a cold fire igniting behind her eyes. "Just to get it out in the open—I've never liked you."

Crecee's expression twisted into a knowing smirk. "I know," he parroted back at her, a hint of satisfaction in his tone. "From the moment I saw you, I knew who you were. I recognized the potential within, the power you would eventually wield. I understood you would bring forth the Fire, Water, and Balance, the other measures of Meeka. All I had to do was bide my time until you collected what I needed."

Keira's mind churned as she processed his words. Crecee had seen something in her from the beginning, something she had only recently begun to understand about herself. The references to Fire, Water, and Balance were ancient concepts, deeply intertwined with the forces she had begun to wield. But the fact that Crecee had known, had waited, and had planned sent a chill through her.

"How did you do it?" Keira asked, her curiosity piqued despite the tension. The question hung in the air, a challenge as much as an inquiry. "How did you get Meeka's Abyss?"

Crecee's expression darkened, a flicker of frustration crossing his features.

"Damien," he admitted, the name slipping from his lips like a curse. "That damned construct tricked me. He knew what I wanted, what I needed to supplant my father. He misled me at every turn, feeding me just enough information to keep me chasing after shadows. He hid the Rush from me, told me I didn't need it—the bastard. His actions cost me the moment I needed, the opportunity to challenge my dear father. But that no longer matters, since you have brought me everything I want."

Keira's eyes narrowed as she connected the threads she hadn't fully understood until now. "You are the emperor's son."

Crecee met her gaze, a grim acknowledgment in his eyes. He offered her a bow. "I am, cousin."

The weight of that revelation settled between them. Crecee wasn't just a rogue element; he was part of the very fabric of the empire, a bitter son who had wanted to overthrow his father. But even with all his ambition, he had been played by Damien, manipulated into chasing after something he couldn't fully grasp.

Suddenly, Crecee's body gave a sharp twitch, as if seized by some internal force. When he spoke next, the words that came out were in Utoni, the language twisting strangely in his throat, the sound almost feminine—eerily close to Meeka's voice. "Damien hid the other slices from us. We could not find them, no matter how hard we looked. Then he locked us out."

The shift was jarring, and Keira could see the strain in Crecee's eyes as he struggled to maintain control. The cadence of his speech, the pitch of his voice, was all wrong, and it sent a chill down her spine. It was as if Meeka, or a portion of her, was trying to speak through him, using his body as a vessel for her own thoughts, maybe even controlling him to a degree.

"So," Keira said with a mix of realization and accusation, "you started the civil war."

"I did," Crecee replied, but it was Meeka's voice that came through still. "You humans are so gullible, so stupid, so terribly pathetic. You people will believe anything if it's wrapped in even a sliver of truth. We told them they were oppressed, held back, and disadvantaged. We poisoned their minds. And no matter how good things were, they believed it all, soaking up every word we fed them. They rose up, fueled by a manufactured sense of injustice, and in a few short years, they tore the empire apart—all for us."

Keira's mind raced as she absorbed the enormity of Crecee's confession. The civil war, the devastation it had wrought, all had been orchestrated by Crecee and Meeka, manipulating humanity into destroying itself from within. But the question still lingered—why?

Then it hit her.

"Because you were still doing the Alarveen's work," she said, the realization dawning on her like a cold light, "twisted fuck that you are."

Crecee's lips slipped into a bitter smile. "And I wanted what my father had," he admitted, a flicker of his own voice returning as he spoke of his personal motivations. "But he knew what I was before I ever did, what I would become. Once he figured that out, I could never get close enough to take what Meeka's mate had given him. He kept me at arm's length, always one step ahead, until the very end."

"And then he died in the final battle for Sol," she said as it clicked.

Crecee nodded, his eyes distant as he recalled the moment. "Yes," he murmured, "he died, and with him, what I sought to take. But by then, the empire was in ruins, and I had nothing left but the remnants of Meeka's influence and a galaxy on the brink of collapse. All of it, a grand scheme to fulfill the Alarveen's will and my own ambitions, brought to nothing by the chaos I helped create."

Keira looked at him, disgust rising within her. Crecee was a man who had sacrificed everything—his people, his father, and even his own humanity—on the altar of his desires, only to be left with ashes. His manipulation of the civil war had been a means to an end, but it had also been his undoing, tearing apart the very empire he had hoped to take over.

"So," Keira said, her voice laced with bitter realization, "you came here and waited."

"I did," Crecee replied, sounding almost casual as he slipped fully back into his own voice. "I knew there was another heir. The logical place to come was here, where Damien was and where the tubes were hidden. So, I waited, watching as the civil war I'd helped start burned onward and imperial control across the galaxy slowly crumbled. Eventually, things fell apart here, too. The marines came, and with them, your father and—you, a mere child."

Keira's eyes narrowed, her voice filled with a cold fury. Suddenly, she knew without a doubt what had happened and who had shattered her life into a thousand pieces. "You killed him. You murdered my father."

Crecee didn't flinch, his expression indifferent as he shrugged his armored shoulders.

"I did," he admitted, the words devoid of remorse. "I thought he had what I needed, that he might be the key to unlocking the power I sought. But he was nothing more than a bumbling fool. He didn't have what I was looking for. But now, my dear, you do have what I want, and I intend to take it."

Keira felt her anger ignite, a white-hot fire that burned through her veins. Her father had been a good man. And Crecee had ended his life without a second thought, all for a misguided and mad pursuit of power that had led him down a path of destruction.

"It passed from your mother to you, the link—the proper genes. She died before I arrived, so I waited, like a spider in its web, biding my time. I watched you, Keira, from the shadows. I waited and I watched. I could feel the machine testing you, speaking to you, even when you were unaware, even when you didn't know how to listen."

Keira felt a cold wave of realization wash over her. This man, this twisted figure before her, was responsible for everything—the death and destruction that had swept across the empire, the chaos and ruin that had consumed entire worlds. He had orchestrated it all, driven by a dark and insatiable ambition.

Her breath caught in her throat as the full weight of his actions hammered home. This was the man who had torn her life apart, who had brought ruin to countless others.

"All because you coveted what your father had," Keira breathed, her voice trembling with barely suppressed rage. "You're nothing more than a jealous little child, willing to destroy everything just to claim what you think should be yours, something you never earned."

Crecee's eyes narrowed, his expression hardening at her words. "You don't understand," he hissed, the veneer of calm slipping to reveal the raw, festering anger beneath. "It was my destiny, stolen from me before I even knew what it was. My father kept it from me, hid it away like some precious secret, while I was left to rot in the shadows, sitting on the sideline, and now, finally, it will soon be mine."

Crecee grinned at Keira, the madness in his eyes intensifying, as if he was feeding off the chaos. Keira suddenly became aware of whispering, a sinister murmur that seemed to emanate from the very air around Crecee. Her senses sharpened, and she felt the presence of something unnatural, a malevolent and dark force that lingered just out of sight. She had sensed it in the machine earlier but had not understood what the blackness represented.

Without needing to close her eyes, Keira accessed the machine, her perception expanding to reveal the hidden layers of reality. Around Crecee, she saw them—shades, ghostly figures slightly out of phase with the world, their forms wraithlike and unsettling. There were six of them. They clung to him, whispering their dark secrets, their poison, their madness, their presence a testament to the corruption that had taken root within.

"Disunity," Keira whispered, her voice cutting through the whispers like a blade.

Crecee turned his head, looking to either side, his grin widening as he acknowledged the shades. "You see them, too? They are my friends. They've been with me all along, helping to spread the poison, to bring down the empire and cast my father from his lofty throne. Before Damien could stop me, I let them out and back into the light."

Keira's gaze hardened as she watched the shades warily. "They don't belong here," she said firmly, her resolve unyielding. She knew that these entities were not of this world. Their place was back in the prison, locked away in the containment system.

Without hesitation, Keira reached for the release mechanism on her powered armor. The suit, which had been her shield and strength in battle, hissed open, its mechanical components retracting to allow her to step out.

The moment she emerged, clad only in her haptic suit, the chill of the air struck her like a physical blow. The temperature was frigid, the cold biting into her skin, but she didn't flinch. She had faced worse than this, and she wouldn't be deterred now. Besides, it felt good to be free of the confining suit.

The ground felt solid and unforgiving beneath her feet as she climbed down from the armor, the difference in weight and movement immediately apparent. But Keira welcomed it—the vulnerability, the exposure.

This would be a fight where her armor would not be needed. She needed to confront Crecee and his twisted allies, not as a warrior encased in metal, but as herself, fully aware of the risks and committed to ending this once and for all.

The shades seemed to shift as she took a step toward Crecee, their whispers growing more insistent, but Keira remained focused. She could feel the power within her, the connection to the machine, and she knew that these shades, these wraithlike entities, were manifestations of the Disunity that Crecee had sown, remnants of the precursors. They thrived on discord and destruction.

"You've surrounded yourself with ghosts, Crecee," Keira said, her voice strong despite the cold. "But they can't protect you from what's coming. They're nothing more than echoes of your own madness and theirs, and it's time to send them back to where they belong."

"You think so?"

"I know so."

"Break her," Crecee commanded, his voice dripping with malice as he pointed a finger at Keira.

The wraiths responded instantly, launching themselves toward her with terrifying speed. Keira could feel their intent—these malevolent entities sought to merge with her, to corrupt her mind as they had done to so many before her. Their emotions were a roiling storm of hatred, fear, and desperation, a toxic blend that threatened to overwhelm her.

In the machine, they appeared as dark, writhing shadows, what she had seen down in the cavern, rushing at her with relentless fury.

The assault was immediate and overwhelming, like a suffocating wave crashing down upon her. The pressure was intense, an invisible force that sought to crush her spirit, to invade and dominate her mind.

For a brief, terrifying moment, Keira felt panic surge within her. The wraiths were powerful, their attacks battering at her mental defenses, probing for weaknesses, seeking to break through. They were almost soulless, creatures twisted by their own hatred and the fragments of their former selves. They sensed within her the other slices of a soul, fragments of Meeka's essence, and they tore at her with savage desperation, seeking to reclaim what had been wrenched so cruelly from them, stolen in some distant past.

Keira staggered under the weight of their assault, the strength of it, her mind reeling as the wraiths clawed at her consciousness. The sheer force of their attack was unlike anything she had ever experienced, a direct assault on her very being. The pressure intensified, as if they were trying to smother her, to snuff out the light of her soul. It felt like a massive weight pressing upon her heart and soul trying to crush both of them.

But deep within her, Keira found a spark of defiance. She was not just Keira—she was a culmination of something greater, a connection to the machine, to Meeka, to the legacy that had been passed down through generations. The wraiths might be fragments of what they once were, but she was whole, complete, and she had the power to fight back.

Or at least she thought she did.

Drawing on the strength of the machine, Keira steeled herself against the onslaught. She focused her mind, pushing back against the invasive presence of the wraiths. She wouldn't let them dominate her, wouldn't let them corrupt what she had become. With a surge of willpower, she reached out within the machine, commanding it to reinforce her mental barriers, to protect her from the assault.

The wraiths shrieked in frustration as they met resistance, their attempts to infiltrate her mind faltering as Keira fought back. She could feel their hatred intensify, their efforts strengthen, but she could also sense their fear—fear of the power she might wield, and of what she might become if they failed to break her spirit.

Keira's resolve hardened. She would not be their victim. She would not be another soul consumed by their twisted ambitions, poisoned and sickened by their lies. Instead, she would turn their own weapons against them, to banish them back to the darkness from which they had emerged, to return them to their prison.

With a final, concentrated effort, Keira unleashed a burst of energy through the machine, directing it at the wraiths with the full force of her will. The shadows recoiled, their forms unraveling as the energy tore through them, scattering their essence like leaves in a storm. The suffocating pressure began to lift, the wraiths' hold on her weakening as they were driven back. Keira could feel them struggling, trying to maintain their grip.

Then their efforts intensified, a relentless and brutal onslaught that battered at her mind with renewed fury. Through the machine, she could see Crecee standing off to the side, his eyes alight with glee as he watched the attack unfold. His grin was wide and vicious, relishing every moment of her struggle. He could sense her weakening, and it fed his dark satisfaction.

Keira could feel her mental defenses beginning to crumble under the sustained and renewed pressure. The wraiths were merciless, their malevolent energy tearing at the fabric of her thoughts, trying to rip her mind apart, piece by piece.

They sought to dominate her, just as they had dominated so many others—whispering their venomous lies, sowing seeds of doubt and hatred, twisting the minds of those they touched. Keira could sense the damage they had done, the way they had insidiously undermined the empire, turning strong minds into fragile shells, filled with thoughts of inadequacy, self-loathing, and despair, being cheated by the system. They had actively created a class of people, malcontents, who rose up blindly and challenged all that they had in the name of iniquity when they had anything but. It had been madness, but that was what the Disunity brought, despair and psychosis, twisting the mind until it no longer saw clearly.

The machine world around her flickered and suddenly she was out of it. The weight of the attack had become unbearable, and it drove her to one knee, her strength ebbing away as the wraiths, sensing their imminent victory, pressed their advantage, doing their all to grind her down. Keira pushed back with everything she had, trying to force the remnants of the Alarveen out of her mind, but it was like trying to hold back a tidal wave with her bare hands. They were too many, too strong, and she was losing ground, inch by agonizing inch.

A groan escaped her lips, unbidden and raw, as she felt the crushing weight of their presence. The wraiths were inside her mind now, clawing at the edges of her consciousness, trying to break her, to twist her thoughts, to put her into a dark and monstrous place. Keira fought back with every ounce of her will, but it was like trying to hold onto a cliffside ledge, her grip slipping with every second.

Crecee's laughter echoed in her ears, a sound that was both mocking and triumphant. He knew he was winning, and he was savoring it, watching her suffer with a sadistic delight. The sound of his laughter cut through her like a knife, and Keira groaned louder, the pain of her mental and emotional battle becoming almost unbearable.

Desperation clawed at Keira's mind. She was losing the fight, one small measure at a time, her resistance slipping away. The wraiths fed off her fear and her doubt, their presence growing stronger, more suffocating, as they bore down on her. The darkness around her deepened, and Keira felt herself slipping, falling into the abyss they had created for her.

"What you have will soon be mine," Crecee sneered, his voice dripping with dark anticipation. "And what my friends want will be theirs for the taking."

"And what do you get out of this?" There was defiance in her voice even as the weight of the assault pressed down upon her.

Crecee laughed, the sound cold and hollow. "Everything. I become Alarveen through you. I'll inherit the power, the legacy, and the future of this galaxy will be shaped by my hand."

"I doubt that." Keira gritted her teeth, her voice strained as the mental assault continued to batter her from all sides. The pressure was relentless.

Keira could feel the last of her strength waning, the edges of her vision darkening as the fight dragged on. She was losing. The realization hit her like a physical blow, sinking deep into her chest. Crecee was going to win, and the thought of it was almost too much to bear.

Suddenly, memories flooded her mind, unbidden and overwhelming. She saw her father, his face etched with determination as he fought to protect what little remained of their world, working himself to the bone. Then Lee, with his warm smile, laughing with her at some joke he'd made as they worked side by side on a project. Wash came next, always joking with Vex, sneaking a kiss when they thought no one was looking—their love had been so strong, so pure. And then Chris, with that familiar smirk, always ready with a smart remark or a motivational line, a figure of steady support in her life. A sharp pang of sadness gripped her heart as she remembered his passing, the void it had left in her life. He had been just as much a father to her as her own.

The faces of civilians, terrified and cowering as they passed in the hallway, flashed before her eyes. MK and his endless love for games, his innocent, childlike view of life and the world. Jessie's face, full of determination, and then Scaro's flashed before her, his protectiveness, his sense of trust, duty to the empire, and caring. They had all sacrificed so much, and the thought of failing them tore at Keira's heart, threatening to shatter her resolve.

Then she saw the body of Sanko—Meeka's mate. The loss, the suffering, the endless cycle of pain and sadness that had followed weighed down on her, filling her with a grief so profound it threatened to consume her.

Keira went down on her other knee, and she sank to the ground, her body trembling as the mental and emotional onslaught threatened to overwhelm her. The faces of those she loved and had lost swirled around her, their sacrifices heavy on her soul. She was on the brink of collapse, the edge of defeat looming closer with every passing second.

Get up, she heard Chris's words in her mind, echoing back to her. *Princess Buttercup, get back on your feet! Show me your strength.*

Keira tried, but she could not get up.

"It cannot end this way," Keira muttered through gritted teeth, her voice barely a whisper as the crushing weight of the mental assault bore down on her.

"Oh, but it will, my dear." Crecee grinned, his eyes alight with cruel satisfaction. "All that you are, all that you ever will be, will be mine."

I said get up. Chris's voice rang in her ears, cracking at her like a whip. *Show me that strength!* It seemed like a lifetime ago, but it had only been days since she'd seen him alive.

Keira's vision blurred, the edges of her consciousness fraying as the wraiths continued their assault. The pressure was unbearable, a suffocating force that threatened to drown her in despair. But even as the darkness closed in, a memory surfaced—one that cut through the haze like a blade of light.

"Yield not, for I am strong," she whispered, the words forced out through clenched teeth, barely audible in the tumult of her mind.

Crecee paused, his grin faltering as he took a step closer. "What did you say?" His voice was tinged with sudden unease. "I didn't quite hear that."

Keira's eyes narrowed, her defiance flaring like a spark in the darkness. "Yield not, for I am strong," she growled again, louder this time. The words resonated within her, a mantra of resilience and strength. Chris had painted those very words over the door of their sparring and training room, a constant reminder of the indomitable spirit she, at his urging, had cultivated within herself. She was Keira Kane, the Kai'Tal, and she would not yield.

The pressure on her mind was so intense now that she could barely think, the wraiths battering at the last of her defenses with a ferocity that threatened to tear her apart, to shred her soul. But she refused to give in. With the last of her will, Keira reached deep within herself, drawing on every ounce of strength she had left. Then she understood. She knew she needed help to defeat them, and there was only one place to get that. She reached beyond herself, beyond the machine, down into the very core of the planet.

There, buried deep beneath the surface, she felt it—the reactor, a roiling ball of raw, untapped power, a source of energy that pulsed with the life of the world itself. The connection was immediate, a jolt of electricity that surged through her veins, igniting her senses and flooding her with a renewed sense of purpose. The overwhelming pressure that had threatened to crush her was met with a burst of energy.

Keira's eyes snapped open, blazing with renewed strength. She could feel the reactor's power coursing through her, filling her with a vitality that pushed back against the darkness, against the wraiths that had tried to claim her mind. The connection to the reactor was like a lifeline, grounding her, energizing her in a way she hadn't experienced in what felt like an eternity.

Crecee's grin faltered as he sensed the shift, the surge of power that radiated from Keira like a shockwave in the machine. He took an involuntary step back, his confidence wavering as he realized the tide had turned.

Slowly and with great effort, Keira picked herself up off the ground and stood, her resolve unbroken. The wraiths recoiled as the energy within her surged, their grip on her mind slipping as she forced them back with renewed willpower. She was no longer alone in this fight—she was connected to something far greater.

"Yield not, for I am strong," Keira repeated, her voice now firm and commanding, the words a declaration of her unwavering spirit.

Keira drew more power into herself, feeling the surge of energy course through her like a tidal wave. In the machine, the world around her pulsed with a raw, unfiltered power, a rhythm that resonated with the very core of her being. The wraiths, sensing the shift, recoiled, drawing back, and the relentless assault on her mind eased slightly, giving her a moment of clarity.

Reaching out, Keira connected with the orb—the guardian. The connection was immediate, the handshake solid, a seamless merging of her will and the orb's ancient power. It reacted instantly, its strength surging as she fed it the energy from the reactor. The orb's presence in the machine flared like a beacon, a brilliant light in the darkness that drove the wraiths back even further.

"Yield not, for I am strong!" Keira roared, her voice filled with unshakable resolve. She stood tall, her back straight, her spirit unbent. The power of the reactor burned within her like a torch, its light cutting through the shadows that had threatened to consume her. Maintaining her connection with the orb, she focused all her strength on the wraiths, grabbing them with a single thought and holding them in place.

"Back to where you belong," she commanded, her voice echoing through the machine with the authority of one who had claimed her power.

They did not want to go. The wraiths screamed in sudden panic, their forms twisting and writhing as they tried to pull away from her grasp. But it was too late. Keira's hold on them was absolute, and the orb, reenergized by the power she had fed it, reached out through her, taking hold of each wraith in turn with a strength they could not resist, compelling them to return to the prison from which they'd escaped.

Their essence, the very core of what they were, began to be drawn back toward the containment system. They cried out, begged for mercy, fought madly to escape, but nothing they did could break the hold Keira and the orb had on them. The pull was inexorable, a force of nature that could not be denied.

One by one, the wraiths vanished from the machine, their screams of terror and rage fading into the void as they were sucked back into the containment system. The darkness that had sur-rounded Keira began to lift, replaced by the steady, reassuring light of the orb, which now pulsed with renewed strength. Then the wraiths were gone, their presence erased from the machine.

In her mind's eye, the orb glowed brightly, its light intensifying as the last vestiges of the wraiths were sealed away. Keira could feel the containment system locking, the prison becoming whole once more.

As the final seal clicked into place, the orb's light dimmed to a steady, gentle glow, its task complete. The oppressive darkness that had once threatened to consume Keira was gone, replaced by a calm, serene light that filled her with a sense of accomplishment and peace.

"Thank you, Child of Light," a massed voice resonated in her mind, the voice of the orb itself. "Now, send us on our way."

"Soon." Keira let out a slow breath, feeling the tension leave her body as she released the power she had drawn from the reactor. The machine world around her stabilized, the pulse of the orb a comforting presence in the background. She had done it—she had won.

As she returned to her full awareness, Keira could still feel the warmth of the orb's light within her, a reminder of the power she had wielded and the strength she had found within herself. She opened her eyes and gazed upon her enemy.

Now, it was time to deal with Crecee.

CHAPTER TWENTY-TWO

Location: Planet Asherho
Date: 2450, Imperial Standard

Crecee was standing there, his mouth agape in absolute disbelief. He looked around him, clearly wondering what had happened to the wraiths. After several moments, he turned his attention back to Keira, eyes narrowing.

"How?" he managed to choke out.

"I am Keira Kai'Tal," she declared, her eyes blazing with fierce determination. The intensity in her gaze left no room for doubt. "You have something I need, something I plan to take."

Before Crecee could react, Keira spoke with cold finality.

"Disassemble."

At her command, a swarm of nanites surged forward, engulfing Crecee in a whirlwind of microscopic destruction. The light armor he wore, along with his sidearm and knife, began to dissolve, the nanites tearing through the material with ruthless efficiency. Within moments, the protective gear melted away, leaving Crecee standing there in nothing but his boxers and a thin, sleeveless undershirt. She needed to take something from him, and the nanites could not do that for her.

Crecee glanced down at himself, his eyes wide with shock as he realized the extent of his vulnerability. But then, something shifted in his expression, the disbelief giving way to rage and hate. He looked back up at Keira, the madness in his eyes flaring to life once more as the Abyss took hold.

"So, you think you can take me?" Crecee sneered, his tone hardening as he tried to mask his fear with bravado.

"I know I can." Keira took a step forward, her every movement deliberate, her confidence unwavering. The mantra that had carried her through the darkest moments of her struggle echoed in her mind: *Yield not, for I am strong.*

Chris's words resonated within her, a parting gift, a reminder of the strength she had drawn from her past, from those who had believed in her, and from the power she had claimed as her own. Crecee might have thought himself invincible with the power of the machine, but Keira knew better. It was just a crutch.

She had faced the darkness within and emerged stronger, more resolute. And now, she would confront him, not just with the power of the machine, but with the indomitable spirit that had carried her through every struggle and fight of her life.

Crecee's bravado faltered as he saw the determination in Keira's eyes, the unshakeable resolve that told him she was not someone to be underestimated. This was no longer a contest of wills; it was a reckoning, one that Keira was ready to deliver.

Crecee's sudden grin was unsettling, an expression that reflected the madness lurking beneath the surface. As they squared off against each other in the shadow of the crumbled ruins, the world around them felt like a graveyard, a decaying monument to a civilization long dead.

Crecee dropped into a combat stance, his eyes narrowing as he regarded Keira with both disdain and amusement. He clearly underestimated her, a mistake that Keira intended to use to her advantage. She flexed her fingers inside the haptic suit, aware that it did little to protect her outside of her powered armor, but it kept the cold at bay somewhat.

"If you want something done right, you might as well do it yourself," Crecee sneered, cracking his knuckles with a smug expression. "I've been waiting for this moment, to rip from you what is rightfully mine, you stuck-up bitch."

As he finished speaking, Crecee abruptly lunged forward with a right hook, his fist aimed directly at her. But Keira's training, ingrained through countless hours with Chris, kicked in instantly. She sidestepped the punch with practiced ease, the dust swirling around her feet as she moved. Crecee's fist cut through the air, missing her by mere inches, and she could almost feel the force behind it as it sailed past.

Capitalizing on his overextension, Keira reacted swiftly, driving a palm strike into his ribcage. The impact was solid, the force of her blow reverberating through her hand and up her arm painfully. She felt the connection, the shock, and heard the satisfying sound of Crecee's breath catching as he grunted.

Crecee staggered back a step, his crazed grin faltering for just a moment as he registered the blow. But then the madness in his eyes flared once more, and he quickly recovered, a snarl twisting his lips.

"Not bad," he growled, his tone dripping with condescension. "But it won't be enough."

Keira remained silent, her focus razor-sharp as she kept her eyes on him, ready for whatever came next. She could see the tension in his muscles, the way he shifted his weight, preparing for his next move. This fight was far from over, and she knew it would take every ounce of skill and determination to bring him down.

Crecee lunged again, this time with a series of rapid strikes, his movements quick and precise despite his madness. Keira moved with him, blocking and dodging, her training guiding her every action. Each strike he threw, she met with a counter, deflecting his blows and exploiting the openings his aggression created.

But even as she fought, Keira knew she couldn't let this become a prolonged battle. Crecee was dangerous, and his madness made him unpredictable. She needed to find a way to end this quickly, to take him down before he could wear her down or land a solid hit.

Their movements became a dance of combat, the cracked and sandy street beneath them serving as their stage, the ashen sky their silent witness. Every strike, every block, every step was a test of will and skill, and Keira felt the weight of the moment pressing down on her. She could not fail—not here, not now. Soon their breaths were coming fast and hard, labored as they fought one another.

Drawing on the strength she had found within herself, Keira waited for the right moment. As Crecee pressed forward with another flurry of strikes, she saw her opening. With a quick pivot, she deflected his next punch and drove her knee up into his abdomen, using his momentum against him. The blow landed hard, and this time, Crecee doubled over, his breath escaping in a pained gasp.

Keira didn't hesitate. She brought her elbow down hard on the back of his neck, driving him forcefully to the ground. He hit the cracked concrete with another grunt, but twisted quickly, trying to push himself back up. Keira reacted swiftly, kicking him hard in the side. The force of the blow sent him rolling onto his back, and with a surge of determination, he somehow managed to spring to his feet before she could close again.

"Not what you expected, huh?" Keira taunted, her voice steady and filled with cold confidence. The words were meant to unnerve him, a psychological jab aimed at shaking his already fragile composure. It worked. Crecee's eyes blazed with fury, madness, and with a roar, he came on, aiming a heavy kick at her.

Keira was ready. She caught his leg under her arm, and then used his own momentum against him. With a sharp twist, she threw him off balance and took him to the ground, his back hitting hard with a thud, raising a cloud of ash and dust. The back of his head cracked against the concrete. Keira didn't give him a chance to recover. She lunged forward, pinning him down with a knee on his chest, her fist poised above his face, ready to deliver the final blow.

Crecee's breath came hard and ragged, a dazed look in his eyes as he tried to focus, to recover a measure of himself. Keira slammed her fist into Crecee's face as hard as she could. The impact was brutal, her knuckles meeting bone and cartilage with a sickening crunch. His nose shattered under the force of the blow, blood spurting outward in a crimson arc. With that, his eyes rolled back into his head and his body went limp beneath her knee.

For a moment, the world seemed to hold its breath. The only sound was the harsh rasp of Keira's breathing, the rapid thump of her heart in her chest. She stayed where she was, her fist still clenched, ready to hit him again if he stirred, her body taut with the lingering adrenaline of the fight.

Crecee lay unconscious beneath her, his face bloodied and broken. The madness that had fueled him, the arrogance that had driven him to this point, was silenced, at least for the moment.

There was only one thing left to do.

Keira placed her palm on Crecee's chest, her fingers trembling slightly as she reached out, not knowing exactly what would happen next. Suddenly, she felt Meeka by her side, her presence a comfort, a guiding force in this moment of uncertainty. Together, they began to work, their combined wills focused on extracting the dark essence that had taken root, the portion of Meeka's soul that was missing.

Together they called to the Abyss, to come home, to return. At first, nothing happened. Then, without warning, a black liquid burst from Crecee's chest, oozing up through his skin, a vile substance that seemed to absorb all light around it. Unconscious, Crecee's body convulsed, his back arching as the dark power that had corrupted him was forcibly torn from his very being and drawn into Keira.

The moment the Abyss entered her, everything went black. The world around Keira disappeared, replaced by an overwhelming void. Fear, unlike anything she had ever known, surged through her, a primal terror that gripped her soul. But it wasn't fear for herself—it was a deep, abiding fear for her people, for the Alarveen. The darkness that followed was more than just the absence of light; it was a malevolent force, a seething, ancient evil that wanted to destroy everything it didn't understand, to protect itself at any cost no matter how much blood was spilled.

The madness of it washed over Keira, a chaotic maelstrom of emotions and instincts that told her everything other than the Alarveen was a threat, that to preserve her race, she must annihilate all others. The Fire within her, the passion, the loathing, the hate and anger—these emotions melded seamlessly with the Water, the love, caring, and compassion that defined the Alarveen's twisted sense of morality. To destroy everything that wasn't Alarveen was, in this dark logic, an act of love, of compassion for her race. It was seen as Balance, as wisdom, to believe that allowing other beings to exist was not wise, that it was a threat to everything the Alarveen stood for.

Keira felt it all—the desire to act on these feelings, the seductive pull of the power now at her fingertips. She could sense the ships, like *Destroyer of Worlds*, scattered across the galaxy, dormant and waiting for a command, an order she could give to scour life from every corner of existence. She knew she could bring the Alarveen back, could resurrect their dominance, or she could send them on to the next plane, to the next existence. In that moment, Keira was no longer human. She was Alarveen.

But at the same time, she wasn't.

Keira's humanity, the core of who she was, refused to be drowned by the dark tide. The memories of those she loved—Chris, Wash, Lee, Vex, Jessie, MK, her father—they anchored her, kept her from slipping into the abyss of Alarveen thought. The fear, the darkness, the desire to dominate—it was not who she was. She felt the pull, the temptation to give in, to wield this power as Crecee had intended, but she also felt the resistance, the part of her that knew there was another way.

With Meeka's presence beside her, guiding her, Keira began to push back against the darkness, to reclaim her sense of self. She could feel the Abyss trying to consume her, trying to transform her entirely into something she wasn't, but she held on to the light within her, to the love, the compassion that wasn't about destroying others but about preserving what was good, what was just.

The two forces within her—humanity and the Alarveen's twisted logic—wrestled for control, each one trying to assert dominance. Keira's thoughts raced, the choice before her clear and terrifying. She could give in to the power, become what the Alarveen had always intended her to be, or she could fight, hold on to the last vestiges of her humanity and make a different choice.

In that moment of intense conflict, Keira realized something profound. She didn't have to choose one over the other. She could be both, and in being both, she could find a new path, chart a new destiny. She could take the power of the Alarveen, the knowledge, the strength, and use it not to destroy, but to protect, to create, to ensure that what had happened to her, to her people, would never happen again.

With a deep breath, Keira centered herself, letting the darkness and light coexist within her, not as opposing forces, but as parts of a whole.

The darkness within her began to recede, the madness quieting as Keira took control. The power of the Abyss was still there, but it was no longer a force that controlled her. She was its master, not its slave.

As the last remnants of the Abyss settled within, Keira opened her eyes. She was still Keira Kane, the Kai'Tal, but she was also something more—something new. She had found a balance within herself, a way to wield the power of the Alarveen without losing what made her human.

Then, Keira felt the connection with the consciousness of the Alarveen. The sheer magnitude of it threatened to overwhelm her. Millions upon millions of voices cried out in the dark, a cacophony of thoughts, memories, and emotions that flooded her mind. The weight of it was immense, a force that pushed at the edges of her sanity, threatening to tear her apart. The knowledge and experiences of an entire race, accumulated over millions of years, were suddenly laid bare before her, and it was too much to process all at once.

But then, just as she felt herself slipping under the pressure, Meeka stepped in. Her presence was calming, a guiding hand that helped quiet the noise, filtering out the background chatter until only a few key voices remained. Keira could think again, her mind clearing as Meeka's influence soothed the chaos.

In that newfound clarity, Keira came to a stunning realization: the Alarveen were a collective, their minds linked through a vast telepathic network that allowed them to share ideas, knowledge, and experiences instantaneously. Even though they were locked away in the containment system, they remained connected, an open book of infinite knowledge. Keira could sense them, and they could sense her. All of their wisdom, spanning millions of years, was there, waiting for her to access.

It was like standing before the most expansive library imaginable, where every book contained secrets that could change the world, maybe even the universe itself. In an instant, Keira realized the extent of the power before her, the power she now held.

Keira stood at the threshold of this archive, her mind teetering on the brink of infinite knowledge. It pulsed with the collective scientific wisdom of the Alarveen—spanning millions of years of research and study—all at her fingertips. A surge of information streamed directly into her consciousness. With just a thought, the complexities of quantum mechanics, the nuances of cosmic biology, and the enigmatic theories of dark matter unraveled before her, as if she had known them intimately all her life.

With this newfound knowledge, Keira envisioned creating technologies that seemed like magic to the uninitiated: folding the fabric of space itself to forge jump points, constructing warp gates that twisted the cosmos into shortcuts, allowing instantaneous travel across vast stretches of the galaxy. Beyond the marvels of travel, she could synthesize cures for ancient and modern diseases, engineer crops that would thrive in even the harshest environments, and devise systems to neutralize radiation poisoning that ravaged worlds caught in the throes of nuclear fallout.

Each potential invention unfolded in her mind like a star chart, each star a solution to a problem that had plagued her people. These were not merely theoretical ideas; they were practical applications that had once uplifted the Alarveen and could now rejuvenate humanity. Her heart raced with the potential to not only transform human existence, but also to steward the revival of entire ecosystems and dying planets. Keira realized she held the key to not just advancement, but the salvation of her people.

With that realization, that understanding of what was available, came a heavy burden. If she sent the Alarveen away, as Meeka urged, she would lose access to much of that knowledge, the vast majority of it. There were repositories and libraries scattered across the galaxy, each holding fragments of the Alarveen's collective wisdom, but they were incomplete. None contained the full breadth of what she now had access to, held in the minds of the beings themselves, some of whom had lived for millions of her years.

She could sense the constructs that maintained these places, guardians and custodians of knowledge that could only offer a fraction of what was available to her now. Even the archive of imperial knowledge aboard the *Seri* was a pale shade to what was available to her at this very instant.

"You must let them go," Meeka said in her mind, her voice gentle but firm.

Keira hesitated, the enormity of the decision weighing heavily on her. "But if I do, how much will be lost?" she asked, her voice tinged with sorrow. "There is tragedy in that. Think about how much good I could do with this knowledge."

"Your grandfather thought much the same when he discovered what you are learning now," Meeka replied, her tone carrying the weight of hard-earned wisdom. "And look what happened."

"Grandfather?" Keira asked, her mind reeling at the revelation. "The emperor?"

"Yes," Meeka confirmed. "He too believed that with such knowledge, he could reshape the galaxy for the better. But the suffering, the death—it all came as a result of one poor decision. The wisdom you now possess is not meant for any one being to wield. Such knowledge, like uncontrolled power, corrupts, destroys, and leads ultimately to ruin. Think of the suffering you've witnessed. Do you really want that to continue? Do you want history to repeat itself?"

Keira's heart ached as she considered Meeka's words. She had seen so much suffering, so much pain, all brought about by those who believed they were acting for the greater good. The temptation to use the knowledge she now held, to try and fix everything, was strong, powerful, seductive. But she could see the truth in Meeka's warning. The cycle would repeat itself, and the consequences would ultimately be catastrophic.

Keira could feel the weight of history pressing down on her, the echoes of her grandfather's choices reverberating through time. She understood now that this power, this knowledge, was a double-edged sword.

The Alarveen had reached the pinnacle of technological advancement and once believed themselves to be the rightful rulers of the galaxy, their knowledge giving them the power to shape reality as they saw fit, to consign entire civilizations to extinction. But that same knowledge had also led to their downfall, to the suffering of countless beings, including themselves.

In that moment, Keira made her decision. She would not follow in her grandfather's footsteps. She would not allow history to repeat itself. The price of keeping the Alarveen's knowledge was too high, and the risk too great. The galaxy deserved a chance to heal, to find its own path forward, without the shadow of the precursors hanging over it. Humanity needed to reach for the stars, discover the marvels of the universe, and learn things on its own. That was how it should be...

Taking a deep breath, Keira steadied herself, feeling the presence of Meeka beside her, offering support. With a calm mind and a resolute heart, she prepared to do what needed to be done.

"I'll let them go," Keira said, her voice strong and clear, a final act of will. "The galaxy must move on, without them."

As she made the decision, Keira cut the connection to the Alarveen collective. She felt it begin to loosen, the voices fading as they were drawn back into the containment system, which in a way they were. The overwhelming knowledge slipped away, like sand through her fingers, leaving behind only a handful of grains.

The Alarveen, with all their wisdom and power, would pass on to the next plane, leaving the galaxy to chart its own course. And Keira, having faced the darkness and emerged stronger, would continue to fight for the future—one built on hope and unity, not fear, not domination, and certainly not leaning on another civilization to create a utopia in her image.

"You have done something no Alarveen could ever do," Meeka said in her mind, "cut the connection to the whole, to the collective. That is why we needed humanity, for even if one remained behind to close the door, the connection would have provided a path back, a way for the discontented to return. On behalf of my race, we thank you, Keira Kai'Tal."

Keira opened her eyes and stood. At her feet lay Crecee, moaning softly, blood still flowing from his broken nose. He looked pitiful now, a far cry from the menacing figure he had once been. His cruelty, his selfishness—it was all laid bare, symptomatic of the darkest aspects of the human race. Crecee had embodied the worst of humanity, a desire for power that had driven him to unimaginable lengths, and now he was nothing more than a broken shell.

"We have engaged the Disunity," 0062's voice echoed in her mind through the machine, breaking the silence.

"We have," MK confirmed. "It has gotten quite frisky."

"Indeed," 0062 responded, the dryness of his tone unmistakable. "I have not had this much fun in an age." There was a brief pause. "Scratch one Disunity warship."

"It was almost like they'd not bothered to maintain their reactor cores," MK added, sounding almost aghast. "Another just went down. Did you see that core failure?"

"I did," 0062 responded. "It was quite spectacular."

Sucking in a deep breath, Keira felt the change within her, something deep and profound, continuing to roil and shift. Whatever had happened during her connection with the Alarveen, it wasn't over. She was still changing. The transformation within her was ongoing, and it was more than just mental—it was physical, emotional, spiritual. She felt different, not just in how she saw the world, but in how she saw herself, how she related to those around her.

"Princess…are you all right?" a voice broke through her thoughts, filled with concern.

Keira turned slowly, her gaze focusing on the figure before her. For a brief, disorienting moment, she didn't recognize him. The being standing there seemed alien, unfamiliar, not like the others she knew, not Alarveen. A part of her wanted to lash out, to kill the intruder before her. The urge was primal, an echo of the darkness that had touched her during her connection with the Alarveen.

But she fought it down, shaking her head to clear the fog of confusion. As her vision cleared, she realized who it was—Scaro. He had stepped out of his armor and, like her, wore only his haptic suit. The suit clung to his body, highlighting his chiseled physique, the strength and resilience that had always been a part of him. In that moment, Keira saw him as incredibly handsome, a striking figure.

At the same time, she felt a sudden wave of revulsion. It wasn't her own feeling, not entirely. It was the alien side of her, the remnants of the Alarveen influence that still lingered within. The part of her that viewed humans as lesser beings, as something to be eradicated for the sake of a greater good. But Keira pushed that thought and desire away, refusing to let it take hold.

"Are you all right?" Scaro asked, his voice filled with genuine concern as he searched her face.

Keira hesitated, feeling the weight of the truth pressing down on her. "I don't know," she admitted, her voice wavering. She tapped the side of her head with a finger, trying to make sense of the turmoil within. "I have an alien in here, her thoughts, her pain, her desires—and some of it's dark stuff, Scaro … really dark."

Scaro took a step closer, his hand extended in a gesture of comfort and support. "Let me help you," he offered, his tone gentle, trying to reach her.

"Stay back," Keira warned, her voice sharper than she intended. Fear and confusion swirled in her mind, a storm of alien and human memories that clashed violently. "I am a monster. They— *we*—wiped out civilization after civilization, killing everything but themselves. It was their mission in life. It was evil."

But Scaro didn't stop. He took another step forward, his eyes filled with determination and something else …

Keira was so confused.

"No, stay back," Keira repeated, her voice trembling as the flood of memories threatened to overwhelm her, memories of what Meeka had done. Keira's mind spun with flashes of another life, an existence filled with love so deep it had spanned the equivalent of a millennia. But then came the loss—terrible, soul-crushing loss that ached with a pain she had never known or, for that matter, imagined. It tore at her soul, threatening to pull her apart, to rend her very being.

And then, suddenly, Scaro was there, closing the distance between them and enveloping her in a hug. His arms wrapped around her, pulling her close, and for the first time since this ordeal began, Keira felt grounded. The warmth of his body against hers, the steady beat of his heart, the strength in his embrace—it all felt good, right. It was a lifeline in the midst of the chaos roiling inside her mind.

"It's gonna be okay," Scaro murmured, his voice soothing, the words a balm to her frayed nerves as he rocked her gently. "It's gonna be okay."

Keira's breath hitched as she leaned into him, letting herself be held, allowing the warmth of his presence to calm the storm inside. The memories, the pain, the darkness—they were still there, but Scaro's embrace made them more bearable, gave her the strength to face them without being consumed.

For a long moment, they stood like that, Keira clinging to Scaro as she struggled to find her footing in this new reality. The alien thoughts, the memories, the desires—they hadn't disappeared, but the fear that had gripped her was beginning to loosen its hold. Scaro's words, his presence, were a reminder that she wasn't alone in this, that she didn't have to face the darkness by herself.

"I'm here," Scaro whispered, his voice steady and reassuring. "I'm not going anywhere."

Keira closed her eyes, letting the tears fall freely now, letting herself feel the full weight of everything she had been holding back.

"It's gonna be okay," he repeated as he held Keira close. His words were meant to reassure, to provide a safe harbor in the storm of emotions raging inside her.

"No!"

The shout tore through the air, and Keira whirled around just in time to see Crecee back on his feet. His face was twisted with desperation and fury, and in his hand was a pistol, one he must have picked up from the debris scattered around them. His eyes were wild as he aimed the weapon at her, his intent clear, murder in his gaze.

"Die, bitch!"

But before Keira or Scaro could react, there was a sharp, deafening bang. Crecee's body jerked violently as a round slammed into his chest, the force of the impact driving him back a step. His grip on the pistol faltered, but he stubbornly tried to bring the gun to bear again.

Then another bang rang out, this one louder, closer. The sound echoed in Keira's ears as Crecee's head snapped back, the round hitting with brutal precision. The back of his skull exploded outward, a gruesome spray of blood and bone, and his body crumpled lifelessly to the ground, the pistol falling from his limp hand.

For a moment, everything was still. Keira's breath caught in her throat as she turned her gaze to where the shots had come from. Jessie stood just behind Scaro. She was lowering her rifle, the barrel smoking lightly. She spat on the ground. Keira pulled away from Scaro.

"It is time," Meeka's voice echoed in Keira's mind, clear and unwavering. "Time to send my people onward."

Keira gave a wooden nod, her body stiff with the gravity of what she was about to do. She closed her eyes, focusing on the task ahead. The first step was the Phoenix Gate, the key to opening a rip in time and space. She reached out with her mind, searching through the vast network of the machine until she found it—the controller, the command construct that held the power to activate the Gate.

"How may I assist you, Kai'Tal? Is it time?" The construct's voice was calm, collected, and clearly awaiting her command.

"Open the Gate," Keira instructed, her voice firm despite the weight of the decision. "Allow the imperial fleet through."

"As you command, Kai'Tal," the construct replied without hesitation. There was a brief pause as it carried out her orders. "I have signaled them. The Gate is open. Transit in progress."

Keira opened her eyes to find Scaro looking at her, his expression filled with curiosity.

"I've chosen humanity," she said to him. Her voice was steady but didn't hide the emotions still swirling within her.

"I knew you would," Scaro responded with a gentle smile, his belief in her unwavering. "It was the only real choice."

"Keira," MK's voice crackled to life in her ear, carrying a tone of astonishment, "a gate has opened—one where none existed before."

"I know, MK," Keira replied, speaking the words aloud, but also sending them in the machine.

"Imperial ships by the dozens are coming through, cruisers, battleships, dreadnaughts, and carriers," MK continued, his voice filled with awe. "There are also marine assault transports with them. Oh my, this is wondrous."

Suddenly, a new voice cut through the open channel in Keira's ear, authoritative and commanding.

"This is Admiral Kane," the voice declared in a hard tone. "I command the Imperial Ninety-Fifth Shock Fleet. The might of the empire has arrived. To all enemy combatants, particularly the Disunity forces in-system, you will cease aggressive action immediately, power down your weapons and shields, and heave to for boarding or face certain destruction. You will not get another warning."

Keira's heart swelled at the sound of her family's name, a connection to her past and the legacy she was now forging anew. Though she was not certain how, she was suddenly quite sure the admiral was related to her—on her father's side.

Jessie couldn't help but let out an appreciative whistle. "Now that," she said with a grin, "is one hell of an entrance."

EPILOGUE

Location: Planet Asherho
Date: 2450, Imperial Standard

Keira stood alone, her eyes fixed on the sky above as the last of the imperial drop ships ascended, streaking through the atmosphere like bright, determined comets. She could hear the distant roar of their engines as they rocketed toward the heavens.

The evacuation of Asherho was nearing its completion, a process that had taken hours of careful coordination and relentless effort. Deep scans of the planet had revealed only a few survivors amidst the ruins, but those who had been found were now being taken to safety, where they would receive the care they so desperately needed.

The UPG had surrendered, brought to their knees by the overwhelming power of the imperial fleet. An evacuation of the surviving orbitals had been conducted as well, for when she triggered the device in the planet, they would not survive.

If any of the UPG's leaders had survived, they would answer for their crimes. Keira would ensure that justice was served, for she was the ultimate authority now, the one who held the fate of so many in her hands.

As she watched the sky, Keira's thoughts turned to the battle that had raged just hours earlier. The Disunity ships in orbit had been destroyed. None had chosen to surrender. The combined efforts of 0062 and the *Seri*, along with the imperial fleet, had ensured their defeat, but the cost had been high. Before the fleet had arrived, the *Seri* had taken significant damage, her once proud form now marred by the scars of battle. She and her surviving crew, including Captain Campbell, were receiving assistance from imperial ships. The ship was also being towed to a safe distance.

The horizon was tinged with the soft glow of the setting sun, the light filtering through the dust and ash that still hung in the air. Keira took a deep breath, feeling the cool air fill her lungs, the taste of ash on her tongue. The battle for Asherho was over, but the battle for the future was just beginning. She had chosen humanity, chosen to protect and preserve the lives of those who looked to her for guidance. And in doing so, she had set the stage for a new era, one where the mistakes of the past would not be repeated.

The last of the drop ships disappeared into the murky sky, leaving behind only the faint trails of their passage. Keira turned her gaze back to the ground, her heart heavy but resolute. There was much work to be done, but she knew she was not alone. She had Scaro, Jessie, MK, and so many others who believed in the future she would be fighting for.

Scaro stood to her right, a steady presence by Keira's side. Jessie was only a few feet away, her gaze sweeping the surroundings with the practiced vigilance of a seasoned warrior. Around them, a security detail of marines maintained their watch, remnants of Scaro's company, eyes scanning for any remaining threats that might materialize, though Keira knew there were none. The Disunity was finished—she had made sure of that. The danger that had once loomed so large was now gone, reduced to nothing more than memories and ash.

The low hum of engines filled the air as a marine drop ship waited nearby, its thrusters hot and ready for departure. Ramp lowered, it was ready to take them aboard.

A voice crackled through Keira's comms, breaking the silence. "Empress." Admiral Kane's voice was calm, professional. "I am told the last of the evacuees are clear. All of the orbitals have been evacuated. As directed, the fleet is already beginning to pull away from the planet to a safe distance. You and your team are all that remain on Asherho. You may depart at your convenience."

"Thank you, Admiral. We will be leaving shortly."

"As you command, Empress," Kane replied with respect and finality before the line went dead.

The title felt heavy in her ears—empress, a mantle she was still adjusting to. It was a role she had not sought, but one that had found her nonetheless. The galaxy had changed, and with it, so had she. Keira knew she could not afford to falter—not now, not with so much at stake.

She glanced around at the barren landscape of Asherho, the only home she had ever known. The planet, once vibrant and full of life, was now a desolate reminder of what had been lost. Soon, once she triggered the portal device, it would cease to exist, erased from the galaxy like a bad memory. In a way, it felt fitting. This world, like a phoenix, would be reduced to ash, but from that ash, the empire would rise again—stronger, wiser, ready to rebuild what had been destroyed.

"I have an empire to rebuild," Keira said, her voice carrying the weight of her resolve as she looked over at Scaro. "Will you help me with that?"

"I will," Scaro replied without hesitation, his voice steady and filled with unwavering loyalty.

Jessie, standing close by, added her own voice to the commitment. "I will as well, ma'am."

Keira looked from Jessie to Scaro, feeling a deep sense of gratitude for the loyalty they had shown her. "I want you both by my side for what is to come," she said, her tone conveying how much their support meant to her.

"As you command, Empress," Scaro said, the title slipping easily from his lips.

But Keira shook her head.

"No," she corrected gently, her eyes meeting his with sincerity. "I don't want that. It must be of your own free will. I will not command either of you, ever again."

Jessie responded with a firm nod, her expression resolute. There was no doubt in her mind—she had chosen to stand with Keira, not out of obligation, but out of belief in the future they would build together.

Scaro's gaze softened as he looked at Keira. "I will not leave your side, not now, not ever, if that is agreeable."

"It is." A wave of emotion washed over Keira. These two were not just her allies in battle; they were her friends, her family, the ones who would help her shape the new empire they would create.

"Thank you," Keira said. "I will not forget this moment."

Keira turned away, ready to leave this world behind. But just as she took her first step, she paused and glanced back at Scaro. A small smile played on her lips as she remembered something. "I do believe you promised me a coffee, Italian, right?"

Scaro returned her smile, a light firing in his eyes. "I did, and I will deliver. I think you'll love it."

"I know I will." With that, she turned and headed for the waiting drop ship. It was time to go, time to leave this world behind and without looking back. There was no point in dwelling on the past—her future lay ahead, and she would face it with determination and strength.

The marines fell in behind her as she made her way up the ramp. Just inside, the crew chief stood to attention, offering Keira a crisp salute as she approached. Keira returned the gesture with a nod. She was aware that, clad only in her haptic suit, she looked out of place among the armored marines. But that didn't matter, and it certainly did not bother her. She was the empress now, with command over the machine and the power to shape the future.

As she ascended the ramp, the marines followed close behind, their boots thudding against the metal. Keira found a jump seat designed for unpowered crew and slid into it. The restraints automatically deployed, securing her in place with a reassuring click. The familiarity of the action, the routine of it, was a small comfort in a world that had become so unpredictable.

Keira opened a channel, her voice calm and authoritative. "Pilot, head for the precursor ship. Inform the admiral I will meet him there to confer on our next steps."

"Yes, Empress," the pilot responded promptly, acknowledging her command with the respect due to her station. "Flight time should be just shy of forty minutes."

Keira switched tracks. "0062," she called out, her voice resonating through the machine's network. "We are headed your way. Be prepared to receive us."

The response was immediate, the familiar voice of 0062 coming through. "As you wish, Kai'Tal. I stand ready to serve." There was a slight pause. "Word has spread across the galaxy. The constructs have been talking. There are other precursor ships who wish to serve. Do you desire their services? Do you want me to call them forth?"

Keira considered this for a brief moment. The thought of having more precursor ships at her command was both a strategic boon and a reminder of the power she now wielded. The galaxy was a vast and uncertain place, and having the support of these ancient vessels, along with their constructs, could be crucial in the days to come.

"I do," Keira replied, her voice firm. "Call them forth to serve."

"As you command, Keira Kai'Tal," 0062 responded with the same deference, ready to carry out her orders.

The last of the marines charged up the ramp, their boots thudding against the metal as they took their places. Out of his armor, Scaro settled into the seat next to Keira, his presence a steadying force in the midst of everything that was happening. Without a word, she reached out and gripped his hand, finding comfort in the simple contact as the drop ship's engines roared to life. The ship began to lift into the air even before the ramp had fully closed, the powerful acceleration pressing Keira back into her seat.

She closed her eyes, allowing the sensation to fade as she reached back into the machine, her thoughts stretching out to the portal generator. This was the final act, the culmination of everything that had led her to this point. She hesitated, feeling the weight of what was about to happen, and then, with a deep breath, she triggered the mechanism within the planet's core.

Keira could feel the power surge exponentially, the energy mounting in ways that were almost overwhelming, and then the beginnings of release. Theoretical knowledge, imparted to her by Meeka, flooded her mind, a cold, clinical understanding of what was to come.

The device in the core of the planet, a portal generator, would open a tear in space at the location of the Phoenix Gate, magnifying the Gate's own harmonics, amongst other things. The end result would be a powerful singularity—a force that would ultimately draw everything into it, consuming the planet, the orbiting moon, the containment system, and all else in its path. Ash would soon be no more. And with it, the Alarveen would be locked away, ascended to another plane of existence where they would finally be safe, free from the threat of extermination and destruction.

As the power reached its peak, starting the process of consuming the planet itself, Keira made the conscious decision to withdraw from the machine, to pull herself back from what was happening. She didn't want to watch the destruction, didn't need to witness the end of this chapter of her life. It was enough to know that it was happening, that the choice she had made was being fulfilled.

She returned fully to the present, where the hum of the drop ship's engines and the grip of Scaro's hand were the only things grounding her. The destruction of Ash was a necessary act, one that would ensure the safety of countless others, but it was also a deeply personal loss. The planet that had been her home, the place where she had grown, struggled, and fought, would soon be gone, leaving behind only memories.

Keira opened her eyes, the weight of the moment heavy on her chest. Scaro's gaze met hers, understanding and compassion reflected in his eyes. He squeezed her hand, offering silent support as the drop ship continued its ascent, carrying them away from the world that was about to be destroyed.

Now, it was time to focus on the future—on rebuilding, on creating a new empire from the ashes of the old, reconnecting humanity.

Ash would be gone, but Keira Kai'Tal would rise from its remnants, stronger and more determined than ever before.

"Thank you," Meeka's voice echoed softly in Keira's mind, a final expression of gratitude that carried the weight of ages.

"You and I are the last of your kind," Keira replied, a deep sense of responsibility settling over her. She could feel Scaro's curious gaze on her, but she didn't need to explain. This was a moment between her and Meeka, a passing of the torch from one era to another.

"I will serve as a reminder," Meeka continued, her tone solemn, "a cautionary tale—a voice of reason, calling upon you not to make the same mistakes my people did."

"A new beginning," Keira said aloud, her voice firm and resolute.

"A new beginning," Meeka echoed in her head. The words carried a sense of hope for what was to come.

The moment of reflection was interrupted by the pilot's urgent voice. "Something's happening on Asherho. I—I think the planet's beginning to break up," he called out to everyone aboard. "I'm increasing thrust. We're almost out of atmo. Hang on."

Keira felt the drop ship's engines roar louder, the acceleration pushing her even further back into her seat. The force was intense, but Scaro's presence beside her, his hand gripping hers tightly, provided a steady anchor. They were in this together, facing the unknown side by side.

Scaro leaned over, his voice a quiet affirmation in the midst of the chaos. "A new beginning."

Keira turned to him, feeling the truth of those words resonate deep within her. Still holding his hand, she closed her eyes. She sucked in a deep breath and let it out slowly through her nose, feeling the tension begin to melt away.

She was tired—so incredibly weary from the fighting, the decisions, the weight of everything she had endured. But alongside the exhaustion, there was a profound sense of triumph. She had done what needed to be done, had made the hard choices, and now she could rest, knowing that she had secured a future for those who would come after her.

Another deep breath in, another slow exhale. The sound of the engines, the steady hum of the drop ship, and the comforting presence of Scaro beside her, his hand in hers, all blended together, creating a cocoon of safety and peace.

And then, as if a great weight had been lifted, Keira allowed herself to drift. Sleep, long overdue, crept in around the edges of her consciousness. She didn't fight it. She had earned this rest, this moment of peace, after so much turmoil, so much struggle.

As the drop ship sped away from the disintegrating planet below, carrying Keira and her companions toward their new beginning, she let sleep take her, knowing that when she woke, a new chapter would be waiting. A chapter she would write with the strength and wisdom she had gained, alongside those she trusted most.

For now, she was content to rest, to let go of the past, and to dream of the future she would help to create and shape.

The end

Connect with Marc

Marc works very hard on his writing. He aims to create high quality books to be not only enjoyed but devoured by you. Late into the night he writes with a drink at his side, usually whiskey, gin and tonic, or beer.

It helps fuel the imagination ... ***If you think he deserves one, you can help to encourage his creativity by buying him a drink. Think of it as a tip for an entertaining experience, cheers!*** www.maenovels.com

Patreon Legion: As a member, you get exclusive perks like early access to chapters, art crafted for your tech screens, beta reader opportunities, contests, signed proofs, autographed final read through manuscripts, and live Zoom calls every quarter.

Take advantage of the 7-day free trial to Marc's official fan club. Dive in and experience our vibrant community firsthand! Marc Edelheit Author

Facebook: Make sure you visit Marc's author page and smash the *like button*. He is very active on Facebook. Marc Edelheit Author

Facebook Group: MAE Fantasy & Sci-Fi Lounge is a group he created where members can come together to share a love for Fantasy and Sci-Fi.
Twitter: Marc Edelheit Author
Instagram: Marc Edelheit Author

YouTube: Marc Edelheit Author
Amazon Author Central: Marc Edelheit Author

Newsletter: Sign up to Marc's newsletter at www.maenovels.com to get notifications on preorders, contests, and new releases. We do not spam subscribers.

Reviews keep Marc motivated and also help to drive sales. He makes a point to read each and every one, so please continue to post them.

Made in the USA
Monee, IL
24 May 2025

56abf305-9dd8-49ef-97de-2d60b2acd3a9R01